"How young she is," was not any younger t out. It was her innoc of the effect her beau her that made her so was she – this doctor's daughter from Divington? How had she managed – without even knowing it – to put him under her spell? He had to know her better. But would he bore her? After all he must be at least ten or fifteen years older than her.

Also by Zia Foxwell in Sphere Books:

NOTHING LASTS FOREVER

ZIA FOXWELL

Borrowed Time

SPHERE BOOKS LIMITED

A SPHERE BOOK

First published in Great Britain by Michael Joseph Ltd 1989
Published by Sphere Books Ltd 1990

Reproduced, printed and bound in Great Britain by
Cox & Wyman Ltd, Reading

ISBN 0 7474 0354 6

Sphere Books Ltd
A Division of
Macdonald & Co (Publishers) Ltd
Orbit House, 1 New Fetter Lane,
London EC4A 1AR
A member of Maxwell Macmillan Pergamon Publishing Corporation

I would like to dedicate this book to the memory of two very dear friends - Tim Walker and Donald Corbett - and with much love to Rosie and Katie.

ACKNOWLEDGEMENTS

I would like to thank Peter Niven, Derek Robinson, Brian Trubshaw and Jeremy Edwards for their very useful information, and also Pat, Barbara and Maggie for everything they have done to help me on my way.

'For what is your life? It is ever a vapour that appeareth for a little time and then vanisheth away.'
The Bible; James, Chapter 4, verse 14.

PROLOGUE: LONDON 1936

'... and so I'll be home after dinner, darling. I thought I'd have a quick meal with Richard seeing that he's my last patient of the day.'

'Fine, darling, but try not to be too late, you've been looking tired lately. I'll have a nightcap waiting for you.'

'You spoil me and I love you for it.'

Anthony Carrington blew a kiss into the telephone and replaced the receiver. "What would I do without Helen?" he thought. She was so perfect – pretty, intelligent and understanding – a tower of strength to an ambitious young doctor. Here he was, at thirty-four years of age, with a successful Harley Street private practice and employed as a consultant to several teaching hospitals. It was mostly a good life and he loved his chosen career. There were, however, one or two occasions when he wished he had chosen something else ... for instance how did you tell a man whom you have known for more than half your life – a man who had been at public school with you and was four years your junior – that he had between three and five years to live? He used to think that Richard Woodward had everything going for him: good looks, a title, wealth and a lovely house in Gloucestershire. True, his marriage had not worked out, but Anthony had never liked Eleanor. She had liked to live in the fast lane and had helped Richard spend a great deal of money. Then one day, after three years of marriage, she had met a German steel baron and had left her husband within a month.

That had been two years ago, but Richard had certainly not been at a loose end since then. He was always surrounded by beautiful women and the gossip columns thrived on his exploits.

'The world is my oyster,' he had told Anthony, not long after his divorce. 'Why should I settle for one woman when I can have the pick of so many? I don't intend to make the same mistake again, old chap. Give me my fill of the good life and tomorrow I'll bear the consequences. I'm going to love 'em and leave 'em from now on.'

At the time Anthony had clapped him on the back and made some trivial remark, but now he shuddered at the memory. Poor Richard, he was obviously – for all his women – a very lonely man, and now his good friend – probably his only real friend – was going to deal him a mortal blow. Richard was running out of time. It was too late now to find happiness with the right woman, there would be no heir and few people to mourn for him. Anthony sighed deeply. He took off his glasses and rubbed his right eye – a habit of his when he felt distressed. He clasped his hands in front of him on the leather-topped desk. "What a waste," he thought, "what an incredible waste."

There was a knock on the door and his secretary popped her head around it. 'Sir Richard Woodward is here, Doctor Carrington.'

'Thank you, Mrs Harper. Please show him in, and then you may go. I'll lock up when I leave.'

'Thank you, Doctor Carrington.'

Anthony unclasped his hands and put his glasses back on his nose. He stood up and walked around his desk, reaching the front just as Richard Woodward walked into the room.

'Richard, dear boy, good to see you.' He held out his hand for the younger man to shake. 'How have you been feeling?'

'Fine, really. Just a little tired from time to time, but then you know me and the kind of life I lead. I suppose I ask for it.' Richard grinned ruefully. 'Well, doctor, what's the verdict? Will I live? Did you actually find anything inside that lump on my neck? To my way of thinking it was probably full of alcohol!' He laughed easily at his own joke as he sat down and crossed his legs in a relaxed manner.

2

"Does he know – has he any idea how ill he is?" Anthony wondered. "Or is he totally oblivious – yet another product of man's belief that he is indestructible when he is anything but?"

'Richard, I'm afraid that the prognosis was not too good.' He walked over to the mahogany drinks cabinet behind his desk. 'Would you like a drink? I'm going to have one as it's the end of the day.'

Richard looked at his watch. 'No thanks, Tony. It's only five-thirty. Mustn't start before six. Shame on you – a professional man!' He grinned. 'Come on, spill the beans. Have I got to have another operation, or something very boring like that?'

'No, you don't have to have an operation, but you do have to have a course of treatment.' Anthony sat down behind his desk and set his glass of whisky down in front of him.

'Well, that's all right then.' Richard gave an exaggerated sigh. 'For a moment you had me quite worried.' He did not look worried at all.

'Richard, I don't think you realise the seriousness of your illness. The diagnosis on the gland we took out of your neck revealed that you have what is known as Hodgkin's Disease. It affects the lymphatic system.'

'Come on, Carrington, now you're trying to frighten me.' The younger man gave a nervous laugh. 'I could almost think that you are trying to tell me my days are numbered.'

'They are, Richard.' Anthony took a long swig of neat whisky and never even felt his throat burn. 'They are. There is no other way to say it.'

'But . . .' The other man gulped. 'I mean, we all know we are going to die eventually. Not now . . . but in time. Not yet.'

'I'm sorry, Richard.' Anthony took off his glasses and rubbed his eye again. This was even more difficult than he had anticipated. 'At this moment in time there is no cure for the disease you have. We will give you a course of deep X-ray

3

treatment as soon as possible to shrink the glands, but I'm afraid we cannot halt its eventual progress.'

The younger man's expression changed and he grew pale. His hands gripped the sides of the leather upholstered chair. 'Good God, man! What are you telling me? What the hell is this? Is it . . .?'

'It's a form of cancer,' Anthony said quietly. 'There's no cure. It's simply a matter of time and then . . .' He unclasped his hands and opened them in a helpless gesture.

Richard was having difficulty in controlling his emotions. His body trembled as he held on to the side of the chair. Anthony had seen it all before, but never this close – never before had he had to tell a friend. He wanted to help him, but what could he say? "Don't worry, old chap. I'll look after you until you die" was not a line to make everything seem all right.

'I'm so very sorry, Richard,' he whispered softly. 'It's the most rotten luck in the world.' He looked up at the ceiling. 'I suppose that He up there must have his reasons. It's just that very often they're hard to understand.'

Richard Woodward forced himself to stand up. He walked shakily over to the window and looked out. It had been raining and a cold evening sun shone down on the glistening wet pavements. The traffic was heavy in the street below. It was rush hour and everyone was going home. But what did he, Richard, have to go home to? An empty house in Cheyne Walk presided over by his butler, Dawkins, or his country estate in Gloucestershire run by Mrs Edison, his cook and housekeeper, and her husband the gardener. It had been a lonely life since Eleanor had left him, but nevertheless he enjoyed it – and at least he had thought he had plenty of time still to come.

'I'll have that drink now, old boy,' he said without turning around. 'Make it a stiff one, will you. I think I need something strong.'

He downed the glass of neat whisky that Anthony handed

to him in one swallow. The liquid burnt his throat and set his insides on fire, but it seemed to quieten the churning feeling in his gut.

He continued to stand silently gazing out of the window for a moment which felt like eternity, then he turned and walked back to the chair and sat down. When he spoke, his voice was normal.

'How long have I got, Tony?' He smiled weakly. 'Obviously I have a few things to get in order.'

'Anything from three to five years. This isn't something that happens overnight!'

'What's going to happen to me?' He was struck by a sudden thought and a look of horror crossed his handsome face. 'Will I become bed-ridden and grotesque?'

'No. It shouldn't be like that. We'll start the X-ray treatment as soon as possible. You will just have one course then there is no other treatment. If you are careful, there is no reason why you shouldn't lead a fairly normal life. Of course, you will get weaker as time goes on and there will be bouts of fever, but in between you will look and feel normal.'

'I see.' Richard picked up a photograph of Anthony and his wife, Helen, and studied it intensely. 'You may not know it, but I've always envied you, Tony, having such a good marriage and wife like Helen. A good marriage is so important in life – and mine was a total failure. Still . . .' He shrugged his shoulders. 'At least there'll be no explaining to do and no loving wife and children to grieve for me. It's probably better that way. I think it will make the situation a lot more tolerable for me.'

'I had no idea you felt that way.' Anthony Carrington was amazed. 'I've always thought you had everything anyone could wish for.'

'We all try to hide our inadequacies, Tony. Even a successful man like you must long for something.'

'Yes, I suppose you are right.' Anthony looked down at his hands which were clasped on top of the desk. 'I've always wanted children, but after nine years of marriage I've given up hoping.'

'You see . . . None of us is allowed to have everything. We have to be reminded of our vulnerability and our dependence. Well, good-night, Tony, I'll be seeing you.'

'I . . . I wondered if you'd like to have dinner with me. I don't want you to be on your own – not tonight.'

'Bless you, old chap. You're a good friend, but tonight is the night that I really think I would welcome my own company. I want to think a few things out.'

'Well, if you're sure?'

'Yes, I'm sure, but thanks a lot, Tony.' Richard walked towards the door. As he opened it, he turned. 'And Tony?' His friend looked up inquiringly. 'If this has to happen to me, then I'm glad it's you that's in charge. If I trust anyone in this world, it has to be you.'

Anthony stood up. 'Thank you,' he said quietly and started to move around his desk.

'No, don't see me out. Stay where you are.'

'I'll have my secretary telephone you next week to arrange for the treatments.'

'Thanks, Tony. I'll be waiting.'

The door closed and Anthony heard footsteps running down the stairs, then the front door slammed.

"Funny," he thought, "you could know a person for seventeen years and really not know them at all." He sighed and picked up the telephone to ring his wife and tell her that he would be home for dinner after all.

PART ONE
1938–42

Jennifer

CHAPTER ONE

Jennifer James jumped off the bus and ran the couple of hundred yards along the road to the stone-built Cotswold cottage in which she lived with her father. It was a beautiful June evening in 1938 and, despite all the gloomy predictions of war in Europe, in the sleepy little village of Divington in Gloucestershire such things seemed far removed from reality.

Jennifer ran because she was excited. Tonight Colonel and Mrs Heywood were giving a coming-out dance for their daughter Madeleine up at the manor and she, Jennifer, had been asked along with her father who was the village doctor. Very few others in the village had been asked as the Heywoods did not mix with the locals, apart from opening the yearly fête and helping to canvass for the local member of parliament at election times. Some people thought them cold and stuffy, but Jennifer knew better. They led extremely busy lives. They spent a great deal of their time in London where Colonel Heywood worked in something called Lloyds and Mrs Heywood was one of the leading Society hostesses.

Madeleine and Jennifer were the same age and had known each other since they were five. In those days Madeleine had been left in the country with a nanny and a governess. The Heywoods had asked whether Doctor and Mrs James would allow Jennifer to share the governess as this would provide welcome company for Madeleine; in Mrs Heywood's eyes, the doctor's daughter would be quite adequate for the few years before Madeleine went away to boarding school.

For the seven years that they did lessons together, the two girls became good friends. Though Madeleine's home comforts were obviously far greater than Jennifer's, they both lived similar lives. At weekends when the Heywoods

9

were at home, Madeleine could be found more often than not at the James's house, for Mrs Heywood believed in children being seen and not heard and, of course, when there were guests, children appeared only after tea to say 'How do you do'. Madeleine loved Jennifer's parents. They were warm and kind and always had time for her. She also adored the shortbread biscuits that Mrs James let the girls help to bake in the tiny kitchen.

However, when Madeleine was twelve, she was sent away to boarding school while Jennifer passed into the local grammar school. After that, Madeleine acquired new school friends who would come to stay and Jennifer couldn't help but feel left out when she listened to their school chatter. Madeleine tried to include her and sometimes it worked, but the other girls were not too interested in the girl from the village. However, the friendship survived in a way. They continued to write to each other, probably because Mrs Heywood usually forgot to write to her daughter more than once a term.

When she was seventeen, Madeleine was sent to Paris for six months and then to Switzerland. When she returned, Jennifer loved to listen to her stories and the descriptions of the places she had visited and people she had met. On the other hand, Madeleine found herself becoming increasingly short-tempered with her old friend when she realised that it was hard for Jennifer to envisage many of the events she was talking about, far less comprehend them.

However, on one subject the girls chattered freely. Boys. Madeleine was always falling in and out of love. In Paris the fashion had been penniless artists and in Switzerland it had been handsome ski instructors. It was all bright and frothy and, as her mother would say, healthy if not taken to excess. Now that she was back home for the London Season, her attentions must be focused upon some suitable young man of unquestionable background and enough money to keep her in the style that she had been brought up to enjoy.

Jennifer's knowledge of young men was very different. She had laughed at Madeleine when Madeleine had told her how lucky she was to be at a school where there were boys as well as girls. Most of them had spots, Jennifer explained, and were either totally taken up with football or liked to tease the girls unmercifully. In fact, Jennifer had been teased especially because of her accent which had none of the local twang.

In her last year at the school, there had been one or two boys who had wanted to take her out. However they had seemed to think that a trip to the cinema involved anything except watching the film, and when Jennifer made her feelings of disagreement clear she was accused of being snobbish and uppity. In the end she had been more than glad to leave school. Because she had worked hard and received a good grounding from Madeleine's governess, she had passed all her examinations with flying colours. For the last six months she had been working in an art gallery in the country town of Cirencester about five miles away. It was a well-paid job and she had a lot of responsibility when the owner was away buying. Jennifer's only regret was that her mother was not there to see how well she had done. Tragically, she had died when Jennifer was fourteen and from then on it had just been her and her father at the little cottage.

Now it was Madeleine's débutante ball. The Heywoods had decided to give it at the manor and not in London, because at this time of year the gardens were at their best. The combination of the floodlit house against a backdrop of the sky full of stars was bound to make an enchanting scene. Tonight was going to be an evening to remember. Lucky Madeleine ... and lucky Jennifer to be included in the festivities, even though she would almost certainly be sitting on the sidelines. She wouldn't know anyone except Madeleine who would be far too busy to bother with her. Maybe somebody would ask her to dance – and there was always her father. Maybe ... "Stop it, Jennifer," she told herself. "Just go there and enjoy the spectacle. It's something you will remember all your life." She opened her bedroom door and drew in her breath sharply as her eyes fixed on the beautiful dress hanging on the cupboard door. Madeleine had insisted on giving it to her. It was of white voile with a tight bodice and a wide frill which came just off the shoulders. The skirt was full and there was a wide pale-blue taffeta sash at the waist which tied in a bow at the back. "For one night, I'll be Cinderella at the ball," Jennifer thought.

A door slammed. 'Jennifer, you home yet?' her father's voice called up the stairs.

'Yes, of course.' She threw her handbag on to the bed and turned around to give him a kiss on the cheek as he walked into the bedroom. 'Did you have a good day? No dramas?'

'Everything's fine. I stopped off on the way home to see Mrs Brett. Her baby's due any day now – in fact, I left her the Heywoods' telephone number just in case it arrives early.'

'Oh, I hope it doesn't. I don't want to have to leave this party early. I don't want to miss a thing.'

'No, I'm sure it won't. If anything, first babies tend to be late.' Doctor James patted his daughter's shoulder. He looked at the dress hanging on the door. 'In that dress you're bound to be the belle of the ball. All the young men will be flocking to dance with you.'

'Darling Daddy, you are so good for my ego, but I doubt that. There will be far more glamorous girls there with much more to say for themselves than I, but I'm sure I will enjoy myself anyway.' She smiled at him and he felt a sudden lump in his throat. Did she honestly have no idea how beautiful she was? She might not have the education and the worldliness of the much-travelled and sophisticated Madeleine Heywood, but she was a knock-out when it came to looks and she was intelligent and very sweet. It would be a combination of beauty and innocence that would make Jennifer irresistible to somebody tonight. He just hoped it would not lead to some young man breaking her very fragile heart.

'Daddy, you're day-dreaming.'

'What, darling?' He shook himself out of his reverie. 'Goodness, it's six-thirty already. Now you hurry up, young lady, otherwise we will be late. You have exactly one hour and ten minutes before we must leave. I know how long you women can take when it comes to titivating yourselves.'

'Don't you worry, I'll be ready.' She made a face at him and he grinned back as he closed the door.

CHAPTER TWO

Divington Manor looked breath-taking when Doctor Derek James drove up with his daughter. A floodlit fountain was playing in the courtyard as the guests arrived, most of whom were dropped at the front door while their cars were driven away by robot-looking chauffeurs. A smartly clad commissionaire stepped up to the car door as Jennifer and her father pulled up between the Georgian stone columns and the front door. As the commissionaire helped her out, Jennifer felt the warm night air on her shoulders. Walking nervously up the steps and into the marble hall, she hoped that her father would not take too long to park the car.

It was obviously a popular time to arrive. The hall was full of people greeting each other like long-lost friends, even though the majority of them had probably seen each other almost every night since the start of the Season. In one corner a trio dressed in the French Left-Bank style were playing background music. As Jennifer looked their way, the accordianist caught her eye and smiled a dazzling smile, then he blew her a kiss. Jennifer felt her cheeks redden and quickly dropped her gaze to the floor. She heard a titter of laughter from behind her and a lot of whispering. Finally a young man detatched himself from the group and walked over to her.

'I say, didn't we meet last week at Maisie Hipwood's bash?' Jennifer looked up still blushing violently to see a tall young man with slicked-back hair grinning at her with an amused look on his face. He held out his hand. 'I'm Teddy Mulholland and who, remind me, are you?'

'I'm Jennifer James, and no, we've never met. I'm not doing the Season.' She put out her hand to shake his.

'Oh!' He looked put-out. 'Aren't you? Pity.' He drifted off, leaving Jennifer with her hand still outstretched and feeling mortified.

'Well, who is she, Teddy?' one of the girls inquired.

'Nobody, darling. Definitely not one of us.'

'Very pretty, though, Teddy old thing. Maybe she's a budding actress,' another young man volunteered.

'Maybe, Jack, maybe. In that case I shall have to find her later.' Teddy winked and the group broke out into laughter once more.

At that moment Doctor James entered the hall. Jennifer sighed with relief. She drew herself up to her full height and glided across the room to meet him, oblivious to the stares of admiration from most of the men.

Dinner was lavish and no expense had been spared. Guests were seated at round tables of eight. Each table was covered with a pink linen cloth, and lit by three candles set in holders embedded in bowls of pink-and-white roses and carnations. The meal consisted of mixed seafood followed by tournedos cooked to perfection and then a wide choice of desserts and, for anyone who still had room for more, there was a tray of assorted cheeses on every table.

Jennifer and her father had been seated with the few locals who had been invited. There was the Reverend Benton and his wife and their son, George, who had his mousey fiancée with him. At first, Jennifer had felt sorry for the poor girl who was obviously very shy as she didn't say a word, but she soon realised that the reason the girl was so silent was because she was intent on eating as much as possible of every dish. Only after she had finished her last mouthful of cheese was Doctor James – who was sitting next to her – then subjected to a long and very boring account of her ideas on how to improve the Women's Institute coffee mornings. The other couple making up the eight were from the next village and helped Mrs Heywood with one of her many charities.

After dinner the dancing commenced. Twelve musicians from one of the top London dance bands played in the ballroom. Jennifer danced first with her father, and then with George Benton who trod on her toes and kept stuttering apologies. The heat from the candles coupled with the warm air had made the house quite stuffy and no one was at their table when George brought her back. He muttered yet another apology and left her to look for his fiancée.

'What do I do now?' Jennifer wondered. She could go and join the vicar who was standing by the bar, but she felt that she had had more than enough of that family for one night. She walked out into the passage and immediately felt cooler. Someone had opened the large French windows that led to the terrace, so she walked outside. One or two couples were draped over the stone balustrade while others talked quietly in little groups. On the right and left stone steps led down to the garden below. No one took any notice as Jennifer started to cross to the right of the terrace. She paused for a minute at the top of the steps and surveyed the scene beneath her. Candles in glass bowls were dotted along a number of paths which converged on a large lily pond in the centre. The pond shone in the artificial light – like a huge sun, Jennifer thought, with the paths marking out its rays. She glanced across at the steps on the other side of the terrace, and saw a man leaning on the balustrade, looking out.

"He's alone too," she thought. "Out of place, like me?" There was something about his stance and the set of his shoulders that suggested a kind of desperate sadness. "Not like me," she decided. "I may be out of place, but I'm quite happy. I'm enjoying myself in my own way and I shall remember this evening always." She walked on down the steps, then ran over to the pond and looked down into it. A ripple beside a water lily suggested the presence of a fish underneath. She trailed a hand in the water and the goldfish, now throughly disturbed, slithered away to take cover elsewhere.

In the left-hand corner – away from the floodlighting –

was a huge cedar tree. Its dark silent presence seemed to dominate the rest of the garden. Even in the daytime, Jennifer recalled, the tree had seemed imposing. When she and Madeleine had been children, a swing had been attached to one of its branches and she wondered whether it was still there now as she felt herself drawn towards it.

"Why, oh why did I come?" Richard groaned to himself as he stood gazing out from the terrace. "I can't enjoy myself with these people any more. They are so silly and superficial, behaving as if they have all the time in the world to squander on such frivolities. Will they never realise how precious that time really is?" He sighed and leaned on the balustrade with his arms folded. But, of course, for them it wasn't, or if it was then they didn't know it. Was he lucky to know? Did it help to make you a better person? It certainly made you act differently. At first he had been defiant. "Why me? What have I ever done that this should happen to me?" But after two years he knew there was no answer to that question. Maybe it would become clear once he reached the other side. But one thing he still regretted was the absence of love in his life – not that there had been any lack of women. They had thrown themselves at him ever since he was a teenager. But he had never enjoyed much parental love. He had been sent away to school at the age of eight, and at twelve his parents had divorced. His mother had remarried and gone to live in America while his father had died of a heart attack two years later due to a surfeit of women and booze.

After his marriage to the flighty Eleanor had broken down, Richard had become convinced that all women were made from a similar mould – cold, like his mother, and fickle, like his wife. He began to identify himself with his father and went on to behave accordingly. Until two years ago. It took a blow like that to make one think – really think – to start asking oneself questions and trying to find the answers. Had Eleanor simply been the wrong woman for him as Tony

Carrington had suggested? Had he not thought hard enough or long enough before asking her to marry him? Had he – without realising it – so craved love and affection that he had proposed to the first pretty girl who had set her cap at him? If so, then perhaps the fault was not entirely Eleanor's. He thought of Tony Carrington. He had always envied his friend's own happy marriage, but had not realised until that ghastly day in Tony's office that even they did not have everything. They had wanted children for so long. "Goddamn it!" Richard brought his fist down hard on the stonework and felt no pain. Tony and Helen had been so delighted when they had discovered she was pregnant at last and then, two weeks ago, Helen had died in childbirth leaving Tony with his longed-for son. But at what cost? And why? Just when you thought you had got close to an answer, something like that happens to start you thinking all over again.

A ripple of light caught his eye and he looked out into the garden. A young girl in a white dress was running across the lawn. She paused for a few minutes by the lily pond and trailed her hand in the water, then she stood up slowly gazing into the darkness. She shook her long blonde hair back over her shoulders and began to glide almost ghostlike towards the looming shadow of a dark cedar tree on her left.

Richard closed his eyes as his heart lurched. For a moment he had thought it was Helen come back from the dead, but that was impossible. He did not believe in that sort of thing ... and yet ...? He opened his eyes to find the garden empty. His heart was beating at what seemed like double its normal rate, and against all reason he found himself compelled to walk down the steps. He had to find that girl – just to prove to himself he was not going mad.

Jennifer found the gentle movement of the swing soothing and relaxing. In the distance she could hear the music coming from the ballroom as the band was playing a well-known ballad. She hummed it softly to herself. Suddenly the tempo changed and she started to swing herself faster – in time to the music. The draught sent her skirt billowing around her.

'I say, should you be swinging so high? You might fall.'

Jennifer wobbled violently as she looked down. A man was standing below her. She brought the swing to a none-too-elegant stop.

'I'm fine,' she said a trifle frostily. 'At least, I would have been if you hadn't made me jump almost out of my skin. Do you make a habit of frightening people half to death?' She took a closer look at him. He was very tall – well over six foot. In the moonlight she could tell that he was thin and had dark hair. He took a cigarette case out of his pocket – opened it and placed a cigarette in his mouth. He struck a match and as he bent his head she noticed a muscle working in his cheek. Something about his carriage reminded her of the man she had seen on the terrace. Had she offended him?

'I'm sorry,' she said. 'That was rude of me. I didn't mean it. You just gave me a bit of a scare.'

'No, no, it's my fault. I had to know if you were real.'

'Real?'

'Yes. I saw you walk across the lawn when I was standing on the terrace. I thought you were a ghost.'

Jennifer laughed. 'Well, I'm not, as you can see.' She held out her arm. 'You can pinch me if you like.'

'Don't laugh.' His voice caught in his throat. 'A good friend of mine's wife died recently, and I was just thinking about them when you crossed the lawn, and from the back you looked so like her. She had long blonde hair.' He lit another match and held it near her face. 'I can see now what an idiot I was. You are much younger.'

Jennifer's eyes were full of compassion as she looked back at him. "How very beautiful she is," he thought. There was a warmth that radiated from her as she said quietly, 'I'm so sorry.' Jennifer thought of her own mother's death four years

19

before. 'It is always so sad when someone we love dies. I understand and I wasn't laughing at you. I think I'm just a little nervous.'

'Of me?' He sounded alarmed.

'Yes – No – I don't know.' She tossed her long hair back over her shoulders. 'Of this whole evening, I think, if I was to acknowledge the truth to myself.'

'Oh?'

'I'm not a debutante and I don't lead this kind of lifestyle. The reason I'm here tonight is because I used to share a governess with Madeleine until she went off to boarding school. My father is the village doctor.'

'And is that something to be ashamed of?'

'Of course it isn't.' She was indignant. 'I was only explaining myself to you.'

'Never explain yourself,' he said. 'You don't have to – least of all to me.'

'You are very nice, and no, I'm not nervous of you.' She put a hand on his arm and felt him tremble at the contact.

'You should be getting back to the party,' he said abruptly. 'You'll be missed, and if you are found here with me it won't do your reputation any good.'

She laughed up at him. 'I suppose so,' she said. She held out her hand. 'Will you come with me?' She was amazed at her own audacity; after all, she did not even know his name.

'No. I'm going to stay here for a while.' He sat down on the swing which she had just vacated.

'Don't brood for too long, it won't do you any good.'

'I won't.' He smiled and looked away.

She turned to walk away.

'By the way, what's your name?'

She turned to face him. 'Jennifer. What's yours?' but he was already immersed in his own thoughts and did not answer her. Jennifer sighed and started back across the lawn.

"Jennifer – a pretty name," thought Richard. "So young – seventeen or eighteen? Sweet and innocent, fresh and unspoiled." He felt a flood of desire course through his veins as he realized she epitomized all the things that had so far eluded him, but now it was too late. He purposely had not told her his name. What would be the point? He found that he was feeling edgy and could not even sit and brood – as she had put it. He stood up and ground out his cigarette in the grass. He shouldn't have come. No, he was glad he had come. He had met Jennifer, even if it was only briefly.

'Well, well, if it isn't the mysterious blonde who isn't doing the Season.' A drunken Teddy Mulholland stumbled over to Jennifer as she reached the top of the steps. 'And where have you been – as if I didn't know? An assignation in the garden – eh?' He winked as he put a hand on her arm. 'I've been looking for you everywhere, darling.' She shivered at his touch and tried to pull away, but his fingers gripped her arm tightly. 'Come and dance with old Teddy. I'll warm you up.'

'I'm sorry, but I have to . . .'

'Excuses, darling, excuses.' He wagged a finger at her and lurched forwards to plant a very wet kiss on her lips.

Jennifer recoiled and tried once more to free herself, but even in his inebriated state he was too strong for her. 'You don't have to be coy with me, darling. I know your sort and I like a woman with a bit of spirit.' With his arms still firmly around her, he started leading her across the terrace. For a moment she almost panicked, but it would have been unthinkable for her to cause a scene at the Heywoods'. She would have to endure the loathsome Teddy as best she could. She hoped that it would not be for long.

'Ah, there you are, Jennifer. I've been looking for you everywhere,' an amused voice called from behind them. As they turned around, Jennifer saw Richard smiling up at her. 'Evening, Teddy. I hope that you've been looking after my girl.'

'Hello Dickie. Didn't know she was with you. We were just going to dance.'

'But you promised the next dance to me.' Richard held out his hand as Teddy released Jennifer's arm. Quickly Jennifer put her arm through his.

'I'm sorry,' she said to Teddy. 'But I was trying to tell you.'

'I say, steady on. First come and all that.' Teddy was indignant. For a moment Jennifer thought she was going to be pulled apart like a Christmas cracker but Richard was in command.

'Teddy!' His voice was curt and authoritative. 'You look very much the worse for wear. I suggest you visit the gentlemen's cloakroom and make yourself less dishevelled. I think that Jennifer had better come with me.'

At that minute Mrs Heywood walked out on to the terrace with a group of older guests. 'Richard, how nice to see you.' She smiled and waved her hand vaguely. 'This is Sir Richard Woodward – Lord and Lady Collerton and Mr Peter Waverley.' Her eyes rested on Jennifer. 'And Jennifer, dear. I didn't know that you two knew each other. How nice.'

Richard took advantage of the situation. 'Jennifer and I were just going to have a dance,' he informed them.

'How nice,' repeated Mrs Heywood as they moved off.

'Thank you for rescuing me. I wasn't quite sure what to do.'

'My pleasure.' Richard inclined his head. 'Besides frightening young ladies in the dark, I also like to rescue damsels in distress.'

'Now you're laughing at me.'

'Only a very little bit.' They had reached the ballroom. He slipped his arm around her waist and took her right hand in his. The band was playing a foxtrot and Jennifer felt as light as a feather in his arms. She was a good dancer, and as Richard twirled her around and around he felt more youthful than he had done for a very long time. They made a handsome couple and heads turned to watch them – the tall dark good-looking man and his beautiful young blonde partner. Under the bright light from the chandeliers, Jennifer could see Richard properly for the first time. The pale translucence of his skin gave his face a sensitive appearance which was enhanced by the sadness in his eyes. She found him very attractive. If circumstances had been different she would like to have known him better, but, and she knew that she must remember this, his world was poles apart from hers. This was merely an enchanting interlude – the most perfect ending to a fairytale evening. In reality, of course, he was only dancing with her to be kind – because she had needed help. How naive he must think she was – so different from the polished sophisticated women he was used to.

"How young she is," thought Richard, although she was not any younger than a great many girls he took out. It was her innocence and her unconsciousness of the effect her beauty had on the people around her that made her so very attractive to him. Who was she – this doctor's daughter from Divington? How had she managed – without even knowing it – to put him under her spell? He had to know her better. But would he bore her? After all he must be at least ten or fifteen years older than her. These thoughts and many more went through his head. The tempo of the music slowed down. Only half aware of what he was doing, he drew her closer and rested his cheek against hers. She did not pull away. She likes me, he thought and felt elated.

From the doorway Doctor James surveyed his daughter and her handsome companion with raised eyebrows. Jennifer looked radiant – a picture of health and happiness. The man she was dancing with was being very attentive – a little too attentive maybe? He was certainly holding her close and she seemed to be enjoying it, judging by the expression on her face. For a second they lifted their heads as she said something to him. As he smiled and answered, Doctor James noticed that the man was older than he had first imagined. A sudden shiver of premonition struck him. "Oh, Jennifer," he thought, "what are you getting into?" Then he shook himself and told himself to be realistic. His daughter was having a good time, and it was a pity that he was going to have to drag her away. He waited until the music stopped and then walked across the floor.

'Jennifer, darling, I'm afraid we have to leave. I've just received a message that Mrs Brett has gone into labour and I must get there as quickly as I can. I'll drop you off on my way.'

'Oh no.' She sounded so downcast that it tore his heartstrings. At the same time, Jennifer immediately reproved herself. It was not her father's fault. She had had her fun and now it was time to go. She had always known that this evening could not last forever. 'Yes, of course I'll come now,' she said contritely.

'I could drop Jennifer home, sir, if you would allow me to.' Richard held out his hand to the older man. 'My name is Richard Woodward and it would be my pleasure to ensure that your daughter gets home safely.'

'Oh, Richard, would you really?' Jennifer's eyes sparkled as she looked up at him. 'Daddy, can I stay? I'm having such a good time.'

The same feeling of premonition struck Doctor James again. The man had his arm around Jennifer's waist and they were both looking at him expectantly.

'That would be very kind of you, Mr Woodward,' he heard himself saying.

By the time he reached the door and turned around to wave they had returned to their dancing, oblivious to anyone else.

'The big bad baronet has cornered Little Miss Muffet, I see,' a female voice said from beside him. A sophisticated young woman with upswept hair was talking to a rather dishevelled young man. 'And he's doing rather better than you attempted to do, darling. She obviously goes for the older man-of-the-world. You, darling Teddy, must have appeared far too crude.'

24

'Oh do shut up, Henrietta. Anyone would think you were jealous.' There was a pause for thought. 'Come to think of it, there was a time when you hoped to become Lady Woodward yourself, wasn't 'there?' Teddy Mulholland laughed cynically. 'But the big bad baronet as you call him always loves them and leaves them, doesn't he? Once was enough for him.'

'Teddy, dear, you are so delightfully droll when you're tight. Everyone knows why Eleanor left Dickie Woodward.'

'Every *woman*, darling. I'm sure he spends long enough regaling them with his so-called hard-luck story. It must make them so pliable.'

'Not me, darling. I'm not the sympathetic type. Now can you remain sufficiently stable in a vertical position to dance with me? I want to get a closer look at her.'

Derek James sighed as he watched the two of them totter towards the dance floor. His intuition had been right. There was something about Richard Woodward – Sir Richard no less – for all his charm. He had obviously been married and was a womaniser of considerable repute.

"I shouldn't have left Jennifer with him," he thought. "I'll tell her now that she must leave with me." He looked around the ballroom but could see no sign of them. "Too late," a voice inside him insisted. He sighed again. It had been too late from the minute he had seen Jennifer's face as she looked up at her handsome dancing partner. He hoped that she would not be hurt. Maybe he would fail to contact her again . . . maybe.

'It's been the most wonderful evening. I've enjoyed every minute of it.' Jennifer kissed Madeleine on the cheek. 'Thank you for inviting me.'

'I'm so pleased, Jen. I didn't think you'd know many people, but tell me, I'm dying of curiosity.' Madeleine lowered her voice to a whisper. 'I didn't know that you knew Dickie Woodward. You dark horse. He hasn't left your side all evening. What have you done to him? You're not his usual type at all. Since Eleanor left him, he's had a succession of very flamboyant and highly unsuitable ladies in tow.'

'Who is Eleanor?'

'His ex-wife, darling.' Madeleine gave her friend a hard stare. 'Just exactly how well do you know our Dickie, Jen?'

'I met him this evening.'

'Good Lord.' Madeleine looked non-plussed.

'Look, Maddy, I hardly know him, but he's been very kind and charming and has offered me a lift home since Daddy had to leave a while ago.' Jennifer turned to walk away as she heard the scrunch of gravel and saw Richard drive up in his car.

Madeleine grabbed her arm. 'Jen, take care. Dickie Woodward's not for you. He'll break your heart. He's totally irresponsible and treats his women abominably.'

Jennifer shook herself free. 'Maddy, I told you I hardly know the man. He's simply giving me a lift home, and I'm a big girl. I can look after myself,' she said crossly.

"Can you?" wondered Madeleine. She had heard of Dickie Woodward's famous charm although she had no personal experience of it. Someone like Jennifer would be a novelty, for him, she supposed, but she did not doubt that he would tire of her as quickly as he tired of all his other girls, and she didn't want to see her old friend hurt.

Madeleine shook her head sadly as she watched Richard help Jennifer into his car and slam the door.

CHAPTER THREE

'Miss Michaels on the telephone for you, Sir Richard.'
Edison, the butler, was standing at the dining-room door.

Richard looked up and frowned. 'But I told you, Edison, I
don't want to speak to anyone at the moment.'

'I did try, Sir Richard, but the lady was most insistent.'

'Yes, she can be.' Richard smiled tersely. 'All right, I'll
take it in the morning room.' He strode out of the dining
room and crossed the hall to his den, the so-called morning
room.

'Good morning, Henrietta. How nice to hear from you.'

'Dickie, darling.' He cringed at her use of his nickname.
'Haven't seen you in simply ages. Not since the Heywoods'
dance and that was well over a week ago.'

'I haven't been well. I've had the flu.'

'Really, darling. In the middle of summer? I thought
you'd deserted me for that little blonde you were paying so
much attention to at the Heywoods'.'

'For goodness sake, Henrietta. What is this? Am I not
allowed to dance with whom I choose? We're both free
agents, my dear. Besides, the poor girl didn't know anyone. I
couldn't be rude, could I?'

Why was he making excuses, Richard wondered. It would
not have mattered to him who Jennifer had known or not
known. He had wanted to be with her that evening and only
her. Damn Henrietta and her possessiveness. It had been a
mistake ever to become embroiled with her, just as it had been
a mistake with all the others before her. They were so
shallow and worthless. He realized now that he wanted
something more. But he could not have it, could he? Not
with so little time left. He had sensed that with Jennifer he

27

might have been able to share something special but, for the first time in his life, he had thought totally unselfishly. He could not ruin this young girl's life for the sake of one, maybe two, years of happiness for himself. It had been a good thing that one of his bouts of fever had struck him the day after the party. It had made him realize how wrong it would be to become involved with the girl. He tried to concentrate on what Henrietta was saying.

'Of course you couldn't, darling. It was very noble of you and I'm sure you were awfully bored. I'm just being silly, but I've missed you, Dickie. When are you coming back to town?'

'Well, it's Thursday today. I'll stay down until after the weekend and come up on Monday.'

'You promise to telephone me as soon as you arrive?'

'Yes, I promise.' He sighed as he replaced the receiver and walked over to the window. It was a glorious day. So far, the summer had been good. The sun shone through the copper beech trees in the park and he could see the farm labourers harvesting the hay. It all looked so peaceful and serene. Funny, how he could be affected by a scene like that which he had taken for granted for so long. Would this be the last summer that he would witness it? He shivered. What now? He was getting very morbid. He had been cooped up in the house for too long, and it was time he went out. He would drive to Cirencester and buy a present for Henrietta. He supposed he had treated her rather badly.

Philip Ellis Art was situated in the market place at Cirencester opposite the church and next door to a reputable jeweller. Jennifer sat at her desk at the back of the shop. She had just finished typing the invoices for two pictures which had been sold to regular customers. It was very quiet that morning for the beautiful weather did not encourage shoppers.

Almost two weeks had passed since the Heywoods' dance

and still she had not heard from him. But had she really expected to? When he had dropped her home they had sat in his car for over half an hour just talking. They had discussed their favourite books and music, many of which they shared in common, and he had been amazed at her knowledge. Jennifer had told him laughingly that it was due to Madeleine's governess who had considered literature and music far more important than some other school subjects. Of course, any gaps in her early education had been more than made up for at the grammar school.

When he had finally walked her to the door he had not attempted to kiss her, but instead had shaken her hand in a quaint old-fashioned way and told her that it had been a pleasure to meet her. He had seemed such a nice man – not a bit like Madeleine's depiction of him, but then he was most probably equally charming to everyone. It was obvious that she had read too much into it from pure lack of experience, for quite clearly he had forgotten all about her. She sighed heavily. He had been so different from any other men she had met – not just because he was older but because he was intelligent and kind and . . . oh, she was being silly. "Stop it," she told herself. "Thinking about him won't do you any good at all. You've got to forget him as he has forgotten you."

Richard parked his car and wandered across the street towards Filby's, the jeweller. A pretty brooch or a pair of earrings; Henrietta would like that, and he would be forgiven immediately. As he reached the pavement, however, his attention was distracted by a painting in the shop next door, a landscape featuring a blonde girl tending a herd of goats. He stopped and stared at it. Why did everything simple remind him of her – of the girl he had met at the Heywoods' party? He decided to inquire about the picture – maybe he would buy it. It was as if he wanted to make sure that it did not end up belonging to someone who would not appreciate what he felt it stood for.

A bell rang above the door as he entered the shop. At first he thought no one was there, then he heard the sound of a typewriter coming from the back of the room and a woman's voice called out, 'I'll be with you in just a second. Please look around.'

Richard studied the pictures on the walls. They were mostly landscapes and animals – attractive and not over-expensive. The owner obviously knew his market.

'I'm sorry to keep you waiting, sir. Now can I help you?'

'Yes. The painting in the centre in the window. I'd be interested in buying it.' He turned around and caught his breath in surprise. Jennifer's welcoming smile froze on her face as her cheeks started to redden.

Richard was the first to recover. 'Good Lord!' he said, 'I didn't know that you worked here.'

'I have done for the past six months.' Jennifer's face was still aflame. She hoped that he couldn't hear her heart hammering. He had caught her completely off-guard and she felt tongue-tied and gauche. To hide her confusion she walked over to the window and gently levered the painting off its easel. She straightened up and held it out to him. 'It's been one of my favourites.' She dropped her eyes. 'If it has to go, I'm glad it's going to a good home.'

He took the picture from her and contemplated it in silence. There it was again – that same way of thinking, his way of thinking. He knew now that he had not been wrong about her. She was something special. Richard had also become a great believer in fate, and, he reasoned, if fate had brought them together again, surely it was for a purpose?

"Why did I say that?" Jennifer wondered. "I'm so nervous that I go and make a silly remark like that. How naive he must think I am."

'It's rather expensive,' she said coolly. 'Fifty pounds?'

'Nothing is too expensive if you want it badly enough.' He pulled a cheque book from his jacket pocket.

'I suppose so.'

Richard realized, too late, how flippant his last remark had sounded "I'm nervous," he thought. For the first time in his life he was nervous of a woman. He did not want to look bad in her eyes.

'I'm sorry,' he muttered. 'I didn't mean it to sound like that.'

'It's all right.' Jennifer had regained some of her lost composure and was wrapping the picture in brown paper.

Out of the blue he heard himself saying: 'It's yours. I want to give it to you.'

'What?' She looked up aghast.

'It reminds me of all the lovely unspoilt things in the world – like you. I think it really belongs to you. Please take it.'

'But you hardly know me, Richard.' It was the first time she had used his name that day. 'And it's terribly expensive. I couldn't possibly accept a present like this.' In her agitation she had subsided on to a chair behind the desk.

'That's easily remedied. Have dinner with me tonight?'

'But, Richard . . .'

'Jennifer, I meant to telephone you – really I did, but I've been ill. I've had the flu and I've felt ghastly for over a week.' There was an urgency in his voice that made him believable. She looked up at his handsome face. There was a pallor about him that served to make him even more attractive, and the fine lines around his eyes hinted at a pain of some kind. Behind the bright and flippant exterior, Jennifer realized, was a far more sensitive person. In that second Jennifer made up her mind. 'I'd love to have dinner with you,' she said. 'But on one condition.' He raised his eyebrows. 'You still don't look fully recovered, so it mustn't be late.'

'Yes, ma'am.' He saluted her. 'I'll pick you up at seven-thirty.' He walked towards the door.

'Richard?' He turned around. 'You've forgotten your painting.'

'But . . .'

Jennifer shook her head and handed it to him. For a brief moment their fingers touched and there was a serious expression on his face. 'Thank you,' he said humbly and closed the door.

As he crossed the street there was a lightness in his tread and he felt better than he had for a long time. He placed the painting carefully on the back seat of his car. It was Jennifer's painting, he told himself. He was merely looking after it for her. One day – hopefully not too soon – it would be hers.

CHAPTER FOUR

The London Season never did see the return of Richard Woodward that summer of 1938. He closed the house in Cheyne Walk and brought the dour Dawkins down to Edgeglow Manor to help the Edisons. Jennifer became a frequent and popular visitor to the manor. The staff thought that their employer's young lady friend was both beautiful and charming and they all agreed they had not seen him looking so relaxed and happy for many a long day. Would there soon be a new lady-of-the-manor, they wondered.

Anthony Carrington and his infant son, Charles, often came for weekends. Nanny Carrington was usually left behind to enjoy a few days off and Mabel Edison looked after the baby. It had been a long time since Mabel had changed nappies, but it all came back as easy as winking. Mabel's two sons were both married now, living far away and so she was pleased to indulge her maternal feelings again.

Poor Mr Carrington, Mabel thought, it hardly seemed possible that his lovely wife had died barely three months ago giving birth to this darling little boy. She looked at the clock. It was six o'clock and time for little Charles' bottle. She picked up the baby who gurgled expectantly and sat herself down in a comfortable chair.

'May I give him his bottle, Mrs Edison?' Jennifer had walked into the room and was smiling down at her.

'Certainly, miss, if you'd like to.' Mrs Edison did not have a jealous nature. She stood up and carefully handed over the baby to Jennifer. Baby Charles, sensing that he was going to have to wait those extra few seconds, started to wail, but as Jennifer rocked him he stopped and blew a string of bubbles, giving her a toothless grin. Did babies smile or was it just wind, Jennifer wondered. She offered him the bottle and he sucked on it furiously with his eyes tightly closed and his tiny fists clenched with the effort of drinking until every drop was gone.

Mrs Edison felt a lump in her throat as she thought what a lovely young woman Miss James was. She should be having lots of babies of her own. Sir Richard was crazy if he let this one go. She was streets above some of the other so-called young ladies who had been down to the manor. But then he did treat her differently from the others, didn't he? He didn't seem to flirt with her but instead was more protective towards her, or so it struck Mabel.

"Oh dear," she thought, "I'm being a romantic old fool. They are probably just good friends. After all, she isn't his usual type, is she?"

The baby finished his bottle – burped to order – and stuck his finger in his mouth contentedly. As Jennifer laid him down gently in his cot she could see that he was already asleep.

'Thank you, Mrs Edison,' she said. 'I thoroughly enjoyed that. Now I'd better go and find everyone.'

'It's a pleasure, miss. You come along any time you want to.'

Jennifer paused for a minute on the landing and leaned against the oak balustrade to survey the hall beneath her. Edgeglow Manor was a fascinating house. It was over three hundred years old and built in true Cotswold style. It was not an old entailed family estate – in fact, Richard had not even been born there. His father had purchased it just before the 1914–18 war. One or two family portraits hung on the walls interspersed with landscapes and at the back of the hall was a large Inglenook fireplace. As it was summer, an enormous arrangement of leaves and flowers adorned the wide hearth. She sighed as she realized how much she loved this house. Even though it was slightly awe-inspiring it was a friendly house. There was something rock-solid and dependable about it. Well, it had been here for over three hundred years, hadn't it? It was a survivor. She was to remember these thoughts at a later date.

It had been a wonderful summer and her relationship with Richard had transformed her life. She had previously known no one like him. They found that their interests were similar and they could talk for hours on a variety of subjects. They teased each other and made each other laugh and not once had he asked anything more of her. Sometimes she wondered if he had any idea of the way she felt about him. Occasionally she had noticed him staring at her – when he thought she was not looking – with such sadness in his eyes. What had caused it? What was he afraid of? She knew that he had been married and that it had not worked out. Was he afraid of another mistake? She was scared to ask him – too afraid of losing what little they already had. She heard movements downstairs and quickly snapped out of her reverie.

Richard and Anthony were reading the newspapers when she walked into the drawing room.

'Where have you been?' Richard spoke without looking up.

'Upstairs with Mrs Edison.' She smiled at Anthony Carrington. 'I've just given your son his tea.'

'I hope he behaved like a gentleman.' Tony put down the paper and grinned at her.

'Of course he did. He's just like his father,' Jennifer teased. 'No, honestly, he's so lovable I could eat him up.'

Richard put down his paper abruptly and stood up. 'Time for drinks,' he said loudly and made his way over to the cocktail cabinet. 'What'll you both have?' His hand shook slightly as he opened the cupboard door.

Tony glanced at him quickly and noticed the telltale signs. Beads of sweat were glistening on Richard's forehead.

'I wouldn't, Richard, if I were you.' Tony spoke quietly. 'Anyway, I don't want one and I'm sure Jennifer doesn't either.'

'No, no I don't, thank you.' Instinctively, Jennifer knew

35

that she must agree. The tension between the two men was electric as they glared at each other. Then, as suddenly as it had begun, it was over. Richard relaxed his grip on the whisky bottle and returned it to the shelf.

'You're right,' he said tersely. 'Maybe it wasn't such a good idea after all.' He turned on his heel and walked briskly out of the room. Jennifer made to follow him, but Tony shook his head.

'Leave him, Jennifer. He'll be all right.'

'But I don't understand . . .'

'No, of course you don't. Bear with him, Jennifer. He has a lot on his mind at the moment.'

'But the drinking?' She had to know.

'He hasn't been well. Drinking doesn't help.'

'Then he's not . . .'

'An alcoholic? No.'

'I'm glad about that.' She laughed nervously. 'Why does he sometimes look so sad, Tony? What happened to him to make him look like that?'

"Oh God," thought Tony, "what do I say to her? I can't tell her the truth. It's against all the ethics of my profession. And I can't let down my friend." What had they got themselves into – this couple who so obviously adored each other? He had seen the looks they gave each other when they thought the other one wasn't watching. He thought for a few minutes and then took a deep breath.

'Richard had an unfortunate marriage to Eleanor,' he said. 'It really should never have taken place, but he was young and she was determined. After it was over I think he mistrusted all women. For instance, I discovered a couple of years ago that he deeply envied me my happy marriage to Helen – I think it hit him nearly as hard as it hit me when Helen died last May. He learned then that, even when you are blissfully happy and contented, something can come along and take it all from you. Be gentle with him, Jennifer. He hurts. Don't push him, just be there. He needs a good friend.'

'Thank you for telling me.' She put her hand on his arm. 'I'll help in every way that I can.'

Dinner was a quiet meal that night. The three of them sat at one end of the vast dining-room table and were waited on by the stoney-faced Dawkins. Mrs Edison's beautifully prepared food was barely touched and they all refused the wine. After the coffee had been served, Richard stood up. 'I'd better take you home now, Jennifer,' he said. 'I can feel a cold coming on. I think I'd better have an early night.'

'Yes, of course.' She was disappointed. Usually, they sat for a while after dinner in the den and talked or listened to music. She looked up at him. He did not look very well and there was a slight flush on his cheeks. 'Shall I come over tomorrow? We were all going to take a picnic to the lake, remember? Do you think you'll be all right?'

'Yes, yes, of course I will be.' Richard spoke more to convince himself than Jennifer.

'Richard, why don't you stay here? I'll run Jennifer home.' Tony spoke quietly but authoritatively. He saw alarm register on Richard's face and guessed why. Richard was worried that, left alone with Jennifer, his friend might tell her about his illness. Tony met Richard's eyes and shook his head sadly. "You should know better, Richard," he thought. "I wouldn't do that – not without your permission."

'No, don't do that. I'll get Edison to take her.' Richard walked across the hall to the kitchen. He returned almost at once. 'That's all arranged. Edison's gone to get the car.' He smiled a little apprehensively at Jennifer. 'Sorry, Jennifer. You don't mind, do you? I really do feel a bit rough. I'm sure I'll be fine tomorrow.'

'Of course I don't mind.' She heard the car draw up outside. 'Take care of yourself and I'll see you tomorrow. Daddy has some calls to make, so he said he'd drop me on his way.'

Richard and Tony stood in the doorway watching as the car drove off.

'You're going to have to tell her, you know.' Tony did not look at his friend.

'No. I don't want her pity.'

'But it's not fair – not when you spend so much time together.'

'She's a friend, Tony. I'm not having an affair with her.' They walked inside and Richard slammed the door with unnecessary force. 'And since when was anything in this life fair?'

Tony remained silent for several minutes, then he asked: 'What are you going to do about tomorrow?'

'I'll telephone her in the morning – tell her I've got another bad bout of the flu.'

'And how many times is she going to believe that one, Richard?'

'Please, Tony.' The younger man looked agonised. 'I know it can't last and I'm not hurting anyone. I haven't even kissed her. It's just till the end of the summer, then I'll pack up and go back to London and face the rest of this farce by myself. No harm will have been done.'

'But . . .?'

'No buts, Tony. I know what I'm doing. Good-night, old boy.'

Ten minutes later Tony knocked on Richard's bedroom door.

'I brought you these to help you sleep.' He held out two pills and a glass of water.

'Thank you.' Richard was sitting up in bed. He swallowed the pills. Beads of sweat had formed on his forehead and some glands had swollen up in his neck.

'Richard, remember that I'm not just your doctor, I'm your friend, and I want to help you all that I can. When the time comes, you won't have to face this alone, I'll be there.'

'Thanks again, Tony.' Richard smiled weakly. 'But I'm not ready to call it a day yet.'

'Atta boy . . . and Richard?' Richard raised his eyes

drowsily. 'You deserve your summer. She's a lovely girl and I'm glad she makes you so happy.' Tony looked down, but Richard was already asleep.

The next day was a beautiful sunny Sunday morning. After attending the ten o'clock service at Divington Church, Jennifer and her father set out in his old battered Morris to drive to Edgeglow. They had to stop for Doctor James to make a couple of calls on the way, so Jennifer busied herself by checking that she had all the food in her basket for the picnic. She had insisted that this was to be her treat and that she would make up a picnic just like her mother had used to make for herself and Madeleine. She had packed cooked chicken legs, sausages, cheese-and-cucumber sandwiches, shortbread biscuits and an assortment of fruit including some Victoria plums freshly picked off the tree in their garden. A feast good enough for a king, she thought happily. Richard and Tony would be bound to enjoy it.

It was half-past twelve when Dr James finally deposited his daughter at the bottom of the drive. As he watched her walk away swinging her basket as she went, he wondered where all this would lead to. He had met Richard on several occasions when he came to collect Jennifer and thought him a nice enough fellow but he worried for his daughter. She was very taken with Richard – and that was putting it mildly – but there was something remote about him, even though he too was quite obviously attracted to Jennifer. Derek James could not pinpoint what it was but he felt deep down that Richard Woodward would never commit himself, and he hoped desperately that Jennifer would not get hurt.

'Jennifer, I've been trying to telephone you.' Tony had opened the door before she had had time to knock.

'Is something wrong?' Jennifer was alarmed. 'How's Richard?'

'Not very good, I'm afraid. He has quite a temperature. It seems to be the flu.'

'Oh no, poor Richard.' She put down the basket of food on the hall table. 'Can I go up and see him?'

'Well, he's sleeping at the moment and he doesn't want you to catch it.' Tony had had strict instructions from Richard that Jennifer was not to see him in his present condition.

'Of course. I won't disturb him then.' She sounded so disappointed as she looked down at the basket. 'I made all this food. What a waste and it would have been such fun. Still . . .' She looked up at him and smiled a little too brightly, 'I suppose there's always another day.' She picked up the basket and turned away.

'Where are you going?' he asked.

'Home,' she said dully. 'I'll wait for a bus at the end of the drive.'

'Don't do that,' Tony heard himself saying. 'Stay and keep me company. We'll take your picnic out on to the lawn and you can play with Charlie.'

Her eyes lit up. 'Are you sure?' she asked. 'I don't want to be a nuisance.'

'Of course I'm sure. Charlie and I would be honoured, ma'am.' He bowed to her in an exaggerated old-fashioned style.

Jennifer laughed. 'Tony, you'd cheer up anyone. That would be lovely.'

'You forget, my dear, I'm a doctor. It's my perfected bedside manner.'

As they walked outside she said, 'Maybe I can see Richard later when he wakes up – just for a second, at a safe distance?'

For a second Tony's heart sank. 'Maybe,' he said softly. 'We'll see.'

It was a lovely afternoon. Baby Charles cooed and kicked his little legs in the air on the blanket. Tony and Jennifer did full justice to the picnic. She told him about her childhood friendship with Madeleine and their early education, and he in his turn told her about his years at Eton and then at Gonville and Caius College at Cambridge where he had studied to become a doctor. Jennifer found herself admiring his dedication to his work and his caring attitude. His was a very sympathetic nature.

From time to time Tony would go in to check on Richard but his reply to her inquiring glance each time he returned was always the same. 'He's still asleep,' he would say. 'It's the best thing for him.'

At the end of the day, Tony ran Jennifer home in his Bentley. He admired the pretty little cottage and Jennifer asked him in for a quick drink. While he was there Doctor James also returned home and was introduced. Jennifer went to brew up some coffee, leaving the two men to talk shop.

'He's a very brilliant and important man – your Richard's friend,' Derek James observed thoughtfully, when Tony had left.

'Yes, he is,' Jennifer smiled. 'And he's not *my* Richard, Daddy. He's just a friend.'

'Aren't you giving him a little too much of your time then, if that's all he is?' he inquired carefully.

'I don't know what you mean,' she said, trying to make her voice sound matter-of-fact.

'Umm . . .' Doctor James kissed his daughter good-night and went upstairs to bed. Maybe it's best to leave things alone, he thought. It would probably all sort itself out if he didn't try and meddle.

CHAPTER FIVE

This time Richard's fever only lasted for a few days. He put it down to willpower. Maybe it was just a question of mind-over-matter. Until very recently he had had no purpose in life. Now things were different and he was going to fight it. Who knew – maybe he'd win?

Since Richard's last bout of fever and the cancelled picnic with Jennifer, Tony and his baby son had not been back to Edgeglow. At the time they had stayed a further two weeks, as Tony had taken his annual vacation and had given the nanny her holiday as well. Mrs Edison had enjoyed looking after Charlie and so had Jennifer when she had been there. Tony had noticed how sweet she was with the baby – a natural mother. It was a rare occasion when Tony let envy get the better of him, but this had been one such occasion. He envied Richard his relationship with this girl. She was another Helen – maybe more determined. He had noticed her strength of character and stamina where her job was concerned. He liked her sense of responsibility and the way she looked after her father. He wondered how she would take the news of Richard's death – if she and Richard were still close – when it eventually happened. They might not – either of them – want to admit to themselves how they felt about each other, but Tony's heart bled for them, and for himself as they reminded him constantly of his own pain. For these reasons and others that he did not understand, he decided not to go down to Edgeglow for a while.

It was well into September before Jennifer suggested the picnic again. The two of them took Richard's car and drove into Wiltshire towards Bath. Even though they had travelled only thirty or forty miles the countryside became dramatically different. They soon found themselves driving along a thickly wooded valley which was complemented by a little stream running along the bottom. Further back there had been sheep grazing on the hills. Not a soul in sight – not a house for miles.

They parked the car in a gateway and laughingly argued about who should carry the picnic. Richard won and strode off whistling as he swung the basket.

'Wait for me!' Jennifer grabbed the car rug and followed him.

They kept to the main pathway in the wood, deciding to see where it would lead them. It was a hot sunny day without a breath of wind, and the only sound was the snapping of twigs as they trod on them and the occasional twitter of a bird. Once a startled rabbit scampered across the path in front of them causing Jennifer to jump and Richard to tease her.

When eventually they came to the other side, a stile separated them from the field beyond. Richard handed Jennifer the basket and vaulted over the fence. He took it back and deposited it on the ground before holding out his hands: 'Come on, lazy-bones,' he said, 'I'll give you a hand.'

'You will not.' She tossed her head with impatience. 'I can manage perfectly well on my own. I am a country girl, you know.' So saying she put one foot on the bar and swung her other leg over. As she transferred her weight the rotten piece of wood gave way and she wobbled violently. Richard was quick to catch her and lift her down safely. For a moment they were motionless as they looked into each other's eyes, his hands still holding her waist. He drew in his breath sharply. He's going to kiss me, she thought, and closed her eyes. Then a dog barked in the valley below and the spell was broken. 'Shall we stay here?' he asked her. 'There's a lovely view.'

43

'Yes, this will be fine.' She made a great show of spreading out the rug for them to sit on at the same time as trying to compose herself.

The awkward moment passed and they both set out to do justice to the picnic. They chatted away in their usual relaxed fashion and laughed at the antics of the dog below them who was now chasing rabbits. After a while it gave up and disappeared.

The sun beat down from above causing Jennifer to feel drowsy, and when she had eaten her fill she lay back and closed her eyes. 'This is the life,' she said sleepily. 'It's wonderful to know that some things will never change.'

'You could be wrong.'

'What do you mean?' Her eyes fluttered open.

'This man in Germany – Hitler. He seems like a madman. He's a potential danger to the whole of Europe. You could find that sometime in the not-so-distant future we may have to fight to preserve our peaceful English countryside.'

'I hope you are wrong.' She sat up and hugged her knees. 'The world has barely got over one terrible war. It couldn't take another. No, I don't think that even Hitler would want that.'

'I think people underestimate him, Jennifer.' Richard spoke seriously. 'He's power-crazed.'

'Well, it won't happen today, and anyway I think that you're being unnecessarily gloomy. It won't happen, Richard. Not here.'

He stood up abruptly. 'I'm going for a walk,' he stated. 'Do you want to come with me?'

'No thanks.' She lay down again. 'I'm very happy just lying here in the sun. You go by yourself.' Let him work off his depression on his own, she thought.

Richard stared down at her. She was so young and so determined that nothing could possibly spoil her own little corner of the world. Alas, he knew better. Maybe it would not happen in his lifetime, but that was not saying much.

Goddamn it! Why did something always have to remind him of his mortality?

He walked for nearly an hour savouring the beauty and the stillness of the countryside. When he returned Jennifer was sleeping where he had left her. He sat down beside her, picked a blade of grass and gently tickled the tip of her nose. Half asleep, she brushed her nose with her hand thinking it was a fly. Her eyes remained closed. He tickled her again and she slowly opened them.

'Rat,' she said, shutting them again. 'I'm asleep.' She turned over and the stretching movement caused the top two buttons of her blouse to pop open. Richard could see the outline of her breasts as she lay facing him and the urge to touch her was unbearable. A lock of hair had fallen across her forehead. He leaned over and brushed it aside, feeling her skin silky and warm from the sun. The temptation was too great. He bent over, intending only to plant a feather-light kiss on her lips, but at the moment of contact her lips parted and he found himself kissing her with all the emotion he had denied himself since he first met her. Her arms had somehow stolen around his neck as she kissed him back. They held each other tightly and she felt the strength of him against her and was overjoyed. He loved her and wanted her as she loved and wanted him. His hand which had been caressing her back moved around and was suddenly inside her blouse stroking her breasts. She caught her breath as the intense pleasure sharpened into a kind of agony. She felt herself grow moist and blushed at her need for him. Hesitantly she took his hand and guided it downwards. Was she completely shameless, she wondered. She felt him tremble as his fingers touched the soft flesh between her legs. He hesitated, and she forced herself to look him in the eyes. 'I love you, Richard,' she said. 'And I want you to love me.'

The effect of those words on Richard was like the effect of a gunshot. It was as if he had snapped out of a trance. He tore himself away from her and sat up.

45

'What's the matter?'

He stood up and ran a hand through his dishevelled hair. 'Damn! Damn!' he said through clenched teeth as he stumbled towards the woods.

Jennifer found him leaning against a large oak tree with a grim expression on his handsome face.

'Richard, what is it?' Her voice was tearful. 'Did I say something wrong?'

'No, you didn't say anything wrong.' He did not look at her. 'It's my fault. I shouldn't have started it.'

'But Richard, I wanted you to. That makes it all right, doesn't it?'

'No, Jennifer, it doesn't. Not when there's no future in it. Not with a nice girl like you.' He turned towards her and for a moment she glimpsed the naked misery in his eyes before he hardened his expression.

'But . . .'

'But nothing, Jennifer,' he said roughly. 'I don't want to make any commitments. I don't want a permanent relationship. I'm not the marrying kind.'

'I didn't mean that.'

'Didn't you? Well, what did you mean then – that you'd be content to have an affair with me?' He spoke harshly.

'Yes – no – I don't know.' Jennifer stared at the ground to cover her embarrassment. Thoughts were whirling around in her head. What had got into him? This was a side of him that she had never seen. Had Madeleine been right all the time when she had warned her about him at the dance? She, Jennifer, had been so determined not to be swayed, but had she walked right into the trap? She had been so sure that he was different from all those stories that were circulated about him. And he was. No, it must be something else that was upsetting him, something to do with the sadness that periodically showed on his face.

'You see?' he said wryly.

In that second Jennifer made a decision. 'Yes,' she said,

holding her head up and looking straight at him. 'I'll have an affair with you, if that's the way you want it.'

'Don't talk like that,' he snapped. 'It's not what I want at all. That would make you like all the rest of them, and you're not, you're, you're different – special.'

'Then why . . .'

'It's a long story and not one that I would enjoy telling you.' He sighed deeply. 'It has nothing to do with you – or anyone else for that matter – and if you knew, it wouldn't change a thing.'

She did not say a word. After what seemed like a very long time he straightened up. 'Come on,' he said, 'I'll take you home.'

It was a long silent drive back to Divington. The sun was beginning to set when they arrived at the cottage. As she started to get out of the car Jennifer saw his hands grip the steering wheel while he kept looking straight ahead and said: 'I think that it would be better if we did not see each other for a while.'

She had known that he had been building up for this all the way home. 'If you say so,' she said in a tense little voice. 'I understand.'

"Oh no, you don't," thought Richard, and his hands gripped the wheel even tighter so that his knuckles showed white. "Thank God, you don't. That would be even harder to bear."

He did not look round as he drove away and Jennifer did not even notice that the tears were coursing down her cheeks as she stood staring after him.

CHAPTER SIX

The six o'clock bus was late, and the people waiting outside the church in the square in Cirencester were stamping their feet to try and keep warm. It was a raw November evening and a light drizzle had started to fall. Jennifer wound her scarf tighter around her neck and burrowed her hands deeper into her pockets. It had been a busy day at the gallery. With Christmas not far away there had been an influx of present-buyers in addition to the normal trade. Philip Ellis was pleased with her – Jennifer knew that. She got on well with his customers and did not mind whatever job he gave her to do. Then why wasn't she happy? Everything was going well for her. She had a job that she enjoyed and a boss who appreciated her, but it wasn't enough.

It was two months since she had last seen Richard on that fateful evening in September. He had not telephoned or tried to make any contact with her at all. For two weeks she had tormented herself with reasons as to why he had dropped her. Had she been too forward? Had that put him off her? She knew that he had a reputation with women, but if that was true why didn't he want her? He *had* wanted her – she knew that. Even the most innocent of women knows when a man wants to make love to her. Jennifer blushed as she remembered the feel of his hands on her body and the headiness of his kisses. Oh yes, he had wanted her as much as she had wanted him – still wanted him. Then what was wrong? She had to know.

After two weeks had gone by she had steeled herself to telephone him. Edison, the gardener, had answered and told her that Sir Richard had shut the house up for the winter and had gone back to London. It was then that Jennifer realised it was over. For some reason best known to himself Richard had thought better of his friendship with her and had gone back to the life of an eligible batchelor around town. She, Jennifer, had been fun for the summer while the London Season was in recess, but obviously after three months he had found her far too provincial and unsophisticated compared to the glamorous, well-travelled and amusing people in the capital city. And yet something wasn't right. She could feel it in her bones.

'Jennifer James, I do declare!' A maroon Standard had driven up and stopped beside the queue. Madeleine Heywood's smiling face leaned out of the window. 'You look frozen, darling. Hop in and I'll drive you home.'

'Madeleine, fancy seeing you here. I haven't seen you since your wonderful dance.' A frantic hooting started as the avenging bus arrived and was unable to park next to the bus stop.

'Get in, Jen, for goodness sake, or there's going to be a fight.' Madeleine was holding the passenger door open.

'That's better.' Madeleine grinned at her friend as she put the car into gear and lurched away from the kerb. 'One second more and that crowd might have turned nasty and thrown things at us.'

'Maddy, you are crazy,' Jennifer giggled. 'Four elderly ladies and a couple of middle-aged men are hardly going to attack us.'

'Don't be so sure.' Madeleine winked at her knowingly. 'People turn into monsters when they are cold and wet and dreaming of log fires.'

Jennifer giggled again. 'Well this is very kind of you and it's lovely to see you. How's it all going? Are you having a fabulous time?'

'Mmmm, it's exhausting though. I simply had to come home for a few days' rest.' Madeleine took her hands off the wheel for a second as an idea struck her, and the car wobbled violently.

'Maddy, look where you are going! We're heading for the ditch!'

'Jen, I've got a wizard idea. Come back to the house with me and we'll have supper. The parents are in London, so I've got the place to myself – except for cook, of course. We'll sit on the floor by the fire and natter like we used to. We've got a lot of catching up to do. Do say you'll come.'

Jennifer thought for a minute. 'Well, it's Daddy's night out playing bridge with his friends, so I don't have to cook a meal for him.' She turned to her friend. 'That would be lovely, Maddy, but I'd better put a note through the door so that he won't worry if he gets back before I do.'

'That's great. It'll be just like old times.' Madeleine changed gear causing the little car to shoot forward at a faster pace. Jennifer clutched the door handle and pressed her right foot to an imaginary brake.

'You're impossible,' she laughed. 'If you don't calm down we'll never get to Divington in one piece.'

'. . . and then there was this Italian count. He had jet-black hair and an olive complexion and the bluest eyes you have ever seen. He was frightfully rich with *palazzos* all over the place. He wanted me to go to Venice with him for two weeks last August to stay with some cousins who have a *palazzo* there. Well, mother was getting very overexcited and thinking that her daughter was practically a countess, and then this ghastly old busybody had to go and tell her that it was all lies and this fellow was a real adventurer looking for a rich wife. There's even a rumour going around that he made Henrietta Michaels pregnant last March right at the beginning of the Season. He thought that way he'd have to marry her, but apparently her parents made her have an abortion rather than let him get his hands on her money.'

'How awful.' Jennifer was shocked but intrigued. 'Thank goodness you found out in time. He could have tried the same tactics with you.'

'Yes, I suppose he could have, but it would have been fun, wouldn't it?' Madeleine winked.

'Madeleine Heywood, don't you sit here and pretend to me that you would have let him ravish you. You'd have been scared to death. You'd hate it if people talked about you like that. You're far too keen on doing the right thing.'

'Jennifer James, you're the only person I would allow to talk to me that way and that's because we've known each other a long time.' Madeleine laughed good-naturedly. 'I often wish I was more like you. You're so sensible and I'm so scatterbrained.'

The two girls were sitting on the floor in front of the fire after dinner. Madeleine picked up an open bottle of red wine and brandished it in the air. 'More wine?' she asked. 'It's very warming on a cold night.'

'No thanks, I feel quite merry as it is. Any more and I'll be tight as a tick.'

'There you are.' Madeleine helped herself to another glass of wine. 'Proves my point.' She took a sip. 'You're right, though. I would have got myself into a terrible mess. I'm not anything like as tough as Henrietta. She just bounced back – not that anyone's supposed to know anything about it. She's had at least two lovers since then, if the rumours are correct. At the moment she's having a bit of a "thing" with Dickie Woodward. I think that she fancies becoming a Lady – if you know what I mean.' Madeleine smiled smugly. 'Not that there's much chance of that. Our Dickie's far too keen on playing the field and having a good time.' A thought struck her and she turned towards Jennifer. 'I say, didn't he give you a lift home after my dance? Come to think of it, he danced with you for ages, didn't he?'

Jennifer was trying desperately to calm the churning feeling inside her at the sound of Richard's name – albeit the nickname which she knew he hated. So now she knew what he was doing. He had obviously totally forgotten her. She would have been a liability. She would have fallen in love with him – correction, *had* fallen in love with him. Madeleine hadn't known what she was saying when she said she wished that she could be more like her, Jennifer. It would be so much better to be like Madeleine and her friends. That way you didn't get hurt and you didn't think too much.

'Jen, what's the matter? You didn't hear a word of what I've just been saying.' Madeleine snapped her fingers in front of Jennifer's eyes. 'I just asked you about Dickie Woodward. You danced with him at my dance and he took you home. Tell.'

'Tell?' Jennifer tried to pull herself together. 'There's nothing to tell, Maddy. He realized that I didn't know many people and he danced with me and then he dropped me home. He seemed very nice.'

'That's our Dickie. Full of charm. Didn't he ask to see you again? He certainly seemed very interested that night.'

'No, he didn't.' Jennifer blushed. Well, it wasn't exactly a lie, was it? He hadn't asked to see her again until he accidentally met her in the gallery.

Madeleine was quick to notice the blush. 'Jen, you're holding out on me. That's not fair. I've just told you my whole life story.'

Jennifer sighed. 'Well, if you must know, I ran into him in the gallery. He came in to buy a picture that he saw in the window. I had dinner with him a couple of times, that's all. He obviously found me far too dull compared with all you sophisticated young ladies.' She managed a weak smile but could not keep a certain amount of bitterness out of her voice.

Madeleine was perceptive. Poor Jen, she thought, fancy entertaining the idea that she could hold the interest of a man like Dickie Woodward. He could eat her for breakfast.

There was a long pause while they both stared into the fire. At last Jennifer stood up. 'He was very nice, Maddy,' she said. 'And before you ask, no, he didn't make a pass at me. I liked him a lot. He didn't seem at all as you have described him.'

'Did he hurt you? I'll kill him if he hurt you,' Madeleine exclaimed theatrically.

'No, he didn't hurt me. I tell you I hardly knew him, so how could he hurt me?'

'Believe me, Jen, you're well rid of him. He can charm the birds off the trees, but there's something strange about him. He doesn't want to get involved. He's a loner. I don't think that he likes people very much. He's certainly got some sort of hang-up.' Madeleine stood up. 'Come on, I'll run you home. Forget someone like Richard Woodward. He's not for you – or for anyone else for that matter. He lives for himself.'

Long into the night Jennifer lay in bed staring at the ceiling. "Forget him." That's what Madeleine had said, even though she had not known anything about what had happened between them. But it wasn't that easy. All the things that Madeleine had said about him – sometimes she believed them but at other times they just didn't seem right.

"Oh Richard," she thought silently and the cry seemed to go out into the night. "I have to know why you hurt so much – because I'm sure that you do. You owe me that much, knowing that I love you. I think that you need me and I know that I need you."

Richard Woodward could not sleep – not that there was anything abnormal about that. It happened all the time when he was alone. He had not had a bout of fever since August and that was three months ago, much longer than usual. Maybe this dreaded disease was in remission? He had asked Tony, but his friend had not been very hopeful. By cutting out alcohol he was feeling better and there had been no cold sweats at night, but Tony's advice was always the same: don't drink, don't smoke and don't get over-tired.

But why prolong the agony? At times he thought that it would be so much more painless to end it all now before it became degrading. At least that way he would not have to think about her – imagine what she was doing, and with whom – knowing that it could never be with him. "I love her," he thought, "and for the first time in my life I've acted unselfishly and put someone else before myself. I should feel good but I don't. I feel empty." He could almost sense her crying out to him – asking him why he had left her so abruptly, just as their relationship had become so special. How could he make her understand? Richard felt that he would feel easier about dying if she knew why he had done what he did.

It came to him that night. He would drive down to Divington tomorrow and explain everything to Derek James. After all, he was a doctor. Jennifer would be miles away at work in Cirencester, so there would be no chance of running into her. He would make Doctor James promise not to tell Jennifer until he was dead.

Richard sighed. He felt as if a weight had been lifted from his mind. She would know and she wouldn't hate him. It was not the perfect solution, but it was the only one and it made him sleep better for the rest of the night.

'Jennifer, these two letters must catch this afternoon's post. Be a dear and run to the post office with them.' Philip Ellis looked at the clock on the mantlepiece. It was quarter to four. 'And then you can go home early, if you can catch the four o'clock bus.'

'That's very kind of you, Mr Ellis. Are you sure that you don't need me?'

'No, no, it's a Friday night and the weather's appalling. You run along home. It's the best place to be on a cold evening like this.' He patted her shoulder in his usual absent-minded way.

Jennifer slipped on her coat and picked up the letters. 'Thanks, Mr Ellis. Have a nice weekend.' She hurried to the door.

'You, too, dear,' she heard him call as she closed it behind her.

The little post office was busy and she had to queue for several minutes. This will be the one day when the bus is on time, she thought. It was, but with much yelling and waving of hands she managed to attract the driver's attention as he was on the point of moving off. He grinned as she hurtled across the street in front of him and threw herself on board.

The journey to Divington took half an hour as the bus stopped at every village and hamlet on the way. It was full and for the first ten minutes Jennifer had to stand. The Christmas shoppers were out in force, and what room was not taken up by bodies was taken up with parcels. People were already in a festive mood which was catching and by the time she reached her village Jennifer was feeling in high spirits. She walked up the road singing quietly to herself.

At first she did not notice anything familiar about the man who was walking briskly down the path from her front door. He was tall and his shoulders were slightly hunched as he strode purposefully towards a car which was parked outside the gate. He jumped in and started the engine and drove quickly away. As the vehicle passed under a street lamp, however, its shape and colour were clearly visible. Jennifer caught her breath as her heart lurched violently. She could swear that it was Richard's car. She started to run, waving her hand and calling his name, but it was already rounding the corner out of sight.

She stood by the gate, her face flushed and her heart beating at twice its normal rate. Richard had come back. He must have come to see her. She had been right to ignore all that vicious gossip about him. She felt elated; but then the doubts started again. Why hadn't he waited for her? He knew where she worked, so why hadn't he come to the gallery? Why had he rushed away? He certainly had not looked as if he had wanted to waste any time. The mood of elation passed. Something was wrong – very wrong. Maybe he had not wanted to see her, but if so, why not? The light was on in her father's surgery, as Jennifer made her way wearily up the path.

Derek James sat with his elbows resting on the top of his desk and his chin in his hands. What a troubled young man Richard Woodward was. He sighed as he remembered the premonition he had had when he had first seen him with Jennifer at the Heywoods' dance back in June. He had felt then that it would all lead to suffering of some kind, though he had never envisaged anything like this. He looked at his watch. It was only half-past four. It would be another hour before Jennifer returned from work, by which time he would be taking surgery. He took his pipe from his pocket and then remembered that he must not smoke in this room. He walked across the hall and into the sitting room. As he packed the tobacco into the bowl, he thought about his conversation with the wretched young man. What a damned awful thing to happen to someone. How dreadful to have your fate hanging over you, threatening to take you away at any time. Derek admired Richard's courage in coping with his situation. It must be especially hard for someone young. At least an older man would be able to say that he had had a good innings – had been able to try to do some of the things that he would have wanted to. But Richard – how old was the boy? Early thirties, no more? No doubt he had made plenty of mistakes in his youth, but like most young people he would have thought that there was a lifetime to correct them in – and so there should have been. Richard had told him that in the last eighteen months he had mentally aged thirty years.

'I've done a great deal of thinking,' he had said. 'I have had to cram into two years – possibly three, or four if I'm lucky – the knowledge and responsibilities that usually come with old age. I've had to change,' he had smiled ruefully. 'I'm a very different person to the person I was before 1936, but I like myself more than I used to.'

Derek had cleared his throat loudly and said nothing as Richard had gone on to explain his feelings for Jennifer. He was very fond of her, he had said, but it could lead nowhere and he did not want her to be hurt. In September he had realised that their relationship was changing and he had not known at that time how to deal with the situation and so he had run away. On reflection, he knew that it had been the coward's way out, but it had seemed the only thing to do. In the last few months it had preyed on his mind. He knew that he had made her unhappy and he wanted to set the record straight, so to speak, so that in time she would know why he had done what he did.

There had been a long pause while both men considered the effect of Richard's speech, then Derek James had looked up and met the younger man's eyes.

'I know that my daughter is very young, Richard – she's only eighteen – but she has had to grow up fast since her mother died four years ago. She is a responsible adult and, although I agree with you that I would hate to see her hurt, I think you owe it to her to tell her yourself!'

'No!' The young man's voice had trembled. 'If you knew how difficult it has been for me to come here this afternoon – you're the only person I've ever told. I couldn't tell Jennifer. There's a limit to how much I can stand.' He had looked down unseeingly at his hands. 'Besides, I don't want her pity,' he had whispered.

'Ah . . .' Derek James' thoughts had been unspoken.

Richard had stood up. 'I know you think I'm taking the coward's way out, but if this must happen to me I want to die a dignified death. I don't want anyone to go through the last few months with me. Surely you, as a doctor, can understand that?'

'Yes.' Derek had sighed deeply and his heart had gone out to this unhappy young man. 'I'm sorry, Richard. Of course I understand.'

'And so you won't tell her?' Richard had paused. 'Not until afterwards?'

'Not if you don't want me to.'

'I don't want you to.' The reply had been emphatic. 'Well, I'll say good-bye.' They had shaken hands.

'Good-bye, Richard, and may I say that it's been a pleasure knowing you. G . . .' Derek's cheeks had reddened. He had been about to say 'Good luck', but how did you say something like that to a man who was dying?

Richard had smiled ruefully and raised his eyebrows, then he had turned, with shoulders hunched, and left the room.

'Daddy, where are you?' Jennifer had not found her father when she looked in the surgery.

'Here.' The voice came from the sitting room and sounded preoccupied. He looked up as she came into the room. 'You're home early, darling.' He looked uneasy, or was she imagining it? 'Something wrong at work?'

'No, Mr Ellis wanted me to go to the post office. He told me I could catch the early bus afterwards. Who was that leaving the house as I was walking up the road?' She tried to make her voice sound casual.

Doctor James tensed. So she had seen his visitor. Damn! Why did she have to choose tonight of all nights to come home early? Thank goodness it was already dark outside as she obviously hadn't recognised him. Still, it didn't leave him with any time to compose himself.

'Um?' he said vaguely. 'Oh, that was someone picking up a prescription.'

He knocked his pipe out on the hearth.

'Anyone I know?'

'Only one of Mr Burrington's farm labourers. Why the sudden interest in my patients?' He was on the defensive.

'No reason, but . . .'

'Darling, you'll have to excuse me. I've got one or two things that I must do in the office before evening surgery.' He tried to leave the room, but she blocked the doorway.

'I don't think that was one of your patients. I think it was Richard.'

'Good Lord, why on earth should you think that? You haven't seen him in months.' Derek's heart sank. He did not think that it was going to be easy to get out of this.

'Daddy, you're a very poor liar. For one thing a farm labourer doesn't have an expensive car the make and colour of Richard's.' He raised his eyebrows. 'I saw the car as it passed under the light from the street lamp,' she continued.

'Ah.' Derek abandoned his thoughts of escape and walked back to the fireplace. He relit his pipe and turned to face his daughter.

'Why was he here, Daddy? Somehow I don't think that he came to see me – he would have waited. Something is very wrong. I can sense it. No, don't tell me I'm imagining things.' She lifted her hand in response to her father's shaking head. 'What I want to know is what is so important that it brings Richard down here to see you and yet he doesn't want to see me. I love him, Daddy, and I'm sure that he loves me. You have to tell me what is going on.'

'He made me promise not to tell you. He didn't want you to be hurt.'

'If he cares about me and there's something to tell, then it's not entirely his decision. Anyway, I'm hurt already.'

'He doesn't want to see you again.'

'That's his prerogative. I still should know why.'

'Oh Jennifer, darling, if it was only that simple.' Derek shook his head sadly.

'It can't be that bad.' She gave a nervous laugh. 'He can't have committed murder or robbed a bank.'

'Sit down, Jennifer.' Her father patted the chair beside him. 'I think you ought to know, but Richard is never going to forgive me for telling you.'

CHAPTER SEVEN

'The train now standing at platform three will stop at Kemble, Swindon, Didcot, Reading ...' The announcer's voice rambled on until it finally reached the word London.

'Are you sure that you're doing the right thing?' Derek James frowned as he looked worriedly at his daughter. 'He doesn't want to see you. You're only making it harder for him and for yourself.'

'I don't know, Daddy. But I do know that I must see him again. I spent a lot of time thinking about it last night after you told me, and all day today. I can't let him face this alone anymore. Not now – knowing the way we both feel about each other. Tony Carrington isn't enough – oh, he's a good friend to Richard besides being his doctor, but he's a busy man and can't always be there when Richard needs him. I don't want him to be alone and afraid. Maybe, if he'll let us be together, we can try and forget it for a while.' Her eyes were unnaturally bright with unshed tears as she tossed her hair back and looked up at her father. 'And who knows,' she added defiantly, 'they might find a cure in the meantime.'

A porter ambled down the platform shutting doors as he approached them. Jennifer took her small suitcase from her father and boarded the train. She pulled down the window and leaned out to kiss his cheek.

'Jennifer, I really don't think that this is wise. Where will you stay? When will you come home?'

The train had already started to move. He walked along the platform trying to keep up with it.

'Don't worry about me. I'll be fine. I'll be back tomorrow. You know that I have to go to work on Monday.'

The train gathered speed leaving Derek James standing at

the end of the platform. He shook his head in bewilderment. Oh, the audacity and the optimism of the young. They thought that love could conquer all, but it didn't – he knew that. No amount of love or prayer had saved his beloved Catherine. One minute she had been bright and healthy and the next she had suffered a massive heart attack. She only lived for three days but they had been the worst three days of his life. He didn't want Jennifer to have to endure suffering like that, and with Richard it would be much worse. She would have to watch him slowly dying over the next few years – or even months. Every time he had a fever she wouldn't know whether it was the end or whether there would be another reprieve. He took out his handkerchief and blew his nose loudly, then turned and walked back along the platform. As he passed the station sign the words Cheltenham Spa stood out brightly and clearly. A Spa – a place where you could take the waters to improve your health. That's what people used to do, wasn't it? Not in this case, though. Poor Richard – and poor Jennifer. It was doomed – their relationship.

Jennifer sat back in her third-class seat on the train. It was relatively empty, being a Saturday evening. She stared out of the window at the rapidly receding lights of Cheltenham and wondered for the first time what she was doing on this train winging her way to London to a man who could well refuse to see her. He wouldn't do that, would he? If he had felt that she had to know eventually about his illness, he wouldn't throw her out unseen. There had to be strong feelings for her on his part. What if he wasn't there? She hadn't thought of that in her haste. What would she do if that were the case? Well, she reasoned, she could go to Tony Carrington and talk to him. He was bound to be in the telephone directory, but supposing he was away for the weekend as well? Maybe she should have telephoned him first. He would have known where Richard was.

Too late now, she told herself, she would just have to take a chance. She shivered and it was not from the cold.

A ticket collector shuffled into the compartment and she handed him her ticket to clip.

'What time do we get to Paddington?' she asked.

The man looked at her in astonishment as if she had asked him how far it was to the moon. He pushed his cap further back on his head and scratched his forehead. After a long pause he answered, 'Reckon it'll be 'bout fifteen minutes past seven.' The words were spoken slowly and with great deliberation, but little conviction.

'Thank you.' She managed to muster a small smile.

'. . . 's all right.' He withdrew, slamming the door behind him.

Jennifer closed her eyes. She had two hours in which to think of what on earth she was going to say to Richard when or if she got to see him.

'. . . So, you see, I thought that if I explained it to him, he could eventually tell her after it's all over. I feel better now that I know that she will be told the truth eventually. I would hate to die thinking that she hated me.' Richard put down his knife and fork and eyed Tony across the dining-room table.

'I can understand your motive, but do you think that it was wise?' Tony took a bite of roast chicken and chewed it carefully while he listened to his friend. 'He might tell her now and not wait. What will you do if that happens?'

'He won't. I have his word on that.'

'She really got to you, didn't she?' As she had to him, Tony thought, as he poured himself a glass of water.

'Yes, she did.' Richard sighed. 'I kept telling myself that it was friendship that I wanted from her and nothing more. I never laid a finger on her until that day in September.' Out of the corner of his eye he saw Tony's eyebrows lift. 'Oh, nothing happened – nothing serious, that is. And yet, something did happen and in a way it was more serious than anything I have ever felt in my whole life. I realised that I couldn't go on pretending to myself that it was only friendship that I wanted from her. I loved her and wanted desperately to make love to her. She wanted it too. It was then that I knew I had to stop seeing her. There was no future in it and she isn't the kind of girl that I could have had an affair with. She's the sort of person that a man marries and settles down with. All that I could have done was ruin her life.'

Tony took off his glasses and rubbed his right eye. That habit again! 'Why don't you?' he asked, trying to make his voice sound nonchalant.

'Why don't I what?'

'Why don't you ask her to marry you? You're not going to die tomorrow and, who knows, living a quiet life in the country with a wife might prolong things for you.'

'How can you say that, Tony? It wouldn't be fair. I'm not that much of a shit.'

'What's fair? And if she loves you, then she's hurt already and it's too late to talk about that.'

Richard gazed at the floor. 'I couldn't subject her to the really bad time – at the end.'

'Can't or won't, Richard?' Tony was warming to his argument. 'Is it her you are thinking about or is it yourself?'

'What the hell do you mean by that?'

'Is it a question of pride, Richard? I don't think you can bear the thought of anyone seeing you helpless or vulnerable. We are all going to die, Richard. Some of us sooner than others, but none of us knows exactly when or where it will happen.'

'I think I have a better idea than most people,' Richard mumbled. 'Don't you think that a man has a right to some dignity?'

'Don't confuse dignity with pride,' Tony said softly. 'After all, you wouldn't be leaving her destitute, would you? She'd be Lady Woodward with a town house and a country estate. She's young and beautiful. You'd be giving her a wonderful new start.'

'Put like that you actually make it sound feasible,' Richard smiled weakly.

'It is, Richard, if she's the girl we think she is.'

'Not quite, Tony,' Richard paused. 'I've led a pretty wild life from time to time, as you well know. I'm not nearly as well off as you think I am. This house is on the market, and I had thought that once it's sold I'd move back to Edgeglow for the time I have left and then – afterwards – it could be sold to pay off the rest of my debts.' He sighed. 'So you see, there would be no money, just a rather tarnished title.'

At that moment the front doorbell rang shrilly.

'I wonder who on earth that can be.' Richard looked at the grandfather clock in the corner of the room. 'Eight o'clock on a Saturday night. None of my so-called friends would let it be known that they were in town on a Saturday night. Have you got a possible emergency?'

Tony shook his head. 'No – anyway, Nanny is at home. She would telephone if anything was the matter.' A thought struck him and he stood up. 'Unless there is something wrong with the phone.'

'Calm down, old boy. Dawkins will answer the door. I'm sure it's nothing important.'

Jennifer stood on the doorstep shivering from the cold night air. Even in her agitated state she noticed that there were lights on in the house, therefore someone was in. Please God that it was Richard. She rubbed her hands together for warmth and to try and stop herself from shaking, then she nerved herself to press the bell. Having done so, she fixed her attention on the river and the few cars that were crossing Albert Bridge. She never heard the footsteps approaching and her thoughts were miles away when the door was flung open.

'Yes?' a voice inquired. 'Can I help you?'

She gasped and swung round. Dawkins' eyesight was not as good as it used to be. He screwed up his eyes and peered closely into her face.

'Good Lord, it's Miss James, isn't it?'

'Y-yes . . .' she stuttered – completely at a loss for words.

He waited patiently for her to continue, but the silence grew longer. Well, this was a turn up for the books, Dawkins thought. In the past few years several of Sir Richard's young ladies had turned up at various times of the day or night when they were not expected – usually to cause a scene. Why, only last week that Miss Michaels had done just that. Well, in Dawkins' opinion, Sir Richard was well rid of that one. Too condescending by half she had been and very much with an eye on the main chance. He sighed as he looked at the young girl in front of him. He definitely had never expected to see this one again – more's the pity. He had liked her and so had all the staff at Edgeglow, but they hadn't really been surprised when the relationship failed to last. Sir Richard preferred the racier young ladies.

'Is Sir Richard in?' At last Jennifer managed to speak.

Now it was Dawkins' turn to be hesitant. He knew that she was not expected. His employer would have told him if she had been. It was usually up to Dawkins to get rid of any young lady who could be difficult, but what should he do in this case? He noted the air of uncertainty about the girl and also the small suitcase that she held in her hand. She had come a long way and it was late. Whatever Sir Richard might say, he couldn't turn her away. Where would she go? Dawkins was sure that she didn't know her way around London.

'You best come in, miss.' He had made up his mind. Sir Richard could fire him in the morning but he couldn't – no, wouldn't – leave this girl out in the cold. He felt responsible for her. 'I'll tell Sir Richard that you are here.'

'Oh, thank you.' She heaved a sigh of relief as she walked

into the hall and Dawkins closed the door. So, he was there. Thank goodness.

At that moment the dining-room door opened and Tony appeared.

'Was that for me, Dawkins?' he asked. 'I thought maybe . . .' He stopped mid-sentence and stared at Jennifer. 'Jennifer, good Lord, what are you doing here?' His heart sank. As if he didn't know. So Doctor James had told his daughter. He wasn't surprised for Jennifer and her father had a very close relationship.

'Tony, I have to see Richard.' Her little face was pinched and her voice trembled. 'Please don't stop me.'

Dawkins coughed discreetly and vanished back into the kitchen. A reprieve, he thought. Thank goodness Doctor Carrington had appeared when he had. He could deal with the situation.

Tony took a deep breath and braced himself for the events that would surely follow. 'I know you had to come,' he agreed. 'In your place I'd have done exactly the same thing.'

'You know?'

'Yes, Richard told me he'd spoken to your father.'

'He should have told *me*, Tony.'

'It's a very private thing, Jennifer – not easily shared – especially not with those you love. He was doing it to protect you because . . .'

She was not listening to him. Her eyes were focused beyond him on Richard who was framed in the doorway.

'I saw you,' she said. 'I saw you as you were leaving the house. I came home early and there you were – leaving before I had a chance to stop you.'

Richard's face was very white. He put a hand on the door frame to steady himself. 'Tony, I don't know how to handle this.' It was an anguished plea for help.

Tony cleared his throat as he felt the tension between them. 'I think that I should leave,' he said. 'This is something that you must settle between yourselves. You don't need me.'

66

'Tony . . .' Richard gripped his friend's arm in panic. 'Please tell her to leave now.'

'Tony, wait a minute.' The tears that had been threatening to fill her eyes had receded and a new note of authority had crept into Jennifer's voice. 'Please tell your stubborn friend that I love him and I'm sure that he loves me.' She looked up and fastened her eyes on Richard. 'I will only leave if he can tell me with his hand on the Bible that he doesn't love me.'

'You know that I can't say that,' Richard said in a whisper. 'You're not being fair.' He tore his eyes away from her.

'Fair? Who's talking about being fair?' She walked over and stood in front of him. 'What's fair about your illness? What's fair about us loving each other and you not telling me?' She put her hands on his arms. 'I love you, Richard, and I want to be with you for as long as is possible.'

'And afterwards?' He still did not look at her.

'Afterwards, I'll survive – the same as I will if you send me away now. We're lucky, Richard, there's still some time left. We can be together for a little while. We love each other and we need each other. Some people – however long they live – never experience that.' She felt him tremble as he digested what she had said, then with a strangled sob he gathered her into his arms and kissed her with all the passion that had been bottled up inside him since he had left her in September.

Tony took off his glasses and rubbed his right eye, then he quietly let himself out of the front door.

Richard and Jennifer were married in Cheltenham Registry Office the week before Christmas. Afterwards they drove back to Divington Church for a short service of blessing. The only people to witness these events were Derek James, Madeleine Heywood and, of course, Tony Carrington.

How beautiful she looks, thought Tony. A serene calm radiated from Jennifer as she stood with her arm linked through Richard's. In her pale-blue velvet suit with the white mink collar and cuffs and the little white mink hat, she looked like a fairytale princess. A stab of pain ran through him as he realised – not for the first time – how much he envied Richard his bride. He mentally chastised himself for thinking such thoughts and raised his glass to toast the happy couple.

'Jen, you are a dark horse.' Madeleine embraced her friend warmly. 'Why, it was only a month ago that we were having dinner together in front of the fire at home and you never so much as hinted that you and Richard were a going concern – in fact you positively went out of your way to deny it.'

'Well, it was all a bit sudden.'

Madeleine frowned. 'You're not pregnant, are you?'

For a moment Jennifer's face dropped as she thought about the baby that would probably never happen, then she forced herself to brighten up. She punched Madeleine playfully on the arm. 'Maddy Heywood, you have a one-track mind. No, I'm definitely not pregnant.'

Maddy giggled. 'Oh well, that's a relief.' She turned serious for a second. 'Are you sure you've done the right thing, Jen? I mean, you know what a reputation he has around town. Can you cope with all that?'

Jennifer caught Richard's eye across the room. He smiled back at her with a wealth of feeling in his eyes. Madeleine noticed the look.

'Yes, Maddy, I know I've done the right thing and I don't have to cope with anything. Of that, I'm sure.'

'Well, you certainly seem to have tamed the lion. Most of the women in London failed. One day you must tell me how you did it.' Madeleine giggled again. 'Mother is amazed. She can't quite believe it. When I told her I was coming to your wedding to Richard, she thought for a moment and then said: "Really, Madeleine, here we are at the end of the

Season and you're not married or even engaged, and Jennifer James, who has never moved out of Divington, manages to catch one of the most eligible bachelors in the country."'

'That sounds like your mother,' Jennifer laughed. 'But I'm sure you won't disappoint her, Maddy.'

'To tell you the truth, Jan, I don't want to settle down for a long time. I enjoy going out and living it up. I'm not a home-body like you.' She changed the subject. 'Well, Lady Woodward, where are you going for your honeymoon?'

Jennifer felt Richard's arm slide around her waist. 'We're not going anywhere at the moment, Madeleine. It's Christmas next week and we can't leave Jennifer's father alone.' He smiled down at his wife. 'We might go away later, mightn't we, darling?'

Jennifer drew in her breath sharply. Even the most innocuous of phrases could take on another meaning when you let your imagination take over.

'There you are,' Madeleine held up her hands in mock horror. 'It's what I've just been saying. You've married a home-body, Richard. She'll love you and spoil you to death. I hope you're ready for this.'

'Yes, I'm ready for it.' Richard spoke lightly, but Jennifer knew what he was thinking. Was it always to be like this, she wondered. Whenever they were with other people, would they be constantly reminded of what lay ahead of them by remarks such as this?

Jennifer would learn in the next few months how much easier it was to be alone with Richard – just the two of them. They could laugh together and even cry together but always they would end up in each other's arms, holding each other and loving each other while they were able briefly to forget the inevitable.

Their three guests had gone. Richard and Jennifer walked back into the house and closed the door. Mrs Edison appeared in the kitchen doorway. 'It's half-past seven, m'lady. Would you like dinner soon? You must be tired.'

Jennifer blushed. She was still mildly uncomfortable at her new form of address. She looked up at her husband and noticed how pale he seemed. For the first time she noticed a frailty about him. He was like a piece of delicate porcelain and as such must be cherished and protected.

'Thank you, Mrs Edison. That would be lovely. We are tired.' She felt Richard give her a squeeze.

'Very good, m'lady. I'll send Edison in to tell you when it's ready.' She paused.

'Yes, Mrs Edison?'

'On behalf of Edison and meself, we'd like to wish you many congratulations. We're sure that you'll be very happy. Sir Richard, your ladyship.' She nodded her head in their direction blushing furiously.

'Thank you, Mrs Edison. I know we will be,' Richard smiled at her.

'Yes, thank you, Mrs Edison. I know I'm going to love being here.' Jennifer walked with her husband into the drawing room.

Jennifer and Richard did not do justice to the excellent dinner which Mrs Edison placed before them. They could feel the tension growing between them – a tension that had not been there all day, but that was building itself up now that they were alone together.

It was three weeks since Jennifer had gone to find Richard in London, and in all the time that it had taken to arrange their marriage they still had not made love. Richard had been very old-fashioned about that, saying that it would not be right until they were married. Jennifer had teased him unmercifully, referring to his reputation in the gossip columns, but he would not be swayed. 'People usually get what they ask for,' he had told her. 'Some live by one code of behaviour and others by another. You, my darling, are very special and I realise how lucky I am to have found you – for however long it will be. Nothing must tarnish our love. Everything must be right.'

At the time and during their brief life together, Jennifer had thought how romantic it all was. It was not until quite a long time after Richard's death that she could look back and put things into perspective. It was then that she realised that the pedestal on which Richard had placed her had subconsciously added one more strain to the already sensitive situation. But now, only hours after their marriage, the only tension came from knowing that it would soon all be released and that soon they would both be together in the true sense of the word.

Jennifer studied her reflection in the mirror as she brushed her long blonde hair. The pale ivory satin nightgown clung to her slim figure. She pinched her cheeks to give herself some colour and her eyes fastened on the reflection of the large four-poster bed – Richard's bed. '*Our* bed from now on,' she thought and blushed violently. She looked up to find that Richard had appeared from the bathroom. Her blush did not fade when she saw that all he was wearing was a towel draped around his waist. He had a good body – maybe just a little bit too thin – with an abundance of dark curly hairs on his chest.

'Let me do that.' He walked towards her and took the hairbrush out of her hand. His eyes fixed and held hers in the mirror and he noticed her high colour. 'My beautiful innocent wife.' His voice was a caress as were the strokes of the brush on her head. She caught her breath and leaned back against him as his other hand began to stroke her shoulder and her neck. She closed her eyes and became mesmerised by his movements so that she was hardly aware when the brushing stopped and he pulled her gently to her feet. She was still lost in a semi-hypnotic trance as he led her to the bed and took her in his arms. She vaguely noticed the straps of her nightgown easing over her shoulders as it fell to the floor, to be joined immediately by his towel. He pressed her naked body closer to him as he kissed her deeply. She felt the hardness of him against her and looked down, and gasped as she saw the extent of his need for her.

'Don't be afraid, my darling.' He pushed her back on to the bed and lay down beside her. 'I love you, Jennifer, and I've wanted you for so long. I won't hurt you.'

'I want you too, Richard.' Her voice trembled with emotion. 'And you know how much I love you.' She pulled his head down to hers and they kissed again. His hands started to stroke her body, kneading her breasts and arousing her nipples. Slowly they travelled downwards across her flat stomach, and then backwards over her buttocks to caress the back of her legs. Slower and slower until they reached the inside of her thighs. Jennifer felt as if her whole body had become liquid. "Don't stop," she told him silently. "I can't bear it if you stop now." And suddenly – had she said it out loud? – his hand was there rubbing gently at that sensitive spot between her legs. She groaned as she gave herself up to the intensity of this new-found pleasure. 'No, don't stop.' Her eyes flew open as he withdrew his hand. 'Shush.' He stroked the damp hair away from her face as he positioned himself over her. She felt his penis nudging her in the same spot and the fire of pleasure intensified. Suddenly she gasped as a violent pain shot through her.

Richard held her still for a moment, savouring the feeling of being inside her at last, then slowly he began easing himself in and out. Oh, the ecstasy of at last being able to love her completely. He came almost at once. It was impossible not to.

When it was over he took her in his arms again, unaware of her shock. 'Darling, I'm sorry that it was all over so quickly. I promise that the next time will be for you.' He buried his face in her neck. 'I didn't hurt you too much, did I?'

'No, of course you didn't,' she lied. 'It was wonderful.'

She folded her arms tighter around him to try and convince herself. Her eyes glistened in the dark with unshed tears. Was this what it was like? She had thought that her wedding night would be wonderful, that a love as intense as hers would banish all pain. Well, she had been proved wrong. But next time would be better, wouldn't it? It had to be.

But there was no love for Jennifer and Richard the next morning, or indeed for several days later. During the night Richard developed one of his fevers which lasted for nearly two weeks. When they eventually made love again Jennifer found that it no longer hurt her, but it lacked the lustre which it should have had. It did not mean that she loved Richard less – in fact she loved him more and was determined that he would never find out about her inadequacy. "I must be frigid," she thought, "and yet I love it when he touches me and when he kisses me. It's just the actual sexual act that doesn't affect me the way I feel it should. It's not that I dislike it or that it hurts me – maybe that would be better than this inability to feel what I want to feel."

It never occurred to Jennifer that possibly Richard was not to be the love of her life or that the pressures upon them could upset and trouble her mind. She was bitterly disappointed in herself and determined that no one should be aware of her shortcomings. She plunged herself into making a happy home life for Richard so that he should want for nothing.

Tony Carrington watched from afar as the dark circles grew under her eyes and she lost weight that she could not afford to lose. Richard had also started to go downhill. The fevers came now with increasing regularity and lasted longer.

In March of 1939 Tony studied Richard's latest X-rays and noticed that his liver and spleen had become enlarged. There were also enlarged glands in his chest. He sighed deeply as he realised that time was running out. Should he tell Jennifer?

He was saved from making that decision when she turned up at his office and asked to be told the latest on Richard's condition.

'I'm sorry, Jennifer.' He took off his glasses and rubbed his eye. 'The X-rays are not good.'

Jennifer's eyes were unnaturally bright and her face flushed. Her movements were jerky, and she reminded Tony of a time-bomb waiting to explode.

'What does that mean?' She drummed her fingers on the top of the desk.

'About two months – maybe less, maybe more.'

Was it a trick of the light or was that relief he saw in her eyes for a brief second? Tony rubbed his hands together thoughtfully. Had Richard been right? Had it been a mistake for these two young people to come together and have to go through something like this? In her way Jennifer looked as ill as her unfortunate husband. She had turned away from him and was gathering herself together. When she turned back to him she looked utterly defeated, and there was an incredible sadness in her eyes. She sank shakily into the leather chair.

'You know, Tony, when we are young we think that we can change the world. We think we know it all and that as long as we have faith and believe in ourselves we can do anything. It's not true, is it?' She nodded at the ceiling. 'He has strange ways of proving that to us, doesn't He? I thought that I could ...' She paused and looked down at her trembling hands. 'Oh, it doesn't matter what I thought.' She sighed and met his gaze. 'The point is that I know better now. I love him very much, Tony, and I hope that I've made him happy. I've tried so hard.'

Tony cleared his throat and tried to swallow. The large lump he found there made it difficult

'You know where I am when either or both of you need me.' Tony's voice was hardly above a whisper.

Jennifer turned around as she reached the door. 'A few months ago I would have said that all we need is each other, but that's not true either. We will need you, Tony, and you can be sure that I'll keep in touch from now on until . . .'

She did not finish the sentence as she closed the door behind her.

On May 23rd 1939, Sir Richard Harold George Woodward, the eighth baronet, died from a chest infection which led to pneumonia. It was three years after Hodgkin's Disease had been diagnosed. As there were no direct heirs, the title passed to a distant cousin.

CHAPTER EIGHT

'For as much as it hath pleased Almighty God of his great mercy to take unto himself the soul of our dear brother here departed, we therefore commit his body to the ground; ashes to ashes, dust to dust; in the certain hope of the Resurrection to eternal life, through our Lord Jesus Christ . . .'

The vicar's voice droned on in its monotonous fashion. Jennifer stood between Anthony Carrington and her father. Her expression was glazed but her eyes were dry, and in keeping with Richard's final wish she was not wearing black. Instead she wore a navy-blue suit and a soft white blouse. Her usually slim figure was now painfully thin and her skin lacked its former lustre. She looked so frail that it was all that Tony could do to stop himself from putting his arm around her to support her, but he knew that she would not want that. When the time came she walked forward by herself, picked up a handful of earth and then let it trickle slowly on to the coffin. 'Good-bye, my love,' he heard her say softly. Then she turned and walked quickly away through the small group of mourners who parted to let her go.

Back at the manor, Mrs Edison had prepared tea and laid it out in the drawing room. Jennifer took off her hat and left it on the table in the hall. She shivered as she walked into the large room. Even though it was the end of May, it was a damp bleak day. Just the kind of weather you would expect for a funeral, she thought wryly. Mrs Edison had had the presence of mind to light the fire in the grate, but it did little to alleviate the coldness and the numbness which surrounded her. She picked up a teacup, but her hand was so unsteady that it would have fallen before she could fill it if Tony had not been behind her. He took it from her.

'Sit down, Jennifer,' he said gently. 'I'll pour it for you.'

'Thank you.' She tried to give him a tired smile as she sank into the nearest chair.

He filled her cup and handed her the steaming liquid. 'Drink it up,' he told her as if he was addressing a child. 'It'll make you feel warmer.' He sat down beside her.

'I don't think that I'll ever feel warm again, Tony. Even my bones feel chilled!' She turned her large haunted eyes on him.

'Jennifer, you know that I'll always be your friend. Let me help you through this.' Tony knew that this was not the time to force himself upon her, but he could not bear to think that now Richard was dead he might never see her again.

'Dear Tony.' She placed her hand briefly on his arm. 'Of course you'll always be my friend. You're the one person that I can talk to. The one person who truly understands. You're like the brother I never had. I value your friendship so very much, but I have to be by myself for a while. I need time to unwind and to find some peace of mind. These last few months have been even more of a strain than I could ever have imagined – if that is possible.'

'You need to get away for a while.' He frowned as he spoke. 'But with all the signs of war brewing in Europe, I wouldn't advise going abroad.' He thought hard for a moment. 'I have an idea.' He took her hands in his and gave them a squeeze. 'Helen and I used to have a cottage in Cornwall. I sold it when she died. Just up the road there was a guest house run by a Mrs Kellow. She was a nice woman who used to take messages for us as we didn't have a telephone. Why don't you go and stay there for a few weeks? I could give her a call and I know that she would look after you. You would be able to walk on the cliffs and be by yourself and have a good rest, and your father and I would know that you were being well cared for.'

'I don't know.' She hesitated. 'Do you really think that there will be a war, Tony? I can't believe that that madman Hitler would be prepared to go so far.'

'You've just answered your question, my d . . . dear.' He

had been about to say 'my darling' but had just stopped himself in time. 'A madman is what he is, and madmen do not act like other people.'

Jennifer looked around the room. She noticed the way people turned away rather than meet her eyes. Most people avoided approaching her – not knowing what to say. Even Maddy kept her distance. "They find death embarrassing," she thought. "It is also distasteful to them. They think if they come and commiserate with me I might cry and that would make them feel very uncomfortable." But for how long would it be like this? Could she stand the carefully angled pleasantries? And could she stand being at Edgeglow – living in rooms that were so much a part of Richard, sleeping alone in their bed? She made her decision and faced Tony.

'Yes, I would like to go to Cornwall, Tony. Thank you for suggesting it.'

'That's wonderful. I'll telephone Mrs Kellow tonight.' He smiled at her. She stood up. 'I'd like to go as soon as possible – tomorrow if you can arrange it. I can't take much more of this.' She glanced at the group of people talking in undertones. 'Do you think that everyone would think me rude if I went to bed? I feel so very tired.'

'Of course they wouldn't.' He walked with her to the bottom of the stairs. 'Would you like me to give you something to help you sleep?'

'No thank you, I'll be fine.'

'I'll telephone you in the morning and tell you what I've arranged, and don't worry about anything here while you're away. I'll be in constant touch with Mrs Edison. Between us we'll look after everything.'

'Tony, I don't know what I'd do without you.' She touched his cheek briefly with her lips before turning to walk up the stairs. 'You're the best friend I ever had.'

Tony sighed deeply as he watched her disappear from view. Best friend, confidant, it was a start, he supposed.

Better than nothing, but would he ever mean more than that to her? When had he first fallen in love with Jennifer Woodward? If he was honest with himself it was that very first weekend when he had brought Charlie down to Edgelow and had watched Jennifer playing with him. Oh, he hadn't realised it at the time – it had been far too soon after Helen's death – but he had envied Richard even then.

'Tony, where's Jennifer? Is she all right?' Doctor James rushed into the hall looking worried.

'She's gone upstairs to rest, Derek.'

'I'll go up and see how she is.'

'No, I wouldn't do that if I were you. She wants to be on her own.' He told the older man what he was going to arrange for Jennifer.

'She's very fortunate to have a friend like you.'

'Not at all, I'm extremely fond of her and I know what she's going through.' The two doctors looked at each other and Derek noticed his companion's drooping shoulders. While Tony was talking about Jennifer he had glanced up the stairs, and for one brief unguarded moment Derek caught sight of the look of naked longing on his face. A sensation of shock ran through him. What was it about his beautiful headstrong daughter that inspired men so much older than herself to fall head-over-heels in love with her? Anthony Carrington must be nearly forty and Jennifer was just nineteen. Would Tony be the next man to claim her, he wondered. Despite the age difference he was a kind man with a son who needed a mother. He was also a highly respected doctor, the top of his field, and there were rumours that he was tipped to be the next royal physician. He was a man totally dedicated to his profession. In fact he worked a little too hard and often appeared completely exhausted – like today. A wife would be good for him. She would make him relax more, but if Tony wanted Jennifer he would have to be prepared to wait and take things very easy.

*

79

The holiday in Cornwall did Jennifer a power of good. Mrs Kellow was a motherly type who liked to make sure that all her guests were satisfied. She was a widow, in her sixties, whose children were grown-up and married. On the death of her husband she had turned the house, which was far too large for her on her own, into a guest house. This, she had told herself, would give her something to do as well as bring in a few pennies. She would also not have so much time to feel lonely.

'There's nothing like folk, my dear, to cheer you up. Why, I have my regulars who come back here year after year. They have become great friends. It's given me a new lease on life.'

It was raining that afternoon and Jennifer was sitting in Mrs Kellow's front room listening to the wireless. Mrs Kellow had just made a cup of tea and had sat herself down for five minutes to chat and enjoy it.

'Very tragic for you at your stage of life, dearie, to be a widow already. It happened to my Maureen, but she was twenty-five. She'd been married for three years when Mat died. Drowned he was, in a fishing-boat accident. Moped around for months she did, but then I says enough's enough. I sent her off to Penzance to work and in no time at all she met a nice young man who was the assistant manager at the Cliff Tops Hotel – he's the manager now, by the way. Well, they've been married these last ten years and have three kiddies. They're as happy as can be. She never stops saying – "Mum, thank goodness I'm not married to a fisherman anymore. Every time he went out I'd wonder if he would come back." I tell you, dearie, there's a lesson to be learned from everything in life.'

Jennifer smiled in spite of herself. There was something about Mrs Kellow which made it impossible to feel sad when you talked to her, whichever way the conversation went. Almost anything that anyone could possibly have experienced had already happened to Mrs Kellow, or to a friend of Mrs Kellow, and however bad it was they had always managed to overcome it. Mrs Kellow set herself out to generate hope and by and large she succeeded.

What really helped Jennifer through was the ease with which Mrs Kellow could talk about death. She spoke openly about it – no hidden undertones and no embarrassment. It was something that happened and had to be taken in one's stride.

'That poor Doctor Carrington. Such a lovely young man. He and his wife often used to come in and see me when they had the cottage up the road. So sad that she had to die so young.' She was silent for a minute as if in deference to a memory, but when she looked up she was smiling. 'But she left him with a beautiful little boy, didn't she? And he's young enough to marry again. We're all put on this earth to be tested is what I says. We have to learn to make the best of things. You'll be all right, my dear.' She looked at Jennifer shrewdly. 'I knows you will be. Just be sure and keep busy. You're young. You've got your whole life in front of you. You're just at the beginning.'

'I don't feel like that at all.' Jennifer gazed at the rain falling outside. 'I feel as if something has been taken from me – not just Richard – something I will never have again.'

'It's called growing up, dearie. It's in the Bible – something about when I was a child I spake like a child, but when I became a man I put away childish things.'

'I suppose so. I know I'll never be a child again.'

'We can never go back, dearie. We must always look forwards and do the best we can.'

Jennifer was to remember this conversation for many years to come. Mrs Kellow became a shining example to her of someone who had triumphed over all her sorrows to emerge as a happy and contented person.

As the days became brighter she took herself for long walks along the cliffs. Her favourite walk was to the Bedruthan Steps, near Newquay, not far along the coast. The steps were large lumps of rock which the sea had torn from the cliffs. Legend had it that a local giant, Bedruthan, used them to step ashore from his morning bathe. The rocks were crumbling all the time which bore testimony of the unending power of the sea.

As she stood looking down at the beautiful wild scene beneath her, Jennifer thought of Maureen's fisherman husband, Mat. The sea was fairly calm now, but she could imagine its ferocity when stormy. Maybe Bedruthan had been angry that day. Poor Mat – mourned for a short while by Maureen, but who remembered him now? "Will I forget Richard in time?" she wondered. Would these feelings of sorrow and guilt ever diminish? Would she ever forgive herself for not being able to feel the need for him that he had felt for her? She had loved him so much – but 'had' was the crucial word. Why was she frigid? What was wrong with her? It was not something that she could ask anyone – not her father nor Mrs Kellow and certainly not Tony. Some women were born like that, weren't they? Well, she wouldn't make the mistake of marrying again. She would get another job and throw herself into her work. She would also have to sell Edgeglow because Richard's financial state when he died had not been such that she could keep it on.

"It's time to go back home," she thought. "It's the end of June and I must start to pick up my life again."

'You can't sell Edgeglow now.' Anthony Carrington sat across the table and surveyed Jennifer over the top of his glasses. She had come up to London to see him and he had suggested that they meet at Claridges for lunch.

'I must. I can't afford to keep it.'

'My dear girl, you couldn't possibly sell it now, however much you might want to. You realize war could be declared at any moment. Nobody is going to be interested in buying anything. You wouldn't be able to give it away.'

'I may have to do just that.'

'Jennifer, relax. Don't be in such a hurry.' He took off his glases and rubbed his right eye. 'Sit tight for the moment and let's see which way the wind will blow. The present situation can't last much longer. Something is bound to happen.'

'And if there is a war, Tony? What then? I could find that the army requisition the house and when they've finished with it, it might be in terrible shape.'

'Not "if", my dear, when. I'm afraid war is inevitable.' He looked at his watch. 'I must go, I've got a very busy afternoon. But try not to worry, Jennifer, I'll think of something.'

As he saw her to a taxi he embraced her briefly. 'Promise me that you won't do anything until I've had time to think? I'll telephone you as soon as possible.'

'I promise.' She climbed into the taxi and he slammed the door. 'Paddington Station,' he told the driver.

'Kiss Charlie for me,' she called as the taxi pulled away.

Kiss Charlie for me. The sentence kept running through his head as he walked back to his consulting rooms in Harley Street. Kiss Charlie for me. It triggered something off in his brain. Why not? She was wonderful with Charlie and she'd be wonderful with other kids too. What a marvellous idea. He hailed a taxi. To walk back now would take too long. He had some important telephone calls to make before his first patient arrived.

'Jennifer, I've got the answer!' Tony Carrington spoke exuberantly down the telephone.

'Tony, I never thought you'd telephone so soon.'

'You like children, don't you?'

'Yes, of course. Why?'

'That's the answer. Children.'

'Tony, will you stop talking in riddles and tell me what this is all about?'

'I'm sorry, my dear, it's just that I'm excited. You know that the government are evacuating children from London in

83

case war breaks out? Well, I've spoken to someone I know in the right department and they could send you as many as you could manage.'

'I still don't follow you.'

'How many bedrooms do you have at Edgeglow?'

She counted quickly on her fingers. 'Ten.'

'That's marvellous. One for you. One for Mrs Edison and one for me whenever I can manage to come down. That leaves seven for the children. I want you to have Charlie – it'll be much safer for him being with you than with me in London.' He did not tell her that he thought he might be called up for active service. 'Nanny wants to leave and go and live with her sister, so I would be happy to pay Mrs Edison's wages, and of course you would get a government subsidy for each child. They would be enrolled at the local school. Well, what do you say?'

'I don't know. I've hardly had time to take it all in.' Jennifer paused to let the idea sink in. Children at Edgeglow. The house would be full of running feet and laughter. There would be jostling around the kitchen table at meal times and little people to love and read stories to in the lonely evenings.

'I'll have to discuss it with Mrs Edison,' she said, 'but if she agrees, I think it sounds a wonderful idea. Tony, I'm always saying this, but what would I do without you?'

Mrs Edison was, as she put it, tickled pink. Of course she would move into the house and Edison could come up for his meals. She and Jennifer worked out that they could take in five other children besides Charlie to start with. They could always increase the number once they were used to the routine.

And so it was that on a hot stuffy afternoon in August five children arrived at Kemble Station and were taken to Edgeglow Manor by Mrs Purton who worked for the Welfare Association.

Each child had a namecard hanging on a piece of string around his or her neck. Paul and Nick Garrett were brothers aged nine and seven respectively. They had dark unruly hair and their clothes looked a size too small for them. Their faces and hands were grubby and little Nick had a large angry scab on his right knee.

Betty Fox was seven. She had not let go of her little brother Tom's hand since they had arrived. He was only four and looked slightly disorientated. They were shabbily dressed but clean and an effort had been made by tying a new ribbon in Betty's hair.

Bridget Lane, though, was a complete contrast to the other four children. She was immaculately turned out and very self-possessed. At ten years she was the eldest. Although her clothes were by no means new, they were starched and ironed to perfection, and her clean shining hair was held in place by two tortoise-shell slides. She had already assumed the role of leader. However, when she spoke there was no difference between her accent and that of the other children.

It was Bridget who first heard Charlie crying. 'That your baby?' she asked Jennifer.

Jennifer blushed. 'No . . .'

'S'all right,' Bridget interrupted her mid-sentence. 'I know it's none o' my business. If I gets too nosey just tell me to shut up.'

'Now then, young lady, that's enough of that.' Mrs Edison was reproving. 'Baby Charlie is an evacuee just like the rest of you.'

'Oops . . . pardon.' Bridget winked saucily. 'I might a' known that there'd be none a' that in a posh place like this 'ere.'

Jennifer laughed. It was impossible not to warm to Bridget. 'Come on now, you lot. Time to get settled in.' Bridget rounded up her little band. She turned to Mrs Edison. 'Is you going to show us where we is?'

Mrs Edison clicked her tongue in slight disapproval and

drew herself up to her full height. 'Follow me, children,' she said. 'Bring your cases with you.'

The other children looked questioningly at Bridget. She nodded at them. 'That's it, saucepan lids. Up the apples and pears.'

Jennifer could not help giggling at Mrs Edison's flawed expression as the little troup picked up their meagre luggage and set off up the stairs.

Mabel Edison had done them proud with her baking for their first meal. High Tea, as she called it, was laid out on the large wooden kitchen table at five-thirty. There were scones with butter and homemade jam, jellies, little individual iced cakes and an assortment of biscuits. There was milk to drink and a jug of lemonade. Tom Fox had to be propped up on three cushions in order to see the food in front of him. His enormous eyes nearly fell out of his head as he viewed the large spread in front of him. 'Cor . . .' was all he could say. After a moment of indecisiveness he stretched out his hand, grabbed an iced cake and shoved it into his mouth. 'Cor . . .' he said again as crumbs flowed freely from each side of his mouth.

'Now then, Tom, that's not the way we do things here.' Mrs Edison took the cake from the little boy's hand and placed it on the plate. 'We don't grab things. We wait until we are told we can start and then we pass the plates to the girls first. You are going to learn manners in my kitchen if you don't know them already. Anyway, before you start eating the cakes you must eat some scones or some bread and butter. You all look as if you could do with some fattening up.'

The children looked at each other and the hands that had been about to make similar grabs hovered in mid-air and then returned to their laps. Little Tom looked nonplussed. 'Yer what?' he stage-whispered to his sister.

'Jus' do like she say,' Betty hissed back. 'Yer do want ter eat, don't yer?' He nodded dumbly and lowered his eyes. For

86

a moment his lower lip quivered, but then he took a huge breath, grasped the plate of scones in both hands and passed it resolutely to Bridget. Bridget caught Mrs Edison's eye. Mrs Edison nodded and Bridget helped herself to a scone. 'Ta,' she said clearly. Jennifer glanced at Mabel Edison and felt a lump in her throat. With the exception of Bridget, they all looked undernourished and all of them – including Bridget – had pasty complexions. Well, that would change now with some good clean country air.

The children settled in quite quickly. The two Garrett boys shared one bedroom and Betty Fox insisted that little Tom shared a room with her. She really was very protective towards her baby brother. Bridget was tickled pink to have a room to herself. 'Never had me own room before,' she told Jennifer one evening. 'Used to have to share wiv me sister and the baby.'

'Oh, you had a baby brother or sister, did you?' Jennifer was intrigued.

'Na, it was me sister Kate's baby.'

'Where was her husband?'

'Oh, she didn't have no husband. She used ter have awful rows with me Mam. Mam used ter call her a trollop, but me Dad said that we had ter look after 'em seeing as how they was o' us so ter speak.' She grinned and shrugged her shoulders. 'That's when I used ter take meself off ter me Auntie Ethel's. Used ter spend a lot a time wiv me Auntie Ethel. She couldn't 'alf tell a tale, she could. Could sit and listen ter her fer hours, I could. She didn't 'alf teach me a thing or two.' Her face lit up as she sat in the armchair remembering.

'Tell me about your Auntie Ethel.' Jennifer was fascinated.

'She was a one, she was. Used ter work as a lady's maid in one o' them smart houses up in the West End. Cor ... the stories she could tell about them lords and ladies and what they got up to was nobody's business. Made our Kate seem almost respectable. Auntie Ethel said that she was just plain unlucky, that's what – seeing as how it was her first time an' all.'

'And was it your Auntie Ethel who washed and ironed your clothes?' That would explain the extra neat appearance of this child.

Bridget nodded. 'She used ter – until I got her ter show me. Now I does it meself. I likes ter look nice. It makes me feel good – especially 'ere in this posh place.'

'You're a funny child, Bridget.' Jennifer smiled at her.

'Funny? I'm not funny.' The little girl looked offended.

'Oh, I don't mean funny in the way you think I mean it. It's just that in some ways you seem so grown-up for such a tender age.'

'Someone 'as ter have a head on their shoulders when everyone around yer is yelling and screaming all day long. I used ter pretend ter meself that I was someone else – act a part, so ter speak. All I've ever wanted ter be when I grow up is a lady's maid like Auntie Ethel.' A thought struck her. 'I seen you and Mrs Edison drawing up a list today of what we could all do ter help. Could I do the washing and ironing? I'd enjoy that and I'm very good at it, though I says it meself.'

'What a good idea. Of course you can, Bridget, and if your clothes are anything to go by you'll prove to be a treasure that we can't afford to be without.'

Bridget grinned delightedly. 'Well, I'll be off ter bed, and thanks, Lady Woodward. You're really nice.' She stood up and then blushed scarlet. 'Ooops . . . I hope yer didn't think I was including you when I talked about Auntie Ethel and her stories about the gentry. Yer ain't like them at all. Yer're a bloody marvel.' She turned and ran swiftly out of the room before Jennifer had time to reply.

Jennifer shook her head in disbelief. When she had first seen the little group of children standing in the hall she had experienced a great feeling of apprehension. The two Garrett boys had looked morose and defensive while the silent Betty Fox had been sizing everyone up and obviously wondering why her parents had seemingly abandoned her and her little brother. But it had been Bridget with whom Jennifer had imagined she would have the most trouble. Her self-possessed attitude and immaculate appearance coupled with her already adopted role as leader of the band made her seem an intimidating character even at the age of ten. It just went to show how wrong first appearances could be, Jennifer thought, as she watched Bridget run up the stairs. Bridget was going to be invaluable – a third pair of hands to deal with the little ones and she was going to love doing it. She sighed contentedly. After only a week, she had taken to all the children. It was going to be fun having them at Edgeglow, whatever the cause.

CHAPTER NINE

On September 3rd, a few days before the children started school, England declared war on Germany. George and Mabel Edison sat at the kitchen table with Jennifer at eleven-fifteen that Sunday morning and listened to the wireless as a solemn Neville Chamberlain told the nation that England was at war with Germany as from five o'clock that evening.

'I never thought that it would actually happen,' Jennifer whispered.

'Had to, didn't it?' George Edison scratched his head thoughtfully.

'Does it mean that everyone in London will die?' Betty was standing in the doorway, her eyes brimming with tears.

Jennifer stood up to go to her, but before she could move Bridget had appeared from nowhere. 'Course not, silly,' she said matter-of-factly. 'Those stupid Germans aren't going ter jump straight into their planes and come rushing 'ere ter bomb us out o' the sky. Nothing need happen fer ages, so stop yer fretting this minute and find yerself something ter do.'

'Yes, Bridget.' The little girl's face brightened visibly as she ran off. Jennifer found herself marvelling once more at the logic of the ten-year-old. She looked out of the window to where Paul and Nick were taking it in turns to mow the lawn. Every so often they stopped and filled a sack with the cuttings which little Tom dragged painstakingly over and dumped in a not-too-neat pile by the bonfire. In the hall were five new pairs of shiny black Wellington boots which Tony Carrington had sent from London. The Edisons and Jennifer had been shattered to learn that none of the children had ever seen the countryside before they had arrived at

Edgeglow. Each child was thrilled to own something brand new and they were all secretly praying for rain so that they could wear them.

Tony had managed to come down one weekend since the children had arrived. At first they had been wary of him, thinking that the presence of a doctor in the house meant nasty medicine and injections, but as soon as they realised the only reason he was there was to see his baby son they became more friendly.

That weekend – the week before war was declared – Tony took the Garrett boys to watch a cricket match on Edgeglow Green. To start with they had been disparaging about the slowness of the game, but after two hours of sitting on the grass in the hot sunshine while Tony explained the rules, they had become interested in spite of themselves. Later on as they sat at a table outside the village pub gulping down large glasses of lemonade, they both vowed that when they grew up they wanted to become cricketers.

Charlie was taking his first steps, and Betty and Tom had made it their business to teach him. Tony smiled with pleasure as he stood next to Jennifer and watched his small son gurgle with happiness as the two youngsters encouraged him in his efforts. He was so pleased that everything had turned out this well. Charlie looked a picture of health and Jennifer looked even prettier than when he had first met her. He took a risk and put his arm around her shoulders.

'You're looking so much better already,' he told her, giving her an affectionate squeeze.

'It's all due to you,' she smiled up at him. 'This was a wonderful idea of yours. I love them all.'

'Don't get too fond of them, my dear. Remember that at some stage they will go home.'

'Oh, I know that,' she said seriously. 'But at the moment it's such fun seeing them all get so much pleasure from doing things that they've never done before.' She slipped her arm through his as they walked back into the house.

'Paul and Nick think you're wonderful and I think Bridget has a crush on you. Will you be able to come down often? We're all going to miss you when you go back to London tonight.'

'I'll come as often as I can,' he promised. 'You know it depends on what happenes. The balloon could go up at any minute.'

On his way back to London Tony wondered whether he should stay away for a while. Maybe he should let her miss him, but he knew that he could not do that. He looked forward to seeing her too much. Besides, he reasoned, Charlie was there. He owed it to Charlie to go down to Edgeglow whenever he could.

However, on September 3rd things were taken out of Anthony Carrington's hands. He was informed that he was too valuable to be sent abroad but instead would become one of the chief medical advisors to the armed forces at the War Ministry. He would be working non-stop with little time for leave.

"Maybe this is for the best," thought Tony, and once again he thanked God that Charlie was down in Gloucestershire with Jennifer.

On September 4th the British liner *The Athenia* was sunk by a submarine and the Royal Air Force raided the Kiel Canal entrance and bombed German warships. War had started.

For a while life in England continued normally. War raged in Europe but not very much happened on the home front. After a few months many evacuees returned to London – lured back by a false sense of security. The five children at Edgeglow, however, were still there in May of 1940. They now fitted well into the village community as the local boys and girls had overcome their first suspicions and doubts and had taken them to their hearts. Bridget was the most popular and she was often to be seen sitting under a tree on the village green regaling a spell-bound audience with stories her Auntie Ethel had told her. Paul was thrilled as he had been chosen to play in the under tens cricket team and Betty had made friends with a little girl who had a pony.

Jennifer and the Edisons watched the children thrive. Their previously pasty faces now glowed with health and vitality and their cockney voices were becoming tinged with a distinct West-Country burr. Bridget kept their clothes immaculate while Paul and Nick had become invaluable to George Edison in the garden. Betty was now an expert at washing up and was beginning to show an interest in cooking. Mabel Edison took great pains to instruct her and was delighted with Betty's results. Little Tom still tottered about trying to help anyone who would let him. He had also given up clinging to his sister – the pony had seen to that!

In all this time Tony Carrington had only managed to come down to Edgeglow twice. His practice plus his specialist advice on some of the early casualties of the war kept him very busy, and when he was not actually being a working physician he was helping to co-ordinate the medical arrangements in the armed forces. It was a gruelling job and Tony could not remember a time during the last six months when he had not felt tired. He also worried about Jennifer and Charlie – though if he was honest with himself, he knew that they should be the least of his worries. Having the children at Edgeglow had done Jennifer all the good in the world, and whenever he spoke to her on the telephone her voice was always enthusiastic and bright. No, if he was really honest with himself, Tony knew that his fears were that Jennifer no longer needed him as much as she had done six months ago. She had pulled through that time of self doubt and recrimination and the children had been there to help her – not him. If only he could get down there more often. He could somehow feel her slipping away from him before he had had a chance to claim her.

He sighed as he realised he had forgotten how young she

was and how resilient the young could be. What right had he to expect – no, to hope – that a girl as beautiful and vital as Jennifer could fall in love with him? He was twice her age. He looked at himself critically in the mirror. At thirty-nine he still had a good physique, but his thin face was lined from lack of sleep and heavy responsibilities, his hair was flecked with grey and he wore glasses. He sighed again. Why was he torturing himself? This war had only just begun. He might not survive it – none of them might survive it. All he could do for the present was to keep in touch and be there whenever it was possible. No good to think of the outcome, there might not be one.

'Bridget, there's someone ter see yer.' Little Tom padded into the kitchen and nodded his head towards the hall.

'I'll be there in just a minute.' Bridget put the iron back on the range and wiped her hands on her apron. It was a Saturday morning and she was just finishing her jobs before going out to meet her friends on the village green. 'Is it Beth or Josie? Why didn't you tell them to come in 'ere?'

Tom looked awkward. 'T'isn't either o' them.' He fidgeted with his hands. 'It's a lady. Cor, she ain't 'alf done up, Bridget. I thinks yer better hurry.'

'You sure yer got it right?' Bridget took off her apron. 'I don't know no fancy ladies.'

'That's what she said.' Tom looked hurt that she should doubt him. 'I've come ter see our Bridget. That's what she said.'

'Well, we'll just have ter go and see, won't we?'

The young woman was standing in the hall looking out of the window when Bridget and Tom rushed in.

Bridget did not know why a feeling of apprehension came over her as she said: 'I'm Bridget Lane. Can I help yer?'

'Well, o' course yer are. That's why I'm 'ere. Mam sent me ter see how yer was.' The girl swung around revealing a heavily made-up face and a too-tight sweater. 'Well, 'ow are yer, our Bridget – as if I couldn't see for myself. Living in clover, aren't yer?'

'Kate!' Bridget stared at her elder sister. 'What are yer doing 'ere? Is something wrong at home?'

'Course nothing's wrong – right as rain, in fact. Very boring. Mam says it's time yer came home – no point yer staying 'ere no more. Mustn't get used ter all this.' Kate glanced around the hall. Her eyes took in the beautiful staircase and the large impressive paintings on the walls.

Bridget's heart turned cold. 'But I can't leave at present, Kate. I'm needed ter help wiv the little ones. I can't let Lady Woodward down.'

'Oh Lady Woodward, is it? I should have guessed – living in a posh place like this.' Kate's eyes narrowed. 'Well, yer'll be far more help ter us at home, our Bridget. No need for yer to stay 'ere no more. London's quite safe. I'm ter tell 'er high-and-mighty ladyship that I's come ter take yer home.'

Bridget stood rooted to the spot. Her lower lip trembled and her eyes filled with tears. Oh no, this couldn't be. To have to go back to the uncomfortable little house in Whitechapel. To have to listen once more to Dad's swearing and Mam's complaining and the endless fights between her parents and Kate.

At that moment Jennifer walked through the front door. She was singing to herself as she swung a basket full of spring flowers on her arm. She stopped as she saw the little group in the hall.

'Hi, Bridget, and who have we here?' She looked at Kate. This was not one of Bridget's usual friends. This overly made-up girl in her gaudy cheap clothes was giving her an insolent stare. What was going on? Bridget uttered a strangled sob and ran up the stairs.

Tom toddled toward the open door. 'Bridget's going ter leave us,' he said. 'I better find Betty.'

*

'It's so unfair.' Jennifer was sitting in the kitchen with Mabel Edison that evening after the children had gone to bed. 'There was nothing that I could do. I telephoned Mrs Purton, but she said that quite a lot of children have gone back to London, and, if Bridget's family want her, then she must go.'

Mabel sniffed. 'One look at that tramp of a sister and I knew we were in for trouble,' she stated. 'A real sour-faced puss, she was. We didn't stand a chance of keeping Bridget. That one wasn't going to let her stay here and enjoy herself. She couldn't bear the fact her little sister was well and happy. No, m'lady, we lost the minute that one walked up the drive.'

'Do you think they'll all go back soon?' Jennifer asked shakily.

'Who knows? Not if the war hots up, they won't. If that happens we'll get Bridget back.'

'Yes, we will, won't we?' Jennifer brightened for a second and then looked horrified. 'Not that I would ever want that, but I have grown to love Bridget very much.'

'Yes, dear, I know what you mean.' Mabel patted her shoulder. The telephone was ringing in the morning room. 'I'll answer it. You sit still and finish your cocoa.' She hurried out of the room.

'It's Doctor Carrington, m'lady.' Mabel appeared back in the kitchen two second later. 'Isn't that nice? We haven't heard from him for a few days. Just the person you should talk to. Maybe he can do something about young Bridget.'

No, Tony told Jennifer, there was nothing he could do about Bridget. If her parents wanted her back, that was it. She was their daughter and at the moment nothing much was happening in London. He was upset to hear Jennifer sounding so down and hoped to be able to get a free weekend soon so that he could come and see her and Charlie.

'Thank goodness I'll always have Charlie,' he heard her say. His heart soared even though he knew what she really meant.

'Of course you will, Jennifer dear,' he said as he thought, "Neither of us will ever leave you."

At the end of the month the British Army was evacuated from the beaches of Dunkirk in one of the most heroic rescue attempts ever staged, but immediately afterwards Hitler proclaimed a war of total annihilation against his enemies. On July 1st the Channel Islands were occupied by Germany, and by July 10th the Battle of Britain had begun.

It was on September 7th that London sustained severe damage in the largest aerial attack since the war had commenced and by a strange quirk of fate, while everyone was celebrating the end of the Battle of Britain and the British victory a week later, news filtered through to Edgeglow that Bridget and her family had been among the casualties when their house had received a direct hit only days before.

The Edisons and Jennifer were deeply shocked. The children were very quiet as they digested the terrible fact that one of their number was dead. In their minds death was only for old people. It did not happen to someone their age and was, therefore, beyond their comprehension.

It was Tom who eventually found the words to comfort them.

'Bridget's gone to live wiv the angels,' he said seriously. 'When I go to church on Sunday, I'm going to ask Jesus to look after her.'

This simple statement released all the pent-up feelings in the others. The tears started to fall but were soon brushed aside as the young minds adjusted to this new conception of Bridget's place in the hereafter. Mabel Edison mopped her eyes and Jennifer felt a large lump in her throat which no amount of swallowing would get rid of. Poor unlucky Bridget. Struck down before she had had a chance to prove herself – and yet she had, hadn't she? She had proved her worth to everyone at Edgeglow and been loved and cherished for herself. It was said, wasn't it, that God took the good to live with him early, hence the saying "Only the good die young". Well, that was Bridget. She had been good, kind, cheerful and above all she had been resilient and had always made the best of things. Looking at it like that, there was nothing else she had needed to prove. She had already earned her place in Heaven. A warm feeling stole over Jennifer as she pictured Bridget in her new surroundings. Maybe it was Lucky Bridget, for who knew how bad this war was going to get? Who would be left at the end of it all, and when would that be?

'Thank you, Tom,' she said to herself.

'What did you say, dear?' Mabel looked up from feeding a hungry Charlie.

'Oh, I was thinking about the children and how simple they can make everything appear.'

'They can that, dear.' Mabel patted Charlie on the back as he choked on a piece of meat. 'Now then, Charlie Carrington, not so fast, it's not good for your digestion.'

Charlie grinned and burped loudly. Jennifer laughed and kissed the top of his head.

'That's better,' Mabel nodded approvingly. 'I haven't seen you do that since . . .' She reddened and put her hand to her mouth.

'Since Bridget died.' Jennifer finished the sentence for her. 'It's all right, Mabel, you can say it. I'm fine now. I loved her very much – we all did – and we'll miss her. I won't forget her the same as I'll never forget Richard, but I've learned that we all have to go on – life has to go on and it will. Thank goodness that the Garretts and the Foxes are still with us and safe.'

'Yes, we must be grateful for that,' the older woman agreed.

Charlie blew a bubble at Jennifer and held out his arms. 'Me go Jennee,' he demanded.

She lifted him out of the wooden high-chair and set him on the floor.

'Come along, young man. You can walk with Jennee upstairs and I'll read you a bedtime story.'

Charlie tottered unstably through the door. Jennifer started to follow him then turned as she reached the door. In the distance she heard him regaling Tom with 'Bed. Story. Jennee.' She smiled at Mabel Edison.

'Do you think that Bridget's with Richard?' she asked. 'She'd be awfully good for him, wouldn't she? He wouldn't have time to feel sad or depressed with her around.' For a moment her face was solemn and wistful, but then she tossed her head resolutely. 'Yes, I'm sure that they're together. Isn't it a comfort to think that neither of them is alone?'

Mabel shook her head after the retreating figure. She was a lovely girl – Lady Woodward. Life had dealt her a few blows in her twenty young years, but she wasn't a one to sit around and mope. Mabel hoped that from now on things would start to go right for her. She certainly deserved it.

It was mid-October when Alison and Vivien Hurst were brought down to Edgeglow by Tony. The two little girls were two-and-a-half years old and three months old respectively. During his work at one of the East End hospitals, Tony had been approached by a harassed young social worker who had told him that the two children would have to be split up as they had no relatives and nowhere to go. Their mother had been very badly wounded in the blitz and would be in hospital for months – if not years – and their father was a fighter pilot based at Millington in Wiltshire. She – the social worker – had heard that Doctor Carrington had a contact with a place in that area which took in evacuees. Mirian Hurst was such a sweet girl – only twenty-one and completely alone in the world except for her husband, Alfred – and he was desperately worried about her and frantic at the thought of his children being separated and put into care.

'Could you just find the time to come and meet her,

Doctor Carrington? She's on the second floor. And if you had a spare moment I could introduce you to the children this evening. I'm sure that, once you've seen them, you'll want to help them. Little Alison is a dear and the baby is adorable. They obviously come from a very loving home.'

One look at Miriam Hurst and Tony was hooked as the social worker had known he would be. She was not a pretty girl, but as she lay in the narrow hospital bed with her black straight hair surrounding her thin face and sallow complexion, her large dark eyes beseeched him to help her.

"Poor kid," thought Tony. "Only twenty-one years old and look at the blows life has dealt her. If I thought that Jennifer was hard done by, it's nothing compared to what this girl is suffering." He took the frail white hand in his.

'I'll do what I can, Mrs Hurst,' he promised. 'I'll make some telephone calls this evening and then speak to Miss Rogers here. Between us we'll see that your children are looked after as you would wish them to be.'

'That's enough for now, Miss Rogers. Can't you see that the patient's exhausted?' A tired overworked nurse shooed them from the bedside.

The two little girls were in one of the children's wards. The baby was fast asleep in a crib and two-year-old Alison was sitting in a cot playing with a battered teddy bear. There were grazes on her face and arms. Tony looked questioningly at Miss Rogers.

'Superficial,' she replied. 'She was lucky. The house next door received a direct hit – blew out part of the adjoining wall. The mother fell on top of the kids trying to protect them. They had to be dug out.'

Tony shook his head. 'Poor little mites,' he mused. 'There must be thousands like them. It doesn't make any sense, does it?'

'No, doctor, it doesn't,' Delia Rogers' voice was curt and clipped. 'But our job is not to brood on that, just to do our best for as many of them as we can.'

'Yes, of course.' Tony looked at his watch. 'Good Lord! Look at the time. If I'm going to organize something for this lot, I'd better get going.' He took his diary from his top pocket. 'Where can I reach you later to let you know what I've been able to fix?'

She smiled a tired smile. 'I'll be here, doctor. Who knows what tonight will bring?'

CHAPTER TEN

Flight Lieutenant Alan Jefferson sat at the crowded bar of the Queen's Head in the village of Millington in Wiltshire. He had just downed his second double Scotch – not that he was normally a heavy drinker. The crumpled letter from his wife, Rosemary, was still in his pocket. As usual she was admonishing him for leaving her and going to England to fight in a war that America had no part in. What if he got himself killed? And all for nothing. Didn't he appreciate how much she loved him? How much she needed him? She wouldn't be able to cope without him. Indeed, she couldn't function properly now, with all the unnecessary worry he was causing her. Alan signalled to the barmaid to refill his glass. What had happened to the pretty sweet girl he had married three years ago?

They had met while he was at Harvard and she was at Radcliffe. They had been the golden couple. Rosemary Prebble was the beautiful but spoiled daughter of a senator from Maine, and the most sought-after girl of her year. In addition to her beauty she was blessed with a sparkling wit, she swam like a fish and played a better-than-average game of tennis. Yes, Rosemary could have taken her pick of any of the men she wanted. But it had not been surprising that she had fixed her eyes on Alan Jefferson. He had been to Harvard what she was to Radcliffe. He had lived and grown up in Boston where his parents were high on the social register. No one quite knew what Alan's father did but it was obvious that family wanted for nothing, and people whispered that it was 'old money' which was very acceptable. Alan had everything. He was six foot, two inches tall with thick blond hair and the body of a Greek god. He led a healthy, outdoor existence, was an excellent sportsman and, more remarkably, was a genuinely likeable person. Far from trumpeting his own attributes, he was actually very modest, and although he enjoyed life he always remained thoughtful of others.

When their college days came to an end, it had seemed totally natural for Alan and Rosemany to get married. Theirs had been the East Coast wedding of the year. The newspapers had named them the Golden Couple and their future was set to be a sunny one. What had gone wrong?

Their troubles had begun with Rosemary's possessiveness. Her parents, permanently caught up in the political whirl, had never had much time for her. To compensate, they had given her everything money could buy, but their lack of attention had taken its toll on their child who had developed a complete lack of confidence. At college, though, her ego had been bolstered by her success, and even more so when she married the Harvard heart-throb and received all the congratulations and envy of her friends. But once they were married, everything changed – the question was now how to keep him. Her lack of confidence reasserted itself, bringing with it a jealousy that rose up the moment any other woman dared to speak to her husband.

At first Alan had been overwhelmed by the near hero-worship of his lovely young wife, but it did not take long for him to feel suffocated. No amount of reassurance on his part could convince her of his faithfulness. Rosemary knew better. People let you down. Life was full of placations. She become very neurotic.

When Alan took up flying as a hobby, Rosemary had had hysterics. How could he do this to her? It was so dangerous and so unnecessary. But Alan would not give it up, because he found he was never happier than when up in the sky in his little plane. It gave him a feeling of peace that he lacked on the ground, and he was able to think more clearly about his problems. He loved Rosemary, but he felt desperately sorry for her. After two years of marriage he thought he understood her neurosis. He knew how much she needed him and relied on him, but he needed space. If only they could have had a baby, but it just did not happen. If she had had a baby to fuss around, maybe she would have changed.

When war was declared in Europe on September 3rd 1939, Alan was at the end of his tether. People were joining up all over the place; and he had thought, why not him? It would give them the break that they both needed and England was crying out for pilots – especially pilots with more than two years' flying experience.

Alan had never stopped to think that he might not come back – that what he was embarking on was more dangerous than anything he had ever done, or ever would do. It was an adventure which had the added excitement of fighting an unseen enemy. His parents were proud of him and so was the senator. Rosemary was told what a hero her husband would be. This idea found a home in her brain, and she had calmed down. After all Alan would be away from all those women who she thought were scheming to take him away from her – she did not consider the possibility that there might be others where he was going.

Now, one year later, here he was, a flight lieutenant in the Falcon Squadron, flying Hurricanes and stationed at Millington. He had taken part in the Battle of Britain and had seen his friends come and go. It was no longer an adventure, it was survival.

Alan pushed his glass back across the bar towards the harassed barmaid.

'One more for the road, Babs honey.' He smiled his natural devastating smile, and the girl felt quite weak at the knees. These pilots were too much, she thought. The pub would never be the same again. So much glamour and excitement, it did wonders for a girl's ego. All the same she subjected him to a small frown of disapproval.

'It's all right, Babs, I'm not gonna tie one on.' He took a

cigarette from a well-worn leather case and lit it up before looking at her. 'No-one ever solved their problems by getting drunk, I think.'

'That's all right then,' she grinned as she refilled his glass. As she handed it to him she became serious. 'Had some bad news, have you?'

'Not really. Nothing out of the ordinary.' He sighed. 'I just feel I need a bit of a pep, that's all. I've got this forty-eight-hour pass, you see, so I won't be flying again till Monday.'

'I suppose you get a bit lonely being so far from home.' Babs leaned her arms on the bar. Should she tell him when she was off-duty? He was ever so good-looking. All her girlfriends would be really jealous if they saw her at the pictures with him. Him being an American and all. She started to open her mouth, then stopped as she saw him hail another young pilot who had just walked in. She sighed. Oh well, there would always be another chance. She turned back to serve the crowd who were jostling around the bar, all trying to get in last orders before closing time.

'Sergeant Hurst, let me buy you a drink.' Alan reached into his pocket for some change.

'That's very good of you, sir. I won't say no.' The young man sat down on the stool next to his superior. He blew on his hands and rubbed them together to get warm. 'Cold out there tonight. We'll get a frost soon, I shouldn't wonder.'

Alan caught the barmaid's eye. 'A pint of bitter for the sergeant, Babs honey.' She nodded, pulling on the lever until the glass tankard was so full that the brown liquid ran down the outside.

'Here's to you, sir, and God bless you.' Alfie Hurst raised the tankard to his lips and drained half of it in one long gulp. 'That's better,' he stated. 'Feel human now, don't I?'

Alan laughed. 'You English. I'll never understand your passion for that stuff. It's barbaric – and so is this currency you have.' He studied the change in his hand. 'I've been in your country for almost a year and still I get it wrong. Why can't you guys be like us Americans and do it the simple way – in tens.'

'Been 'ere longer than you Yanks – if I might make so bold, sir. We 'ave no trouble wiv it. It's a young country like yours that needs must simplify everything.' Alfie looked up comically at his senior officer.

Alan chuckled good-naturedly. Sergeant Pilot Hurst always had an answer for everything. He was a real good sort. He was also an extremely fine pilot and in the same flight as Alan – in fact they were paired together. It made one feel secure, Alan thought, to know that a man as capable as Alfie Hurst was covering him from behind during a dog-fight.

The two men had taken a liking to each other from the moment they first joined the squadron. It took a war, Alan thought wryly, for you to meet and form friendships with people from other walks of life whom under normal circumstances you would never come across at all. On the base there were separate messing facilities for commissioned officers and for non-commissioned officers, but off the base everyone got together in the Queen's Head – that was, all the flying crews. The ground crews had their own watering hole, the Jolly Miller, at the other end of the village.

They looked a strange pair sitting at the bar together – the suave blond American aristocrat and the short wiry East End cockney. Culturally and socially complete opposites, yet drawn together in so many ways. Both were courageous and dedicated, both were flyers of the highest calibre, totally committed to winning this war, and both believed that they were indestructible.

'How's your wife coming along?' Alan had heard that Hurst's wife had been badly hurt in the blitz.

'As well as can be expected, sir. She took a hell of a punishing, but she's a survivor like me, is my Miriam. She'll come through. It'll be a long slow haul, but she'll do it.' Alfie took another swig of his beer. 'In anover couple o' weeks they're going to move 'er out of London which will be a weight off me mind. Only trouble is, it's up north somewhere, so I won't get to see her much. But you can't 'ave it all and she'll be much safer there, won't she?'

'Oh, sure she will,' Alan agreed. 'Don't you also have a couple of kids, Hurst? What's happened to them? They weren't hurt too bad at the time, were they?'

A large grin lit up Alfie's face. 'That's just what I come out to celebrate,' he said and pulled a typewritten letter out of his pocket. 'I heard today that they've been evacuated together to a place not too far from 'ere. This posh doctor who works at the hospital where Miriam was taken managed to fix them up at . . .' he looked down at the page in front of him, 'Edgeglow Manor. It's near a place called Cirencester. I looked it up on the map and it's only forty miles or so away from 'ere. I thought that seeing as we've got this forty-eight-hour pass, I'd get myself up there tomorrow and see the little blighters. I don't 'alf miss 'em.'

At that moment the landlord called time. Both men downed their drinks and stood up.

'Well, I'm real glad things are working out for you, Hurst. Lord knows, you deserve it.'

'Thank you, sir.' Alfie held the door open for his commanding officer. A wave of cold air hit them as they walked outside. Compared with the pub's smoky oppressive atmosphere it was almost refreshing. A thought struck Alan.

'How are you fixed up for transport tomorrow, Hurst? You haven't got a car, have you?'

'No, sir, but I'm saving up for one. I'm told that one month as messing sergeant and I'll have enough,' he laughed. 'But tomorrow I'll 'ave to take the bus. It's not too bad. I 'ave to change twice, but it'll only take a few hours.'

'I've got a car. I'd be happy to give you a ride, if you like. I've nothing planned for this leave.'

There was a silence while Alfie digested this offer. When he spoke he stuttered slightly. 'That's very good of you, sir, but I wouldn't want to put you to any inconvenience. I can easily get the bus, no problem.'

'Sure you can, Hurst, but really it's no inconvenience to me, I promise you. Besides it will give you more time with your kids, and me the chance to see some more of your beautiful countryside. Shall we say ten o'clock?' He strode away quickly before Alfie had a chance to reply.

Alfie looked after the retreating figure. Poor bugger, he thought. He must be even more lonely than the rest of us. His family are thousands of miles away across an ocean. They were real good chaps – these few Americans who had joined the war. After all it was not as if their country was involved. Yes, he was a real good bloke – the lieutenant. It was a pleasure to be in the same squadron and on the same flight. He, Alfie Hurst, would make sure that the lieutenant had an enjoyable day.

It was a beautiful sunny morning when they set off the next day. Gone was the feeling of approaching winter and instead the air was that of an impending Indian summer. Dressed in civvies, the two young men felt instantly more at ease with each other. Alan threw his comfortable old camel-hair jacket into the back of the Standard which he had bought as soon as he had arrived in England and rolled up the sleeves of his Brooks Brothers shirt.

'Gonna be a glorious day, Alfie.' He looked up at the sky and breathed in deeply. He expelled the air from his lungs with a loud 'Ah'. It was on a day such as this that he actually managed to feel he was still only twenty-four. Usually, the everyday pressures of wartime and the overwhelming sense of responsibility for his team when they were engaged in combat made him feel so old. He glanced at the little man who stood beside him. Alfie Hurst could not be more than twenty-one – twenty-two at the most. Sometimes Alan felt that there was a whole generation gap separating him from his pilots, not just the two or three years that really existed.

'Have you got the road atlas?' he asked as they drove off. 'Not that it will do us much good. I haven't seen a signpost in months.'

'Yes. sir.' The younger man seemed slightly flustered by Jefferson's use of his first name.

'Oh, and Alfie, don't you think that seeing as we're off-duty you could call me Alan? It's so much more informal.'

'Yes, sir. If you say so, sir . . . I mean . . . er . . . Alan,' the young man stuttered. Bli'me, he thought, this bloke was a real top-hole toff and he was asking him, Alfie Hurst, to call him by his Christian name. It wasn't really right, was it? Never would happen – even in civilian life – not here. He scratched his head. But these Yanks were different, weren't they? More informal like. He shook his head in amazement and gave a nervous little laugh.

'Anything the matter?'

'I was just thinking, sir – I mean, Alan. If my Miriam could see me now – hob-nobbing wiv a toff like you and on first-name terms – I wonder what she'd say.'

'You British, you're incredible. Never underrate yourself, Alfie. It's what we are, not who we are, that counts. You try and remember that.'

'Yes, sir . . . I mean . . .'

They both laughed as Alan started the engine and they motored off through the quiet countryside.

It was midday when they approached Edgeglow village. Being a Saturday morning, there were plenty of children to be seen playing on the green. Alan noticed how Alfie tensed up now that they were near their destination.

'How about breaking here for a quick snack and a drink, then we can ask someone the way to the manor?' he suggested.

'Yes. Good idea,' the younger man replied gratefully.

Alan pulled the car up in front of a little Cotswold stone pub. The sign above it read The Cricketer's Arms. As they walked inside he was struck by the peaceful atmosphere – so different from the noisy crowded pubs near the base. Here, the room was almost empty. One or two old men stood at the bar nursing pints of beer, while four middle-aged women sat at a table by the window gossiping. They all looked up when the strangers entered, but after a brief stare they resumed their conversations.

'Just passing through?' asked the landlord.

'No, we're looking for an Edgeglow Manor,' Alan answered, as Alfie appeared to be tongue-tied.

The landlord handed them their drinks and took two freshly cut sandwiches from a shelf. 'Just made ten minutes ago,' he stated.

Alan paid him. 'Thanks,' he said. 'They look great. Won't you have a drink with us?'

'That's very good of you. I don't mind if I do.' He poured himself one and raised his glass. 'Cheers! You boys in the services?'

'Airforce.'

'Wonderful job you are doing. You don't sound English though?'

'I'm an American.'

'Ah!' The man's eyes took on an even greater look of respect. 'Marvellous, bloody marvellous.'

'Not really.' Alan spoke very quietly. It always embarrassed him when people looked at him that way. It made him want to question his motives as to why he had joined up.

'You boys are too modest.' The landlord laughed. 'Edgeglow Manor, is it, that you're going to? That's Lady Woodward's place. Know her well, do you?'

'No, not at all.' At last Alfie had found his voice. 'My kids are there. Me wife was hurt in the blitz and they've been billeted there.'

'I see.' The landlord smiled. 'Well, they couldn't be in better hands. Wonderful woman, Lady Woodward. Her husband died just before the war, but she has kept right on. Never had no children of her own, but she's got lots of other people's now. They all love her.' He gulped down his drink. 'She's another bloody marvel.'

As they walked out into the sunlight Alfie was whistling. Alan grinned to himself. One should never underestimate the value of a drink. The boy looked better already. His nervous tension had gone and he was much more relaxed. Now, to meet Lady Woodward. Well, she sounded a nice old lady, obviously someone with a heart of gold. In his mind's eye Alan pictured a straight-backed grey-haired woman in her sixties. Very much the county lady and very capable.

The iron gates leading to Edgeglow Manor were impressive and so was the parkland which was dotted with oak, chestnut and copper beech trees. The house itself was typical of its kind. It was built of Cotswold stone with a tiled roof and beautiful lattice windows. Across the drive from the main entrance was a large expanse of lawn where croquet hoops had been set up. Two boys and a girl were in the middle of a game while a smaller boy watched them. At the other end of the lawn a tall blonde girl sat on a tartan rug playing with a baby. With her were two toddlers – a little boy and a little girl.

'That's my Alison!' Alfie pointed excitedly out of the car window. 'There, sitting wiv the young lady.' He was out of the car almost before it had stopped. 'Alison,' he called. 'It's your Dad. Alison, oh Alison.' He ran across the gravel and scooped up the little girl as she toddled towards him.

'Dada.' The child buried her head in his neck. 'Dada come back.'

Alfie's eyes were full of tears as he walked over to where the blonde girl sat. She had picked up the baby and was smiling at him as he approached.

'You must be Sergeant Hurst. We've been expecting you.'

'Yes. I came as soon as I could.' He looked down at the baby who smiled and gurgled up at him.

'They've settled in so well,' the girl said. 'Alison is very helpful and baby Vivien is so good. Everyone loves her. She's such a contented baby.'

The little boy who had been standing quietly all through this exchange now piped up, 'Of course she's not really smiling. Mrs Edison says it's wind.'

'Thank you, Tommy.' The girl laughed and tossed her magnificent blonde hair back over her shoulder. 'Why don't you go and rescue Charlie before he gets hit for six by that croquet ball?'

'OK, Jennee.' The little lad ran off across the grass.

Alan held out his hand as she started to get up.

'I'm sorry. This is . . .' Alfie paused, then continued, 'my friend Alan Jefferson. He's also my flight commander.'

'Pleasure to meet you, ma'am.' Alan gave a small salute.

'You're American.'

'Yes, ma'am.'

'One of the few. Everyone over here appreciates so much what you are doing for us.' She passed the baby to him as she stood up. 'Would you mind? I don't want to drop her.' She dusted herself off and then reached for the baby who had just decided to show that she could cry if she felt like it. 'Now now, Vivien, don't you go letting me down when I said how good you always were.' She rocked her in her arms and Vivien, now happy in the familiar arms, cooed delightedly.

How lucky Lady Woodward was to have a girl like this to help her, Alan thought as he tried to catch Alfie's eye. It was time to find Lady Woodward and introduce themselves, but Alfie was completely wrapped up in his elder daughter. Once again he, Alan, would have to take the initiative. 'Excuse me, ma'am, but I think we really ought to make ourselves known to Lady Woodward,' he said. 'Do you know where she is?'

'Oh, I'm sorry. How thoughtless of me. I know your names but you don't known mine. I'm Jennifer Woodward.' She held out her hand. Without thinking, Alan grasped it, then his mouth fell open. Alfie, who had been deep in conversation with his daughter, nearly fell over.

'Bli'me!' He looked up comically from where he was kneeling on the grass. 'Who would'a thought it?'

'Obviously, I'm not at all what you expected.' She laughed and looked down at her hand which was still imprisoned in Alan's.

'Excuse me.' Alan released it quickly. He felt himself blush. That was something he hadn't done for years. Well, it was nice to know he was still human and that a beautiful young woman could still affect him.

'Come into the house and have some tea,' she said. She turned to Alison. 'And afterwards, Alison, you can show Daddy your bedroom and the rest of the house.'

As they followed her across the gravel, Alison toddling along beside her father clutching his hand, Alfie raised his eyebrows at Alan. 'Wouldn't mind being billeted 'ere meself, old mate,' he said with a wink. 'The dustbins 'ave done right well for themselves.'

'Pardon me?' Alan looked puzzled.

'Dustbin lids – kids. Savvie?'

'No, I'm afraid I'm lost.'

'Oh dear, you foreigners.' Alfie sighed in mock exasperation. 'Where I come from in the East End of London we've got our own special language. I'll teach you if you like on some of the long winter evenings we're in for.' He clapped Alan on the back. 'When I've finished wiv you, nobody will know you're not a genuine cockney.'

Alan laughed. 'You do that, but alas I fear you'll never rid me of my telltale American twang.'

'I know!' Alfie stopped as if blessed with a brilliant idea. 'You can be the first American cockney. You never know, the idea might catch on!'

The two young men were still grinning as they entered the house.

It turned out to be a wonderful weekend. When Jennifer heard that they were not expected back at Millington until the following evening, she insisted that they stayed the night at Edgeglow. 'There's plenty of room,' she told them. 'Mabel, my housekeeper, will welcome the opportunity to go back to her cottage and stay with her husband, and one of you can have Tony's room.'

Betty was dispatched upstairs to the store room and came back brandishing two toothbrushes and some toothpaste. Mabel Edison was delighted that her young employer would have some company of her own age for a change. She bustled around making beds and then made sure that dinner would stretch to include the two guests.

Later Alan found himself wondering who Tony was as he stood in the little room he had been allocated. The wardrobe door was half open and he could see evidence of a man's clothing hanging inside. He experienced a sudden irrational stab of irritation. Who was this man who obviously came down to see Jennifer all the time? Was he a lover? Yes, he must be. Well, the poor girl had been a widow for eighteen months or so, so it was hardly suprising. Alan couldn't help thinking that Jennifer Woodward would never write the kind of letters to her husband that Rosemary wrote to him. The British were a marvellous race, he mused. They never gave up, no matter what trials they had to face. He was sure that Lady Woodward would be a tower of strength to any man in her life. Lucky bloody Tony – whoever he was.

After supper the three of them spent the evening talking in the drawing room. In contrast to the hot sunny day the air had now become quite chilly. Gone for another year were the warm light evenings of an English summer. Now there was a distinct nip in the air by six o'clock.

Alan and Alfie regaled Jennifer with stories of the lighter side of the war. She laughed until tears ran down her cheeks as they described escapades that some members of the squadron had got up to in their off-duty hours. Nothing serious was mentioned. No one needed to be reminded of the horrors that happened from day to day whenever the squadron was airborne. For the two young men tonight was a night to relax in this unexpected luxury away from all their everyday worries. To crown it all they would have the best night's sleep they would get for weeks in a comfortable bed and with a room to themselves. Yes, luxury indeed.

The telephone rang and Jennifer ran out into the hall to answer it. Silence descended in the room as both men could not help straining their ears to listen.

'Tony, how lovely to hear from you.' Alan stiffened as he heard the name. 'Yes, he's fine . . . Yes, I'm fine too . . . Yes, I think he understands how busy you are. Will you be able to get away soon? . . . No, I'm not lonely – I don't have the time to be. Oh, and by the way, Sergeant Hurst, the father of the two little girls you sent me, is here to see them. He has brought a friend with him from his squadron and they are staying the night as they don't have to be back at their base until tomorrow. I'm thoroughly enjoying their company . . . No, don't you worry. Everything's fine. You let us know when you're going to be free and you know that you are always welcome. Good-bye, Tony, and take care, won't you.'

Hardly the conversation of two lovers, Alan thought wryly. He lit a cigarette, drew on it and then exhaled noisily.

'All right?' Alfie looked across at him.

'Sure, just tired as usual.'

Jennifer walked back into the room. 'That was Charlie's father,' she said as she poured herself a cup of the rather tasteless Camp coffee. 'He's an old family friend. He was at school with my husband.'

Neither of the men said anything as they waited for her to continue.

'He, Doctor Carrington, is a very well respected doctor in London.' She smiled at Alfie. 'In fact, it was through him that Alison and Vivien came here. He met the social worker in the hospital and she introduced him to your wife, Alfie.'

'Bli'me! Who would a' thought it?' Alfie grinned. 'Miriam

said she met this posh bloke who pulled some strings. Fancy 'im being a friend o' yours.'

'He's a very good friend of mine.' For a moment her expression was sad as she said, 'He looked after my husband when he was ill and he helped me tremendously after his death. It was he who suggested that I take in the evacuees, and I started with Charlie because Tony did not want him to be in London. You see his wife died when Charlie was born. He feels much happier knowing that his son is safe in the country.'

As he lay in bed that night waiting for sleep to envelop him, Alan wondered about Jennifer and her friend the doctor. In order to hold such a high professional position, he couldn't be a young man. He must be in his late thirties at least – perhaps even forty. Had the husband also been so much older than Jennifer, then? As he thought about her he felt a stirring within himself. She was so breathtakingly beautiful and seemed so soft and innocent. In the last year he had come to know what it felt like to lose someone close to you – it didn't bear thinking about – but she had survived and obviously enjoyed what she was doing. He sighed. Why couldn't Rosemary be more like that? She had been blessed with everything and yet still she was discontented. He would never leave her – Alan knew that. He was an honourable man and she was his responsibility, but why, oh why couldn't life be more simple? Why did things have to turn sour? Why did dreams always fade? On this last thought his brain ceased to function and he fell into an exhausted sleep.

CHAPTER ELEVEN

On their way back to Millington the next evening both young men agreed that it had been the best and most relaxing leave they had spent in a long time. After a wonderful night's sleep they had sat down to a hearty breakfast with Jennifer and the children. After that, while she and Mrs Edison prepared lunch, they had made themselves useful by chopping wood and then by kicking a football with the boys. Before lunch they insisted on taking Jennifer down to the Cricketer's Arms for a drink. It had been a happy day with plenty of laughter, and Alfie had had tears in his eyes as he kissed his children good-bye.

'Come again as soon as you can.' Jennifer had put a hand on his arm which told him that she knew how he felt. 'We'll take good care of Alison and Vivien, and you know that you'll always be welcome. You too, lieutenant.' She turned to Alan and shook his hand. Alan felt a sharp spark of electricity ignite within him at her touch. Oh God, she was so beautiful. He looked down at her, and for a moment he saw confusion in those lovely eyes as she started to blush, then she looked away quickly. 'Take care,' she said in a softly controlled voice.

"Yes, ma'am, I surely will," he thought to himself as he put the car in gear and drove off.

During the next few weeks Alan spent hours inventing reasons as to why he would be unable to accept another invitation to Edgeglow Manor, were it proffered.

"Be fair," he told himself. "She's not the sort of girl to have a wartime fling with. I'm married – heavily married –

to a wife who needs me and who I feel responsible for. I can't play around with this girl. I can't risk hurting her."

"And yourself?" asked a small voice within him.

"Anyway," he told himself, "she has the good doctor who is obviously in love with her and will one day marry her and give her all the security and love that she should have – and she adores his son. It would all be most satisfactory."

"You don't know that," said the small voice. "He might be old and unattractive and just a father-figure."

"I won't go. I don't want to get involved and I have enough strength of character to say no." He ground out his cigarette and glanced at his watch. It was nine-thirty. If he was quick he could get to the Queen's Head for a drink before closing time. There was a good movie at the local this week. Maybe he'd ask that jolly barmaid – what was her name, Babs – to accompany him one night. He grabbed his jacket and rushed out of the room before he could change his mind.

The Queen's Head was crowded and smoky as usual. Alan made his way to the bar and caught Bab's eye. She broke off from what she was doing and measured out his customary double Scotch.

'Thanks, honey.' He gave her a smile and a nod of encouragement as he downed half of it in one gulp. 'I haven't seen you in a while. We must get together some time.'

'Been visiting my sister, love,' she grinned at him. 'Back to the grind now, though. I'll just finish pulling these pints and then we'll have a nice natter.' Things were looking up, she thought. Play her cards right this time and the handsome young flight lieutenant would ask her out.

'Evening, sir. You're just the man I wanted to see.'

Alan turned around to see Alfie Hurst at his shoulder. 'What'll you have, sergeant?' He reached into his pocket for some more change.

'That's very kind of you, sir. I'll 'ave a pint of best bitter if I may.'

'Babs. A pint of best bitter here, please.'

The barmaid glanced up, and for a second her cheery expression dropped. Damn. He had company now. Foiled again, she thought, but then her good nature got the better of her. 'Coming up,' she said brightly as she pulled yet another pint.

'I'm going to see the dustbins on me next leave at the end of the week. Spoke to Lady Woodward this evening, and she said to tell you she'd be so pleased if you could come too.' Alfie did not look at his senior officer as he spoke. He was still very much in awe of his rank while on the base.

'I . . . I don't know.' Alan hesitated. 'I was thinking of going to London.'

'That's all right, sir. Not ter worry.' Disappointment showed in the younger man's voice.

'You OK for getting there, sergeant?'

'Yes thank you, sir. Just finished me turn as messing sergeant. Made meself a tidy sum.' Alfie grinned and winked at his superior officer. 'Bought meself a little runabout for twenty-five quid.' He paused for a second before trying a new tactic. 'Be my pleasure to drive you, sir, if you decide to come.'

From a long way off Alan heard a voice saying: 'Why not? London can wait. Thank you, Hurst, there's nothing I'd like better.'

Alan gasped. It was his own voice speaking, and he had just done what he had promised himself for the last month that he would on no account do. He had accepted another invitation to go to Edgeglow and he felt marvellous. If he hadn't been in this crowded smoky little room he would have jumped six feet in the air and whooped with joy. He was brought back to earth by Sergeant Pilot Hurst's voice.

'That's great, sir. Wouldn't be the same somehow if you wasn't there again. We 'ad a great time, didn't we?'

'Yes we did, Alfie.' Alan spoke softly and sincerely, the strict formality suddenly gone from his voice. 'I'm already looking forward to this leave.'

'Me too.' For a moment Alfie's expression was serious. 'Believe me, Alan, when I tell you that me and the other chaps in our flight count ourselves bloody lucky to have you as our leader. You're the best. The very best.'

Alan's throat constricted. He picked up his glass and drained it of the remaining whisky. 'Thanks,' he said quietly.

It was another cherished forty-eight hours which was to set the pattern for several more throughout the winter. Alan began to wonder why he had wound himself up so much over the beautiful young Lady Woodward. If she thought of him in any other way than that of a friend she did not let it show, but he was always slightly on guard with himself. He left the friendly gestures to Alfie, who put his arm around her at least ten times a day and told her what a bloody marvel she was.

Jennifer also thought about the young officer. He had became increasingly formal since his first visit – and quieter too. It was no fun fighting a war – she realised that, of course – but there was an aloofness about him that had not been evident before. Had she imagined that spark of electricity between them? She did not think so, though she could have been wrong, but whatever it may or may not have been he certainly was not in the mood to pursue it. And who could blame him, she reasoned. Being a fighter pilot must demand all his concentration, and leave no time for other relationships. "Besides," she thought, "I really know nothing about him. He may be married with six children for all I know." She laughed at the improbable thought of the young man, who could only be in his early twenties, having so many children, but then she drew in her breath sharply. "What I really mean is that I don't want another relationship with someone who could be here one moment and gone the next. If my house can provide comfort for these two whenever they can come here, then I will be more than happy. At least they can forget the pressures and responsibilities for a few hours, and that is enough." She sighed. "Who am I kidding?" she asked herself. "I want to see his handsome face, I want to feel this breathless feeling whenever he smiles at me and, more than anything, I want to hear his voice and the sincerity in it when he talks about the things he believes in."

And Alan thought: "I was being silly when I worked myself up over a brief communication. War does strange things to people. It makes them overreact. I felt the way I did because I haven't made love to a woman for well over a year, and this girl is so attractive that I started to fantasise about her." But he had never been a man to indulge in casual affairs. That was why he knew that he would not begin a liaison with Babs from the Queen's Head, however much of a good sport she might prove to be. He tried thinking of Rosemary, but that only depressed him more.

"I like coming here," Alan told himself. "I like the happy relaxed atmosphere. I like walking in the fields without hearing the sound of aeroplanes above. I like getting a warm comfortable night's sleep and decent wholesome food to eat. It is all that I need." Then he laughed. "I'm not very convincing," he told himself. "What I really like is to look at her beautiful face and hear the love in her voice as she talks to the children. I admire her for being so brave and for managing to stay so soft, and what I really want . . . no, I mustn't even contemplate it because it's not possible, and even if it were possible it would be wrong – an entirely selfish move. I must control these feelings. I know the rules and I have my integrity. I'll not show myself to be the weak-minded creature that Rosemary believes all men to be. I'm going to survive this war and all its pressures, whatever they are."

The dawn of 1941 brought frustration and unrest to the pilots of the Falcon Squadron. There were long periods of inactivity due to bad weather conditions caused by snow, ice, fog and rain. Tempers were short – not surprisingly – as the young men were cooped up in the small space of their quarters at the base at Millington.

The German blitz was now directed at many other cities besides London. The Falcon Squadron was on night-flying duty and would take off whenever possible and make its way towards local cities looking for the enemy. Sometimes they saw bombs falling past them from enemy aircraft which were above. Alan grimaced as he thought of this new hazard to a fighter pilot's life. Not a glamorous way to go – killed by an enemy bomb while in the air.

In the spring they started sweeps over northern Occupied France. At least this was more interesting and their lives seemed to have a purpose again.

'Happy Birthday to you. Happy Birthday to you. Happy Birthday dear Alison. Happy Birthday to you.'

Alison Hurst stared around her in wonder, then her eyes fixed on the cake with its three candles that Mabel Edison had placed on the table in front of her. She sat at the end of the table on one of the rickety wooden-backed chairs, with three cushions under her to make her tall enough to see over the top.

When the other children finished singing, Betty leaned over and whispered: 'Now you must make a wish and blow out all the candles with one breath. It's lucky.'

Alison glanced tentatively at Jennifer who was sitting opposite her with Vivien on her knee. Jennifer nodded and smiled. The little girl leaned forward and placed her tiny hands on the table. She screwed her eyes tightly closed and drew in a deep breath which she held for several seconds. When she released it, it came out like a long sigh. The candles flickered and went out. Alison opened her eyes and let out a whoop of joy.

'Dada and Uncle Alan will come and see us again soon,' she announced confidently, and then as an after-thought, '. . . and Mummy too.' But she did not sound so sure about that.

Jennifer swallowed a lump in her throat as she heard

Mabel blow her nose loudly. It was April 7th 1941, and they had just heard that Greece and Yugoslavia had been invaded by German troops. The news seemed to get grimmer by the day. The two young pilots had not been able to come to Edgeglow for months. At first it had been because of the bad weather conditions, and now – well, God knows what dangerous missions they were flying, Jennifer thought. She was thankful that nothing serious had developed between her and the handsome Alan Jefferson. In a way it was a relief that he had not been able to come to Edgeglow for a while, even though it was sad that the Hurst children had missed seeing their father. She looked around the table as the children relished this birthday treat and savoured every mouthful of Mabel Edison's delicious cake.

'My birthday next,' said Charlie.

'Yes, you'll be three in May.' Jennifer smiled at him.

'My Daddy will come to my birthday,' Charlie announced to Alison. The little girl's eyes filled with tears.

'That's enough, Charlie,' Jennifer admonished him. 'You know perfectly well that Alison's Daddy would be here if he could, and it's by no means certain that your Daddy will be able to come down here for yours. He works extremely hard.'

Charlie pouted and looked defiant. He hated it when Jennifer told him off, which she was apt to do with increasing frequency. Jennifer sighed. Charlie was becoming a problem. His obvious adoration for her was causing him to resent the other children. To Charlie she was the mother he had never known and he did not want to share her with anyone. Whenever Jennifer showed love or affection for any of the others, Charlie became difficult. As he got down from the table he pinched Alison on the arm. 'Owch,' she screamed and started to cry.

'It's all right, Alison.' Nick Garrett, who had been sitting the other side of her, put his arm around her and fixed Charlie with a stern glare which made the little boy quake as he looked up at the eight-year-old. 'At least Alison has a

Daddy *and* a Mummy – not like you. You've only got a Daddy.'

'Yes I do, don't I?' Alison brightened up immediately.

Charlie's lip quivered. 'I do have a Mummy. Jennee's my Mummy.' He ran over to Jennifer and threw his arms around her legs.

'Stop it, all of you,' Mabel Edison intervened. 'It's time that you were taken in hand.' She extracted Charlie gently but firmly from Jennifer. 'You go upstairs and put Vivien to bed, m'lady, while I give this little lot a piece of my mind. It's long overdue.'

Jennifer looked at her gratefully. As she made her way to the stairs she could hear Mabel's voice saying. 'Now sit down, children. I want to have a little chat with you.'

Later that evening after kissing the last of the small children good-night, shutting off the light and closing the door, Jennifer thought that she heard a car in the drive. As she walked along the corridor she wondered idly who it could be. Not many people came to visit – especially at this time of night. If Tony had been able to come down from London he would have telephoned. As she reached the top of the stairs she saw Paul Garrett already opening the front door, then she drew in her breath sharply. There, framed in the doorway and looking more handsome than ever in his uniform, stood Alan Jefferson. He was alone. It was all she could do to stop herself from running down the remaining stairs and throwing herself into his arms. She pulled herself together and walked sedately towards him.

'Alan, what a lovely surprise, but isn't Alfie with you?' Alan had never come to Edgeglow on his own before. As she looked up at him she noticed how tired he seemed to be. It was the first time that he had appeared in his uniform and he seemed to be on edge.

'No, he's not.' The reply was terse and he glanced at Paul who was shutting the door.

"Oh God," thought Jennifer, "so that's it. Something has happened to Alfie." Her heart sank, but she turned to Paul and managed to speak normally. 'Paul, dear, will you round up Nick and Betty and go and have your supper. Mrs Edison must have it ready by now.' The child nodded and disappeared. 'Come into the drawing room.' She led the way and closed the door after them. 'I have one bottle of whisky left from Richard's cellar. You look as if you could do with a drink.'

'I sure could, it's been the hell of a time.' Alan unbuttoned his jacket and deposited his cap on a chair.

'What's happened?' She almost did not dare to ask.

He took a large swig of the double whisky she handed him and felt the strong liquid warm the back of his throat as he began to relax. 'Alfie was shot down over northern France ten days ago.'

'Oh no!' Jennifer's hand flew to her mouth.

'It's not as bad as you think,' he said quickly and put an arm around her trembling shoulders. 'He was able to bale out. I saw that. We heard today that he's a prisoner of war. That's why I came here at once to tell you. Otherwise, it could have taken weeks for you to find out.'

'That was very kind of you.' Her voice was a little shaky.

'No, no, it was the least that I could do.' He gave her a lean smile. 'You see they would only tell his next of kin which is his wife – and we both know that she is still a very sick lady. You might not have heard for months.'

'Poor Alison.' Jennifer spoke quietly remembering the incident at teatime.

'She'll get over it. She's barely old enough to understand. Children are very resilient, you know.'

'Yes, I suppose so.' She smiled sadly at the young officer. How could you explain to someone who doesn't have a family of his own at what age complexes start to form? 'You look exhausted,' she said. 'You can stay the night, can't you?'

'Not a chance. I have to get back. I shouldn't really be

here at all.' He stood up and passed his hand wearily over his forehead. He closed his eyes momentarily to allow the sudden feeling of dizziness to go away.

'Alan Jefferson, I can't allow you to leave this house in your present condition. You'd never make it back to Millington. It's a two-hour drive.'

'But I have to.' He could have fallen asleep on his feet he felt so tired.

'Well, if you must go tonight, I insist on feeding you first.' Jennifer looked at the clock on the mantlepiece. It said eight o'clock. 'The three elder children are having supper in the kitchen with Mabel and I was just about to join them. There will be plenty for one more and I won't take no for an answer.'

'All right, bossy lady.' The thought of good wholesome cooking and the warm cheery kitchen was enough to persuade him – besides, it would mean that he would be with her for a while longer. He sighed as a thought struck him. Now there was no excuse to come down here anymore. There would be no Alfie to hide behind and it would not be fair to put their emotions to the test. He wasn't – and never would be – a free man.

'Alan! Great to see you.' The three children sprang to attention as he walked into the kitchen behind Jennifer.

'Hi kids. Sit down and finish your dinner.' He smiled at them as he joined them at the table. Jennifer had done well with these kids, he thought. Their manners were impeccable. He wondered if it would be appreciated when they went back home to the East End of London.

'How long can you stay?'

'Will you play cricket wiv us?'

'I've learned to jump on Maisie.'

'Will you come and watch me?'

All the children spoke at once.

'Calm down. Calm down.' Jennifer gave a tight little laugh. 'Flight-Lieutenant Jefferson can't even stay the night. He just came here to tell me something . . .'

'Oh no!' There was groans of disappointment from them all and before she could continue, Paul's voice could be heard above the others. 'Where's Alfie?'

The chatter stopped and three pairs of eyes turned towards Alan. Mabel Edison drew in her breath sharply. She had a feeling they were going to hear something unpleasant.

'That's why I'm here, kids.' Alan leaned his hands on the table and spoke earnestly. 'Alfie's been taken a prisoner in France. His plane got shot down but he was able to parachute to the ground. Unfortunately, the Germans were waiting for him, though, so he's a prisoner of war.'

'Cor . . . it sounds terribly exciting.' Nick Garrett's mouth fell open and the piece of toast that he had been about to eat dropped back on to his plate.

'It sounds frightfully romantic.' Betty rested her elbows on the table and clasped her hands together. 'Just think, 'e probably landed in a cornfield and then tried to escape and found 'e was surrounded.' She sighed as her imagination took over. 'Just like the pictures.'

'Will 'e be all right, Alan?' Paul asked.

'Oh yes, sure he will, Paulie.' Alan spoke with a conviction that he did not entirely feel. 'For him the war is over. He'll have to sit it out in some prison camp until one side wins, and then we can all go back home again.'

'We are going to miss him,' Paul said quietly. 'It was great having you both come down 'ere and play wiv us.' He looked away, not wanting to catch Alan's eye as he felt a lump form in his throat. 'I suppose you won't feel the need to come down 'ere no more, now that Alfie won't be coming to see his kids.'

'Oh no!' Betty roused herself from her reverie. 'You've got to come and see us Alan. We look forward to your visits so much.' Her eyes filled with tears.

'Hey, hey,' Alan ruffled her hair, 'That's not very kind to Jennifer or Mrs Edison, is it?'

'That's not what she means, Alan.' Paul stood up. 'It's just that it's nice to 'ave a man around sometimes.' He went red as he spoke.

Alan looked at Jennifer. 'But Charlie's father comes to see you, doesn't he?' Jennifer shivered. Was he asking her or simply answering Paul's question? Was she really never going to see him again?

'Charlie's father don't come very often. He's very busy and they need 'im in London. Besides,' Paul walked behind his brother and Betty and put a hand on each of their shoulders, 'he's much older. He doesn't play cricket and football wiv us . . .'

'. . . and he doesn't understand ponies like you do,' Betty chipped in.

'Don't get us wrong, Alan. We really like 'im. He's a right good bloke, but we do appreciate you coming to see us. You won't stop now, will you?'

Three pairs of eyes fixed him yet again with pleading looks. Jennifer caught her breath and busied herself at the sink to hide her confusion. She wasn't going to lose him. The children had just made sure of that, for she knew that he would never be able to refuse them.

'Well . . .' Alan felt the tension building inside him. Of course he wanted to go on coming to Edgeglow. He enjoyed playing with the kids – it helped to relax him and took his mind off all the unpleasant things he had to cope with every day. He wanted to keep on seeing Jennifer and he knew that it wasn't fair. But what was fair? "I can't justify it," he thought to himself. "I just know that I want to do this and I can't fight it any more." He turned to look at Jennifer. She was placing a jug of custard on the table. As she straightened up, she caught his eye. She smiled hesitantly and his heart almost turned over. Was she aware of the effect she had on him? Did she feel anything for him?

'Well . . .' he continued, 'if that's OK with Jennifer, I'd love to.'

'Hooray . . .' All the children jumped up and started capering noisily around the kitchen.

Amid the chaos, Alan smiled tentatively at Jennifer. 'It can be very lonely in a foreign land,' he said by way of explanation.

'Yes,' she said softly. 'I can understand that.'

As she walked with him to his car she felt a warm glow inside her. 'Do you know yet what your plans are regarding your next leave?' she asked.

'I'm due for a two-week break at the end of the month. I'll probably go to London and I'll come and see you all for a few days towards the end.'

'No, don't do that. London can be a very lonely place. Come here for the fortnight.' She blushed at her boldness and was glad that the darkness hid her face. 'That is . . . if you would like to . . . I mean, we could always find things for you to do to help us . . . I mean . . . oh dear, how awful of me. Obviously you would prefer to spend time in London. I don't know what came over me.' She hung her head in confusion. Alan stopped beside his car and took her hand between his and squeezed it gently.

'You know that there is nothing more that I would like to do than to spend the whole of my leave here, don't you? I just don't know whether I should.'

'Of course you should,' she replied. 'The children need you.'

"But do you need me?" he wondered. "The way I need you? And if you do, where can it lead us? All we can do is hurt each other. I've got myself into this and I can't get out – I don't want to get out, anyway, but I don't feel good about it. I feel like a heel – except that I love you."

'I'll see you then at the end of the month. I'll call you when I know the dates.' He kissed her very briefly on the cheek and jumped into his car.

'We'll all look forward to seeing you.'

'Will you?' He stared at her meaningfully.

'Yes.' She met his eyes.

'Me too.'

As he let in the clutch and drove off, Alan felt his spirits soar. He had made the decision and there was no going back now. He had a feeling that this war would continue for many years but he would have Jennifer to come home to. He would take life one step at a time, for who could tell what the future might bring. So many things could change; but he owed it to Jennifer to tell her about Rosemary. A terrible thought struck him – if she knew she might tell him not come down any more. He sighed. No, she wasn't like that. Who was it that said it was better to have loved and lost than never to have loved at all? Jennifer had already experienced the loss of a loved one – and in a way so had he. Rosemary was definitely not the same girl now as she had been when he married her. "Yes," thought Alan, "so many things can change – especially in these days of war and uncertainty. Life is precious. Love is precious. We must all take things one step at a time."

CHAPTER TWELVE

Tony Carrington was exhausted – mentally and physically. His brain was on alert for eighteen – sometimes twenty – hours a day. When he collapsed into bed it took him ages to unwind, then he would fall into a heavy sleep for those few hours that were left until his alarm clock rang to announce yet another jam-packed day. But he was glad that he was busy. It would be easy to sink into an unbearable depression if he had any time on his hands. After so many months of looking at the results of man's inhumanity to man – the severed limbs, atrocious burns and disfigurements, the paralysis and disease – he was amazed at the ability of the afflicted to keep cheerful. Most of them were so young; it was dreadful that they would have to pass the majority of their lives as invalids. And then there were the victims of the blitz – the women and children and the older people. No, it did not bear thinking about. The best thing that he could do was to devote himself to trying to ease their pain and lessen the misery that must rage beneath their brave exteriors.

Interspersed with his work at the hospital was his work at the War Office where he helped to organize the medical corps. Here he was privy to a great deal of highly secret information which added mental stress to physical strain. It was the end of April and it had been suggested – politely, of course – by one of the military bigwigs that he needed to take a few days off. The hospital had endorsed this. 'Otherwise,' they said, 'Doctor Carrington will become one of our patients.'

And so here he was walking through the gardens of Edgeglow arm-in-arm with Jennifer and with his son Charlie holding his hand. For the first time in six months – had he really not seen them since October? – Tony felt at peace. Charlie was ecstatic and Jennifer was – well, she was Jennifer. She was a wonderful woman and Tony realised how very lucky he and Charlie were to have her as their friend. He was so proud of her. It could not be very easy sharing your house with strangers and children could be very difficult, but she had done wonders with these rough kids from the East End and they obviously worshipped the ground she walked on. There was a new glow of serenity about her which made her seem even more beautiful than before. She looked fulfilled. What a wonderful mother she would make to children of her own one day.

Tony sighed with contentment. Jennifer glanced up at him and smiled. Charlie released himself from his father's grasp and ran on ahead to join the other children who were setting out the croquet hoops on the freshly mown grass. Tony smiled back at her and patted the hand that was linked in his arm. It was like being a family – him and Charlie and Jennifer – they knew each other so well and he loved her so much. He could admit to himself now that he always had, even when she was married to his friend. Of course he had never told her – he still had not told her. Now wasn't the time, but when this awful war was over he would ask her to marry him and then they would be a real family at last.

'. . . and so we have a guest.'

'What's that, my dear?' Tony had been so deep in his thoughts that he had not been listening to her.

'Tony, love, you're miles away,' she laughed. 'I was saying that Alfie Hurst's friend, Flight Lieutenant Jefferson, is coming to spend his long leave with us. He arrives tonight.'

Tony stiffened. 'But I thought that Hurst was a POW. This chap is an American, isn't he? No relation or anything. Why would he want to spend his leave here?'

'Well, I rather think that he was press-ganged by the children,' she answered, apparently oblivious to his irritation. 'The boys told him that they would miss not having a man to play games with them. They wouldn't take no for an answer.

He's very good with them, as was Alfie.' She paused for a moment and then continued. 'I think he's lonely. He's so far from home, and although I'm sure he's a popular young man I don't think that he's one of the boys. I think he likes coming here and being able to be part of a family. You'll like him, Tony, I'm sure.'

Tony relaxed. For a minute he had been jealous of the unknown airman who was obviously so much closer in age to Jennifer than he was, but the way she had just spoken about him was almost maternal.

'You speak of him as if he was one of the children, not someone of your own age,' he admonished gently.

'Do I? I suppose I feel a sense of responsibility for them all the time. While the children are here I want them to be happy and contented, otherwise I'm not doing a good job.'

'You push yourself too hard. No one could help but be happy here with you.'

'Thank you.' She kissed his cheek and smiled at him affectionately. 'Dearest Tony, you are my very best friend. What have I done to deserve you?' Her mood changed as she continued: 'And who are you to talk of pushing yourself too hard? If the powers that be had not decreed you had to take a break, you wouldn't be here now.'

'Probably not.' He gave her a rueful grin. 'I love being here with you and Charlie and all the others, but I can't help feeling that I am needed so desperately at the hospital.' He took off his glasses and rubbed his right eye. 'I don't like the way this war is going. What with Athens being captured by the Germans yesterday, who knows where it will all end. I must get back soon so that I can help.'

'You've only been here two days. You're to stay at least a week. You've got to rest, otherwise you'll be no good to anyone.' Jennifer had a determined look on her face as she folded her arms and stared him in the eyes.

'Yes, boss.' He gave her a mock salute. 'I'd better conform or I'll never get out of here.'

Jennifer threw back her head and laughed. 'You know, that's the second time this month that I've been accused of being bossy,' she said.

'Really?' He was amused.

'Yes. Alan Jefferson told me I was a bossy lady when he came to tell me about Alfie. He looked so tired that I told him he'd better stay the night. He couldn't, though, but I wouldn't let him leave without having something to eat, and he called me bossy. But he did look better when he left.'

'Oh.' Tony's lighter mood dissolved. Why did the mere mention of that name manage to depress him? He didn't even know the man, but already he felt antagonistic towards him. Was he really so insecure where Jennifer was concerned? He had sworn to himself when Helen died that he would never love anyone so completely again, and now, without quite knowing how it had happened, he was feeling this way about Jennifer. But now was not the right time to mention it. He would have to allow time for her own feelings to develop. She already loved him as her best friend, so that was a start. Given time and lots of love and support from him, and with Charlie on his side, he was sure he could win her eventually – and he was damned if some young American was going to come between him and his dreams of the future. These young airmen diced with death every day. It was an admirable thing that they were doing, particularly someone like Jefferson whose country was not even at war, but that did not entitle him to an affair with his, Tony's, girl, for that is how he now thought of Jennifer. At the end of the war Jefferson would go home to America – probably to a girl that he had left behind there.

"Why am I torturing myself by imagining all this?" wondered Tony. "He could be short and fat and buck-toothed and happily married with a wife and kids."

He sighed. No, one thing he wouldn't be was a family man. If he was, he certainly would not be fighting a war that did not involve his own country. As for the rest – possible, but not probable. Jefferson was a threat, of that he felt sure. Well, there was not long to wait. They would meet tonight.

Try as he did, Tony could not bring himself to dislike Alan Jefferson. The young man was charming – quiet and well-mannered and not at all like most Englishmen's idea of a brash American. He obviously came from a good family and was well educated and intelligent – no wonder he enjoyed coming to Edgeglow. It was probably what he was used to back home. He was strangely reticent about himself and his life before the war, but Tony put this down to the fact that he probably came from a rich family and had not done very much. This obviously embarrassed the poor boy now. When Alan let it slip that he had been at Harvard, Tony was not really surprised. Well, that accounted for his not talking about his job. He had obviously come straight to England after he graduated. If he was rich maybe he had learned to fly at university or before. What bigger adventure could a young man want? And yet he did not seem like a devil-may-care type of character. It was also strange that he should have been friends with the East Ender as they came from such different backgrounds, but then war created strange bedfellows. Tony was determined to learn more about this young man who seemed too good to be true.

As for Alan, his first reaction when he walked through the door and was introduced to Tony was a sudden disappointment at the realization he would have to share Jennifer – but this was quickly followed by the feeling of being granted a reprieve. There would be no awkward moments, no wrestling with his conscience. He had already built up a mental picture of Doctor Carrington and he had not been far wrong. He was a thoroughly decent man. Alan watched him play with his son whose little face shone with happiness at having the two people he adored – Jennifer and his father – here with him. They looked just like a family. The thought depressed him. How selfish it was of him to feel this way, he mused. Jennifer was lucky to have the good doctor. It was plain to see that he adored her and she was very fond of him. Fond, but not in love. Well, that was no bad thing. Love could land you in so much trouble. Surely it was better to be good friends and love one another gently than to experience the grand passion of 'falling in love'. Being in love could bring so much heartache, and it was a flimsy thing that could be damaged so easily. The other kind of love was the love that stood more chance of lasting and it could grow.

"I'm in love with her," Alan admitted to himself. "I want her so much that it hurts and I'm sure that she feels something too." He sighed. All he could do was hurt her and ruin her chance of happiness with Tony Carrington. Silly Tony. How typical of an Englishman to be so cautious – so afraid to show his feelings and risk rejection. If Tony had asked Jennifer to marry him six months ago, she would have done so. Of that Alan was sure. Now, without a word being said, it was too late. Even if nothing happened between himself and Jennifer, the feelings were there and that would make it impossible for someone like Jennifer to consider a proposal from Tony. He knew that, but what could he do? He had not even told her he was married. He wanted to forget his family problems until he had to go home and face them. Whenever he thought about Rosemary he felt so depressed – and so sorry for her. He looked across the drawing room at Tony who was sipping his glass of port – another luxury from Richard's cellar which was kept for special occasions. Tony smiled and raised his glass.

'Nothing like a glass of good port to make one feel a whole heap better.'

'Must be. I've not had a cigarette since before dinner,' Alan replied.

'That's good. You smoke too much,' Jennifer admonished. She refilled their glasses and then put the decanter back in the cupboard. 'That's enough or you'll both have headaches in the morning.'

'Never, not on a port of this quality. Anyway, we could always blow the cobwebs away by going for a brisk walk after breakfast.' Tony glanced at Alan. 'What do you say to that, Alan?'

'Oh . . . sure. I'd like that.'

'Good, then that's settled. I've been here almost a week and so have you. It's time we took some exercise.'

'Well, I think I'll turn in.' Alan stood up. 'The thought of all that exertion tomorrow has made me sleepy. Good-night.'

After he had left the room, Tony turned to Jennifer. 'I must say, he's a very pleasant young man,' he stated.

'Yes, he is. I'm glad you like him.'

'What did he do before joining up?'

'I don't know. He doesn't talk much about himself. I've never liked to pry. All I know is that his family comes from Boston and that he went to Harvard.'

'Aren't you curious?'

'Not really.' Jennifer busied herself with the empty glasses. 'If he doesn't want to tell us, I can hardly put him through the Spanish Inquisition, can I?'

'No of course not – don't get me wrong. I just . . .'

'Tony, don't worry.' She slipped her arm through his and smiled up at him. 'He's a perfectly ordinary man who likes to keep himself to himself. I sometimes wonder why he spends so much of his free time with us, but if we can help to take his mind off some of the terrible things he must witness every day, then I'm happy, and I do enjoy his company and so do the children. We don't see you nearly enough, and it's nice to have a visitor.'

'You're a wonderful girl, Jennifer.' Tony gave her a quick hug. 'Of course it's good for you to have company. I'm just envious because I can't get down here more often to be with you and Charlie and the others.'

'We understand and we still love you.' She grinned at him.

'Likewise.' He spoke lightly. Maybe he was worrying unnecessarily. There certainly did not appear to be anything between the two young people. 'Let me help you with the clearing up.'

As she lay in bed later that night Jennifer stared into the darkness and thought how lucky she was to have Tony for a friend. He cared for her so well. At first she had thought that he did it out of a sense of loyalty to Richard, but since then he had shown her how fond he was of her and she knew that she had a lifelong friend. As for Alan – had she imagined that there could be something between them? With Tony staying, there was no way of finding out. Every night Alan retired to bed early before Tony and herself. It was as if he did not want to be left alone with her – and yet he liked coming to Edgeglow. He had said so. Well, he didn't have to come, did he? And yet the children had made it very difficult for him to refuse. Jennifer blushed as she remembered trying to make him spend his full two weeks' leave with them, particularly as he had told her on his arrival that he would in fact be unable to stay the whole time. Apparently he had things he had to do in London and so would be leaving at the same time as Tony.

"I shouldn't have suggested it," she thought. "He obviously has other things to do and other people he wants to see. I made a fool of myself." She sighed. "It's probably just as well that Tony is here. The last thing I need is to become involved with someone who could be killed tomorrow. I've been through that before and I don't think I could stand it again."

'Going to be a beautiful day,' Tony announced as he and Alan left the house the following morning.

'You could have fooled me.' Alan surveyed the thick mist that enveloped the valley.

'You town-folk are so ignorant.' Tony grinned at his young companion. 'There's been a sudden change in temperature – hence the heat haze. When it clears, it'll be a lovely sunny day; you mark my words.'

138

'You reckon?'

'I most certainly do.'

They walked across the parkland and into the wood. The air smelled good and peace prevailed. The stillness was only broken by the occasional flutter of a bird in a tree and the breaking of the odd twig underfoot.

It took them half an hour to walk through and emerge in the open again, and by then the mist had cleared slightly allowing the sun to come through.

'Jesus! What the hell is that?' Alan strained his eyes to the far side of the field. A house was perched on the top of the hill and embedded in its roof was the remains of a small aircraft.

Tony followed his glance. 'Oh that. That happened back in the winter. One of ours. Came from one of the Welsh bases, I think. The woman in the house had an amazing escape. As luck would have it she was downstairs feeding her baby. She was able to grab the child and rush outside before the house caught fire. Of course, it was completely gutted.'

'Can we go take a look?'

'If you like, though we must be careful. I don't think that the structure is very safe.'

They set off across the field and climbed the hill.

'Rather spooky, isn't it?' Tony gazed at the remains of the gallant little Spitfire. 'I wonder what went wrong.'

'Any amount of things.' Alan shivered as once more it was brought home to him how precarious his future was. 'Fog, misjudgement of fuel – maybe engine failure. I bet the poor bastard didn't stand a chance.'

'You're right. He didn't.'

They were both silent for a minute in homage to the dead pilot, whoever he had been.

'If I remember rightly, Jennifer had terrible trouble with the kids.' Tony was trying to lighten the mood. 'They all wanted to come and see what had happened – which was fine, but trying to keep the boys away from all the hazards of the debris was not an easy task. They were quite fascinated. I believe the local policeman had to speak to them very firmly.'

Alan grinned. 'I can understand that. I was very inquisitive as a small boy – I still am.'

'Is that why you joined the airforce?'

'Umm?' Alan's thoughts were miles away.

'Is that why you joined up? I'm curious as to why someone in your position would want to come and fight in a war that did not involve his country. Don't get me wrong – I have the utmost respect and admiration for you boys from America, but it still puzzles me as to why you are here.'

'We all have our reasons, Tony.'

'Of course, but you don't strike me as the kind of hot-headed young man who wants to go down in a blaze of glory.'

'I'm not.' Alan spoke quietly.

'I'm sorry.' Tony was contrite. 'I had no right to say that and it's none of my business why you do what you do.'

Alan took a cigarette out of his pocket and lit it up. He leaned against the stone wall which surrounded the overgrown garden. 'You're wrong, Tony. In a way it is kind of your business. I need someone to talk to and you being a doctor could help me.'

Tony felt an icy feeling grip his heart. 'Good God, man! You're not going to tell me you're suffering from some dreadful illness, are you?'

'Relax, Tony.' Alan laughed mirthlessly. 'I'm no Richard Woodward. If I was, I never would have passed my medical. No, there are other things that require a doctor's advice.'

Tony heaved a sigh of relief. He sat down on the wall and folded his arms. 'I'm listening,' he said. 'Fire away. You know I'll help if I can.'

'. . . And so you see, that is my reason for being here. I thought it might give us some breathing space and help Rosemary to stand on her own feet. When I get home things may be different.' Alan looked around him for the first time since he had begun his story. 'It's so lovely here,' he said. 'I feel so peaceful and relaxed. I love playing with the kids. The whole set-up reminds me of when I was a child and we spent the summers with my cousins in New England. They were a large family and we all got on so well. It's funny how things change, isn't it? They're all scattered through the States now. Two are divorced and one became a nun. Nothing lasts, does it? I always vowed than when I grew up I'd make a life for myself based on those summers I spent in New England, but nothing is ever what it seems. We kid ourselves, don't we?'

'You are too young to become a cynic, Alan.'

'No one is young any more, Tony. We've all had to grow up in the last couple of years whatever age we may be – even those kids at Edgeglow are older now than they ever would have been if the war hadn't started.'

'I suppose you're right,' Tony sighed.

'I'm right.' It was said bitterly. 'And look at Jennifer. She's only twenty-one and already she's been a wife and a widow and now has all the responsibility of running that large house and looking after other people's children.'

'I try to make things easier for her.'

'Of course you do and she's so very lucky to have you. I'm sure she appreciates that, but it doesn't alter the facts, does it?'

'No. You are right.' Tony rubbed his offending right eye. 'Have you talked to her about your problems?' He was fishing for a reaction, as he knew perfectly well that Alan had not said a word.

'No, I don't usually discuss my private life.'

'Then I'm honoured that you trust me -- even though I am a doctor.' Tony looked hard at the other man. 'Would you like me to mention it to her?'

Alan met his eyes. He shrugged his shoulders, helplessly. 'Just tell her I'm married,' he replied.

They started back to Edgeglow, each deep in their own thoughts. Tony felt sorry for the young man who walked beside him. He was a good man who was aware of his responsibilities. He had married too young and was paying the price for it, but his decision to stick by his neurotic wife was an honourable one. Tony could see that he had not been wrong when he had imagined that Alan was attracted to Jennifer. Having heard Alan's story, he realized that Jennifer had to be everything that Rosemary was not – courageous, independent and trusting, all very attractive qualities for a man in a strange country who was risking his life from day to day. Would anything happen between the two young people? He thought not. Alan was a gentleman – that did not mean that he would not have the occasional affair while he was over here, but Tony had the feeling that he would not play around with Jennifer. He respected her too much and would not want to cause her any pain; and Tony realized another thing – Alan would not be able to stand the guilt. It's funny, he thought, you could look at a man like Alan Jefferson and be so envious. It was only if you bothered to dig deeper that you found God did not give all to one and nothing to another. Poor Alan. Tony hoped that things would work out for him in the end. Surviving the war was only one of his problems.

By the time they reached the park, Alan felt as if part of the weight inside him had been lifted. He liked and trusted Tony Carrington. He wished that he could get to know him better, but circumstances would not allow for that. Their free time would probably never overlap again. It was good to have been able to talk to him and he was glad that Jennifer would at last get to know that he was married, as he would have found it very difficult to tell her himself. Well, that had been taken care of. Now they could be good friends and nothing need be said. It made him feel better about coming here in the future. They would be like brother and sister – his family while he was in England.

CHAPTER THIRTEEN

Jennifer found the evenings quiet and long after the two men had left. She had not really been surprised when Tony told her that Alan was married. It explained quite a lot of things that had puzzled her. Of course, being a married man he obviously missed the comforts of home. Tony had said that he came from a large family and that was something that she, Mrs Edison and the children helped to re-create. "He's a nice person," she thought. "A genuine person. I like him a lot, but now that I know about him I shan't let my feelings get out of control. I won't allow myself to grow too fond of him – in the same way that I won't grow too fond of the children. One day they will all have to go home – and so will he."

For a moment she allowed herself to feel sad. It would be very hard to send Charlie back to his father, even though she would see him often. Supposing Tony married again? A new wife would not want Jennifer around too much. Ah well, she'd cross that bridge when she came to it.

The telephone rang and she went out into the hall to answer it.

'Jennifer, is that you? I've got a forty-eight-hour pass on Friday. Can I come up and see you all?'

'Alan, how lovely to hear you.' She felt quite lightheaded. 'I was just thinking how quiet the evenings were around here. Of course you must come. When shall we expect you?'

'I should make it in time for supper, if that's OK?'

'Marvellous. We'll look forward to it.'

She put down the telephone and smiled to herself. The children would be delighted. The weather was lovely at the moment and they would have him out playing cricket and croquet in the garden. Nearly a month had passed since they had last seen him and Jennifer was determined that it should be a wonderful weekend – relaxed and happy and with no undertones. Friendship was all that was needed and that's all that there would be.

When the children arrived back from school that Friday they were in high spirits. The two Garrett boys and Betty took it in turns to mow the lawn with the inadequate hand-mower. Petrol was rationed and in very short supply – it definitely could not be used for mowing lawns. Tom followed after them, raking up the cut grass. There was no way that Mabel Edison or Jennifer could tempt them to come inside for tea; one by one they dashed into the kitchen and grabbed a piece of bread and margarine, then rushed back outside to continue their work.

By seven o'clock they had finished and the croquet hoops were in place as was the carefully measured cricket pitch with a homemade wicket at each end. Betty's friend was under strict instructions to see that her pony, Maisie, was groomed to perfection when she brought her up the next day to show Alan how far Betty's riding had progressed.

'Can I stay up for supper tonight, Jennee, please?' Tom's large brown eyes looked at her pleadingly.

Jennifer thought for a moment. 'Yes, just this once as there's no school in the morning,' she smiled.

'Whoopee!' The little boy jumped up and down with excitement. 'Thanks, Jennee.' He rushed off to wash his hands and brush his hair.

Mabel shook her head. 'You spoil them,' she admonished. 'He's only five and he's had a long day.'

'I know, but they do so love it when Alan or Tony is here. They are able to entertain the boys so much better than you or I can.' She patted Mabel's shoulder. 'If he's tired tomorrow, he can have a rest in the afternoon.'

'Some chance of that!' Mabel snorted, but she was smiling. She glanced at the clock on the kitchen dresser. 'When do you think Lieutenant Jefferson will arrive? It's nearly eight o'clock.'

'Let's give him until half-past eight.' Jennifer got up from the kitchen table where she had been sitting. 'I'll just go and check on the little ones. They should be asleep, but you never know. If he's not here by the time I get back, we'd better start without him. I'm sure he won't be long. He'd let us know if his plans had changed.'

But when the clock said eight-thirty, Alan still had not arrived. The disappointed children sat silently around the table not doing justice to Mabel's delicious stew. At half-past nine, Jennifer sent them to bed.

'Go along now,' she said firmly amid their cries of indignation. 'Otherwise you won't be in a fit state to enjoy the weekend. It's been a long day and you are all tired. You can see Alan in the morning.'

It was well after ten o'clock when Jennifer and Mabel finished clearing up. As they sat nursing cups of tea at the kitchen table, Jennifer voiced the thought that they were both thinking.

'Supposing something has happened to him?'

'Now don't you go getting yourself in a state.' Mabel was forever practical. 'He's probably just running late. There's any amount of things that could have happened to delay him.'

'But he would have let us know.'

'Maybe that was impossible.'

Jennifer shook her head. 'Mabel, I know you mean well, but it is worrying. Alfie got shot down, but he was lucky . . .'

'Now don't go imagining a whole lot of things that I'm sure haven't happened. If he doesn't arrive by eleven, I'm sure that he'll wait until tomorrow. The telephones are very unreliable. He probably couldn't get through. He'll be here tomorrow, you'll see. Would you like me to stay the night? I could run over and explain to George?' Mabel usually spent at least two nights a week at the cottage with her husband and tonight was one of them.

'No, I'll be fine. It's not as if I was here alone, is it?' Jennifer smiled weakly. 'You go, Mabel, otherwise George will be disappointed. He doesn't see much of you as it is. I'll wait up for an hour, just in case.'

'All right, dear, and don't you worry. I'm sure he's fine. Men just don't think. They don't realize how much we women worry.'

Jennifer sat in the drawing room for what seemed like ages. It was not warm and cosy like the kitchen, but she could hear if a car should drive up from there. Twice she had gone into the hall and picked up the telephone just to see if it was working. It was. At half-past eleven, she had to admit to herself that he would not be coming now. She locked the door, switched off the lights and went upstairs to bed.

But it was impossible to sleep. Visions of planes being shot down and burning wreckage floated in front of her closed eyes. No one would let her know, would they? No one would know of her existence. If something had happened to him, she might never know. For a while she tossed and turned in the large bed. She was cold – even with three blankets and an eiderdown. She curled herself up into a tight little ball, but all that served to do was to give her cramp. As she stretched out she felt a strange ache spread throughout her body. "I want him so much," she thought. "I've never felt like this before – not even with Richard!"

She sat up in bed and switched on the light. As the room blazed with light she rubbed her eyes and brushed her hair back from her face. "I'm going crazy," she told herself. "I have no business to feel this way. He's married to someone else and he intends to stay married. He doesn't feel this way about me. I'm building up fantasies in my mind, I've obviously been alone for too long. God . . ." She blushed as she remembered her relationship with her husband. "I loved Richard so much. I longed for the consummation of that love, yet when it eventually happened I felt so let down. I didn't love him any less – or did I? I just felt so inadequate."

She sighed deeply. Maybe all the love inside her was maternal – that love she had for the children and Tony and had had for Richard. Passion was obviously not for her – and yet this feeling she had for Alan did not seem maternal at all. "It's just as well that I'll never find out," she thought. "Either way would be impossible to bear."

She got out of bed and put on her cotton dressing gown. Maybe, if she went downstairs and made herself a hot drink, she would be able to get some sleep.

As she walked down the stairs, she thought she heard a noise. It sounded like a door slamming. She felt a tingling at the base of her spine. Surely no one was about at this hour? She shivered and told herself to stop imagining things. She had probably left the kitchen door open when she went to bed, and a draught must have just closed it. As she continued on down the stairs and across the hall a different noise brought her to an abrupt halt. Someone was tapping on the front door. She froze and kept silent. There it was again. She tiptoed over.

'Who's there?' she asked hesitantly.

'It's me, Alan.' The voice was low and husky.

Suddenly she came to life. She threw back the bolts – almost forgetting to turn off the light before flinging open the door. He stood on the gravel bathed in moonlight.

'I was so worried. What happened?'

'It's a long story.' He attempted a small smile. 'I'm sorry, I had no idea it was so late. What time is it?'

'Half-past twelve.'

'Really?' He looked disorientated.

'It doesn't matter. You're here now.'

Neither of them ever knew who moved first – whether Alan stumbled from exhaustion or Jennifer swayed from the combination of fear and relief. Somehow they found themselves in each other's arms and he was holding her so tightly that she could hardly breathe. His lips were on her hair, on her eyes and on her cheek until at last they found her mouth. It was not a gentle kiss, but was impelled by long pent-up emotion – demanding and hungry in its intensity. Jennifer wound her hand through his thick blond hair as she responded to his passion. "I don't want this moment ever to end," she thought, as they clung to each other as if their very lives depended on their closeness.

They stood locked together in the doorway for what seemed like an eternity. Eventually a small shiver of cold ran through her. Alan released her gently and they gazed at each other still bemused.

'For goodness' sake, it's freezing cold out here. Come in.' She gave a shaky laugh.

He picked up his small suitcase and followed her inside. Once she had closed the door, she switched on the light.

'I think we need a drink, don't you?'

'You don't know how much.' He followed her into the drawing room.

'We're almost out of whisky. When this is finished it'll be difficult to get more.' Her hand shook as she tried to pour the liquid into the glasses.

'Here, let me do that for you.' He took the bottle from her and she noticed that his hand shook nearly as much as hers had.

He walked across the room and flung himself down on the sofa.

'What happened?'

'Bad day.' He leaned his head back and closed his eyes.

'Do you want to talk about it?'

'No.' Christ, how did you talk about some of the horrors of war? This afternoon one of his pilots – a kid of barely nineteen – had crash-landed on the airfield. By the time they had got to him the crate was on fire and he had had to watch the wretched young man burn to death. No, he definitely did not want to talk about it.

'That's all right.' She sat down beside him.

'I'm sorry.'

'It really doesn't matter.'

'You don't understand – how could you? There are things I see from day to day that don't bear talking about. You just have to put them out of your mind in order to survive.'

'I do understand – believe me.' She took his hand in both of hers and felt him shiver. He leaned forward, gently extricating himself from her touch.

'Jennifer, what happened just now should never have happened. You know I'm married. I'm truly sorry.'

'Are you?' It was said tremulously.

"Oh God!" he thought desperately as his eyes held hers. "How strong am I expected to be?"

Her little face looked pinched and pale and her eyes were as large as saucers. Bright pink spots had appeared on her cheeks and her mouth quivered slightly, but she held herself rigidly erect.

He looked away and took another sip of his whisky. 'No,' he heard himself whisper.

Jennifer stood up and walked over to the fireplace. She kept her back to him while she gazed fixedly at the unlaid hearth.

'I've been thinking a lot about us since you were last here – I've had a lot of time to do that. The evenings can be very long when you are on your own. I think that we've both felt something between us for a long time now . . .' She raised her hand to stop him from interrupting. 'No, don't say anything. Let me finish. I know that you're married. Tony told me everything and I understand your loyalty to your wife. I would expect nothing less of you – but, Alan, this is different. Circumstances are different. Who knows how long this war will last or who will ever go home? I think you need me and I know that I need you, and if we can give each other comfort for even a short time it will be worthwhile.'

'But it's not fair to you. I don't want to be the cause of any unhappiness.'

'What isn't fair, Alan, is for you to make the choice for me. If I choose to want to be with you, that is my decision.

149

Your choice is only to decide whether you want to be with me.'

'You know that I do.' His voice was thick with longing. 'But you're not just anyone, my dear, you are you. This wouldn't just be a casual affair. We both know that.'

She laughed shakily. 'It could go on for years the way this war is going.'

'That's the first good thing I've heard in its favour.' He stood up and in two strides she was in his arms again. This time he held her tenderly and Jennifer was sure that he must feel the frantic beating of her heart against his chest. She pulled away from him slightly and looked up at him. 'There are rules,' she said seriously.

'Oh yes? And what are they?' He smiled down at her.

'When the war is over and you have to leave, we must both promise to let go.'

The smile left his face. 'I know.' He sighed deeply. 'That's the way it must be.'

'It's late,' she said. 'You must be tired.'

'Not any more.' He saw her blush. 'I adore you, my Jenny.' It was the first time that he had used the diminutive form of her name and she liked it. 'You make me feel indestructible. We'll survive – you and I – whatever happens, but in the meantime we'll make each other happy for as long as possible.'

'Yes, we will, won't we?'

As she walked up the stairs beside him, Jennifer wondered what they both really expected of this relationship. They were attracted to one another physically and they both liked each other as people, but what was the other essential ingredient for each one of them? In her case, was it a need to prove herself as a woman – to be fulfilled by physical love? What was it for him? Call it woman's intuition, but she was sure that he was not a man who indulged in light affairs. He needed to belong. Well, for a while they could pretend that he belonged to her.

*

It was half-past four in the morning. Jennifer stood by the window with the curtains slightly parted looking out into the park. It was still dark, but the moonlight gave an eerie glow to the trees. Behind her she could hear Alan's even breathing as he slept. She smiled. Soon she would have to wake him and send him back to his own room. It would never do for the children or Mabel to know what was going on. Mabel would be most disapproving as she adored Tony – why did that thought come into her head? Jennifer put it out of her mind as she remembered yet again the wonder of the last few hours.

There had been nothing gentle about their love-making – not until afterwards. They had shed their clothes and fallen on the bed, each desperate with their need for the other, the unspoken thought being that if they waited it would never happen. They could not hold each other tighter. They could not kiss each other deeper. When at last they were one and he was inside her, their relief was so great that they both climaxed at once. As he heard her soft cry and felt her shudder beneath him, Alan was overwhelmed with a tenderness such that he had never known before. He held her gently in his arms and stroked her hair. 'Oh, my love, my Jenny,' he whispered. 'What have we started?'

She did not answer, but just pressed herself more tightly against him. He kissed her cheek and tasted the saltiness of her tears. 'Are you all right? I didn't hurt you, did I?'

She shook her head, still too overcome to speak. Her hand caressed his back, then ran down his leg. He felt himself grow hard again. This time it was a far more gentle act, as they both sought to please the other – touching and caressing each other as they learned the pattern of each other's body. Alan's nerve-endings felt almost raw with pleasure as he touched her warm smooth skin. She had a beautiful body, lean and firm, and it seemed to him at that moment that it had been made for one purpose only, for him to love. She was his Jenny, his love. The passion between them increased – was it possible? She surprised him with her capacity for love, or did she? Now there was nothing gentle about their seeking for fulfilment. Desire was met by desire. This time he was not afraid that he would hurt her. Her body was demanding as much and more.

As he lay beside her afterwards, she cradled his head against her breasts. A delicious feeling of warmth and safety washed over him. He sighed as he fell asleep in her arms. Nothing must be allowed to cut short their precious time together.

'Are you all right?' Alan's voice floated across to Jennifer as she stood by the window.

'Yes, I'm fine.' She turned towards the bed. He had raised himself on one elbow and she could see his face in the slice of moonlight cast from the open chink in the curtains. He looked younger, she thought. The lines of tension had eased. Her heart pounded just looking at him. He seemed so vulnerable.

'Why are you over there?'

'I couldn't sleep. There was so much to think about.'

'You don't regret this, do you?' His voice was unsteady.

Why should he feel so insecure, she wondered. He, who had grown up with everything. The golden college boy to whom everything had come easy ... except love, she realized. 'Oh no.' Her voice was thick with emotion. 'I'll never regret this.'

'Then come back to bed.' He patted the pillow next to him. 'I need you beside me.'

'Only for a few minutes.' She closed the curtain and walked over to the bed. 'You must go back to your own room soon. It will be daylight in an hour or so.' She sat down and turned on the light.

'Jenny, what is it? What have you been thinking?'

'So many things.' She smiled down at him tenderly. On an impulse she took his hand in both of hers and kissed it, then held it to her cheek. 'You have done so much for me in just a few short hours. I thought that I could never experience those feelings. I thought that I was cold and frigid and that I was not capable of feeling sexual passion. It had never happened for me before.' She blushed. 'I used to tell myself how inadequate I was. I prayed that in time I would feel something, but I never did. You have proved to me in one night that I can be a real woman. I have so much to thank you for. I need you, Alan, I didn't realize how much until now. Please take good care of yourself for my sake. I'm being totally selfish when I say that I want you here for as long as possible, so don't go trying to be a hero. Our time together will be all too brief as it is.'

Alan pulled her into his arms and held her quietly. "Oh, my Jenny," he thought. "You haven't got a selfish bone in your body. You were never in love with your Richard. You loved him, but you weren't in love with him. We cannot order ourselves to fall in love with someone – it just happens whether we want it or not. With you and Richard the chemistry obviously wasn't right." He sighed and held her tighter. "I was never in love with Rosemary," he realized. "I thought I was, but I wasn't. I was in love with an extension of myself. Golden boy meets golden girl. Conclusion – they are bound to live happily ever after. I should have waited. I was too young to realize that all that appears on the outside is just superficial, and that it's what is on the inside that truly matters. Why do we only find out when it's too late? Now I am tied to a woman I don't love by feelings of guilt and responsibility. I didn't have to marry her – I chose to do so – and now I must reap what I have sown."

And why had he had to meet Jennifer? Was it to show him how vulnerable he was? Was God showing him what he might have had for keeps if he had not been so hasty – if he had taken the trouble to find out more about life before rushing blindly into marriage at so young an age? Or was he being handed a bittersweet bonus – an offering like that given to the gladiators the night before their ordeal in the arena? One night of love before almost certain death the following day. "Those who are about to die salute you." Alan shuddered with apprehension. For the first time since he had arrived in England he felt that he was not indestructible. Suppose that he should not survive this war? "But I have to," he told himself. "Too many people depend on me – on my ability to win through. I can't let them down."

But the seed of doubt had been sown and it remained embedded deep down in his subconscious. The chink was already there in his armour and one day it would affect his judgement and cost him plenty.

CHAPTER FOURTEEN

It was a summer of snatched happy interludes and golden private moments. In June Alan's squadron was moved to Farrington Chase in Hampshire. This put another hour on to his journey to Edgeglow, but nothing would have kept him away from Jennifer whenever he was free. He had thought that at Edgeglow he would find peace, but that formed only a small part of this relationship. Mostly it was a raging torrent which had to be held in check during the day for appearances' sake. When, at last, they were alone in her bedroom late at night, it became an unquenchable fire whose flames were permanently fanned by the unspoken thought that every time could be the last. Peace came briefly after the violence of their love-making. Peace was the unspoken understanding they had between each other.

On the rare occasions that Tony was able to visit, he noticed the change in Jennifer. He could see it in her eyes and in the bloom on her cheeks.

"It's happened," he thought. "They are lovers. Alan doesn't have to be here for me to see that. It's written all over her face." His heart felt as if someone had tied a stone to it and dropped it in the ocean. "I've lost her and it hurts so much."

Suddenly he felt angry at these two young people – the young officer whom he admired so much and the young woman whom he loved. They thought that they could only hurt themselves, but that wasn't true. When the war was over Alan would leave her; if he hesitated, Jennifer would make sure that he did the honourable thing and stood by his wife. They thought that they were so noble. An idea struck him. How silly, he hadn't lost Jennifer at all. All he had to do was wait for the war to end. When eventually Alan Jefferson went back home – that is, presuming he survived – Jennifer would turn to him again, and this time he would not hesitate to make her his wife.

On July 24th the Falcon Squadron took off to fly to Brest. They were to give cover to bombers who were to attack the German pocket battleships *Scharnhorst* and *Greisnau* sitting in Brest Harbour. It was a day that Alan Jefferson would remember hazily in his mind for ever. What had distracted him from his usually careful vigil? Why hadn't he seen that Messerschmitt 109 before it got so close to him? What had he been thinking about – as if he didn't know. Sergeant Pilot Hurst would have covered him but Alfie Hurst was in a prison camp and his replacement was erratic and not as seemingly infallible as Hurst. The crippled Hurricane coughed and spluttered. Did he have a hope in hell of nursing it back to base? If so, could he land it safely? He was losing height and rolling dramatically as he saw the Cornish coastline loom up in front of him. All he could hope to do was to put her down in the nearest field.

'God in Heaven.' He spoke out loud and crossed himself. 'Don't desert me now. I promise in the future always to do what is right and what it is my duty to do.' He gripped the joy-stick so hard that his knuckles went white. 'Come on, old girl,' he coaxed the Hurricane. 'You can do it.' Then they began their erratic descent.

'Tony? I'm so worried. I don't know what to do.' Jennifer's voice was slightly hysterical on the other end of the telephone.

'Calm down, my dear, and tell me what's bothering you.'

'It's Alan. I haven't heard from him in six weeks. I waited a month before calling the base, but they can't tell me anything – or they won't. Something's terribly wrong – I know it is. Oh Tony,' she gulped, 'do you think he's dead?

I'd be the last to know, wouldn't I? . . . I mean, I'm not a relative. They've got no reason to tell me. They probably don't even know of my existence.'

Tony felt a cold ring form around his heart. So soon? He almost felt that he had willed this on the poor young man. He pulled himself together.

'You really must calm down, Jennifer dear. Now start at the beginning and tell me what has happened.'

Jennifer took a deep breath. 'I wish I could,' she said shakily. 'Tony, this will come as a shock to you, but Alan and I meant a great deal to one another. He came down here whenever possible, though recently his squadron was transfered to Farrington Chase. He used to telephone at least once a week. Well, you can imagine how I felt when I hadn't heard from him for a month. I've never liked to telephone the base, but two weeks ago, after a month had passed, I just had to.' She started to cry gently. 'They couldn't tell me anything. They didn't even seem to know the name. At first I thought that it was because he had been there such a short time. If something had happened so soon, some junior officer might well not know his name, but then I realized that that was impossible. They just were not going to tell me. They didn't know who I was and they were not going to give out any information. Tony, please help me. I've got to know what has happened to him.'

Tony took off his glasses and rubbed his offending right eye. 'Jennifer darling' – the endearment slipped out without him noticing it and she certainly did not – 'I'll do what I can. Now stop thinking the worst and try and relax until I can find out something. He may just be wounded and in hospital somewhere. I'll be in touch as soon as I have some news.' He replaced the receiver and shook his head. He called through the open door to his secretary: 'Miss Harper, get me the War Office on the telephone. I want to speak to a Wing-Commander Grenville-Bailey.'

'Yes, doctor.' His secretary was pure efficiency. If she had overheard his conversation, she certainly did not betray the fact.

Tony glanced at the clock on the mantelpiece. It said five o'clock. He hoped that Grenville-Bailey would still be there. Mrs Harper appeared in the doorway.

'Your call, doctor,' she announced. 'The wing-commander is on the line.'

'Jennifer, I've managed to find out a little.'

'Tell me, oh please tell me.' She spoke tremulously into the receiver.

'He's alive . . .' He heard her gasp of joy.

'That's wonderful . . . Where is he? . . . When can I see him?'

'I don't know that yet. My friend at the War Office is finding out.'

'Is he badly hurt?'

'I don't know that either. Apparently he was taken to a hospital in Cornwall, but the wing-commander doesn't think he's there any more.'

'Why was he taken there? It's miles away?'

'My dear, I really don't know.' He spoke wearily. 'I'll be able to tell you more when he calls me back tomorrow.'

'I'm sorry, Tony.' Instantly she was contrite. 'I didn't mean to keep plying you with questions. It's just that I'm so relieved.'

'Don't get carried away.' He couldn't help speaking dryly. 'We don't know how bad it is yet.'

There was a pause on the other end of the line. Eventually she said: 'I won't.' It was little more than a whisper. 'Thank you, Tony, for all your trouble. I know how busy you are, but you always seem to find the time to come to my rescue. I really don't know what I'd do without you.'

'That's what friends are for.'

'You're more than just a friend, Tony. You mean everything to me.'

"Not quite," Tony thought wryly as he put down the telephone. "You're an inconsiderate bastard, Anthony Carrington, trying to make her feel bad just because of your own disappointment. There is nothing to be gained out of other people's unhappiness. You must be happy for her and Alan Jefferson. Now is their time. Later it will be your turn."

He turned off the lights and locked his consulting room door, then ran down the stairs and out into the cool evening air. In the distance a clock chimed eight o'clock. It was only September 20th and already the summer was on the wane. As he reached the corner of the street he glanced at the billboards behind a newsboy. Some were headed 'Crimea Cut Off From Mainland' while others informed him 'Kiev Entered by Germans'. Where was it all going to end? He was supposed to be dining with a colleague but he didn't feel hungry. He was tired – not physically but mentally. He was tired of these two years of war which showed no signs of abating. He was tired of making decisions, and more than anything else he was tired of being on his own. He reached in his pocket and pulled out a coin. He handed it to the boy. 'Ta, Guv,' the boy grinned and passed him a paper. 'Not too good, is it? Jerry seems to 'ave it made.'

'We'll win in the end,' Tony said with a conviction that he did not feel.

'Course we will,' the boy replied earnestly.

"He really believes that," Tony thought. "Ah, the enthusiasm of the very young. How old could the boy be? Fifteen – sixteen at most. In a year's time he would be off fighting for his country along with the rest – maybe he'd be dead?" It was a very sobering thought.

'Good morning, Doctor Carrington. You've just missed a telephone call from the War Office. Wing Commander Grenville-Bailey wants you to call him back as soon as possible.'

'Thank you, Mrs Harper.' Tony braced himself. Now he

would hear it. He hoped that it would not be too bad. He dialled the number and waited to be put through.

'That you, Anthony?' the wing commander's voice boomed down the telephone. 'I've got that information for you. Not too good, I'm afraid, but it could be worse.'

Tony listened as the wing commander droned on, giving him the facts. At the end of the conversation he thanked him profusely and replaced the receiver. Now what was he to do? He opened his appointment diary and glanced down at the heavily filled page. Patients for most of the morning, two hours at a hospital in the East End after that, a meeting with some of the Army Medical Corps at three o'clock and a visit to another hospital in the West End at five. If he was lucky he would be finished by seven and could be down at Edgeglow by nine. He could stay the night and drive back up to London first thing in the morning. He wanted to give Jennifer this news in person, for she might well need a shoulder to cry on – and, if so, he would like it to be his.

'Doctor Carrington, what a nice surprise. Her ladyship must have forgotten to tell me you were coming.'

'She didn't know, Mabel. I didn't telephone because I have some news I think I ought to give her face to face.'

'Oh dear, is it that bad?' Mabel Edison closed the door and her hand flew to her face. 'That nice young Flight Lieutenant Jefferson – it's about him, isn't it? We've been so worried. Not a word, you know, for weeks. Oh dear. Oh dear, oh dear.' She shook her head and sniffed loudly.

'There, there, Mabel.' Tony patted her arm. 'It's not fatal, but yes it is about him. Where is Lady Woodward?'

'She's upstairs putting the younger children to bed. I'll fetch her.'

'I'm here. What's going on down there?' Jennifer had appeared at the top of the stairs. She took in the scene below her. 'Tony, what are you doing here?' Suddenly her face drained of colour. 'What's happened?' she whispered. 'When someone appears on my doorstep unannounced at night, it is usually bad news.' She flew down the stairs and grabbed his arm. 'It's Alan, isn't it? What's happened to him? He's dead, isn't he? Oh God.'

Tony put his arm around her and led her towards the drawing room. He nodded over his shoulder to Mabel who took the hint and disappeared quietly back to the kitchen. 'No, my dear, he's not dead.' He sat her down on the sofa and took both her hands in his. 'He's going to be fine – more or less – but I thought it would be better to come down and explain everything to you. It's easier than doing it over the telephone, and I thought you might like me to be here as a friend.'

He felt her tense up. Her eyes were bright with unshed tears. She drew in a deep breath. 'Tell me,' she said. 'Don't try and dress it up. Tell me straight.'

Tony squeezed her hands. 'He crash-landed in a field somewhere in Cornwall on the way back from a mission. You didn't hear from him because he was quite badly injured. The force of the landing gave him a spinal injury and he also badly damaged his eyesight.'

'Will he be all right?'

'Yes, I've already told you, he's going to be fine.'

'When can I see him?'

'That's the point, Jennifer dear. You can't see him. They've already shipped him back to America.' He heard her gasp as he continued. 'You see, he's no good to the RAF any more. Eyesight is the most important thing for a pilot and Alan's will never be that good again. Our hospitals are overcrowded and every bed is needed, so when it was safe for him to be moved, they sent him over on the first available boat.'

Jennifer closed her eyes tightly as if the very effort of squeezing them together would shut out the truth.

'You'll have to face it, my dear. He's gone. There's nothing you can do.' He took off his jacket. 'Be glad for him,

Jennifer, if you can. He's out of this awful war. He's alive and he will get well and he won't go blind.'

'I am, oh I am.' She sighed. 'I'm being totally selfish. I thought that we would have more time together, that's all. I knew that it wasn't permanent – nothing is forever, is it? I know that and you know that, but I didn't think that God would begrudge me just a little more time. He has, though. Perhaps this is His way of telling me that it was wrong? Alan belonged to someone else and I had no right to him.'

'Don't be so hard on yourself.' Tony stroked her hair as he would a child. 'It does take two, you know, and the circumstances were out of the ordinary. He understands.' As he spoke, Tony wondered if he sounded convincing. Why this war? Why this senseless killing? Why so many things? And not least, he wondered why he should be the one to benefit from this unfortunate young man's demise.

Jennifer sat back and smiled at him tremulously. 'You are so good to me, Tony,' she said with feeling. 'When everything crumbles around me, you're always there to pick up the pieces. I don't know what I'd do without you.'

'You'll never have to,' he said quietly.

She stood up and walked over to the fireplace. 'I've felt sick with worry for the last few weeks. I've hardly been able to eat at all. At least it's a relief to know that he's all right. I must stop feeling sorry for myself, for we both knew that it was only ever to be a temporary relationship. I must be happy for the short time we had together, as I was with Richard.' She paused as a wave of guilt washed over her. Oh, how she would miss the feel of his body next to hers, the passion of his kisses and the exquisite fulfilment of their desire. In that moment Jennifer made a vow to herself. "I'll never let my heart rule my head again," she told herself. "It's too painful. Next time – if there is a next time – I'll have a steady relationship, nothing volatile. A love that endures must be built up gradually. There will be no more wild abandon – that is for the young and fancy-free. I'm an adult now, and I need security and peace of mind." She looked at Tony. "I need a family of my own and so does he. Maybe one day we'll settle down together." She sighed. It was too soon to think about something like that, and at the moment life was far too unpredictable.

The following morning Jennifer did not appear until Tony had nearly finished his breakfast. As she walked through the kitchen door, he noticed how pale she looked.

'Did you have a bad night?' he asked. 'Would you like me to leave you some sleeping pills? It won't do you any harm to get a good night's rest.'

'No thanks, Tony. I just don't feel very well this morning. All this worry has been taking its toll, and now I suppose it's the reaction to your news last night. I'll be fine later, don't you worry.'

Before he could ask her more the Fox children and the Garrett boys dashed through the door grabbing their coats from the pegs on the wall and rummaging in their satchels to make sure that all their school books were there.

'Bye, Doctor Carrington. We're going to be late.'

Little Tommy stopped and turned around. 'You won't leave us too, Doctor Tony, will you?' His face looked pinched and his eyes enormous. 'People we like always go away and never come back. First it was Alfie and now it's Alan. Do we do something wrong, Doctor Tony?'

Tony swallowed a lump in his throat. 'No, you don't do anything wrong, Tom.' He gave a smile. 'I know it's hard for you to understand, but neither Alfie nor Alan wanted to go away. Sometimes people have to do things that they don't want to do. They have to fight in this war to keep us safe.'

'But they say at school that it's wrong to fight – even in the playground.'

'I know, Tom, I know.' Tony ruffled the little boy's hair. 'It's a funny old world. I won't desert you – in fact I'll try my hardest to come down more often. I promise.'

Tom nodded seriously, then turned and ran off after his sister. Jennifer linked her arm through Tony's as they watched the little foursome wend their way down the drive.

'Will you really be able to get down more often?'

'I fully intend to.' He patted her hand. Damn it, he was entitled to some time off, and he was going to make sure he took it from now on.

'You're so good to me. How many times do I tell you that?' She leaned forward to kiss his cheek. 'Ooooh . . . I feel so peculiar.' She swayed and instinctively he caught her before she could fall.

'Jennifer, what's the matter?' He looked down at her but her eyes were shut. He swept her up and into his arms and carried her to her bedroom, calling to Mrs Edison on the way.

As he laid her down, her eyelids fluttered and opened. She looked slightly disorientated. 'Where am I?' she asked. 'What's happened?'

'You had a dizzy spell.' He put his hand on her forehead. She was not hot. 'You've had a shock, Jennifer. I think that you should stay in bed today and rest.'

'But I can't.' She tried to sit up. The room swam before her eyes and she sank back on the pillows. 'Oh God, I feel sick.' She sat up and reached for Mabel Edison's hand. 'Mabel, help me to the bathroom. I'm going to be sick.'

Mabel met Tony's eyes for a second as she busied herself helping the ill young woman out of bed. What was she trying to tell him, he wondered. What was the matter with Jennifer? Was she over-doing it? Was the strain of looking after all the children too much for her? Was she even more distraught than she had appeared to be over Alan Jefferson's departure? What was wrong?

He walked over to the window and looked out. Then it struck him – like an arrow straight through his heart. Of course! All the symptoms were there. "Doctor Carrington, you're really not very bright," he told himself. "Still, there are none so blind as those who just don't want to see." He turned back at the sound of footsteps. Jennifer walked into the room leaning on Mabel's arm.

'I feel better now.' She gave him a weak smile and got into bed. 'If I stay here this morning, I'll be fine by lunchtime.'

'Jennifer, I think that I should examine you.' He spoke quickly before he lost his nerve. Mabel nodded approvingly and left the room.

'I'm fine, really I am. You're talking as if there was something radically wrong with me.'

'I don't think there's anything wrong with you – not unnatural anyway.'

'Well then, don't be silly. Tony really . . .'

'Jennifer, I think you may be pregnant.' There, he had said it.

She gasped and was silent while she digested his words. Alan's baby. She would have a part of him with her forever. She felt warm and loved and fulfilled. Her eyes shone as she looked up at Tony. 'Then you had better examine me, doctor,' she told him.

Two months pregnant. Jennifer was two months pregnant. Tony sat at his desk with his hands clasped in front of him. He rubbed his right eye until it grew red and angry – rather like he felt. Damn Jefferson. Now what could he do? Tony had seen clearly the radiance on her face when he had confirmed her pregnancy.

'What are you going to do?' he had asked.

'Do? I should have thought that was obvious,' she had replied. 'I'm going to have a baby.'

'But, Jennifer, have you thought of the problems involved in having an illegitimate child?'

'I don't care. He's my baby and I'm going to have him.'

'Him?'

'He's going to be a boy. I know he is.'

'But Jennifer . . .' He had been at a loss for words. 'It will be very difficult for you. People won't be understanding. You and your child will have a great deal to put up with.'

'Then we'll put up with it. Do you think that I'd kill Alan's baby? You're a doctor. You wouldn't want me to do that, would you?'

He looked at the floor and shook his head miserably.

'There you are, then.' She had taken his face in her hands and had made him look at her. 'I can put up with people ignoring me and gossiping about me. The ones who will do that won't be worth knowing anyway, but you won't think any less of me, will you, Tony? That, I couldn't bear.'

Tony had thought deeply about the question. Would he think less of her for bearing Alan Jefferson's son? At the moment he felt betrayed. Yet why should he feel that way? He had known that they loved one another and that they had consummated that love. No, he felt betrayed by their thoughtlessness, the selfishness in their love. They had not been aware of the pitfalls while they sought only to please each other. And now how could he protect her? All that could protect her would be a husband. He drew in a sharp breath and his heart started to hammer double-time. Could he live with Jefferson's little ghost running around every day? She knew that she could never marry Jefferson, but would she always be mourning the fact? Time was a healing factor, so they said, and it was true. He knew that from his own experience after Helen's death, and Richard's. Suddenly, he was struck by the thought that his own circumstances were really not much different from Jennifer's. Every time she looked at Charlie she would know that he was Helen's son, no matter how much she loved him.

Tony made up his mind. "I love her and I want to marry her," he told himself. "Jefferson's child will be my child in as much as Charlie will be Jennifer's. Nobody will ever know anything different. They will be brought up as brothers, so that even they believe it. Everyone knows that I go down to Edgeglow a lot and have been doing so for years. They will all believe that her child is mine – except Mabel, and she would never voice a different opinion."

'But Tony, it isn't fair to you.'

'Yes it is.'

They were sitting in the garden the following weekend.

'No it's not. I can't ask you to be a father to another man's child.'

'I have Charlie. Can't I ask you to be his mother?'

'That's different. I love Charlie. I've loved him ever since I've known him.'

'And I'll love your baby. He'll be mine too – all but genetically. Damn it, Jennifer, I'll be the only father he will ever know.'

Her eyes glistened with unshed tears. "Damnation!" he thought. "I've gone too far."

'Charlie needs a mother,' he said quietly. 'Your baby will need a father. I'm extremely fond of you, Jennifer, and I think you are of me. Together I think we can be very happy.' How he wished that he could tell her how much he loved her, but he was afraid it would frighten her. He hesitated before adding: 'Of course, I wouldn't force you to do anything you didn't want to do.'

Jennifer gave a little sob and flung her arms around his neck.

'What have I ever done to deserve you?'

'Sh . . .' He rocked her gently. 'Everything's going to be all right – just you wait and see.'

She moved her head slightly and pressed her lips to his. Tony was surprised when he felt them part. He kissed her softly, his tongue gently exploring her mouth. She sighed and relaxed in his embrace. She had surprised herself. She was enjoying his kiss – oh, it had none of the urgency and frenetic excitement that had existed with Alan, but she felt safe and loved. It was as if she had been a ship caught up in a bad storm and had now suddenly found her way back to harbour.

"This is where I belong," she thought and knew that it was true. "I'm so lucky to have Tony – so lucky that he wants me. I'll be a good wife to him. I know I will. He's right when he says that we can make each other happy."

The notice in *The Times* birth column read: CARRINGTON – to Anthony and Jennifer (née James) a daughter, Alaina, born on April 1st 1942. A sister for Charlie.

PART II
1955–1962

Lainey.

CHAPTER ONE

'It all sounds frightfully romantic.' Alaina Carrington sat at the foot of her best friend Vivien Hurst's bed with her knees drawn up to her chin and a far-away expression in her eyes. The two girls were discussing Vivien's first experience of the local Pony Club dance. 'What happened next?'

'Well . . .' Vivien – the elder by some twenty months – revelled in being able to impart her more worldly knowledge to such a receptive listener who had yet to find out the basic pleasures of teenage love. 'Well, someone turned off the lights and suddenly we were dancing in the dark to this slow romantic tune and then he kissed me – really properly. He put his tongue right into my mouth and . . . and . . .' Vivien shivered with excitement as she recalled her first kiss. She remembered a line from a novel she was reading . . . 'I felt a tingling up and down my spine and I almost fainted with desire.' She paused dramatically and waited for a reaction from her friend.

'I think that's disgusting.'

'What?' That was certainly not the reaction she had been expecting.

'How could you?'

'How could I what?'

'Let him do that to you – put his tongue in your mouth?' Alaina blushed at the thought. 'It's so . . . unhygienic. You could probably taste what he had for dinner. Ugh!'

Vivien stared at her in amazement for a second and then started to laugh. 'Lainey, don't they teach you anything at that fancy boarding school you go to? That's what boys and girls do when they kiss – if they really like one another. It's very exciting. You wait until you start going to dances. You'll find out and you'll like it too.'

'No I won't.'

'Oh, yes you will. Anyway, you don't kiss anyone who has bad breath or is unattractive 'cause that could put you off for life.'

'Have you done it lots of times?' After her initial horror, Lainey was curious.

'Once or twice.' Vivien crossed her fingers under the bedclothes and tried to look nonchalant as she gazed out of the window. 'It improves all the time.' She hoped that God and her mother would forgive the little fib.

'Your mother wouldn't like it if she knew.'

Vivien jumped and faced her friend guiltily. Surely Lainey had not realised she had just told a fib. But one glance at Lainey's face satisfied her. The other girl was still referring to the kiss.

'Only because she'd think I'm too young. Things were different in her day. This is 1955.' She put her head close to Lainey's and whispered in a conspiratorial way. 'Anyway, she's not going to find out, is she? I've only told you because you're my best friend.'

'You know that I won't breathe a word to a soul.' Lainey was indignant.

'That's all right then, I'll always tell you everything.'

'Oh, you must. How old was this . . .'

'Julian?'

Lainey nodded.

'He's eighteen.'

'Vivien! That's older than Charlie!'

'Yes, I'm going in for men from now on. They're more sophisticated.'

'But why would someone of his age want to be bothered with you?'

Vivien struck a pose which she hoped looked alluring.

'Maybe it's because I'm sexy.'

There was a pause before both girls dissolved into a fit of the giggles.

'Don't laugh. It's a very serious matter.' Vivien was still laughing herself. 'I could become a *femme fatale* like Marlene Deitrich in all those forties movies.' More hysterical laughter. At last Lainey sat up and dried her eyes. A thought struck her. 'I wonder how long Charlie has been doing all this?' she mused.

'Oh ages.' Vivien gave another hysterical hiccup. 'Boys start earlier than girls. They've got nothing to lose except their virginity.'

'Vivien!' Lainey blushed again.

'Well, it's true. No man ever had a baby that I'm aware of.'

'Babies . . . Do you mean . . .?'

'Why not? He's seventeen. I'm sure he's tried it out by now. You should ask him.'

'Oh I couldn't. I'd be much too embarrassed. Besides, he wouldn't be amused. He's frightfully protective about me. He'd be horrified if he thought that I was interested in that sort of thing.'

'The trouble with your brother is that he's a bit old-fashioned and prudish. Just like my sister. I bet that Alison's as innocent as the day she was born. Oh, I love them both dearly . . .' She raised her hand as Lainey tried to interrupt, 'but they've got no spirit of adventure. They both take life too seriously. All Alison wants is to be a nurse and your brother just wants to be a doctor – not a Harley Street specialist like your father, just a good old-fashioned country doctor.'

'There's nothing wrong with that.' Lainey came to her brother's defence swiftly.

'I didn't say there was, but we're only young once, and it seems such a shame not to take advantage of everything that's going for you.'

'What do you mean?'

'Well, we've got so many opportunities. Our parents are well-off. Daddy's got a very successful company and your father is doing very well with his Harley Street practice. Both our families have nice houses, and we also have London flats. I know that Mattingham House isn't as big as Edgeglow was, but that was much too big for a family of four and much too far away from London to be practical for your father. Having you here in Surrey is super. It makes our friendship so much easier. We are very lucky, and I for one intend to take advantage of it all. When I leave school I'm going to live in our London flat and get myself an interesting job where I meet all kinds of people and have a jolly good time.'

'Charlie's not really a stick-in-the-mud.'

'Oh Lainey, I'm sorry. It's not that. He's lovely – really he is – so is Alison. It's just that they're so serious when this is the time they should be having fun.' Vivien scratched her head. 'You know something? They should get married. They're perfect for each other, even down to their chosen professions.'

'Don't be so silly, Viv. They're only seventeen.' Lainey spoke quite crossly.

'Keep your hair on. It was only a joke.' Vivien held up her hands in mock despair. 'Though you must admit that they get on well together and I'm convinced that Alison has had a secret crush on Charlie for years. She goes all pink when I mention his name.'

'You're imagining things.' Lainey jumped off the bed. 'I'm going to bed before your mother comes up here and tells us off for talking so late.'

'Lainey, what's the matter? Are you cross with me for saying that?'

'Don't be ridiculous. Of course I'm not. I'll see you in the morning. Night.'

'Night.' Vivien shook her head as the door closed behind her friend. She sighed. Even at the tender age of 'almost fifteen' she saw problems ahead for Lainey and Charlie. They were so close, even though there were four years between them in age. Lainey was a hothead – always determined to get her own way. She adored her elder brother almost to the point of obsession, but they were constantly arguing. No, that was wrong, Charlie didn't argue. It was Lainey who argued. He was very protective of his little sister. Vivien had to agree that Charlie would indeed be horrified if he thought that at the age of thirteen Lainey was kissing boys.

He wasn't handsome, Vivien thought as she turned off the light and lay back in the darkness, but there was something very attractive about Charlie Carrington. He wasn't very tall – about five feet eleven inches with a nice open face and large honest brown eyes. Rather like a spaniel's, she chuckled to herself, utterly dependable and faithful. She had been right when she made the comparison between him and her sister Alison. They really were very alike. She, Vivien, was more like Lainey – a bit more down-to-earth though. "I've got my feet on the ground," she thought "whereas Lainey permanently has her head in the clouds. It's not just because I'm that bit older, it's always going to be like that. I'm nearly fifteen and I know what I want, but I have a feeling that Lainey will always be searching for the unobtainable." At that moment she felt considerably older than her years. Poor Lainey. She had probably realised for the first time tonight that there were some things Charlie didn't tell her – things that he did not consider it right to discuss with a sister who was only thirteen years old. She was obviously feeling sore and left out, but she'd get over it as soon as she started to have boyfriends, of that Vivien was sure.

There was a tap on the door. Vivien pretended to be asleep. If it was her mother, the chances were that she would go away if everything stayed quiet. The tapping came again and then the door opened slowly.

'Viv Hurst, don't you pretend to be asleep. I know you're awake.' Lainey came in and closed the door.

Vivien sat up and switched on the light. 'What do you want? It's after midnight.'

'I forgot to tell you what I want when I grow up.'

'Well make it quick. Mother'll hear us and then there'll be hell to pay.'

'I want everything. That's what I want.' Lainey leaned against the door and focused her brilliant blue eyes on a spot behind Vivien's head. 'I want to mix with important people and go to exciting places. I want to be beautiful and in demand everywhere I go. I want to be somebody.'

'But you are somebody. You're Anthony Carrington's daughter and you already know a lot of important people through your parents.'

'No, you don't understand. I want to be me, not just someone's daughter. Charlie would understand what I mean.'

'Would he?' Vivien was cynical. 'He's not a bit like you, Lainey. He's quite happy to be who he is.'

'Oh you . . .' Lainey stamped her foot and shook her long blonde hair so that it became a cloud around her face. She clutched her pale-blue cotton nightdress around her tightly. 'One minute you're saying that we should take advantage of all our opportunities and the next you're inplying that I shouldn't.'

Vivien surveyed her petulant friend. There was no doubt about it, Lainey was already beautiful. She had a wonderful skin – completely flawless, no sign of the spots of puberty. Her hair was a thick, white blonde, but it was her eyes that were really distinctive. They were a brilliant cobalt blue, and when they focused on you they could send shivers up your spine. What man would be able to resist them in years to come?

'It's not the same thing, Lainey.'

'Why not?'

'I want to do what is best for me. I want to enjoy my life to the full and I want my parents to be proud of me whatever I choose to do.'

'Well, that's all I want too, silly.' Lainey gave her bright smile and slipped out of the room.

Vivien switched off the light and lay down again. "No, that's not what you want at all," she mused to herself. "Your problem is that you've been cossetted all your life by your parents and by Charlie. I'm lucky that way. I may not be beautiful," she smiled to herself, "but at least I've been brought up to be in touch with reality. Nothing has ever been hidden from us. I know how hard Daddy had to work to achieve everything we have now. That's the real difference between Lainey and me. I want to make my parents proud of me because I am so grateful for everything that they have done for me, and I'm sure Alison feels the same. But Lainey takes her way of life as a matter of course. She wants to be a golden girl – better than everyone else. The difference is that she's doing it for herself and not for them. It's almost as if she feels she's got to do it in spite of them." She felt her eyelids becoming heavy with sleep. "I'm talking nonsense," she thought hazily. "I'd better go to sleep."

'Morning, lids.' Alfred Hurst looked up from his close scrutiny of the *Sunday Times*. 'Help yourselves to some breakfast. Mrs Trigg has done us proud this morning.'

Mrs Trigg was the Hursts' 'treasure'. She was a plump jolly character who had worked for the Hursts ever since they had moved to Doves Place in 1951 and was now very much one of the family.

'Morning, Daddy.' Vivien bent down to kiss the top of her father's head.

'Morning, Uncle Alfie.' Lainey kissed his cheek.

'Where's the strife then?'

From behind her father's chair, Vivien raised her eyes comically towards the ceiling. Lainey grinned at her. Uncle Alfie was a scream. He hadn't changed at all, despite all the money he had made. He still spoke with his original cockney accent and its quaint rhyming slang. It was so funny listening to the father and his two daughters. No-one meeting them for the first time would guess that they were related. Alison and Vivien sounded so different with their educated voices acquired at their exclusive day-school in London. Lainey knew that Alfie was extremely proud of his daughters – proper young ladies, he called them. She wondered what he would think of Vivien's admissions last night and quickly stifled a bubble of laughter.

'Mother's on her way down.' Vivien helped herself liberally to eggs and bacon. 'She said that she's feeling a bit slow this morning.'

'She's all right, isn't she?' Alfie started to get up.

'Sit down, Daddy.' Vivien pushed him back down into his chair. 'She's fine. You know that there are days when she feels very stiff. No-one could take the sort of battering that she took in the blitz and not have any after effects. She's fine, really she is.'

'Yes, I suppose you're right, love, but I do worry about her.'

'Who worries about who?' Miriam Hurst walked into the room smiling.

'Are you all right, darling?'

'Oh Alfie, stop it.' She patted his shoulder. 'I'm perfectly OK. Just a little soreness now and again, but that's to be expected. I'm lucky to be 'ere and to be walking again.'

'You're a very brave lady and I love you very much.'

'Alfie, I said stop it. You're getting maudlin and it's only nine o'clock in the morning.'

At that moment the door from the kitchen swung open to reveal Mrs Trigg brandishing a tray.

'Oh Mrs H, you're down already,' she puffed. 'And here was me just about to prepare a tray and bring it to you up-stairs.'

'Well, as you can see, 'ere I am. Thanks all the same, Elsie.'

'You all right, Mrs H?' Elsie Trigg sounded concerned. 'Don't want to overdo things, do we?'

Miriam threw up her hands in mock horror. She appealed to her daughter.

'Will you try convincing your Dad and Elsie once and for all that I am not an invalid, and that Uncle Tony said it was good for me to be active.'

'I tried, really I did, but you know what Daddy's like when it comes to you.' Vivien winked at her mother. 'Come on, Lainey, let's get lost and leave the two love-birds to argue. Mrs Trigg can be referee.'

'Oh, you two. No respect for your elders.' Mrs Trigg swiped at them good-naturedly with a napkin as they scuttled out of the room. 'Growing up into fine girls,' she told her employers.

'Yes, they are,' Alfie nodded contentedly. 'Viv's a good girl – a bit more scatterbrained than Alison, but a right good girl none-the-less. That Lainey, though.' He shook his head. 'She's going to be a beauty, just like 'er mother, but much wilder. She's very strong-willed already.'

'She's only thirteen, dear. So she's a bit 'ead-strong now. She'll outgrow it. Don't you think so, Elsie?'

'There's them that does and them that doesn't.' Mrs Trigg nodded her head wisely. 'She's a dear, though. They get on really well, those two. It's nice for Miss Vivien to have such a good friend. And if Miss Lainey is a bit fiery, her elder brother will keep her in check. Right fond of him, she is and he of her. Does your heart good to see families like yours and hers all getting along so well.' She sniffed loudly and disappeared back into the kitchen.

'She really is a dear, isn't she?' Miriam smiled at her husband and squeezed his hand across the table. 'I don't know how we'd do without 'er.' She finished her cup of coffee and glanced at the clock on the mantlepiece. 'I nearly forgot. I promised Jennifer I'd ring and tell 'er when you were going to run Lainey 'ome.'

'Tell 'er I'll get Lainey back around teatime. You going to come with me?'

'No, I don't think so. You know what a rush it is on Sunday nights, getting ready to go back to town and all that.

Besides, Alison should be coming home sometime this afternoon, so I should be 'ere to meet her.'

'OK, little mother. You stay 'ere and I'll make the journey to the lovely Jennifer on my own.'

'Idiot, you'll have Lainey for company one way, and you know she never stops talking.' She gave him a quick hug and left the room.

Alfie shook his head as he looked after her. She was a remarkable woman, his Miriam. She looked so frail and yet she had the heart and courage of a lioness. She was only five feet two inches tall with heavy long almost black hair and an olive complexion. A good Jewish girl was how his father had described her when Alfie had first started dating her. Alfie lit a cigarette and grinned to himself as he remembered. Her father had kept the corner shop at the end of the street and they had both gone to the same school as children. But he had not noticed Miriam until that fateful Saturday morning when he had gone to buy a packet of fags to smoke illegally in the park with his friends. He had seen her helping her parents behind the counter, and been struck between the eyes right then and there. Here was a beautiful little miniature person who needed protecting. He had been protecting her ever since.

He had been frantic with worry during the war. As a POW there had been little he could do but worry. Would she recover from the dreadful injuries she had sustained during the blitz? If so, would it be as a cripple? But his Miriam had proved how strong and determined she could be and had fought her way back to health. It had been a long and, he knew, very painful process. After leaving the London hospital, she had been sent to a nursing home in the north of England where she had remained for four long years. She had only been allowed home six months after Alfie's release.

They had a great deal to thank Tony and Jennifer Carrington for, Alfie reflected. Not only had they looked after the girls during the war, but they had insisted that he and Miriam should stay with them until they were back on their feet.

That had taken six months. Alfie was a worker and he still had a couple of good mates from the old days. Between the three of them, they were able to start a small business making cheap but good-quality men's and women's clothing. No-one was more surprised than they at their almost overnight success. England had suffered five – nearly six – years of rationing and depression. Now people wanted to spend. Hurst, Lever and Kirkman were catering for the needs of the ordinary household. The three young men had pored over endless magazines and newspapers, producing designs that were almost the same as the high fashion houses but in fabrics that brought them within reach of the average pocket.

At first they had sold to the trade, but in an incredibly short time – two years to be precise – they had opened their first store. At the same time Kirkman, the only one who was not married, had died in a car crash leaving his share in the business to be split between his two partners.

By 1951 there were two Hurst and Lever stores in London, and by 1955 four other major cities had been added to the chain which was still expanding rapidly. Alfie Hurst and Jack Lever were rich men. Their children went to the best schools and they lived in the best neighbourhoods. But they never forgot who they were or where they had come from. Their employees loved them, but knew that they would not stand for slackness or shoddy workmanship. They demanded complete loyalty and they got it. They also gave more than their fair share to charity, and promoted schemes and scholarships for young people. The press adored them and so did the public. Alfie and Jack were still amazed when they had the time to ponder their success. All this and they were both still only in their mid-thirties. 'Must be doing something right,' they agreed.

Alfie sighed and took a deep drag on his cigarette. Life had been good to him and he was mighty grateful. He thought for a moment about Jennifer and Tony Carrington. He had not really been surprised when he heard they had married. It had been obvious when he had visited Edgeglow at the beginning of the war that the doctor had been really smitten with her. In fact, it had been Tony Carrington who had set her up with all the evacuees – thank goodness. He had put his Charlie there and all. He was no fool. He'd known how to get her. Well, it had worked a treat, despite the difference in their ages – he was sixteen years older than Jennifer. They were a very devoted couple. "Beats me how they produced that little fire-cracker though," he thought to himself. "She's a sweet kid, but I'm sure she'll be a handful when she's older."

'Can I clear away the breakfast things, Mr H?' Mrs Trigg was hovering beside him.

'Um? Oh, sorry Mrs Trigg. I was thinking.' He stood up.

'You do enough of that during the week. It's not right on a Sunday. It should be a day of rest.' She surveyed him severely with her hands on her ample hips. He raised his eyebrows comically. 'Oops!' She put her hand to her mouth. 'I forgot. For you it's Saturday, isn't it? Oh, never mind.' She waved her hand dismissively. 'I'm sure it's all the same to Him up there.' She glanced upwards. 'He don't really care. It's man that makes all the distinctions, isn't it?'

Alfie let out a gawf of laughter. 'Mrs Trigg, you're the salt of the earth. His prophet on this planet. What would we do without you?'

'Now you're laughing at me.' She looked hurt.

'Never, Mrs Trigg.' He sobered up quickly. 'Your value to us all is quite beyond price.' He patted her arm.

She brightened up. 'Isn't that a nice thing for you to say,' she beamed. 'I knew that I would not regret taking this job.'

As he walked out of the door she called after him, 'Now remember what I said. No working at the weekend. Stop all that brainwork and go for a nice walk or something.'

CHAPTER TWO

It was the last day of the Easter holidays. Charles Carrington's trunk sat in the hall waiting to be loaded into the shooting brake for the journey back to school the next day. The family sat around the dining-room table, eating his favourite dinner of roast beef and Yorkshire pudding. They had made it a family tradition that on the last evening of the holidays, whoever was going back to school chose his or her favourite dish. In three days' time it would be Lainey's turn and she would choose roast chicken followed by lemon pancakes. It was always the same. Both children swore that school food was disgusting. Vegetables were slushy and puddings were stodgy.

'It's not fair, you having to go back before me,' Lainey complained.

'It works out the same in the end,' Charlie replied. 'I break up before you do.'

'You're missing the point as usual. I mean, what am I going to do without you around for my last three days?'

'Oh, am I so dreadful to be with?' Jennifer Carrington smiled ruefully at her daughter.

'What the squirt means, Mum, is that without my bright ideas as to how to fill her time, she is completely at a loss,' Charlie grinned.

'Oh Mummy, I didn't mean that at all. You're a pig.' Lainey glared at her brother. 'And don't call me that any more. I'm a teenager now. I'm catching you up fast. Soon I'll have boyfriends and then I won't need your company and you'll be sorry.'

Charlie let out a gawf of laughter. 'You with boyfriends, squirt? Not for a while. You're far too young.'

'Don't you be so sure.' Lainey gave what she hoped was a knowing look.

'Stop it you two.' Tony Carrington put down his knife and fork and surveyed his two troublesome offspring. 'Charlie, don't you think that you are too old now to be sparring with your little sister?'

'Yes, he is.' Lainey smiled angelically and then turned when she thought no one was looking and made a hideous face at her brother.

'Lainey, that will do,' Tony admonished. 'You are being thoroughly provocative.'

'The squirt's just being a squirt, Dad. Squirts can't help it. They're all the same. Ooooh . . .' Charlie was already on his feet and ducked to avoid the napkin which had been hurtled in his direction. He ran out of the door, hotly pursued by his sister. There were sounds of grappling in the hall mingled with shouts of 'Squirt? I'll give you squirt, you pig. Take that and that . . . Ouch!'

Tony looked questioningly at Jennifer. She shook her head and continued drinking her coffee. 'Leave them alone,' she said. 'They always sort it out. They're going through a bad stage. Charlie is nearly grown-up and Lainey is only just entering puberty. She's beginning to feel left behind and so she is attracting his attention in the only way she can. Charlie's a sensible boy and he's just as fond of her as she is of him. It's best if we don't interfere.'

Tony sighed. He took off his glasses and rubbed his eye.

'She's becoming quite a handful, isn't she?'

'Not really. All girls go through a stage like this. She'll be all right – you wait and see. Hillsford Abbey will rub the corners off her – give them a chance. She's only been there a couple of terms.'

The sounds from the hall had changed to hysterical laughter, then they heard Charlie say, 'Come on, I'll play you my new Elvis Presley record.' Two pairs of feet tramped up the stairs.

*

'Charlie, would you mind very much not calling me squirt any more?' Lainey surveyed her adored elder brother from her position cross-legged on the floor of his bedroom. 'I'm thirteen now and some people say that I look even older than that. You've called me squirt for as long as I can remember. I know you mean it affectionately, but I don't want it to catch on now that I'm growing up.' She gazed at him earnestly with her brilliant blue eyes, while Elvis sang 'Don't be cruel to a heart that's true' in the background.

Charlie stopped stacking his records and turned around. As he noticed the serious expression on her upturned face he felt a strange sensation pass through him. He shivered without knowing why. Her eyes held his. My goodness, but she was becoming a beauty – his little half-sister. Those beautifully chiselled features, that heart-shaped face and cloud of white-blonde hair which hung completely straight in a pageboy style to her shoulders. Yes, she had been right when she had stated at dinner that there would soon be boyfriends. Charlie felt an unpleasant twinge. Was it jealousy? Would he find any man good enough for his perfect sister?

'Charlie?'

'Sorry.' He came back to reality. 'Well, what shall I call you! Alaina?'

'Lainey will do,' she smiled.

'OK. And you're right. You are growing up. You are getting quite pretty.'

'Am I?' Her face lit up. 'You are quite the nicest brother.' She jumped up and threw her arms around his neck and hugged him.

Again Charlie felt those strange sensations. Quickly he untangled her arms from around his neck. 'Hey, no need to overdo it just because I pay you a compliment.'

'What's the matter, Charlie?'

'You've got to learn that you can't go throwing your arms around every man you know.'

'I wouldn't. You know I wouldn't. Only you and Daddy.'

'Yes, well.' For some reason he felt awkward with her. 'See that you don't.' The record had finished. He busied himself with looking for another, glad of something to do.

'Ugh! Handel. Why didn't you put on something modern?'

'I happen to like Handel.'

'You're too serious. Vivien agrees.'

'You and Vivien are frivolous. You should learn to appreciate the finer things in life.'

'Like Handel?' She paused. 'Charlie?'

'What now? Can't you listen to the music?'

'When did you first kiss a girl?'

'What!?'

'When did you first kiss a girl – I mean really properly, with your tongue?'

'For God's sake, when did you learn about things like that?'

Lainey put on a prissy expression. 'Mother wouldn't like you taking the Lord's name in vain.' She wrapped her arms around her legs and put her chin on her knees. 'Vivien says that she's kissed several boys that way.'

'Then she's either very forward or she's lying.'

'Vivien wouldn't lie. She says it gets better every time.' She looked down at the floor. 'I can't wait,' she added and waited for a reaction.

'Don't you start doing things like that at your age.'

'Why not?' She looked up innocently.

'Because you . . . you could get more than you bargained for. That's why not.'

'Like what?'

'Lainey, if you want to know all about the birds and bees, go and ask Mother.' Charlie's face was bright red.

'But I don't want to ask Mother. I want you to tell me. Do you kiss Alison?'

'Mind your own business.'

'Why won't you tell me?'

'It's private. Some things are private, Lainey.'

'Why? Are you in love with her?' Suddenly she was alarmed. Was she losing him? Would Alison become his confidante from now on?

'Of course not. I'm far too young.'

Lainey relaxed. Not for long though. His next words made her clench her teeth.

'I'm very fond of her though.'

'More fond than you are of me?'

'Lainey, you're my sister. I love you.'

'Do you? Do you really, Charlie?' She fixed him with those magnetic eyes. Charlie felt a churning in his stomach. Try as he would, he could not break away from her gaze.

'Yes, I do,' he whispered.

Suddenly Lainey's mood changed. 'That's all right then,' she said and stood up. 'It's nice to know that I still have a hold on you.' She blew him a kiss. 'Night, brother dear. I've had enough culture for one evening. I'll leave you and Handel together.' She waltzed out of the room, slamming the door behind her.

Charlie shook his head trying to clear his confusion. A hold on him! Did she really have a hold on him? What was it about her that made him feel the way he did? She was strong-willed, hot-headed and determined to get whatever she wanted. She was also beautiful, loving and she adored him. They were closer to each other than they were to their parents. Why was that? Their parents were good parents, but there was something between him and Lainey that was inexplicable. It had been a warm loving relationship – until recently. Now they were always arguing and having to make up. Why? It was all so puzzling. It was a good thing he was going back to school tomorrow. Only one more year and then he'd be going up to Cambridge and following in his father's footsteps at Gonville and Caius. He wanted to be a good doctor – but not in a fashionable London practice like his father. It wasn't that he thought there was anything wrong with his father's way of life, he just wanted to work in a country practice and care for ordinary people in a small community. A thought struck him. That would not be the life for Lainey, would it? When she was older she would want to go to parties and live the high-life. She would be a burning candle attracting all the moths to her flame. He sighed. When the time came he would need to be around to keep an eye on her. But by then he would probably be doing his internship at a London hospital anyway. Why did he feel so responsible for her? Well, she was his sister. Correction – half-sister. And yet there was more between the two of them than between most full brothers and sisters.

"Lainey, Lainey," he thought. "What a problem you're going to be, but I wouldn't be without you for the world."

Tony Carrington and Lainey stood on the doorstep waving good-bye as Jennifer started the car. Charlie, looking very neat and tidy in his school uniform, was sitting beside her.

'Are you sure you don't want me to come with you?' Tony asked his wife.

'No, darling, you've had a hard day. You sit down and relax. I'll be back before you know it.'

Charlie stuck his head out of the window. 'Bye, squ . . .' Lainey glowered at him. 'Sorry. I mean – bye, Lainey.' He grinned.

'Promise you'll write?' She ran around the car.

'Yes, if I have time.'

'Not good enough. Once a week. Promise?'

'Yes, yes, if you do.'

'You know I will.'

'And behave yourself.' He wagged a finger at her.

'Fat chance of anything else.' She winked at him.

'You're impossible.' He gave her arm a friendly punch. 'Come on, Mum, we'll never get there.'

Jennifer slid the car into gear and they set off down the drive.

'Well, Lainey, what now?' Tony looked down at his daughter.

'Come inside, Daddy, and put your feet up. I'll pour you a drink and you can tell me all about your day.'

Tony smiled to himself. She was trying so hard to be grown-up. He watched her as she poured the whisky carefully into a glass and added a splash of soda – just the way he liked it. She was growing to be quite a beauty, this daughter of his – well, she was his daughter, wasn't she? Everyone thought so, including Lainey herself and Charlie. The only people who knew differently were himself and Jennifer – and maybe Mabel Edison, but she was long gone. She had died, so they had heard, not long after they had moved to Surrey. No, nobody knew about Lainey – and anyway, he felt that he was her father in every way that mattered. After all, he had known her since before she was born and he loved her as his own.

For a moment he wondered what had happened to Alan Jefferson. Poor chap, he would never know what a lovely daughter he had produced. Lovely, wilful Lainey who was bursting with health and vitality. She was a golden girl just as her father had been a golden boy. Everything had come so easily to Alan Jefferson. Would it be the same for Lainey, or would she make unnecessary problems for herself?

Did Jennifer still think about Jefferson, he wondered. How could she help it? Every time she looked at Lainey, there was the reminder.

She was a wonderful wife, warm-hearted and loving and they were very contented. Yes, it was a happy marriage – despite the difference in their ages. He was fifty-one now and Jennifer was only thirty-five. She was still a girl and extremely beautiful. Her hair had retained its natural blondeness, though now she had cut it and it was set in soft curly waves around her face.

Lainey would look just like her mother when she was a few years older. But would she have the softness that her mother had always had? And the eyes. They were different – quite amazing in the intensity of their blueness, the colour of a cloudless sky on a hot summer day. They would shape her destiny, he thought with a shiver. They seemed to speak of a burning desire hidden within her, but for what? It was frightening to behold in one so young. He was glad that Charlie did not have that light in his eyes, as he had the feeling that it could make or destroy one. What had it done to Jefferson? They were his eyes, weren't they? He wished they had a photograph of the young pilot so that he could compare the two of them. But in the move from Edgeglow so many things had been lost. There were a few wartime photographs, but none had Jefferson in them. Had Jennifer got rid of them on purpose? No matter, it did not do to dwell on the past. Jefferson was long gone – back to America and the neurotic wife that he had left behind. Maybe it had all worked out well for him. Maybe even at this very moment he was sitting in his splendid house with his wife and many children, thanking his lucky stars that he had been forced to go home when he had. His wife had in all probability recovered from her neurosis and the kids were probably model children. Maybe that was so. Maybe.

CHAPTER THREE

'Rosemary, I'm home.' Alan Jefferson slammed the door of the Park Avenue duplex and threw his briefcase on a chair.

'In here, dear,' his wife's voice called from the living-room.

Alan's spirits rose. She sounded quite normal today. He took off his camel-coloured cashmere coat and hung it in the hall cupboard. New York was experiencing a cold spell, even though it was the end of April.

'Well, what have you been . . .' He stopped mid-sentence as he reached the doorway and viewed his wife. She was lying on the sofa with cushions piled up behind her and a rug thrown over her legs. A half-finished box of chocolates sat on the coffee table beside her. 'What's the matter? Don't you feel well?'

'I've got one of my migraines.'

Oh God, not again. The psychiatrist said that most of Rosemary's problems were psychosomatic. It was her way of opting out of whatever she did not want to do – whatever she could not cope with.

'You shouldn't be eating chocolates.' He could not help the sharpness that crept into his tone of voice. 'You know that chocolate isn't good for migraines.'

'That's right. Go on, scold me.' She sounded peevish. 'You don't want me to have any pleasure in this miserable life of mine.'

'That's not true, and you know it.' He sat down wearily. 'But you are never going to get well, dearest, unless you do as the doctor tells you.'

'That silly bloody doctor. He doesn't know anything.' She pouted and looked at the floor.

'What did he say to you when you went to see him this morning?'

She did not answer.

'Rosemary, answer me. You did keep your appointment, didn't you?'

'No, I didn't,' she replied sullenly.

'Rosemary!' He was exasperated. 'Doctor Hasler is the best in his field. He can help you far better than I can, but you must let him try. You do want to be helped, don't you?'

'Doctor Hasler, Doctor Hasler. That's all I ever hear.' Her voice rose. 'Fuck Doctor Hasler.'

'Rosemary, stop it. You're becoming hysterical.' He gripped hold of her hands. For a moment they stared at one another and then her face dissolved into tears. She threw her arms around his neck sobbing loudly.

'Oh Alan, what is the matter with me? Why am I the way I am?'

'I don't know, my dear.' He held her close and rubbed her back. 'I just don't know.'

'Thank goodness I've got you, darling. You're so good to me, Alan. If I didn't have you, I think I'd kill myself.'

Alan shivered involuntarily. 'Don't talk that way, honey. You know it's wrong.' In her unstable state he knew that she was capable of trying to fake suicide purely to draw attention to herself. By rights she should be in a nursing home, but the Prebbles had been against that. Alan knew that the senator was not keen to have the world find out he had a mentally unstable daughter. It would not do his career any good. Alan had to admit that he had not wanted it either, as he knew what these places could be like – even the most expensive. He did not want Rosemary to be confined in a mental home for any length of time.

When Alan had been shipped back to America at a moment's notice in 1941, Rosemary had played the part of the wounded airman's wife to perfection. For the weeks that he had been in hospital, and when he first went home, she could not have been more loving and attentive. Alan had been completely taken in. Here was the Rosemary that he had married – or so he thought. By a tremendous force of will he had managed to put Jennifer Woodward out of his mind more or less. Rosemary was really trying – Alan had to admit that. She was so pretty and sweet these days, and different from Jennifer – that was important. Alan would have had to have been made of steel to be able to resist her, and Rosemary knew it.

Two months later she had announced to him that she was pregnant. Alan was overjoyed. Here at last was the baby they had always wanted – but his joy was short-lived. From the day that her pregnancy started to show, Rosemary's new-found confidence left her. She became convinced that she was ugly and that Alan wouldn't like her. She formed a hatred for the baby long before it was born, and this turned to jealousy afterwards.

Alan realised for the second time, and too late again, that he was trapped. He was caught once and for all in a marriage to someone whom it was impossible to love and who was bearing his child. Even if he had wanted to leave her, he knew it was out of the question. The Prebbles were not without influence. If Alan wanted his child to grow up with some kind of normality around him or her, he would have to be there to provide it.

And so it had come about that, although he still felt pity and compassion for his wife, all the love he had to give was lavished on his daughter, Mary-Beth.

The sound of a door slamming brought Alan back to earth. Running footsteps crossed the hall and the living room door was thrown open.

'Mommy, I'm back. Daddy, you're home already.' Mary-Beth rushed across the room and flung herself into her father's arms.

'Such a noise.' Rosemary put a hand to her head feebly.

'Hi, sweetheart.' Alan hugged his daughter. 'We've got to be very quiet. Mummy has got one of her headaches.'

'Oh sorry, Mommy.' Mary-Beth grabbed her father's hand and pulled him towards the door. 'Daddy, I brought Jeannie back for tea. Lorelei said I could.'

Lorelei was the coloured maid employed by the Jeffersons.

'I can't stand it.' Rosemary's voice had risen shrilly. 'Screaming children running all over the apartment while I'm lying here in agony.'

Mary-Beth looked at her mother in amazement. 'Mommy, Jeannie and I are both nearly thirteen. We haven't run around screaming since we were little kids.'

'Run along to the kitchen, honey, and you and Jeannie can help Lorelei get the tea.' Alan patted his daughter on the shoulder. 'Just remember to keep the noise down, OK?'

'Sure, Dad.' She looked up at him. 'Can we all go to the movies tomorrow? You promised we could this weekend.'

'I can't possibily go.' Rosemary had turned sulky. 'I know I won't feel well enough.'

'Oh, Mom, you never come with us.' Mary-Beth said in exasperation. 'Jeannie's Mom takes her all over the place when she's not at school. Don't you ever want to be with us?'

'Oh why are you always picking on me? First your father, and now you. What have I done to deserve this?'

Mary-Beth looked at her father for guidance. He signalled to her to keep quiet.

'I saw that. Don't think that I didn't. You're ganging up on me. It's not fair.'

'Rosemary, that will do.' Alan spoke quietly.

'No, no, you hate me – both of you. You'd be much happier without me.'

'Mom, you're sick. Really you are.' Mary-Beth's bottom lip quivered.

'Oh, so now you think I'm mad, do you?' Rosemary's eyes flashed.

For a moment there was silence, then Mary-Beth burst into tears. 'Yes I do,' she sobbed and ran from the room.

'Rosemary, for God's sake what are you trying to do to your daughter?' Alan forced himself not to raise his voice.

'My daughter. You have to be joking.' Rosemary was becoming hysterical. 'She hasn't been my daughter for years and you know it. She's yours and yours only. I hope you feel proud of taking her away from me.'

'That will do, Rosemary.' Something in his voice stopped her hysteria. 'You have only yourself to blame for your relationship with our daughter. I pray to God that she doesn't end up with a lot of psychological problems as a result.'

'What do you mean by that?' Her tone had changed. Now she was simply curious.

'If only you could understand. If only I could explain it all to you.'

'Darling, what's there to explain? There's nothing wrong with me. I'm fine.' As he sat down beside her she moved her hand to stroke a lock of hair back from his forehead. She closed her eyes. 'I'm so tired,' she whispered. 'I think I'll sleep now.'

CHAPTER FOUR

Lainey stood in front of the mirror in her bedroom and surveyed herself quizzically. She was wearing a lemon-organdy evening dress which was embroidered with little white daisies. It was boned and self-supporting, though it had two thin shoe-string straps in the same material. Lainey's white-blonde hair was cut in a fringe and fell thickly to her shoulders. It was held in place by a lemon-coloured velvet band.

"Do I look more than fourteen?" she wondered. She grabbed the head-band and pulled it off, shaking her head as she did so. "That's better." She smiled knowingly at her reflection. The white cloud of hair had settled in just the right way. Casual but appealing.

"You'll do," she told herself. She shivered with anticipation as she contemplated her first dance. Would she be a wall-flower, or would she be the centre of attention? At school she was a popular girl who was known for her devil-may-care attitude. In fact, she had always been a bit of a tomboy. "Good old Lainey." Good at sports – better than most, including the boys. Would the boys now begin to see her in a new light? She certainly hoped so. Was it really over a year since she had sat on the end of Viv Hurst's bed and discussed kissing? She laughed now as she remembered her initial reaction to her friend's behaviour. "I thought it sounded awful," she mused, "and now I can't wait for it to be my turn." Would someone try to kiss her tonight? Would he be tall, dark and handsome like they were in books? He'd take her into the garden and tell her how irresistible she was. And he'd be older. If Viv could attract eighteen-year-olds when she had been fourteen, so could she. She'd have none of those groping fourteen- or fifteen-years-olds. At eighteen boys were sophisticated. That's what Viv had said, and – much more important – they knew what they were doing. She blushed. Well, someone had to, didn't they?

'Lainey, are you ready? We're going to be late.' Charlie's voice from downstairs brought her back to reality.

'Coming.' She grabbed her coat and evening bag and gave herself one last appraising look before hurrying along the corridor.

She paused for effect at the top of the stairs. As she looked down, she drew in her breath sharply. Charlie stood in the hall with Jennifer and Tony beside him. As the two young people's eyes met, Lainey's heart began to pound. Charlie looked so romantic standing there in his dinner jacket. "I'm so lucky," she thought. "I have the most wonderfully attractive brother in the world. I will always adore him." A strange light came into her eyes. "And he must always adore me."

Charlie felt a tingling in his spine as he gazed at his beautiful half-sister. 'Come on, Lainey,' he said gruffly. 'This thing starts at eight. We'd better get going if you want your money's worth.'

'Darling, you look lovely.' Jennifer kissed her daughter as she reached the bottom of the stairs.

'Thanks, Mummy. Daddy, will I do?' Lainey turned her shining eyes on her father.

'You look wonderful, poppet. Quite the young lady.' Tony turned to his son. 'You look after your little sister and make sure that she has a good time.' He took off his glasses and rubbed his eye. 'Drive carefully, Charlie. You've not had your licence for very long. I want you both to come home in one piece.'

'Don't worry, Dad. I'll look after her – haven't I always? Not that she's going to need it, looking the way she does. And I'll drive carefully, you know that!'

As she watched her daughter get into the little Austin beside Charlie, a small sigh escaped from Jennifer's lips.

'Makes one feel old, doesn't it?' Tony put an arm around her and squeezed her. 'She's no longer a little girl, is she?'

'No, she's become a young woman almost overnight. She's so . . .'

'Like her father?'

'Oh, she's really not like you at all.' It had come out without thinking.

'I didn't mean me.' He said it very quietly.

'Oh Tony, dearest, I'm so sorry. I didn't think. At least, I always think of you as her father.' She was stuttering in her confusion.

'It's all right, love, I know what you mean.' He looked at her seriously. 'The truth is, though, that neither of us knew that much about Alan Jefferson, did we? He seemed to be a charming likeable chap with a strong sense of responsibility – and I'm sure that he was all of those things – but we don't know what skeletons there might have been in the family cupboard, do we? There's a half of Lainey that we can't account for and never will.'

She looked at him curiously. 'You've hardly mentioned Alan Jefferson in fifteen years.'

'I thought it better not to.'

Jennifer was silent.

'Do you think about him often, Jennifer? Do you ever regret how things turned out?'

'Yes, I think about him – but only when Lainey does something to remind me of him, and then not for long.' She turned towards him and cupped his face in her hands. 'And no, I don't regret how things turned out. You are the best thing that ever happened to me. I love you very much.'

'But what about Jefferson?'

'Alan was a beautiful interlude, but we knew that it couldn't last. At the time we gave each other what we both needed. I don't regret knowing him. With him I learned to feel like a woman again. I'll always be grateful to him for that, but it's you that I love.'

'Why?'

'I just do. You've always been there for me and I know that you always will. It's a feeling of trust that goes very deep. I feel warm and safe and comfortable and loved.' She wrapped her arms around him tightly.

"Oh Jennifer," he thought. "We may not have had the passion, but we have so much more. We do not demand great things of each other, but we are content."

'I'm glad you decided to take me.' Lainey glanced at her brother as he concentrated on driving along the country roads.

'Consider yourself lucky. Pony Club dances are not my style.'

'Oh, you think yourself too adult now that you've left school?'

'I suppose so.' He grinned at her as he stopped at a halt sign. 'No, not really. There'll be lots of people there tonight who are my age, but they're all so terribly . . . horsey.'

'I'm horsey.' She frowned at him.

'Yes, but when you start to bang on about fetlocks and forelocks I can beat you up and you'll stop.'

'Pig.' She made a face at him. 'Anyway, you'll have Alison to talk to. You can discuss the merits of everything from stethoscopes to bedpans. Should be a fascinating conversation to keep you going all evening.'

'You shouldn't be so scathing,' he answered. 'If it wasn't for Alison, I wouldn't be going.'

'Are you keen on her?'

'She's OK – and why do you always see everything in that light? Can't one have friends?'

'I think she's rather dull.' Lainey glanced sideways at him through lowered lashes.

'You think everyone's dull, if they're not frivolous like you.'

'I don't think you're dull.'

Charlie felt that odd fluttering in his stomach. 'That's because I'm your brother,' he said quickly.

'Half-brother,' she corrected him. She paused for a moment. 'Sometimes I don't think of you as my brother at all. Sometimes I think of us as . . . oh, I don't know . . . as just two people. Do you know what I mean?'

He shivered. Oh yes, he knew what she meant. He ignored the question.

'We're here.' He turned into the drive of Canley Manor where the dance was being held. 'I'll drop you at the door and go and park the car.'

'Viv, Viv, hi!' Lainey bounded up the steps and tapped her friend on the shoulder.

'Gosh, Lainey, don't you look terrific.' Vivien gasped as she stared at the younger girl. 'Doesn't she, Ali?'

'Thanks.' Lainey managed a demure look.

'Where's Charlie?' Alison asked.

'Don't worry, he's here. He's parking the car.' Lainey noticed that Alison's face had flushed.

After giving their tickets to the man on the door, they stood in the crowded hall waiting for Charlie. Several young people came up and spoke to them and Lainey found that she knew a lot of them. She also noticed looks being thrown in her direction from several young men that she had never seen before. It was very gratifying.

'There's Julian Fenner.' Vivien nodded her head in the direction of a fair-haired young man. 'He's just been picked for the inter-branch team.'

'Is he the one who . . .?'

'Yes, he gave me my very first kiss. Here. Last year.'

'You said you'd been kissed masses of times before that.'

'Did I?' Vivien looked vague. 'You must have got it wrong.'

'Viv Hurst, you lied to me!' Lainey was indignant.

'No, I didn't. I just fibbed a little.' She grinned. 'Anyway, I've had lots of practice since.'

'How do I know? You're probably fibbing again.'

'What are you two arguing about?' Alison had turned away from the friends she had been talking to.

'Nothing. I say, Ali, who is that gorgeous creature with Julian Fenner? I've never seen him before. He can't be a local.' Vivien was staring at a tall self-possessed young man standing next to Julian Fenner who was paying court to four pretty girls, all obviously hanging on his every word. His dark straight hair was brushed sleekly back from his face and was just a shade too long. Underneath thick black eyebrows his eyes appeared almost half-closed as he spoke. The effect was one of utter self-confidence.

'That's Harry Wrightson. He's staying with the Fenners,' Alison volunteered. 'I've met him a couple of times in London, but he doesn't bother with the likes of me. He's only interested in the top débutantes.'

Lainey glanced in his direction. For a moment the stranger's eyes left his admiring crowd as he looked up and met her gaze. His eyelids lifted, revealing cynical grey eyes. He raised one eyebrow quizzically and gave her a crooked smile. Lainey felt a shiver of expectancy shoot through her. With difficulty she tore her eyes away from his and turned back to the Hurst sisters who were still chatting and had noticed nothing.

'He looks fascinating,' she said.

'Yes, well, he isn't going to waste his time on us when he can have the pick of that lot.' Vivien indicated the group of giggling girls. 'They must all be seventeen at least.'

'Who must be what?' Charlie had come up behind them.

'Those girls surrounding Julian Fenner and his friend,' Vivien replied.

'Good Lord, that's Harry Wrightson.'

'Do you know him?' Lainey was interested.

'Yes, he was at school with me. He was a year ahead of me, but he was expelled before his final year. He had to go somewhere else to take his exams.'

'Why was he expelled?'

'Never you mind.'

Lainey fixed her eyes on the young man again. This time he did not look up, but somehow she knew that he was aware of her. It was an exciting feeling. She felt pricked by a sense of challenge. Somehow she must get him to dance with her. That would show Charlie she was not a child any more and it would wipe that satisfied smile of superiority off Viv's face.

'Come on girls, let's get this show on the road. I'm famished. There's a buffet in the dining room. Why don't we go and eat?'

It was eleven o'clock already, but although there had been no shortage of dancing partners as far as Lainey was concerned she was not enjoying herself. Her feet had been trodden on by at least three fifteen-year-olds. Her last partner had sweated profusely as he held her clumsily to him, and it had not helped to see the suave Harry Wrightson drifting by with a contented blonde in his arms. "You could almost hear her purring," Lainey thought crossly.

She had finally got away from the sweaty fifteen-year-old by escaping upstairs to the loo. When she returned she found the lights had been turned down and couples were dancing cosily together. Now here she was, late in the evening when everyone had paired off, without a partner and with nothing to do. She wandered into the bar and was about to get herself a drink when she heard a voice behind her.

'To coin a phrase, what is a beautiful girl like you doing alone at this hour in a place like this?'

She turned around to find herself face to face with Harry Wrightson. She felt herself starting to blush. How stupid and gauche he must think she was. "Come on, Lainey," she told herself. "This is what you've been waiting for. Don't blow it now." She drew in a deep breath and brought her eyes up to meet his.

'I was escaping from someone. I was just about to get myself a drink.'

'Let me.' He walked over to the bar where they were serving spirits. 'What would you prefer? Gin? Whisky? Or something else?'

She had been about to get herself an orange juice, but he would think that very tame. She had never tasted gin, but, well, there was a first time for everything, wasn't there?

'Gin would be fine, thanks.'

He paid for the drink and handed it to her. 'Salute.' He raised his glass to her. 'What's your name? I'm Harry Wrightson.'

'Alaina.' She took a sip of the clear liquid. It tasted funny at first but afterwards she liked the warm feeling it gave her.

'Alaina what?'

'Just Alaina.' She didn't want him to know that she was Charlie's sister.

'Ah, a mystery lady.'

She smiled.

'Would you like to dance, mystery lady?'

'Yes, I would.' She finished her drink. The warm feeling was spreading. She felt much more relaxed.

He led her on to the dance floor, putting one arm around her waist while his other hand grasped her right hand to his chest. She started to speak.

'Don't talk,' he whispered and placed his cheek against hers. 'Let's just enjoy the music.'

He was a very competent dancer – not that they moved very much. It was more like swaying to the music. Over his shoulder she spotted Charlie and Alison in the dim lighting, and as they turned she caught a brief glimpse of Alison's face. Her eyes were closed and her expression was that of pure ecstasy. Lainey's stomach knotted. They were both oblivious to her conquest. She waited until they were nearer, then she wrapped both of her arms around Harry's neck and pressed herself a little tighter against him. She felt him tremble slightly. Did Charlie see? She hoped so.

'It's getting hot in here. Shall we go outside?' Harry whispered in her ear.

She nodded.

The French windows had been opened and there were a number of couples reclining outside on the grass.

'Come on, I know somewhere we can be alone and talk.' Harry grasped her hand and set off across the lawn.

My goodness! It was all happening as if she had already planned it.

A small wooden summer-house emerged from between the trees. He pulled her up the steps.

'Come in quickly and shut the door.'

She did as she was told. She could hardly contain her excitement. As her eyes grew accustomed to the darkness she could just make out a wicker sofa with padded cushions. Harry leaned against the door and put his arms around her.

'Of course, you know that you are the best-looking girl at the party, don't you?' She said nothing. 'And I've been wanting to get you to myself all evening.'

'Well, it took you long enough.' A forthright note crept into her voice.

He laughed softly. 'One should always save the best till last, don't you agree, Alaina?' He ran a hand up and down her back. It felt delicious. She flung her arms around his neck and closed her eyes. She felt him shudder as he bent his head forward and touched his lips to hers. Oh, she thought she would melt. She parted her lips slightly and felt his tongue dart inside. At first it felt funny and ticklish as it probed the inside of her mouth. She experimented with her own. Um . . . that was nice. She felt strange sensations in parts of her body that had never happened to her before.

'Let's sit down.' He led her to the sofa and fell on top of her. 'You're incredible,' he murmured 'You love it, don't you?'

A warning note sounded in her head. She tried to move but his weight on top of her was too great. His grip on her, which before had seemed gentle, now seemed like a vice. His hand moved up her leg pushing her skirt aside as it went. When it reached her suspenders his passion grew.

'No, don't do that.' Alaina struggled as she tried to push the offending hand away. 'No, I don't want to. Stop, please stop.' This had gone much further than she intended.

'Don't play games with me, Alaina. I don't like it. Relax. You know you'll enjoy it.'

'No, I didn't mean ... I mean I've never ...' She was struggling violently now.

'Don't be coy. It doesn't suit you. You can't expect me to believe such protests after the way you've been leading me on all evening?' His hand had reached her knickers and was trying to push its way inside. 'What the hell?' He stopped suddenly as the door was thrown open. A man stood silhouetted in the frame.

'That's what I'd like to know. What the hell do you think you're doing, Wrightson?'

Lainey saw her chance and, hurriedly smoothing her skirt, scrambled over to the door. An arm reached out and grabbed her. Charlie's voice was low and controlled but she had never heard him so angry.

'Get your coat and wait for me in the hall. We're going home.' He let her go and she ran outside. She paused at the foot of the summer-house steps and smoothed back her hair. Phew! That had been a close shave. Thank goodness for Charlie's intervention – even if it did mean that there was going to be hell to pay. She could hear raised voices in the summer house behind her, and crept closer to listen.

'What do you mean by barging in here like that?' Harry was shouting.

'You bastard, I could knock your head off.'

'I wouldn't try if I was you, Carrington. You know who'd come off the worst.'

'You haven't changed since school, have you, Wrightson? Not since you knocked off the junior matron and got expelled. And I believe that this isn't your first visit here tonight, is it? I'm sure you've done the rounds. Why did you have to pick on her?'

'Bloody attractive bit of stuff. Just crying out for it too. She'd been leading me on all evening.'

'Lying bastard.'

There were sounds of a struggle, then, 'For God's sake, Carrington, that hurt. Just because the lady obviously preferred me to you. If she means so much to you, then you're welcome to her. She wasn't that great anyway.'

Lainey's eyes glistened as tears of frustration and anger welled up inside her. "Charlie's right," she thought. "You are a lying bastard. I saw the way you looked at me and I know that's not true. One day I'll make you pay for saying that. You're used to getting everything and everyone that you want, Harry Wrightson, but not me. When I'm older I'm going to haunt you. You'll never have me, but by God you'll want me." She walked back across the lawn towards the house. "I've learned a lot tonight," she told herself. "I won't make the same mistake again."

'By Christ, Carrington, I'm sorry. I didn't realize that she was your sister. Only fourteen? Bloody hell. My sister was still a kid at that age.'

'So is Lainey, really.'

'She sure didn't act like it. Sorry, sorry.' Harry held up his hands in mock surrender. 'Even if she is your sister, it's true. You'll have to watch that little fire-cracker.'

'I'm warning you, Wrightson. Stay away from her. She's not for you, ever.'

'All right, all right, I'm not a child-molester.'

'And don't you breathe a word of this to anyone. If I hear that so much as one word had been repeated, I'll cause you so much trouble . . .'

'Charles, you may think that I have the morals of an alley cat – and I probably do – but I'm not a complete sod.' Harry smiled ruefully and held out his hand. Charlie shook it reluctantly.

As they walked into the hall Lainey kept her eyes averted.

'Come on.' Charlie stomped out of the door in front of her.

As Lainey turned to follow him she looked up and caught Harry's eyes on her. "Jesus!" he thought. "What eyes." They exercised an almost hypnotic effect on one. Was there a slight look of triumph on that beautiful face? Was she as yet aware of the power she could wield over men? No, she was still only a child. She had, however, managed to ruin the rest of the evening for him. What would she be like in three or four years time, he wondered. "I must make sure that I'm around to find out." He walked back into the bar and ordered a double whisky.

For once Lainey was lost for words and she and Charlie drove home in silence. She could tell how angry he was by the way his fingers gripped the steering wheel and his knuckles gleamed white. When at last they arrived, she heaved a sigh of relief. After parking the car in the garage, he unlocked the back door and they tiptoed quietly into the kitchen. The clock on the wall said a minute before midnight. "I must say something," she thought. "I can't let this silence go on. I must make him understand."

'Charlie . . .?' she ventured tentatively.

'Go to bed, Lainey, before I say something I'll regret.'

'I just wanted to say thanks for rescuing me.'

Something inside him snapped. 'Rescuing you? You didn't look as if you needed rescuing to me. You were behaving like a common little tramp. I never would have thought it of my own sister.'

Lainey's eyes filled with tears. 'I didn't mean to,' she whispered. 'I only wanted to know what it was like – to be kissed, I mean.'

'Why the hell did you go to the summer house with him?'

'It seemed so romantic,' she gulped. 'He really seemed to like me, but then it all changed and I couldn't stop him doing things that I didn't want him to do.'

'But surely you realized what would happen?'

'No.' She shook her head. 'I tried to ask you, but you wouldn't tell me.'

'I told you to ask Mother. Didn't you do that?'

'No.' She looked up at him with tears running down her face. 'Oh Charlie, don't hate me. I couldn't bear it. I'm not what you said I am – really I'm not.' She ran to him and flung her arms around his neck, sobbing as if her heart would break.

At first he held her loosely as his hand patted her back in what he hoped was a comforting gesture, but as she squeezed him tighter he felt those strange unsettling sensations yet again.

'There, there, it's all right.' He said it more for his own benefit than for hers. He closed his eyes. He felt as if all the breath had been knocked out of him and he was suspended somewhere in space. His hand stopped stroking her and he hugged her firmly against him.

From a great distance he heard a voice saying: 'Oh Charlie, I love you so much.'

He gasped and pushed her away from him.

'What's the matter?' She almost stumbled. 'What have I done now?'

What had she done now? Did she really not know? As he looked at her, he saw that her eyes were innocent and questioning. He shivered.

'Nothing, Lainey. You've done nothing. Go to bed. I think I just overreacted.'

'And you're sure that everything's all right? You understand and you don't think badly of me?'

'No, no, everything's fine. Good-night.'

'Night.' She ran up the stairs, turning as she reached the top. 'And thanks again for being so terrific.' She vanished down the corridor.

Charlie stood at the foot of the staircase. "I don't know what's happening to me." He shook his head in bewilderment and sat on the bottom step. "Correction" – he put his head in his hands – "I do know and I don't like it. It frightens me and I hate myself for it. The way I feel about her is wrong. It's far stronger than the feelings I have for Alison or any girlfriends – but it's not just a brotherly feeling. It's wrong." He beat his head against the bannister. "I'm perverted. She's my sister! Tonight I was jealous – jealous that another man wanted her, and that she could want him. Oh God. I'm torturing myself. She's only fourteen. Yesterday, I saw her as a child – or did I, if I'd bothered to look? I've had too much to drink and I'm thinking crazy thoughts. Everything will look different in the morning."

Lainey lay in bed with her arms behind her head. "Men like me," she told herself. "I know they do. I can feel the power I have over them. Even Charlie. I've always been able to wrap him around my little finger, but now I know that it's not just him. I can do it to other people too."

What did she really think of Harry Wrightson? He was very good-looking. Smooth – that's what Vivien would call him. His ardour had given her a bit of a fright, but what had really dented her pride was when she had listened afterwards and realized that she was just another would-be conquest. That had hurt. It wasn't until she looked up and met his gaze as she was leaving that she realized that power of hers. There had been no mistaking the look in his eyes. That was when the look of triumph had entered her eyes.

And what about Charlie? Was he just being protective towards her? She knew that he adored her as she adored him. Sometimes she didn't feel that he was her half-brother. Sometimes – like just now – she felt . . . Oh God, what did she feel? When they had stood with their arms around each other, she had felt warm and safe and loved, and there had been this feeling of exhilaration – almost of danger. Why? With Harry the sensations had been delicious and exciting, until she realized that she couldn't stop him. Then she had panicked, but it wasn't too late. They could be delicious and exciting again, but next time she would be calling the tune. In a few year's time . . .

CHAPTER FIVE

'Where's your Mom?' Jeannie Mason looked around the tidy living room of her friend Mary-Beth Jefferson's home.

'She's gone away for a while.' Mary-Beth sounded purposefully vague.

Jeannie raised her eyebrows quizzically: 'You mean they've split up?'

'No, silly.' Mary-Beth was cross. 'I mean that she's not very well and has gone to some nursing home for a rest.'

'Oh.' Jeannie paused. 'You didn't tell me. Why didn't you tell me? I thought I was your best friend.'

'You are. It was just something that I didn't feel like talking about – you know.'

'I suppose so.' Jeannie nodded. 'It must be rough having a Mom like yours. She's awful odd, isn't she?'

'She can't help it.' Mary-Beth rose swiftly to her mother's defence. 'She's going through what Daddy calls a nervous breakdown.'

'I heard Daddy trying to tell Mom how to make the spaghetti sauce the way he likes it the other day. Mom told him to get out of the kitchen before he drove her crazy. She said that between him and the three of us kids we'd end up giving her a nervous breakdown – then she threw a pan at him.' Jeannie thought for a moment. 'Maybe my Mom should go away for a rest?' She shrugged her shoulders and grinned. 'Ah, maybe not. It was the best spaghetti sauce we'd had in a long time.'

'Your mother's great,' Mary-Beth sighed. 'I often wish that mine was like her. She cooks terrific meals and takes you all over the place. You're real lucky, you know.'

'It's because she's Italian,' Jeannie stated. 'They're very

family orientated – and they reckon that the way to a man's heart is through his stomach.'

Mary-Beth burst out laughing. 'Jeannie, you're too much. If you all treat your poor mother like that, no wonder she throws pots and pans around.'

'It's true,' Jeannie was serious. 'Mom sees life as a continuing comedy series – like on TV. In our house there's always plenty of gesticulating and arm-waving so that someone will pay attention over all the noise. Every day must be dramatic, with Mom in the lead role giving it all she's got. It's all very exhausting, but there's certainly never a dull moment.' She slumped into a chair, feigning tiredness, then winked at her friend. 'Daddy thinks she's great. He plays up to it real good, considering that he's a full-blooded American.'

'You are awful,' Mary-Beth giggled. 'Fancy talking about your parents like that.' She rested her chin on her hands 'I wish we had as much fun. It's so quiet here. Even though Mom's not around, I still feel that I should be tiptoeing about the place.' She gazed out of the window. 'When I come over to your place it's so relaxed. There's so many of you and you are all laughing and teasing each other. I wish that happened here.'

'You get along OK with your father, don't you?'

'Of course, he's wonderful and he tries so hard to make up to me what is missing from Mom.'

'Well then?'

'It's not that. Ever since Mom has been ill – and I can't really remember when she wasn't – Daddy's been devoting more and more time to his work. It is almost as if he believes that Wall Street would collapse without him being there. I'm sure that it started as an excuse to be away from Mom's tantrums, but now he's so high-powered that it occupies nearly all his time.'

'But he takes you out on weekends, doesn't he?'

'Sure, and we have a great time – just the two of us.'

Mary-Beth shook her head. 'I'm being very ungrateful and I know it, but it can be so lonesome sometimes. You know, I had this dreadful feeling only last night that Mom would never come home again, and do you know, Jeannie, I don't know whether I cared or not.'

'That is bad.'

'I know and I feel so guilty. Daddy's so young – he's only forty and he looks even younger. He shouldn't be sitting in on the nights that he isn't working late. He should be having some fun.'

'He must still love your mother very much, otherwise he would have divorced her a long time ago. At least half the kids in our grade have divorced parents.'

'No, I don't think he does any more – love her, I mean. She's ruined his life, hasn't she? I think he's desperately sorry for her and worried about me. He might feel that I could turn out to be just like her – but I won't, of course.' She smiled ruefully. 'This is 1956 and I'm fourteen. Next term I'm going to boarding school. I understand a lot more than he thinks I do. I'm not the neurotic type.'

'You're what Miss Crighton would call "well-adjusted", though God knows how!' Jeannie rolled her eyes towards the ceiling.

'Coming from a schoolmistress, that ain't bad. She obviously has class,' Mary-Beth giggled. 'Anyway, what's well-adjusted? Look at the way you all behave in your house.'

'The day that chaos is overruled at home, that's the day I'll go crazy.' Jeannie gave her friend a comical look. Both girls collapsed into peals of laughter.

'What's going on in here?' Lorelei stood in the doorway with her hands on her hips trying to look stern. 'Who's going crazy?'

'Nothing, Lorelei, nothing.' Mary-Beth gave another uncontrollable gulp of laughter. 'Say, have you made any of your cookies for us today?'

'I might have done. What about your homework?'

'All done.' The two girls grinned at her brightly.

'You sure?' Lorelei attempted to glower at them.

'Would we lie to you?' Mary-Beth gave her a wide-eyed stare.

'No, but you could bend the truth a little.' Lorelei gave up trying to be strict and capitulated to their sunny mood. 'Come on then, I's got cookies galore on the kitchen table. You better hurry up and eat them before Mr Jefferson gets back and tells me off for spoiling you.'

'Will Daddy be late tonight, Lorelei?'

'No, child, he's gone to see your mother, but he said he'd be home for dinner.' Lorelei took a large jug of iced tea from the refridgerator and poured them all tall glasses of the cold liquid.

'How is Mrs Jefferson, Lorelei?' Jeannie was making conversation.

'She's getting along just fine, Miss Jeannie. Mr Jefferson says that it'll be no time till she's back here with us.'

'You think so?' Mary-Beth's mood had changed. It was as if a gust of cold air had suddenly penetrated the room.

Jeannie shivered. She put her arm around her friend protectively. 'I'm sure that Lorelei's right, MB. Your Mom will be back before you know it and she'll be fine – just as you'd want her to be.'

Lorelei felt a lump in her throat as she watched the two girls. Tears threatened her eyes. She turned her back on them and busied herself at the sink. She did not believe in what she had just said and neither did Mary-Beth or Jeannie – she knew that. Why did they all have to pretend? It would be much better for Mary-Beth and Mr Jefferson if that poor crazy Mrs Jefferson didn't ever come back. At least their lives would be more normal. In fact, it would be a blessed relief if they could be rid of her for ever.

"You's terrible to think like that, Lorelei," she reproached herself. "The Lord will wreak his vengeance on you for thinking thoughts like that. You'd best go to church first thing tomorrow morning and beg his forgiveness for the evilness of your mind."

CHAPTER SIX

'Darling, are you nearly ready? We're going to be late,' Tony Carrington called to his wife through the open door of their bedroom.

Jennifer jumped. She had been day-dreaming while putting the finishing touches to her make-up in front of the bathroom mirror.

'Coming right now.' She picked up a comb, fluffed up her short blonde hair, and walked into the bedroom.

Tony felt his heart beat a little faster when he saw her. Even after seventeen years of marriage she still managed to affect him that way. Tonight she was dressed in ice-blue chiffon. If was a very romantic dress with a full skirt which was cut to make her movements seem almost ethereal.

'You look beautiful.'

'You're biased, Tony dear.' She smiled up at him, and cast a quick eye over his own attire. 'Oh look, your tie is crooked as usual. You'd better let me do it. There.' She re-tied his black bowtie. 'You look so distinguished in your dinner jacket. I'm sure that you'll be the toast of the evening.'

'Minx.' He tapped her lightly on the bottom. 'Come on. Mrs Barrington Craig went to great lengths to tell me that she hates latecomers.'

They drove down Oxford Street towards Hyde Park, the Christmas illuminations blazing overhead. It was an exciting time of year in the capital city. London sparkled in so many different ways in the two months leading up to Christmas, Jennifer thought. The shop windows looked inviting and the people in the streets seemed so much better humoured than they were at other times of the year. October, November and December had come to be known as the mini-Season, for by this time most of the foreign visitors who came over for the summer months had left and London Society entertained itself. It was the most intimate time of year – warmer in everything but climate.

'Do you realize that it's only three weeks until Christmas?' Jennifer suddenly commented, as Tony steered the car through the heavy traffic.

'Only too well.' He smiled at her as he pulled up at a red light. 'I've been so busy I haven't thought about my Christmas shopping yet.'

'You won't get any sympathy from me,' she laughed. 'You only have to buy three presents. One for each of the children and one for me. I do all the rest for you and . . .' She held up her hand to stop him from butting in. 'I know that you'd be impossible to live with if you weren't busy all the time.'

'They're hardly children any more.' He swerved to avoid a taxi which had stopped without any warning. 'Bloody taxis. They think they own the place.'

'Relax, darling.' Jennifer patted his knee. 'We want to get there in one piece.'

'As I was saying, they're not children any more. Charlie's twenty and Lainey's sixteen.'

'I know. It's incredible how much they've changed in the last few years.' Jennifer smiled at her husband. 'Do you remember that summer two years ago when Charlie took Lainey to her first teenage dance? It seems to have been no time at all and yet she'll be leaving school next term. Here we are in December 1958 and I don't know where the last few years have gone.'

'It's one of the penalties of growing older,' he replied. 'Time goes by so much faster than it used to. You look wonderful, my darling, but I can't think what you see in an old man like me.'

'Still looking for compliments,' she teased. 'I couldn't possibly start to tell you now. We're nearly there and I would have only just begun.'

'What would I do without you?'

'You'll never have to,' she said softly.

'Dear Doctor Carrington. How very good of you to come to my little soirée.' Joan Barrington-Craig descended on her latest arrivals like a ship in full sail. 'And Mrs Carrington. How charming to meet you at last.' She extended her hand regally. 'Although we've never met, I feel that I know you intimately, having seen your photograph so often on dear Anthony's desk. He's so proud of his family, and now I can see why. How pretty you are, my dear.' Still gushing, she led them over to a group of people who were assembled in front of the fireplace. 'Darlings, this is my wonderful doctor, Anthony Carrington, and his beautiful wife ...' For a moment she looked blank. 'Janet.'

'It's Jennifer actually.' Jennifer was trying hard to keep a straight face.

'Darling, how simply awful of me.' Joan Barrington-Craig posed, stage-struck. 'Bimbo would turn in his grave if he'd heard me do that. "Joanie," he always used to say, "always bone up on names. You must never get your introductions wrong. It is the worst social *faux-pas* you can make." Please, please forgive me.'

'That's quite all right. I don't mind at ...' Jennifer was cut off in mid-sentence by her hostess who had spied more guests arriving.

'Bless you, my dear, and now I must go and greet my other guests.' And with that she sailed away to the other side of the room.

'Bimbo, as I'm sure you must have realized, was her late husband.'

Jennifer turned towards the speaker. A tall, thin, upright woman smiled at her. She was not expensively dressed, but her immaculate deportment lent her an air of grandeur which was accentuated by her neatly coiffed grey hair. She must have been in her late sixties, Jennifer thought.

'Yes, I did guess that,' Jennifer smiled back.

'I can imagine Bimbo saying that – that is, if he ever got a word in edgeways. With Joan it can be difficult.' The grey eyes twinkled. 'Known them for years, you know. Bimbo was at school with my husband – of course they're both dead now, have been for ages. When it comes to stamina, we gels have it over our men time and time again.' She sat herself down on the sofa and patted the seat next to her. 'Sit down and talk to me, my dear. Us old things can't stand for too long.'

Jennifer laughed as she joined her on the sofa. Already she was warming to this forthright character.

'Now, where were we? My name's Lavinia Wrightson, by the way. I have managed to gather through all that fracas that you are Jennifer – not Janet – Carrington and that your husband is Joan's marvellous Harley Street doctor. Which is he?' She looked vaguely around the room.

Jennifer pointed discreetly to Tony who was standing talking to two other men opposite them. At that moment he turned and caught her eye and smiled.

"Quite an age difference," Lavinia thought. He must be nearly twenty years older than his pretty young wife. She caught the look that passed between them and it warmed her heart. Whoever said that age didn't matter was right. It didn't – at least, it didn't when the chemistry was right and the feelings were genuine.

'How long have you been married, my dear?'

'Seventeen years.'

'Really? You hardly seem old enough.' Lavinia raised her eyebrows.

'I'm thirty-eight.' Jennifer anticipated the question. 'It was a second marriage for both of us. Tony's first wife died giving birth to their son and my first husband died six months after we were married when I was nineteen.'

Why was she telling a complete stranger all this, Jennifer wondered. It was something she hadn't talked about for years. She glanced at Lavinia Wrightson who was sitting, ever upright, beside her. There was something about her – a strength of character laced with a sense of fun and sharp wit – that made her endearing. Jennifer felt that she was talking to a woman of exceptional courage and endurance, and something told her that Lavinia Wrightson had survived hard times.

'Do you have any children of your own?' Lavinia asked.

'Yes, we have a daughter. She's sixteen.'

'Goodness! Next year she'll be a débutante.'

'Oh, I don't think so.' Jennifer laughed. 'I don't come from that sort of world at all and Tony wouldn't know where to begin.'

'My dear, we all owe it to our daughters to launch them properly into Society.' Lavinia patted Jennifer's knee. 'Meeting the right people and making the right marriage is still terribly important. I should know. I had three daughters of my own and one son. Sadly, my son was killed in the war, but my three gels have turned out very well.' She thought for a minute, then added: 'My son didn't do so badly either. He did at least marry and produce an heir before he died.'

Jennifer was saved from having to reply to this onslaught by the arrival of a smartly dressed woman who perched herself on the arm of the sofa.

'Lavinia, darling, how's business?' The American accent was noticeable.

'Booming, Annabel.'

'Is this another of your products?' the cool voice continued as the eyes gave Jennifer an appraising stare.

'Good Lord, no!' Lavinia gave a gaff of laughter. 'Unfortunately I can't claim responsibility for every beautiful lady in London. And this one has an almost grown-up daughter of her own.'

'Really? I'd have never guessed.'

'Jennifer, dear, forgive me. This is Annabel Clover from Texas.'

'Pleased to meet you. I'm from Houston.' She pronounced it 'Hewsten' as she held out her hand.

'Annabel, this is Mrs Jennifer Carrington. She's the wife of Anthony Carrington, a very well-thought-of physician in Harley Street.'

'Really?' Annabel repeated as she took out a cigarette from her heavily beaded evening bag. 'Ma husband's in shoes.'

Jennifer looked nonplussed.

'What Annabel means, dear, is that her husband owns one of the largest shoe-manufacturing companies in America.' She winked at Jennifer while Annabel was engrossed in lighting her cigarette.

'Lavinia is bringing out our daughter, Grace, next spring in London. Ah know that you all are just going to have a terrific time.' She blew a perfect smoke ring. 'Is your daughter doing the Season next year too?'

'Oh no, I hadn't even thought about it.'

'Oh.' The word was spoken slowly, and as it tapered off so did the interest which had been in Annabel's eyes. She stood up. 'Must circulate, darling,' she said and drifted away.

Lavinia's eyes followed her. 'Was it Oscar Wilde who said that America was a very young country?' she asked as she grinned at Jennifer.

Jennifer thought for a moment and then burst into a fit of uncontrollable laughter. 'Oh, you are naughty,' she said as she wiped her eyes. 'You have a wicked sense of humour and I feel as if I've known you for years.'

'Well, was it?'

'No – and you know it – he was talking about Australia and the fact that Mr Hopper made his money from packing food into circular tins.'

'Just testing.' The eyes twinkled. 'I like you, Jennifer dear, I think that we are going to be great friends.'

'I'm sure that we will be. By the way, what is this business of yours?'

Lavinia Wrightson sobered up. 'When my Teddy died I

was left very hard up,' she said. 'He was typical of his family. They played hard, drank hard and generally spent money like water. He left me with a great many debts and very little in the bank. I needed to work, I wasn't trained for anything and I was middle-aged which didn't help. It was then that I struck on this idea of bringing out gels whose parents either didn't have the time or who didn't have the connections.

'I take about four or five gels a year and they live with me in my house in Ennismore Gardens. I make sure that they get asked to all the débutante parties and I give a dance in my ballroom for each one of them – oh, and of course I present them all at court in March.' She sighed. 'It's such a shame that the presentations stopped this year. It's all Prince Philip's fault, you know. He told the Queen that it was becoming a rat race.' She smiled wryly. 'I suppose he didn't like people such as myself presenting the shoemaker's daughter from Houston etc. But they're all nice gels. I only take on nice gels – rich, I grant you, but when I've finished with them, you could put them anywhere and they could cope.' She sighed again. 'Of course, it's only a matter of time now before the whole scene changes. It won't happen at once, but in five or six years from now it will all be different. The thing that really annoys me is that some foreigner should have the power to change our English heritage.'

'It sounds as if you really enjoy what you do.' Jennifer was intrigued.

'Oh, I do, dear. It makes me feel useful in my old age. I feel that in this hard tough world we live in, I'm actually helping to keep up some standards.'

'Ladies and gentlemen, dinner is served.' A butler resplendent in white tie and tails stood in the doorway.

'Before we go into dinner, here's my card.' Lavinia fished in her brocade bag and retrieved one of her visiting cards. 'Do telephone me next week and bring your daughter to tea. I'd like to meet her.'

'I'd love to.' Jennifer took the card and glanced down at it.

It said: 'LAVINIA, LADY WRIGHTSON' and gave an address in Ennismore Gardens in Kensington.

'Well, what did you think of this evening?' Tony Carrington took off his dinner jacket and loosened his tie.

'It was fun.' Jennifer turned her back to him so that he could unzip her dress. 'Are all your private patients like that these days?'

'You know they're not,' he laughed. 'Our Joan's quite a character, isn't she? She's been dying to meet you ever since someone told her what a young attractive wife I had.'

'I hope that I lived up to her expectations.' She stepped out of the dress and hung it in the wardrobe.

'From where I'm standing, you couldn't fail to.'

'Idiot.' She kissed his cheek and slipped her dressing gown around her. 'I met a fascinating woman.' She sat down at her dressing table and started brushing her hair.

'That woman you spent hours talking to on the sofa before dinner?'

'Yes. She's got a wonderful sense of humour and I think what she does is amazing.'

'Well, don't leave me in suspense. What does she do?'

'She launches young girls into the London social scene – or to put it her way, she brings them out. She gets paid for it. I suppose she's a sort of paid hostess. She has girls from all over the place. The parents pay her for ensuring that their daughter goes to all the important social events on the calendar and all the best parties – she even gives a dance for them.'

'Sounds like a Madame to me.'

'Tony, don't be ridiculous. You're making fun of her. She's not that at all. These girls have a marvellous time. They meet masses of other young people and learn all the social etiquette. She wants me to take Lainey to tea with her next week. It might be nice for Lainey to do the London Season,' she mused. 'At first, I didn't think so, but I've been thinking about it ever since she mentioned it. I didn't come from that sort of background myself, but that doesn't mean that Lainey shouldn't have some of the things I didn't have. You come from that kind of world – even though you don't socialize a great deal. You and Richard went to Eton and . . .' She paused.

Tony walked up behind her and put his hands on her shoulders. 'And Alan came from an old Bostonian family and went to Harvard.' He felt her tremble as he spoke. 'It's all right, Jennifer. I understand what you're saying. You're right, Lainey should have her chance. It's just that sometimes I'm frightened for her. She is such a determined young lady and she's got that wild streak in her, but I dare say that with you and Lady Wrightson supervising her she'll come to no harm – and, anyway, we can't go on protecting her for ever. She has to be allowed to grow up.'

'You are forgetting Charlie.' She smiled up at him. 'Elder brothers are far better than parents when it comes to protecting a girl's honour. Those two adore each other. Charlie won't let her behave too wildly.'

'That's true.' He laughed. 'Charlie's the Rock of Gibraltar.'

'Just like his father,' she replied.

'You know, there's something that bothers me over the name Wrightson.' Tony frowned as he sat down on the bed and pulled off his shoes. 'It rings a bell way back in my memory, but I can't think why.'

'Well, I don't think that she was a chorus girl back in the twenties,' Jennifer giggled. 'She seemed terribly county to me.'

'No, it's nothing like that.' He shook his head. 'I feel that I know the name from somewhere. I've got a *Who's Who* in my consulting rooms. I'll look her up in the morning.'

'Darling, you sound positively snobbish.'

'You know me better than that.' He looked up and found that she was teasing him. 'Sorry.' His expression was contrite. 'I just know that I remember that name from somewhere.'

He patted her hand. 'Telephone her tomorrow and fix a day when you can take Lainey to tea. It all sounds very exciting.'

'Tony, if we let Lainey do all this, she must still get some qualifications. I think that is very important. I'm going to insist that during the week she does a typing course or something like that.'

'I agree.' He turned off the light. 'Now forget about it until tomorrow. I have a busy day ahead and so do you. We must get some sleep.'

'How good to hear your voice, Jennifer dear, and wasn't it a nice evening we shared last night?'

Jennifer smiled to herself as she held the telephone to her ear. From the little she knew of Lavinia Wrightson, the adjectives good, nice and dear featured strongly in her vocabulary.

'Now, about bringing your lovely daughter around for tea,' Lavinia continued. 'The diary looks very full next week, but after that most people have left for the country for Christmas. I'm not going myself until just before the holiday. I can't stand to impose myself on relations for too long. It always ends in tears if one does. In fact, this year I'm going to stay with my daughter-in-law and my grandson. She's married again, you know, and has got three uncontrollable children under ten. It's always very exhausting – though I must say that when I tell them to be quiet they do take heed, even if only for a short while.' She paused for a minute to catch her breath. 'Would Thursday of the following week be all right? Shall we say four o'clock? Good, good. That will be very nice. I'll look forward to seeing you both then. Good-bye, dear.' The phone went dead.

Jennifer stood up. She consulted the list in her hand. There were so many things she had to do before Lainey came home from school. It was incredible to think that she would be going down to Hampshire to collect her at the end of the week.

Before she could leave the room the telephone started ringing again.

'Jennifer, you're not going to believe this.' Tony's voice came down the phone.

'What is it, darling? Is something the matter?' She was concerned.

'Nothing's the matter. It's just that I've looked up Lady Wrightson. I knew that I'd come across that name from somewhere and I was right.'

'Well, who is she?'

'I tell you, you're not going to believe this.'

'Tony, don't keep saying that.' She was exasperated.

'She's Richard's father's first cousin. That means that she's Richard's first cousin once removed. A bit vague, I grant you, but never-the-less a relation so to speak. It says here she's the daughter of George Woodward who was the younger brother of Sir Robert Woodward. Robert was Richard's grandfather. She was born in 1892 which makes her sixty-six. In 1912 she married Edward Wrightson, the third Baron Wrightson. He died in 1949. They had three daughters and one son who was killed in 1940 at Dunkirk. The title has passed to the grandson, Henry, who was born in 1937.'

'Good Lord!' Jennifer felt weak at the knees. She sat down hard on the chair. 'That's incredible. What do I do?'

'What do you mean, what do you do? She's a marvellous character. I remember now how Richard used to talk about her. He didn't know her very well as there was some sort of split in the family, but I think his mother used to tell him stories about his eccentric cousin. Now that I recall, I think that she drove an ambulance in the First World War. Extraordinary woman.'

'I mean, do I tell her who I am?'

'Of course you must. From what I've heard of her, she'll love it. You'll become family at once.'

'Oh dear, this is all too much to take in.' Jennifer shook her head trying to clear it. 'I must admit that I did take to her from the moment I started talking to her, but to find that she is related to Richard . . . well, it seems so weird.'

'Don't worry, darling. We'll discuss it when I get home.' He rang off.

Jennifer sat for a long time with her chin on her hands, thinking. Tony had seemed really excited and pleased. She knew how much he had cared for Richard, and realized that it was important for him to make contact with his old friend's family. And what about her? Did she want to – now that she knew who Lavinia Wrightson was?

"I have nothing to worry about," she told herself firmly. "Richard died nineteen years ago." Although she had done nothing wrong, for the first time in years Jennifer felt a pang of guilt. "I didn't love him the way I thought I did and I'm sure that he knew." A tear rolled down her cheek. And then there had been Alan. All that passion and tenderness made more acute by the sense of danger and the feeling of impermanence, the thought that it could all end tomorrow. And it had. A lifetime of loving all crammed into a few months, but what a legacy he had left her. How sad that Lainey's father could never know that he had helped to produce such a perfect daughter.

'Well, well, isn't that just amazing. Fancy you being poor Richard's widow. It really is a small world, isn't it?' Lavinia Wrightson had taken Jennifer's story in her stride and was now pouring the tea from an elaborate silver teapot. 'Of course, I hardly knew him – tremendous split in the family, you know. They hadn't spoken for years – my father and his brother. Consequence was that the two branches of the family were completely separate. I never even knew of Richard's death until well after it had happened and I must admit that it didn't really register as I hadn't seen him in years.' She offered the cucumber sandwiches. 'Do have one, they're very good. Oh, this is such fun.' She clapped her hands in delight. 'I already feel that you're part of my family.

We are going to have a simply splendid year.' She beamed at Lainey, who was sitting next to her mother on the sofa. 'Lainey, dear, you are so pretty. You'll be a great success, I'm sure. Maybe, you'll even be "Deb of the Year".'

Lainey smiled a little uncertainly. 'It sounds very exciting,' she said.

'It will be. It will be.' Lavinia smiled at her fondly, then turned and addressed herself to Jennifer. 'I shall be giving a ladies' lunch sometime in January for the mothers of various débutantes so that they can meet each other. You must come to that. Oh, and I must see what I can do about the Berkeley Dress Show. Lainey would make a perfect bride.'

Jennifer looked startled.

'Oh, don't worry, dear.' Lavinia patted her arm. 'The Berkeley Dress Show is one of the main events on the débutante calendar. Each year a different designer chooses the top ten or twelve girls to model his clothes for charity. This year my friend the Countess of Berescombe is organizing it. Her daughter, Candida, is coming out.'

Jennifer put down her teacup. 'Lavinia, I want to make it clear that if Lainey does the Season, she has to do something else as well. Neither her father nor myself intend that she should sit back all summer and just go to parties. She must learn some skills – do a course and get some qualifications.'

'Oh, Mother.' Lainey turned the force of her magnetic blue eyes on Jennifer. 'I will have only just left school in March. Can't I have a few months off before I start bashing a boring old typewriter?' She smiled beseechingly at Lavinia Wrightson. 'There must be more exciting things to study. I'd love to be a model,' she mused. 'I'm sure I could do it and I'd make lots of money, wouldn't I?'

'Lainey, I . . .'

'Wait a minute, Jennifer.' Lavinia held up her hand to prevent the argument from developing. 'What about enrolling Lainey for a course at Lori Lawley's for the summer?'

'What's that?'

'It's a modelling agency – oh, not just any modelling agency. They run a course that also includes cooking and flower-arranging. It's more like a finishing school. It would be quite a good idea for Lainey to do that and it wouldn't tax her too much while she is coping with a lot of late nights.'

'Well, I don't know.' Jennifer was cautious.

'Oh, Mother, go on. Please say yes. It would only be for the summer and I would really enjoy it,' Lainey implored.

'We'll see. I'll have to discuss it with your father.'

'You do that.' Lavinia rose from her chair. 'I'm sure you'll find that he will approve. After all, a gel must be capable of running a house – more so than an office.' She winked at Lainey who impulsively kissed her on the cheek. 'Now, now, dear, nothing is arranged yet. All in good time.' She turned to Jennifer again. 'I'm so pleased that you have decided to let Lainey do the Season. I know that she will benefit from it.' She turned back to Lainey. 'The next time that you come here, I will give a little dinner for my gels to introduce them to some nice young men. My grandson helps me provide them, you know. He works in the city.' Her eyes twinkled as she continued. 'You must be careful of him, he's got an eye for pretty gels and he's too good-looking by half!'

Lainey flashed her a dazzling smile. 'I can't wait to meet them all.'

Jennifer looked at her sharply. Oh dear, she wondered, was this going to be a big mistake? Was her headstrong young daughter going to lead everyone a dance and worry them to death with her impulsive behaviour?

Lainey sensed her mother's doubts and immediately changed her tactics. Her eyes widened and a slight note of awe crept into her voice as she said: 'I'm so lucky to have parents like you. I'm going to have a wonderful time and I'm going to make sure that I do you all credit.'

'Dear gel,' Lavinia beamed.

"She puzzles me," Jennifer thought as they walked out into the hall. "One minute I think I understand her and the next minute she has changed. She's good and kind and I love her so much, but Tony was right when he said that there's one side of Lainey we don't know at all and probably never will."

As they walked down the steps and out into the street, Lainey's thoughts were quite different. Wrightson. She'd never forget that name. It wasn't a common one. Was Harry Wrightson the grandson by any chance? She smiled enigmatically to herself as a feeling of intense excitement washed over her. "Oh, am I going to learn things, Mother," she thought. "I'm going to take London by storm. I'll be a glamorous and successful model one day, and Harry Wrightson will be wild about me and I won't care, which will really upset him. He thinks he can get any girl he wants — well not me. I'll have whoever I want, when I want and how I want, and I'll play him like a fisherman playing a fish." Another thought struck her. It would drive Charlie crazy. For a moment she frowned, then her face cleared and she tilted her head upwards. "So it will," she said thoughtfully. "So it will."

CHAPTER SEVEN

Mary-Beth Jefferson sat on her bed in the room that she shared with her friend Jeannie Mason. It was the penultimate day of term at Miss Porter's School at Farmington, Connecticut and tomorrow would see the start of the Christmas vacation. Two whole weeks and Jimmy would be in New York for a few days. Mary-Beth re-read a paragraph of the letter that she was clutching in her hand. A vague pink tinge crept into her cheeks as she lay back on the bed with her hands behind her head. A delicious feeling washed over her – it did every time she thought of Jimmy. It wasn't just physical attraction, it was a warmth and a sense of complete trust and great happiness. Mary-Beth was a mature girl for her sixteen years and she knew that she was very young to have these feelings. At her age it was normal to fall in and out of love with great frequency. Infatuations usually depended on whether the boy was good at sport, looked like a film star or owned a fantastic sports car. Jimmy Foxton had none of those attributes.

Mary-Beth had met Jimmy when she was in her freshman year. The Glee Club had had a dance and he had been one of the boys imported from various schools nearby. Thank goodness she had been able to sing. If you joined the choir, you could join the Glee Club and only the Glee Club were allowed to give dances.

Jimmy had cut in when she had been dancing with one of the 'local heroes' who, though brilliant on the hockey field, certainly had not shown the same prowess on the dance floor. Mary-Beth's feet had already been smarting from his clumsiness. Initially, Jimmy's appearance had also belied his greater capability in this direction. He was tall and thin and

231

wore glasses. The studious type, she had thought, probably very intense and not a lot of fun, but how wrong she had been. From the minute that they had started to dance together, she had realised that she was with an expert. He was a master of jive and rock and roll and had thrown her from side to side, catching her deftly each time. It had been such fun that she had felt desolate when the music had ended.

'Where on earth did you learn that?' she had asked him breathlessly.

'I don't know,' he had grinned back at her. 'It's just something you feel, I guess. It's in the music.'

'Are you a musician?' She had been curious.

'I play the piano a bit,' he had replied.

She had found out later on that that had been a gross understatement. He could play anything from jazz and pop to classical music. They had spent the rest of that evening together.

Mary-Beth had discovered that Jimmy hated sports, loved the theatre and, above everything, wanted to win a music scholarship to college. It had been the beginning of a great friendship based on mutual respect. Although Jimmy was two years older than Mary-Beth, it did not matter. To him she did not seem any younger – on the contrary, in many ways she was older than he in her outlook. It was probably because of her mother's illness, he had reckoned. She had a sense of responsibility and patience that was rare in someone so young. Jimmy had warmed to that. It had made him feel tender and protective towards her from the start of their relationship. During Mary-Beth's first two years at Farmington they had written regularly to each other, and met up at the few school dances that took place. In the vacations Jimmy had found many reasons for visiting his cousins in New York so that he could see Mary-Beth.

At first Alan had been alarmed at the attention this young man was paying to his daughter. She was so young – they both were. Neither of them seemed the slightest bit interested in having other boyfriends or girlfriends. And yet, it seemed an innocent love. It was as if by unspoken agreement they knew that they could wait until the time was right to develop other sides of their relationship. He had therefore decided not to interfere. Jimmy Foxton was a nice young man and good for his daughter. He teased her and made her laugh – and they mixed with a great crowd of kids, swimming, playing tennis and going to barbecues. Alan was happy for his daughter and willed himself not to be jealous of the fact that she no longer spent the majority of her vacation with him.

On the one rare occasion when he had tried to warn her about becoming too involved and maybe getting hurt, she had looked at him seriously and said: 'That will never happen to Jimmy and me, Daddy.' Somehow, he had known that she was right.

Mary-Beth sighed as she lay on her bed. Jimmy had won his music scholarship and was at Harvard now. She glanced down at the letter she was still holding. He had sent her a poem written by one of his fellow students. It was called 'Always walk beside me' and Jimmy was setting it to music. The words were quite beautiful. It could almost be about the two of them, she thought, and knew immediately that she was probably right and that Jimmy must have confided in his friend. That was when the blush had come to her cheeks. Silly, there was nothing to blush about really. They had done nothing to be ashamed of and never talked of love in 'that' way. Yet the very things that were unspoken were known to them both. They knew without telling each other but these thoughts could not be voiced as yet.

'Learn the words,' Jimmy wrote in his spidery handwriting. 'When I come to New York next week, I'll bring the music and you can sing it for me.'

Mary-Beth smiled to herself. 'Always walk beside me.' It was OK if you said it in a song, but they knew, didn't they?

Only a few more days and then she would see him again. She kissed the letter softly and closed her eyes.

'Oh, there you are.' Jeannie burst into the room. 'I've been looking for you everywhere. The Principal wants to see you. He looked awful serious. What can you have done?'

Mary-Beth swung her legs to the floor and stood up. She folded the letter carefully and put it in the drawer by her bed.

'I can't imagine.' She was still thinking of next week.

'Another letter from the faithful Jimmy?' Jeannie had seen the letter.

'Um.' Mary-Beth was vague.

'You two aren't on this planet.'

'Eat your heart out.' Mary-Beth came back to earth.

'Don't get mad. I'm just the poor little left-out room-mate.'

'Don't come that one with me. You'll get no sympathy. You've got so many boys after you that you don't know which one to date first.'

'Chance would be a fine thing in this prison. Just wait until next week. My brother, Victor, has this fabulous-looking friend . . .'

'Jeannie, you're too much.' Mary-Beth gave her friend a good-natured punch on the arm. 'I'd better go and see what the Principal wants.'

'Maybe he'll make you wash dishes after supper as a penance.'

'Quit, will you,' Mary-Beth called over her shoulder, laughing as she ran along the corridor and down the stairs.

'Come in.' The headmaster of Miss Porter's School raised his eyes from the paperwork that he had been studying on his desk. 'Ah, there you are, Mary-Beth. Sit down, dear. Mary-Beth . . .' He folded his hands in front of him and cleared his throat – something he always did when he was unsure how to proceed. 'Mary-Beth, I'm afraid that I have to be the bearer of very sad news.' He coughed and

234

shuffled the papers into a neater pile. 'I'm afraid that your mother has had an accident . . .'

'Oh, my God . . .' Images and thoughts whirled through Mary-Beth's head. The colour which had been in her cheeks faded as her face became chalk-white. 'How bad is it?' she asked shakily.

The tall angular man stood up and walked around the desk to put his hand on the young girl's shoulder. 'My dear, I hate to say this, but your mother is dead.'

There was a stunned silence.

'I'm so sorry, my dear.'

'How did it happen?' Mary-Beth was staring at a small spot on the otherwise immaculate carpet.

'I don't have the details.' The headmaster swallowed nervously. After all, it wasn't up to him to tell the wretched girl what had happened. 'Your father is at the nursing home and a car is being sent for you within the hour to take you back to New York. You'd better go and finish packing. In the meantime, is there anything I can do for you?'

Mary-Beth shook herself and tried to concentrate on what was being said to her.

'No . . . thank you.' She felt remote – numb. Her eyes were dry but her stomach felt knotted.

The headmaster had seen shock many times before. 'Is Jeannie in your room? I don't think that you should be by yourself, dear.'

'I'm OK, but, yes, Jeannie's there.' Mary-Beth walked towards the door. When she reached it she turned and stared unseeingly at the middle-aged man. 'Isn't it strange?' she said softly. 'It's Christmas next week. It should be the happiest time of the year, but something usually happens to spoil it.'

The headmaster sighed as the door closed behind Mary-Beth. Poor child. He knew something of Mary-Beth's problems at home. Alan Jefferson had thought it fit to inform him of his wife's illness and how it could affect his daughter.

It was amazing, he thought, how normal and well-adjusted Mary-Beth was. He hoped that the poor girl could cope with this terrible situation.

Mixed emotions raged inside Mary-Beth as she crossed the hall. Her mother was dead. How she had died was still a mystery which would not be revealed until she got back home. Somewhere she felt guilt at not having loved her as she should have done, but her mother hadn't loved her, had she? No, her mother had been jealous of the fact that Alan loved her, Mary-Beth, so much. "Mom didn't love me – she saw me as a threat," she thought. "All her life Mom opted out of anything she didn't want to face up to. She never had any confidence, so she just kept running away, and in the end there was nowhere to run." A cold shiver ran up her spine as the realisation suddenly hit her. "It was no accident," she thought. "Mom finally ran away from herself." A deep sorrow welled up inside her, but still the tears didn't flow. A need to be held and comforted overwhelmed her – not by her father, although she loved him so much, but . . .

She had reached the half-landing between the floors on the staircase. The pay phone beckoned in front of her and she could see that someone had left a twenty-five cent piece on the ledge. It was meant to be, wasn't it? She slipped it into the box and dialled.

Harvard's term had already finished. Please God that he was at home.

'Hello?' It was his voice. She sighed with relief.

'Mother's dead.' Her voice was flat.

There was a pause, then . . . 'Are you all right?' he asked.

'I don't know.' Her voice cracked. 'I'm going back to New York tonight.'

'I'll be there first thing in the morning.'

'I knew you would.'

'Hold on, Mary-Beth. I love you.'

'I know,' she said softly. 'I love you too.'

She walked on up the stairs in a daze.

'Well?' Jeannie was standing in their bedroom riddled with curiosity.

'Mother's dead.' Mary-Beth sat down on the bed.

'What?' Jeannie was aghast. She sat down beside her friend and put an arm around her. 'Oh, my God, how awful. What happened?'

Mary-Beth did not hear her.

'Isn't it odd?' she said. 'On the worst day of my life, something wonderful happened. We finally admitted it, we made a commitment. Our relationship will never be the same again.'

'I don't understand.' Jeannie was baffled.

'I know you don't.' Mary-Beth looked at her friend sadly. At that moment she felt a generation older. 'But you will, one day.'

'What are you going to do now, Alan?' Karen Prebble sat between her husband and her son-in-law at the dining-room table in their house in Washington. It was three days after Christmas and the Prebbles had insisted that Alan and Mary-Beth spent the holiday period with them as arranged before their daughter's death.

Rosemary's funeral had taken place the week before Christmas and she had been laid to rest in the family plot near their home in Maine. Throughout the time beforehand, Jimmy Foxton had been with Mary-Beth. Alan had had so much to do that he had welcomed the presence of the young music student. However standing beside his daughter at the interment he had become aware of her hand tightly clasped in Jimmy's and had noticed the strength of the look that passed between them. Was it jealousy or hurt – or a mixture of both – that had made him realise his beautiful daughter no longer relied totally on him? What he had to give her was no longer enough. This tall thin young man with his serious eyes had more power to comfort Mary-Beth than he – her father – was capable of. They were so young – sixteen and eighteen – and they had looked so loving together. But would it stand the test of time? Alan had sighed deeply. He was nearly forty-three years old and he had never had a relationship like that – or had he? Would he have had a chance with Jennifer? Or would those intense feelings of love and passion have played themselves out? Oh God! What a time to be thinking thoughts such as these. It was too late – seventeen years too late. The future now meant taking one day at a time and working to the best of his ability to make a home for himself and Mary-Beth until such time when she would marry and leave him alone.

'Alan, did you hear me? I said, what are you going to do now?' Karen Prebble repeated her question and turned her grey eyes in his direction.

'I'm sorry. I was miles away.' Alan abandoned the food on his plate. 'I shall carry on working and look after my daughter.'

'That's what we want to talk to you about.' Karen tinkled the silver bell which was beside her. The maid appeared and started to clear the plates away. Karen waited until she had left the room, then continued: 'Neil and I think that it would be in Mary-Beth's best interest if she came to live here for a while. She needs to meet other young people. In particular, her relationship with that boy is far too intense for someone of her age. It can only lead to trouble. Someone needs to see to it that she mixes in the right circles and has some more fun.'

'Karen, I know that you mean well.' Alan rested his elbows on the table and folded his hands. 'But Mary-Beth is my daughter and she's going to live with me. She has another year and a half at school, and in the holidays we will be together.'

'Is she with you now?' Karen smiled a thin cold smile to prove her point. 'You've let her go off and stay with that boy's family for New Year. It's all very well, Alan. Neil and I saw the way they were looking at each other last week.

What do you think they will get up to? Do you want a sixteen-year-old pregnant daughter on your hands? He's only eighteen. He's got two and a half years to complete at Harvard and then what is he going to do?'

'He wants to be a composer.'

'Grow up, Alan.' If it was possible to snort politely, Karen Prebble achieved it. 'Do you want to see your daughter living in a garret with an out-of-work musician?'

'I trust Mary-Beth.' Alan spoke quietly. 'She's not an irresponsible girl. In fact, she's much more grown-up than most kids her age.'

'That is not the point.' Karen sighed in exasperation. 'Neil, for God's sake say something.'

Throughout this conversation the senator had kept silent. Now he took a long sip from his wine glass and looked thoughtfully at his son-in-law.

'To all of us our little lambs seem perfect,' he said solemnly. 'We can blind ourselves to what we don't want to see and in hindsight say what we might have done if we had only realised, though whether we would ever have done any different is another matter.' He stared at the silver candlestick in front of him for what seemed an age. When eventually he looked up there was a haunted look in his eyes. 'Our grand-daughter is a great little lady,' he said. 'She's all that we could ever have wanted – and more. We know how much you love her, Alan, and of course she must live with you ...' He held up his hand to prevent his wife from butting in. 'But why don't you let Karen organise her début next Christmas and the following year. You are hardly equipped to do it yourself. Karen has the time and the know-how. She'll keep Mary-Beth so busy partying that she won't have the time to remain so deeply involved with one person. The whole thing will blow over, you'll see.'

'At least agree to that, Alan.' Karen's tone was earnest. 'Mary-Beth is entitled to a social life before she ties herself down to some penniless boy.'

'You're right,' Alan sighed. 'Mary-Beth is entitled to everything you say she is. After Farmington, I want her to go to Radcliffe. I want her to have all the things that her mother and I had when we were young – though little good it did us.' The two Prebbles exchanged a look but did not interrupt. 'I want her to have some fun and live the life of a young girl with not too many responsibilities. Thank you, Karen, for offering to organise her début. I'm sure you will do it splendidly, but until then Mary-Beth stays with me. I need her as much as she needs me.'

Karen Prebble nodded her head. 'That's settled then,' she said and allowed herself to smile in an almost friendly way. 'You look tired, Alan. Why don't you go to bed. We've all had a terrible time, but none more so than you.'

They walked along the beach on the New Jersey coastline. A cold east wind was blowing and it was trying hard to rain. It was New Year's Day – the first day of 1959. No one was in sight except a dog who scampered by, purposefully intent on where it was going. Further along they stopped and stood facing the sea watching the breakers thunder on to the sand.

'I meant what I said when I told you that I loved you.' Jimmy gazed intently at the sea.

'So did I.' Mary-Beth did not look at him.

'Things will never be quite the same between us again.'

'I know.'

'I wish we were older.'

'So do I.'

'Three years is a long time.'

'Yes, but it will pass. Time always passes.'

He turned her towards him and saw the tears glistening in her brilliant blue eyes – so like her father's. Her short dark hair clung damply to her face. He smoothed it back and cupped her face in his hands. She trembled slightly as her eyes beseeched him silently. Slowly he bent his head, kissing her eyes and tasting the salt of her tears. She turned her head

240

and his lips found hers, for a second they hovered tentatively over hers, then the flame of desire unleashed itself in both of them and they kissed each other deeply with all the passion of the young. Oblivious to the heavy rain which was now falling, they stood on the deserted beach, clinging tightly to each other and feeling totally as one. Then gently Jimmy drew himself apart.

'You see now why we must see less of each other for a while?' he whispered.

'I suppose so,' she answered shakily.

'Mary-Beth, I love you. I want to marry you when I graduate from Harvard. You're only sixteen. I don't want anything to happen to you because of me. You do understand, don't you?'

'Yes.'

They turned their backs on the angry waves and walked silently and separately back the way they had come.

CHAPTER EIGHT

Harry Wrightson looked contentedly into the mirror as he straightened his bowtie and smoothed back his thick dark hair. He was under no apprehension about his desirability where young women were concerned – or for that matter older women as well. He examined his reflection once more. Yes, he would do. Formal clothes suited him, and the elegant cut of his Saville Row dinner jacket set him off to perfection.

At the age of twenty-two Harry had been at the top of every deb's mum's list for the past four years. His tall athletic physique, dark saturnine features and heavy-lidded eyes lent him an air of dangerousness which most women found irresistible. His title was also an advantage, as was his adequate income – not that he was rich. He wished to God that he was. Harry had realized very early on that, despite his job in the city, if he wanted to live in the style to which he was rapidly becoming accustomed, he would have to marry a rich girl. There was also the fact that when the family home came into his possession on his twenty-fifth birthday he would have to maintain it. He had three years to find himself a rich wife – and where better to look than the London Season? He looked at his Cartier watch and saw that it was already quarter to eight. Time to go. Aunt Lavinia hated people who were not punctual and he had to pick up Candida Leach on the way. He wondered what his aunt's crop of girls would be like this year. He knew that there was a Texas heiress whose father made shoes. Chance would be a fine thing if she turned out to be a raving beauty, but the odds were about ninety per cent against that. Then there was a doctor's daughter who sounded insignificant and the daughter of some department store mogul – probably from the north with a strange accent. There were two other girls, but he couldn't remember what their backgrounds were, which said it all. He glanced around his bedroom to make sure that it looked inviting – well, you never knew your luck but he didn't hold much hope, not unless he went on to the Stork Room afterwards, and there would be no need to bring one of those girls back here.

Just as he was about to leave, he remembered the Hermes scarf neatly packed in its box in the sitting room which he had bought that day. He rushed back into the flat and grabbed it before setting off down the stairs. The scarf was a birthday present for Lady Candida Leach. Harry was not giving it to her because he particularly liked her, but rather because he had heard her say how much she loved them and how expensive they were. If he gave her one for her birthday it would be all around London by the next day and could only serve to enhance his reputation.

Harry smiled to himself as he unlocked the door of his red Austin Healey. In order to catch the big fish you had to bait the trap. Hence the sports car, the Cartier watch and the impeccably tailored clothes. It was also essential to have a decent bachelor pad in a good part of London and not to have to share it with anyone – that would certainly cramp one's style. Expensive though these assets had been to acquire, he looked on them as leading to his future security. It was also just as important that he be seen to escort 'La Leach' tonight, for she had already been tipped by Paul Tanfield of the *Daily Mail* and William Hickey of the *Daily Express* as a more than likely choice for 'Deb of the Year'. It would look good in the eyes of any prospective heiresses. He lit a cigarette and slammed the car into gear, revving it up as hard as possible, and set off with a squeal of his tyres.

'Do you think that this evening will be amusing?' Lady Candida Leach sat back and arranged the folds of her dress as Harry closed the door of the car. He got in beside her and started the engine.

'I don't see why not. Aunt Lavinia always entertains in style.'

'Yes, but who are these girls that she brings out and why can't their mothers do it themselves?'

'Not all people have as much time on their hands as your mother, Candida darling, neither do they have the entrée into so-called Society.'

'That's not very nice of you, Harry. Mummy is an extremely busy person.'

'I quite agree. She's busy trying to marry you off. Once that's been achieved she'll revert to the tiring job of opening endless bazaars and attending fashion shows and charity balls.'

'You are awful.' Candida gave a loud giggle. 'I can't think why everyone puts up with you.'

'For that very reason, dear heart,' he said with great affection. He leaned across and placed his left hand heavily on her knee through the folds of her dress. 'They think I'm exciting – and I am.'

The car wobbled as they sped along the Embankment.

'Harry, for God's sake, we'll end up in the river if you don't put two hands on the wheel.' She looked down her long aristocratic nose at his offending hand.

'There you are! You agree.' He laughed and removed his hand.

'No, I don't.' She tried to pout alluringly. Two high spots of colour had appeared on her cheeks.

"Oh God," he thought, "it's so easy and so boring."

'I've got something for you.' He said it in a throw-away manner. 'Reach over into the back. It's in the square box.'

'Gosh, how super.' She didn't seem surprised. He supposed that she was used to being showered with presents.

As she drew the brightly coloured scarf out of its box she gasped.

'A little bird whispered that it was your birthday soon,' he said smugly. 'I do hope that you like it.'

'Oh, I do. It's beautiful.' She smiled at him radiantly. 'It's so sweet of you, Harry.' She kissed him impulsively on the cheek.

He brought the car to a halt a few yards down the street from his aunt's house. He turned and looked at her in the dim light from the nearest street lamp.

'You can do better than that,' he said softly as he took her face in his hands. He touched his lips to hers. Her lips did not part although he could feel that she was holding her breath. It was as he had thought. The Lady Candida may be self-assured in many ways but in the arts of love he felt sure she was a novice. Gently and expertly he forced her lips apart with his tongue. She didn't pull away. He probed more deeply into her mouth and heard her sigh with pleasure. He wondered why. It was rather like kissing an ice-maiden – if such things existed. It did nothing for him at all – not even causing an erection. He wondered idly what she would be like in bed, but couldn't summon up any great interest at the thought.

He pulled away from her and straightened his tie. 'Half time,' he said heartily and jumped out of the car, running around to open the door for her. She was still in a daze – well, he had known that she would be. He intended that she would walk into that drawing room with eyes only for him. It would look very complimentary.

Lavinia Wrightson stood in the doorway of her ballroom and surveyed the beautifully laid table. The placements were for twenty. She would sit at the far end of the table and her old friend and stalwart partner, Ambrose Middleton, would be opposite her. The rest of the party was to be made up of her five girls, four other top débutantes, her grandson Harry and eight other young men. Of course you couldn't really call Eric Symmington-Smythe that young. He had been on the débutante circuit for at least twelve years and admitted to being thirty-two, saying that his hair had gone prematurely grey. Lavinia imagined that he sat permanently under a sun lamp as he always had a deep tan. He wasn't a great brain and of course he was a sponger of the first order, but he was a good man to get for a party at the beginning of the Season. The young girls were always very impressed that a man of his age should want to talk to them and it gave them confidence.

'Is everything to your liking, m'lady?' The butler, sent by Searcy's, was waiting for her approval.

'Yes, Higgins, everything looks lovely as usual.' She smiled. Searcy's always did the catering for her big parties and she made sure of this by booking them well in advance. In addition to Higgins there were three parlour maids to help with the serving. The spring flowers gave out a beautiful scent and the silver tableware winked and gleamed in the soft candlelight. Thank goodness she had been able to hang on to it, Lavinia thought. Due to her little job, as she called it, she had been able to keep all her treasured family possessions as well as refurbish the house. Life was exciting and fun nowadays. Yes – if she dared to admit it – even more fun than when Edward was alive. No, that wasn't fair. It was different now and just as enjoyable.

She thought about the five girls she was launching this year. The Bishop twins from Yorkshire were a lovely pair. They were not beautiful, but they were rosy-cheeked, healthy from country living and attractive with their red hair, freckles and sunny smiles. Their mother had insisted that they must do the Season as she had done, even though she herself hated London and refused to come anywhere near it. Lavinia had no doubts that the twins would be a great success. They were good fun and unaffected and certain to be popular.

Grace Clover, on the other hand, was shy and rather nervous. She wasn't an unattractive girl but she did not make the best of herself. Lavinia was not really surprised. Having a mother like Annabel must be, to say the least, a bit inhibiting. Still, Grace had her assets. She wasn't brash or loud like a great many American teenagers and neither was she out to prove that she was a blue-stocking. Of course, her biggest asset was her fortune. She would be all right – especially if Annabel didn't make too many appearances.

Vivien Hurst was a pleasant down-to-earth girl. She was a little bit older than the others – she would be nineteen in July – but it was fun for the Carrington girl to have her best friend doing the Season with her. Lavinia had liked the Hurst parents when she had met them. They were honest people who did not try to hide their humble origins which she admired.

It had been Jennifer Carrington's idea that the two girls should do the Season together, and Lavinia suspected it was because the sensible Vivien would influence the wild and very beautiful Alaina. At first Lavinia had questioned the wisdom of giving only one Hurst daughter a chance to do the Season, while the other – who was older – was studying to be a nurse. Would the elder daughter, Alison, feel that she had been passed over? No, Alfie Hurst had been adamant, Alison was a completely different character from her sister. She would not have enjoyed this sort of thing at all, he had assured her.

And what of her star turn – for that is how Lavinia thought of Lainey. The girl was the most beautiful and exquisite creature she had ever seen. Everything was right about her. She was tall and elegant with that wonderful long blonde hair which would be the envy of many. Her skin and features were flawless, and those enormous cobalt blue eyes were almost mesmerising in their intensity. She also had an air of fragile innocence about her, tempered by a hint of potential wantonness that would drive most men wild with desire.

Alaina would be a problem – of that she was certain – but the press would adore her. She would be the sensation of the Season and the object of much jealousy. She would be

247

Lavinia's *pièce de resistance*, and Lavinia looked forward to launching what would almost certainly be her first 'Deb of the Year'. With such pleasant thoughts in mind, she walked back to the hall just as Higgins opened the door to admit the first guests.

Harry felt an air of expectancy as he entered the drawing room. It was nothing that he could put his finger on, but somehow the atmosphere seemed charged. Maybe it had something to do with the anything-but-subtle expression of adoration in Candida's eyes fixed firmly on him.

The room was already crowded – so much for trying to be early. Candida had kept him waiting for at least twenty minutes and he had had to spend that time drinking and conversing with her father the Earl of Berescombe, to whom he had taken an instant dislike. Harry grinned now as he remembered a story about the earl which had been told to him by a little Australian actress only the week before. At the time he had thought it very funny, but it had been far too compromising to repeat at his club. Now it was locked in his memory as potentially useful information. God, if the press got hold of it they would have a field day. If he ever needed a favour from Candida it would certainly hold a great deal of persuasive power.

He looked around the room and spied Julian Fenner talking to two redheads. He walked over and joined them. They were nice girls – so alike that they had to be twins. Thank God that they did not dress alike as well. They were talking about horses, a subject which Julian was equally keen on but which did not inspire Harry at all. Just as he was about to move on he felt his arm clutched by his Aunt Lavinia.

'Harry dear, I want you to meet Grace Clover. She comes from Houston, Texas.' A small dark girl was standing beside her. Not bad-looking, Harry thought, but her hairstyle was much too severe. It was scraped back from her face and pinned in a chignon. Only a very beautiful face could carry off a style like that, and the fact that she wore practically no make-up didn't help either.

'Hello.' The girl held out a hand which shook slightly.

Well, at least she didn't shriek out 'Hi, y'all' and slap him heartily on the back. Harry took the outstretched hand and flashed her one of his most charming smiles. 'It's a pleasure to meet you, Grace.' Would she blush, he wondered. She didn't. It was as if she was used to hearing those words but did not believe them. He did not know quite how to continue the conversation and the American girl appeared to be tongue-tied. Harry let his glance rove around the room again. There was not much talent about, but he hadn't expected there to be. That ghastly man Symmington-Smythe was standing by the fireplace ingratiating himself with a rather attractive brown-haired girl and a blonde who had her back to him. The blonde was tall with long hair which almost reached what seemed to be a very slim waist. Back views could be deceptive, Harry knew that, but the brunette also looked quite promising. He decided to go over and annoy that smooth bugger Eric Symmington-Smythe.

'Evening, Eric. Still sitting under the sunlamp I see.'

Something that passed for anger crossed the elder man's face, but it was hastily replaced by the famous capped-tooth grin.

'Good-evening, Harry. I might have guessed that you would be here.' Eric's tone of voice indicated that it would have been far more pleasant if he hadn't been. 'Girls, may I introduce Lady Wrightson's grandson, Harry.' He waved his hand dismissively.

The blonde turned around, and Harry drew in a sharp breath as he immediately recognized the exquisite young girl he had tried to seduce at a Pony Club dance three years ago. The memory came flooding back to him. At the time he had been so carried away by her response and her loveliness it had never occurred to him she might be as young and naive as she was. She had seemed so experienced. When her brother Carrington had barged in and told him her real age, he had been frankly amazed. He had also felt a bit foolish – and even ashamed. It was certainly not his style to try and knock off fourteen-year-olds – for a start it was illegal as far as he knew.

As he stared at her, the brilliant blue eyes met his directly and the mouth curved into a slightly mocking smile.

'Lord Wrighton and I have already met some years ago. How are you, Harry?' she said.

For a moment he thought that he was going to let himself down and appear helplessly gauche. He just managed to pull himself together in time to say: 'Good Lord! Alaina Carrington. How you've grown.'

If he was trying to put her at a disadvantage, it didn't work. The infuriating little smile was still on her lips as she replied. 'Oh I have, Harry, I have.' An intense feeling of excitement welled up inside him. He had not been wrong about this girl. She was incredible. Just looking at her now he could see how perfect she was with her flawless complexion and beautiful face. As he talked to her he was barely aware of what was being said. She mesmerised him like a cat might mesmerise a canary. He had to shake himself back into reality when the butler announced that dinner was served.

His eyes followed her as she left the room with the other young women in front of the men. Did she realize the effect she was having on him? Probably not – and yet there had been that mocking little smile. With other girls he would have called it flirtatious but not with her. The conundrum served only to excite him more. "No woman has ever made a fool out of me," he thought, "except her, three years ago when she was just a kid. It won't happen again." He raised his glass of champagne and took a long sip. "May the best man win, Alaina," he vowed, and never even contemplated losing.

*

'Who was that, darling?' Jennifer Carrington walked into the drawing room just as her daughter was putting down the telephone.

'Eric Symmington-Smythe. He's asked me out to dinner after the Hodells' cocktail party tonight.'

'But I thought I heard you telling Harry Wrightson that you couldn't go out with him tonight because you were already busy.'

'You couldn't have done.' Lainey looked vague. 'I've only just fixed tonight up with Eric.' She looked at her watch. 'Good Lord, look at the time, I must go and change or I'll be late.' She dashed out of the room and up the stairs.

Jennifer shook her head in bewilderment. She could not keep up with Lainey these days. She was never in. There were lunch parties, tea parties and now cocktail parties and young men vying to take her out to dinner. As yet the dances had not started, but that would not be long now.

Jennifer was very proud of her beautiful popular daughter. This morning the photographs which had been taken by Lénare had arrived in the post and there wasn't a bad one amongst them. One was scheduled to appear in *Country Life* magazine the following week. Soon Lainey would be starting her course at Lori Lawley's modelling school, and Jennifer suddenly had the feeling that this could be the start of something very big for her.

She wondered what Charlie would think of his very social sister. So far he had not seen much of her, as he was working hard for his examinations at Cambridge. He had promised, however, that he would get down to London to watch her model in the Berkeley Dress Show in two weeks' time.

Jennifer was almost as excited as Lavinia Wrightson that Lainey had been chosen to take part – she was to model the bride's dress as well. She would look absolutely devastating. Monsieur Lefauvre had apparently gone into ecstasies when he had seen her.

Lainey appeared to take it all in her stride. She was

pleased about the dress show but was showing it in a quiet way. It was as if she had expected nothing less. Jennifer knew that her daughter set herself goals to achieve – she always had – and that this was simply one more. She never contemplated losing. Jennifer wondered what would happen when she did. Lainey was going to have to learn to cope with not always getting what she wanted. So far her life had been too easy.

CHAPTER NINE

As he climbed the last few stairs to his flat, Harry yawned and belched loudly. He was just the littlest bit tight, he thought. It had been a long evening, and although the three double whiskies he had consumed at the Four Hundred had helped to keep him awake at the time, now he felt knackered.

Grace Clover had not been the most inspiring companion. She hadn't had much to say for herself and Harry had had to make an effort to keep the conversation going. It had been hard work and he'd had to keep reminding himself how rich she was. When he danced with her – which had been frequently as it spared the need for conversation – she had allowed him to hold her close and did not tread on his toes or trip up, but he had not felt she was excited by his close proximity.

They were all the same, these American girls, his friend Julian Fenner had once told him after some horsey trip to the States. They always wanted to dissect everything. Julian had been very funny about it.

'In the middle of a kiss they'll pause, and you can almost hear them as they wonder whether they should stop there or whether it would be beneficial to their education to continue. It's guaranteed to take all the passion out of the moment. The other thing they're good at is talking about what they call "meaningful relationships". They always have to complicate things. Give me an English girl every time. You can have fun with them. They don't take themselves so seriously.'

Harry had laughed at the time, but he had thought about what his friend had said afterwards. Julian was lucky. He didn't need a Grace Clover. He didn't have an estate to keep up and an ancient lineage to preserve. What it boiled down to was that when it came to marriage Harry knew where his duty lay. He considered himself to be in a similar position to the royal family in that he had to marry a girl who would fit the job. In his case she would have to be very wealthy. A sudden thought struck him – maybe Grace was thinking along the same lines. Maybe she was planning to use her fortune to buy herself a titled husband. Well, in that case, at least they would understand each other. For a second he felt a pang of – he didn't know quite what. He shook himself. There was still time for a lot of fun, even if he did decide that Grace was the inevitable outcome. He could still take out pretty girls while he romanced Grace on the side. He felt a shiver of excitement run up his spine as he let himself into his flat and closed the door. Tonight, before dinner, at the Hodell girl's cocktail party, Alaina Carrington had agreed to go out with him the following night. By God, the girl was beautiful. He had already asked her out twice, but she was so popular that she had been unable to accept. He had vowed then that he wouldn't ask her again for a while, but when he had found himself talking to her this evening he hadn't been able to stop himself. In fact he had had the devil's own job not to look aghast when she had accepted.

He took off his suit and hung it up with his spotted silk tie. The rest of his clothes he tossed carelessly on the floor, then walked into the bathroom to brush his teeth.

As he lay in bed, unable to sleep, he wondered where to take her. He would have liked to book a table at the Connaught Grill, but his wallet told him evenings of that category could only be spent on a prospective bride. Eventually he decided he would take her to the Berkeley. He was a member of the club there which for people under twenty-five was very good value. You could eat cheaply but well, and Bobby Harvey on the piano, sweating away as he sang his heart out, was guaranteed to make the evening a success. He smiled contentedly as he turned over and drifted into a dreamless sleep. How could he know that wheels were already in motion which would cause their evening to be not as perfect as he had planned.

'It's so terribly unfair.' Lainey was talking on the telephone to Vivien. 'Everyone knew that he had allocated the wedding dress to me and I was so thrilled that I was going to wear it. Now people will think dreadful things and my name will be mud. They'll think that I've behaved badly and been demoted.'

'No they won't, I'll make sure of that.' Vivien was indignant. 'What I don't understand, though, is that Candida wasn't even chosen to be one of the models. How is it now that she is not only in the show but modelling the star outfit?'

'She manged it somehow, just as she has managed to take away all my other outfits. Originally everyone was going to model three things. Now, because she's been added to the show, I've ended up with only two, and they're both ones I hadn't tried on before. They're not nearly as nice as the outfits I had to begin with.'

'I think that she's jealous as hell of you. I've noticed the the way she looks at Harry Wrightson. It's obvious she's bonkers about him and if that's clear to me it must be equally obvious to her that he fancies you rotten.'

'Viv, you are a tonic.' Lainey attempted a laugh which came out as a gulp.

'Hey, come on. Cheer up. It's not as if you weren't still in the show.'

'I know, but it's terribly disappointing. When I asked Monsieur Lefauvre he was very evasive and looked rather embarrassed.'

'Well, there you are.' Vivien was triumphant. 'Someone's put pressure on him. I'll bet it's that old cow of a mother of Candida's. Darling Candida wanted to be in the show and model the wedding dress, so Mummy, as chairman of the committee, saw to it that she did.'

255

'Oh, she wouldn't do that, I'm sure. No, I think that for some reason he just changed his mind.'

'Don't be so sure,' came the tart reply. 'Anyway, you go in there wearing whatever he gives you and make quite certain that you steal the show.'

'I could try, I suppose, but at the moment I feel like chucking the whole thing in.'

'Whatever you do, don't do that. If you do, then Candida wins hands down. She's not bad-looking but she doesn't hold a candle next to you in terms of sex-appeal or charm.'

'You really are good for my battered ego, Viv.'

'Well, it's true. Now, what are you doing today?'

'Nothing. I was going to a lunch and a tea party, but I cancelled them.'

'Whatever for?'

'I didn't feel like coping with all the whispers when I walked in. I'm sure that Candida hasn't wasted any time telling everybody about her good fortune.'

'Don't be so silly.' Vivien spoke crossly. 'You're going to have to deal with her sooner or later.'

'Yes, but tomorrow it'll be stale news and I'll have gathered myself together.'

'Well, do so if you must, but for heaven's sake go out tonight if you can.'

'Goodness, I completely forgot. I told Harry Wrightson I'd have dinner with him. Oh dear, he's the last person I want to see while I'm feeling like this.'

'Nonsense, of course you must have dinner with him. He is the best person there is to cheer you up tonight. Not only is he dashing and frightfully handsome and titled, but ninety per cent of the girls doing the Season – including Candida – have erotic dreams about him. Anyone that you run into will be madly envious. He's the perfect cure.'

'But he's so very smooth. I feel that I should be at my best to cope with him – and he takes out Candida, so heaven knows what he will have already heard by tonight.'

'Two fingers to Candida. All the more reason for going, and I'm sure that she won't have said anything to him. As I said before, she knows that he fancies you. She won't push her luck. Go. Have a wonderful time, and spend all evening thinking about how cross Candida will be when she finds out.'

'She won't find out. He's hardly likely to tell her.'

'She'll find out.'

'Viv, you wouldn't?'

'I don't know what you mean,' the reply came innocently back down the line.

'Viv, be fair.'

'All's fair in love and war.'

'For goodness' sake. I'm not in love. I hardly know the man. It's Candida who you seem to think is dewy-eyed for him.'

'Exactly, and for you it's war. You can't let her get the better of you. I thought you liked a challenge.'

'I do, but . . .'

'Go. Promise?'

'All right, if only to keep you quiet.'

'Good. Have fun, but remember that he's terribly fast and ever so NSIT.'

'What are you talking about?'

'Heavens, Lainey, don't you know anything? Not Safe in Taxis. Some of last years' girls compiled a list of NSITs and he was at the top.'

'He won't try it on with me.' Lainey felt herself blush as she remembered all too well the scene in the summer-house three years before.

'Don't be so sure.'

'I'll be OK. I can look after myself. Maybe what I need tonight is a good fight.'

'You might get more than you bargained for.'

Lainey laughed. 'Bye, Viv,' she said and put down the receiver. "Never," she thought. "Never again." Vivien didn't know about her episode with Harry. No one did except for Charlie, and she hardly ever saw him these days as he had stayed up at Cambridge this vacation, studying hard for his finals. She wished that he was here now. She had always been able to talk to him – much more so than to either of her parents. She let out a big sigh. He was coming down to London especially to see her in the dress show and now she wouldn't be the star.

"I miss you, Charlie," she told him silently as she prepared to go out.

'I've booked a table at the Berkeley,' Harry said as they sped along Piccadilly in his sports car.

'Oh, did you.' Lainey did not sound very keen.

'Don't you like it?' He was concerned. He wanted this evening to go well.

'I've never had dinner there,' she said dispiritedly. He looked at her quickly as he paused for the lights to change opposite Green Park. She was not her usual bubbly self. In fact, she had been very quiet ever since he had picked her up.

'Then it's time that you did. It's great fun and there are usually people there that one knows. Besides, I gather that you are the star of the dress show, so the sooner you become acquainted with its location the better.'

She did not reply. Something was wrong, Harry thought. Maybe she had had an argument with her parents, or maybe she was regretting having said that she would have dinner with him?

'Is something the matter?' he asked her tentatively.

For a moment it was as if she had not heard him, then she turned her head and gave him that wonderful smile of hers which never failed to make him catch his breath.

'No, Harry, nothing's wrong, and having dinner at the Berkeley will be lovely.'

*

The evening was progressing well and Lainey seemed to have recovered her good spirits. She ate well too – not like some girls, Harry thought, who just picked at their food and pushed the rest into a corner where they hoped that it would go unnoticed. It made a chap feel good when he saw that the meal he had spent his hard-earned cash on was being appreciated.

Strangely enough he felt that he could relax with her. There seemed to be no need for idle conversation, and yet there were no awkward pauses. Very different from last night with Grace.

When they got up to dance, he became aware of how graceful she was. The band was playing a rock-and-roll number. Harry prided himself on his ability as a dancer – well, he'd had enough practice, hadn't he? – but Lainey was just as good. She was as light as a feather and quite at home with the rhythm. No matter how much he twisted and turned her she never missed a beat. People turned to watch them, and Lainey's eyes began to sparkle. At last she had thrown off her glum mood and was thoroughly enjoying herself.

When they stopped a few people clapped, causing a vague pink tinge to come to her cheeks.

'That was fun,' she said breathlessly.

'You're very good.' Harry was impressed.

'Thank you.'

He liked the fact that she did not pretend false modesty.

'We must do this again,' he said, wondering what she would say.

'I'd like that.' She smiled at him, then he saw her stiffen as she looked towards the door. He looked up to see Cynthia Pugh, one of Candida Leach's great friends, walk in with a crowd of people.

From that moment onwards Lainey's mood reverted to its former dejection. When they danced again – this time to a slow number – he felt her tremble slightly. "It's not for me," he thought instinctively. "Something has been bothering her all evening. It left her for a while but now it's back, and it must be something to do with that lot over there."

When they returned to their table, she leaned forward and said, 'Harry, would you mind taking me home. I'm not feeling very well.'

'Of course.' It was an automatic response. He glanced furiously at Cynthia and her friends who were laughing and giggling loudly at their table. Somehow they had managed to ruin his evening. He was sure of it.

Harry was helping Lainey on with her coat in the foyer when a slightly tipsy Cynthia tripped towards the powder room. She stopped when she saw them.

'Hello there, you two. We saw you sitting tucked away in that corner.' She giggled, then turned her attention to Lainey. 'I hear you've been demoted. That's bad luck, but Candy's absolutely thrilled. I wonder why the Froggy changed his mind. Did you upset him?'

'Of course not,' Lainey snapped coldly. 'It's his show, so it's his prerogative, isn't it.'

Harry saw her discomfort. He took her arm protectively. 'Come on, Lainey, if we're going to the Four Hundred, let's get a move on.'

Lainey realized at once that he was trying to help her. She smiled up at him gratefully.

'It may be his prerogative, but . . .'

''Bye, Cynthia, I'm afraid that we really must go.' Harry propelled Lainey out of the door, leaving Cynthia staring after them with raised eyebrows.

'Do you mind telling me what that was all about?' he asked as he paused before starting the car up.

'It doesn't matter. It's not important.' She sounded depressed.

'It does matter. I'm incredibly nosey and my curiosity always has to be satisfied.' He kept his tone light. 'Besides,' he added, 'I heard enough to get it all wrong, and that would be far worse than telling me the truth, wouldn't it?'

'Oh, all right. I heard today that I'm not to model the bride's dress in the show. Candida is to do it.'

'Candida? I didn't know that she'd been selected to model at all.'

'She wasn't – not until today.' Lainey's tone was bitter. 'Now she's not only going to model the bride's dress, but she's been given my other two outfits as well. I've been given two new dresses that aren't nearly so nice.'

'I wonder how she managed that?' he mused.

'Oh dear, I shouldn't have told you. You're a friend of hers.' Lainey looked at him in the dim light which came from the street lamp outside. 'Please forget all about it. It's not important. I knew that it was a mistake to come out tonight when I felt a bit low.'

'I'm glad you came,' he said quietly. 'I'm just sorry that those idiots spoiled what was a very nice evening.'

He started the engine, then said recklessly: 'Well, now that it's off your chest, maybe we can continue to enjoy ourselves at the Four Hundred?'

'You don't have to do that, Harry.' She was embarrassed. 'I know that you were just being supportive when you suggested that in front of Cynthia.'

'I know that I don't have to.' He grinned at her. 'I want to, and you need cheering up. It wasn't a very nice thing to happen to you.' He put the car into gear and released the brake. His bank manager was going to write him another nasty letter about the state of his finances, but that was too bad. It would be worth it, if for no other reason than to see her smile.

Candida Leach had been delighted when Harry Wrightson telephoned her earlier that morning and asked her out for lunch. She was to meet him at the Stock Pot in Basil Street. It wasn't a very expensive place, but plenty of people whom she knew were guaranteed to be there, so word would get around.

He had said he wanted to see her as soon as possible. Well, she supposed she had that effect upon men. She had never lacked admirers, even when at school, and when she had been at that Swiss finishing school the ski instructor had got into terrible trouble for trying to take her out. Candida shivered with delight as she remembered the bronzed, athletic young man. On the ski slopes he had looked magnificent. She had been absolutely furious when the headmistress had found out about her intended night on the town and put a stop to it. When, however, Rudi had turned up out of the blue on her doorstep in London last March, her reaction had been dismay. Without his dashing ski clothes and skis, he had looked decidedly less-than-average. What a pity that he had chosen this time of year to come over, she had told him coldly, she was extremely busy and hadn't a free moment.

Harry Wrightson, though, was a very different proposition. He was terribly attractive and he had a title and a stately home. Of course his title wasn't quite as grand as her father's – he was an earl and Harry was only a baron – but it was better than the courtesy title she had that went with being the daughter of an earl. If she was to marry Harry she would become a baroness. Candida saw herself as the perfect wife for someone like Harry Wrightson. She was used to gracious living, having been brought up on a beautiful estate, and she would therefore be completely at home in such surroundings. She also wanted to make sure she continued to live in such surroundings. He must be interested in her, she thought. After all, he had given her that divine Hermes scarf for her birthday and kissed her in his car before that evening at his grandmother's. "Play your cards, right, my girl," she told herself, "and in time he can be yours."

She didn't really mind him taking out other girls at the moment. She wanted to play the field as well. She would become his confidante – someone with whom he could laugh and share private thoughts. It was usually that sort of person men turned to in the end. Of course, he must have heard by now that she was to be the star of the Berkeley Dress Show. That was probably why he was in a hurry to take her out. He wanted to get in quick with the girl who was tipped to become the 'Deb of the Year'.

Candida did not consider that she had any serious rivals for Harry's affections, though she had been a bit irritated when her friend Cynthia Pugh had told her she had seen Harry out with the doctor's daughter two nights ago. Apparently they had beat a hasty retreat when Cynthia and her party arrived at the restaurant. Good old Cyn had got one in about the dress show. Well, you had to show these *nouveaux* who was who, didn't you? Candida still firmly believed that people who were involved in the professions were 'in trade'. They didn't come from the right background, and after all that was what counted in the long run.

It was trying to drizzle when Candida left her parents' house in Cadogan Square. She hailed a taxi and gave a self-satisfied smile as she settled down. It was only a few minutes' ride. She could just as easily have hopped on a bus – or walked with an umbrella – but she was a great believer in style. With a man like Harry, style was all important – and besides, she had her own image to keep up.

So far the lunch had been a success – not that Candida had eaten much of it. She knew that she had to watch her weight. She had had to learn to live with her height, but she was determined not to end up like her mother who resembled a large ship in full sail.

After a young waitress had served them coffee, Harry leaned back in his chair and surveyed her from under his heavily lidded eyes.

'Well, Candida, you look positively radiant,' he observed. 'The Season is agreeing with you already. I hear that you are also to be the star of the Berkeley Dress Show.'

'Yes, I am.' She gave him what she hoped was a demure smile.

Suddenly he leaned forward with his elbows on the table and his hands clasped in front of him. 'Why is it you, now, instead of Alaina Carrington?'

For a moment he caught her off-guard and she looked thoroughly irritated, but she collected herself quickly and managed to put on a worried expression.

'I don't really know, Harry. It was a bit hard on Lainey, I suppose, but Monsieur Lefauvre must have reconsidered. There was nothing any of us could do. It is his show after all.' She lowered her eyes. 'I do feel sorry for her, but I am absolutely thrilled that he chose me.'

'That's not the way I heard it,' he said quietly.

'What do you mean?' She became wary.

'I spoke to Marcel Lefauvre yesterday and he gave me to understand that you had demanded the right to wear those clothes.'

'What are you talking about?' Her voice was beginning to rise.

'He told me that you almost threatened him. He doesn't want any bad publicity, so he felt that he had to agree.'

'How dare you meddle in things that don't concern you. The man's exaggerating. Surely you're not going to believe some stupid story he told you in order to justify changing his mind?'

'Oh, I think you and I know that he wasn't exaggerating, Candy.' Harry took a sip of his coffee and leaned back lazily in his chair. 'I've got to hand it to you, you're a real go-getter, aren't you? I admire that. I'm a bit like that myself.'

Candida looked at him doubtfully for a moment. Did he mean what he had just said, or was he deliberately baiting her? She decided on another tactic.

'I had to be in that show, Harry. The bloody little man didn't even pick me to be one of the models. I simply said that I thought he should, seeing that my mother was chairing the committee. He just went a bit overboard, that's all. I never expected to be given the wedding dress as well.'

"I'll bet," Harry thought. He smiled as he said: 'You don't have to make excuses to me, Candy. I wouldn't presume to pass judgement on you.'

'And you won't think badly of me?' She was worried.

'Of course I won't.' He patted her hand across the table.

She sighed with relief. That had been a close shave, but she had got away with it. It just went to prove how alike she and Harry were. They understood each other perfectly.

As the waitress refilled their coffee cups, he said: 'By the way, I heard something the other day that I thought you should know. I took that little Australian actress, Brenda Patterson, out to dinner a week or so ago, and she had been staying with your parents at Canningfield for the weekend for some charity ball. Well, it seems that your father was quite smitten with her, and apparently, since he and your mother now have separate bedrooms, he has been known on occasion – so the rumours go – to fool around.' He paused.

'Why are you telling me this?' Candida's face had gone green.

'If you allow me to continue, dear heart, you'll find out and be everlastingly indebted to me. Well, it so happened that your mother got up early on the Sunday morning and went to your father's room to ask him something. Needless to say, he was in bed with the luscious Brenda, who sat up clutching a sheet to her prize knockers and said, "Oh, Lady Berescombe, I didn't think you minded!" Poor dear Brenda.' He laughed as he continued. 'She's quite a simple girl really. There's not much up top – except for the knockers that is. She wants to become a serious actress, but I'm afraid that her figure is against her. Anyway, and this is the crunch, I told her that serious actresses could not afford to become mixed up in any scandals, and that meant she mustn't breathe a word of this to anyone in case it got into the papers.'

'Oh God,' Candida breathed. 'Sometimes Daddy's such a fool.'

'Don't worry, Candy.' Harry folded his arms and fixed her with a hard look across the table. 'I promise you that I'm the only one she has confided in, and I put the fear of God into her. Of course, I knew what a laughing stock it would make of your family if it hit the gossip columns.'

'You wouldn't ever say anything to anybody, would you, Harry?' She looked ill at the thought.

'How could you think that I would?' He leaned forward. 'And you won't wear the wedding dress, will you? Be in the show by all means, but tell Lefauvre that you don't want to wear that dress.'

'So that's what all this is about.' She stood up, trembling with anger. 'How do I know that you haven't made the whole thing up, just so that stupid Lainey Carrington can wear the best dress. What's the matter? Are you finally smitten? I don't think you know anything about my father.'

'Are you willing to try me, Candy?' He threw some money on the table and followed her outside.

'I hate you, Harry Wrightson.' She gave him a look of pure venom.

'No you don't.' He grinned and gave her a peck on the cheek. 'And I'm not smitten as you call it. You girls just have to be kept in order every so often. You can't always be allowed to have everything you want. It diminishes male superiority. Now be a good girl, Candy, and ring Lefauvre and tell him.'

'Don't call me Candy. Nobody does. And I'll get even with you for this.'

He raised his eyebrow. 'That should be interesting. Anyway, I'll come and watch you in the show, and if you're a good girl I'll take you out for dinner afterwards.'

'What on earth makes you think that I'd come?' She felt a shiver of excitement run through her.

'You will,' he said confidently as he started to walk away.

'Harry,' she called after him. 'Are you to be allowed always to get what you want?'

'Of course,' he called out without turning round and disappeared around the corner.

CHAPTER TEN

The day of the Berkeley Dress Show dawned at last. Marcel Lefauvre was up early in the morning checking that all the outfits were in order for his twelve models to wear. As soon as the workmen had finished positioning the catwalk, there was to be a rehearsal before lunch, leaving time for everyone to relax before the actual show started at four o'clock.

Marcel feasted his eyes on what he considered to be his perfect creation. It was the ivory silk wedding dress. He had heaved a merciful sigh of relief when the young Lord Wrightson had telephoned him and told him that everything would be fine. He had talked to the Lady Candida Leach and she no longer wished to wear the bride's dress. Marcel would be hearing from her soon. And so he had – that very evening.

Marcel smiled to himself as he recalled how the young Lord Wrightson had come to his hotel and asked to know why the girls had been switched. At first he had been loathe to confide in him as he hadn't wanted any trouble. This show in London was meant to be helping his career with good publicity, not hindering it.

Eventually, though, the young man's charm had got the better of him, and, because he was not happy with the thought of the Leach girl wearing his prize dress, he had admitted what had happened. Harry had listened quietly and then told him not to worry. He would sort it out. Marcel thought how wonderful it was to be young and in love – for it was obvious to him that the young man was crazy about the Carrington girl. Well, who wouldn't be? Marcel had felt breathless the first time he had seen her, and she had a rare innocence and natural confidence which suited his wedding dress so perfectly. But he had also been worried that Harry's ardour might stir up a hornets' nest.

It hadn't. Neither had it promoted a love affair, as Harry Wrighton had made him swear he would not divulge that Harry had had anything to do with this. Ah well, *c'est la vie*, and right now Marcel had more important things to worry about.

The show was progressing well. The audience, which was mostly women, was made up of débutantes and their mothers and friends. Marcel was pleased to see that many of them were making notes on their programmes when they liked a particular outfit. Good. That meant that he would probably sell quite a lot from his collection.

The photographer from the *Tatler* magazine was busy snapping away, and so were the rest of the press. But for every one picture that was taken of the models, at least three more must have been taken of people in the audience. Marcel smiled wryly to himself. Well at least some of the older women were wearing his clothes. His attention was caught by the flurry of someone arriving late. It was Harry Wrightson. He was too late for a seat, so stayed at the back of the room, lounging against the wall.

All too soon it was time for the finale. As Lainey stepped out in the ivory silk wedding dress an awed silence fell over the entire room. Lainey continued her graceful walk to the end of the catwalk. Two high spots of colour appeared on her cheeks and her brilliant blue eyes seemed misty. She paused at the end of the platform and smiled a gentle smile, then she lowered her eyes becomingly. The applause was deafening.

"I feel wonderful," she thought. "I've never felt so exhilarated in my life. I love wearing expensive clothes and I love knowing that people appreciate seeing them on me. If only this moment could go on for ever."

Slowly she turned towards the eleven other models who were filing out to join her. She raised her head and in that split second decided to do something completely unrehearsed. With one deft movement she threw her bouquet of spring flowers at the other girls where it was caught by a startled Candida. The press cameras flashed, recording Candida's look of surprise and Lainey's radiant smile. Marcel Lefauvre choked. What a performer she was. Had he read her wrong? Was she more worldly than she seemed? Suddenly he was aware of a hidden streak in the beautiful Alaina which he could not quite pinpoint. No one would shoot her down – least of all someone like the Lady Candida Leach.

As soon as the models had changed, they came to join their families. The Carrington table was near the main entrance, just in front of where Harry was standing. When Lainey appeared, she made her way through the room smiling at everyone who stopped her to congratulate her. Suddenly her eyes lit up and she broke into a run. Marcel followed her with his eyes as he stood talking to some enthusiastic ladies. *L'amour*, he thought. Lord Wrightson must be very proud of his lovely girlfriend. Suddenly he frowned. A tall serious young man wearing spectacles had stood up from the table directly in front of Harry. He held out his arms as Lainey rushed into them and swung her around in the air before setting her down and clasping her to him. After a few seconds he held her away from him, and as they smiled at each other there was such love in their eyes that Marcel felt a lump in his throat. It was plain to see, he thought, that this man was the love of her life, as she was his.

'Don't you agree, Monsieur Lefauvre?'

'*Pardon?*' Marcel tried to concentrate on the conversation around him.

'We wondered if you agreed.'

'Oh . . . er . . . *certainment.*' He had no idea what they were referring to.

'Really? I'm surprised to hear that.' One of the ladies he had been talking to looked quite put out.

'*Excusez-moi.*' Marcel extricated himself. 'I see someone I must speak with.'

He walked across the room to where Harry was standing.

'Lord Wrightson, I want to thank you for your help. It is due to you that my show has been such a great success.'

'My pleasure, Monsieur Lefauvre.' The younger man nodded his head. They both looked across to where Lainey was sitting chatting avidly with her friends.

'She is very beautiful. She has a certain . . . *je ne sais quoi.*' Marcel spoke almost to himself.

'I know what you mean,' Harry said quietly.

'Oh, *pardon.*' Marcel realized how the other man must be feeling. 'Love. It is very strange, *n'est ce pas?*'

Harry looked towards the table and then he threw back his head and laughed: 'That's not love, monsieur . . . well, it is of one kind. That's her half-brother who is studying to be a doctor. He goes back to Cambridge tomorrow, so I can't begrudge him an evening of her undivided attention, can I?' He patted the little Frenchman's arm and walked away. He stopped briefly at Lainey's table and said a few words. She smiled up at him prettily, and then returned her full attention to her brother. Was that a frown of irritation that crossed the Carrington boy's face as Harry stood there? Marcel sighed deeply as he had a sudden premonition.

"*Mon dieu,*" he thought. "*Quelle tragédie.*"

Harry sauntered up to Candida with a cynical smile on his face. She was surrounded by a group of giggling girls who were obviously teasing her about the wedding bouquet.

'Don't forget our dinner date,' he whispered in her ear. 'You were just perfect, Candy dear, but then I knew you would be.'

She gave him a set smile. 'I'm going to Laura Davenport's cocktail party first.'

'So am I.' His grin encompassed all the other girls. 'Wouldn't miss it for the world. If you look half as good as her mother when you are forty, you'll have nothing to worry about.' He winked at them, then turned and left the room.

*

William Hickey reproduced the photograph of Lainey and Candida as his leading story the next day. The caption underneath read:

Alaina Carrington the model bride throws her bouquet to her self-styled maids of honour at the Débutante Dress Show at the Berkeley Hotel yesterday. It was caught by Lady Candida Leach who is tipped to become the Deb of the Year. Watch out, Candida, you could have a serious contender in the beautiful Lainey, as she likes to be called.

By the end of April the dances had started, which meant it was no longer necessary for the young men to spend so much money on the girls. For the next three months there would be at least six dances a week and sometimes two on one night, with dinner parties arranged beforehand so that no one had to turn up alone.

Young eligible men were much in demand. Not all of them were well-off, but, as long as they were presentable and ex-public school, all they needed was a white tie and tail coat, a dinner jacket and a few evening shirts. They could survive on one good meal a day, courtesy of their hostesses, while drink flowed freely at the dances and sometimes there would be breakfast provided as well.

Lainey and Vivien were having a wonderful time. Both girls were very popular and never lacked for partners. In May they were both picked in the ballot to be maids of honour at Queen Charlotte's Ball. Queen Charlotte had been the wife of King George III and the story was that every year on her birthday she liked to have her maids of honour bring in her birthday cake to the strains of Handel's *Judas Maccabeus*. The ball, an annual event held at Grosvenor House Hotel, was a must for every débutante, and the chosen maids of honour would troop down the impressive staircase into the ballroom and process behind the massive cake as it was wheeled to the centre of the room – with all its candles blazing. There they would halt and on the given signal curtsey to the cake – a great honour indeed!

Lavinia Wrightson was pleased with her girls. They were all having a good time and doing her credit. She had also arranged to take them to the Derby and to Royal Ascot, both of which were 'absolute musts' on the social calendar.

Harry Wrightson had taken the day off work especially to go to the Derby, accompanied by his friend and racing mate Julian Fenner. It was always profitable going racing with Julian, he thought. His connections in the horse-world usually provided him with a few good long-shots, which – if they came in – made the day more than just socially worthwhile.

It was quite customary for young men to go racing together. That way they could survey the scene – women and horses – and agree to meet anyone who took their fancy in the bar for a Pimms after a given race, while having the certain escape route of needing to place bets on the next.

Today Harry was determined to concentrate on Grace Clover. The girl had expressed an interest in horses which made him think that talking to her might be easier in these surroundings. Julian was being a bit vague about his plans for the day, but Harry supposed he would gravitate towards one of the Bishop twins. He had noticed him in a tight clinch with one at the Burns' dance the night before. Difficult, that, he thought. How did you get one away from the other? And when you did, how did you know which one it was?

The best-laid plans can always go astray, as they did that day. Lavinia Wrightson had told her girls that, if they became split up, they should meet at one end of the members' enclosure just before the last race. Then she suggested that they go to the paddock to watch the horses parading before the first race.

Lainey looked at Vivien. 'I want to go the loo,' she said pointedly.

Vivien immediately took the hint. 'So do I,' she said. 'We'll catch you up.'

As they walked into the ladies' cloakroom Lainey grinned and spread her arms wide. 'Freedom,' she said theatrically.

'You are naughty. We'll probably never find them.'

'That is the idea, my dear Viv.' Lainey looked down at her friend from her greater height. 'I have no intention of spending the day in a group of five females with an elderly chaperone.'

'Just what do you intend doing then?'

'Finding someone frightfully glamorous to escort us.'

'I wish.'

'Think positive, Viv. Maybe Julian Fenner's here. You can't fool me. I know you're nuts about him.'

'Lainey!' Vivien blushed.

'Oh, your secret's safe with me – guide's honour.' Lainey held up three fingers and winked. 'Now, will you hurry up and have a widdle, then we won't have told a lie.'

As she pushed open the lavatory door, Vivien turned around. 'You were never a girl guide,' she accused.

'Yes I was. I went to one meeting. It was ghastly. I never went again.' Lainey disappeared into the next-door lavatory and bolted the door.

The sun was shining as the two girls walked towards the paddock. It was extremely crowded with people running in all directions. There was no possibility of getting anywhere near the ring, so they stopped for a moment to consider where they should make for instead.

'Hold on to your hat.' Lainey was gazing past Vivien. 'Guess who's coming our way?'

'Who?' Vivien turned around. Her eyes focused on two young men who were walking towards them. 'Oh my God!' she breathed. 'It's Julian – and he's with Harry Wrightson.'

'This is our lucky day, Viv. We're just about to bag us two of the most eligible escorts around. Everyone is going to be madly envious.'

Vivien wished that she felt as confident at that moment as Lainey did. 'At least they will have to stop and talk to us,' she told herself. 'If they don't, it will be awfully rude.'

'Hello, Harry. Julian.' Lainey smiled sweetly.

The two men stopped and raised their hats. As Harry looked down at Lainey, he was aware once more of her incredible beauty. He could never control his reactions when he was close to her. She seemed to have some strange effect on him.

Julian was trying to say something. Harry forced himself to concentrate.

'Would you both like to join us?' Julian's face was just the slightest bit pink as he spoke and he was looking at Vivien Hurst.

'I . . . yes, that would be lovely.' Vivien was trying her hardest to remain cool.

So that was it. Harry smiled to himself. Old Julian fancied the little Hurst girl. Well, she wasn't a bad looker and Daddio was doing very nicely – not that Julian need worry about money, he had plenty of his own. He turned back to Lainey. Julian and Vivien had already started to walk on ahead.

'It looks as if you are saddled with me.' He gave her his charming, slightly rueful smile.

'I could do worse.' Her eyes danced.

'So could I.' He looked at her admiringly. She was wearing an elegantly tailored red-linen suit and a white blouse covered with red polka dots. Her long slim legs were encased in the sheerest of stockings and on her feet she wore a pair of simple red court-shoes. She held a red handbag in her white-gloved hands. The whole outfit was off-set by a large picture hat in red with a single white silk rose pinned to the side of the crown.

She was also wearing her hair up. It was the first time that Harry had seen her without it falling over her shoulders, and it made her look much more sophisticated. He wasn't sure whether he liked that, but as he stood there he noticed the millions of other young girls with straggly hair poking out from beneath their hats. He sighed. She was right, of course. The rest looked a mess while she looked a million dollars.

'Ma'am.' He gave her a little bow and proffered his arm.

'Thank you, sir.' Her eyes sparkled as she smiled up at him and placed her hand on his sleeve.

From nowhere a flash bulb exploded. The next day Paul Tanfield's diary was to carry the picture with its write-up on Derby Day, informing the world that Lord Wrightson, one of England's most eligible bachelors, had escorted débutante Miss Alaina Carrington.

While they were watching the first race, Lainey asked Harry what happened on the other side of the race track.

'That's where the gypsies are,' he told her. 'They come from miles away just for Derby Day. There's a fairground and fortune-tellers over there. It's all very informal and fun.'

'I'd love to see it,' she said. She looked at him out of the corner of her eye. 'Would you take me, Harry?'

'Maybe, some day.'

'Not some day. Now.' She faced him, her eyes were very bright. 'Oh, come on, Harry. It would be an adventure – much more exciting than staying here.'

'I came to watch the racing.'

'Did you? Well, you can watch it just as well from the other side.'

'We haven't seen the big race yet.'

She waved her hand in the direction of Tote Investors. 'Place your bet now and let's go. Come on, Harry, don't be a stick-in-the-mud.'

'But we're all dressed up.'

'Snob.' She turned on her heel and started to walk away. 'Well, if you won't take me, I'll go on my own.' She knew that that would goad him.

'Wait.' He ran after her and grabbed her hand. 'You can't go over there on your own.' She looked up at him defiantly.

'Oh, all right then.' He pushed his way through the crowd, pulling her after him. 'But only for a short while.'

'Thanks, Harry. You're terrific,' she said contritely and squeezed his hand.

What had he been doing, Harry wondered afterwards. He had spent his valuable time at the Derby cavorting with a wild teenager on swings and roundabouts and the big wheel and he hadn't enjoyed himself so much for ages. Lainey had abandoned her hat and the pins which were holding her hair in place. Instead, as they went soaring through the air on the big wheel, her hair had fanned around her face like a misty haze. They had shared a large stick of candyfloss, and Harry had had a go on the shooting gallery and won a teddy bear which he proudly presented to Lainey. She in her turn had been to the fortune-teller – a real gypsy with gold-hoop earrings and a red kerchief – who told her that there was a tall dark stranger in her life and that she would be very successful. The afternoon had passed so quickly that when she rejoined Harry he had to remind her of the time, which was nearly five o'clock.

'Heavens!' She had put her hand to her mouth. 'I have to meet your grandmother in the members' enclosure before the last race.' With that she had produced two hairpins out of her pocket and deftly wound her thick hair into a knot and stuck them in, and then, firmly clamped her hat back on to her head.

'Ready,' she had announced and set off at a brisk pace.

Harry had smiled and shaken his head. The girl who was now well on the way to becoming 'Deb of the Year' was still an enigma to him. The press would have loved to have seen her that afternoon, but maybe it was just as well they hadn't.

By the time they walked back into the members' enclosure Lainey was once again the cool sophisticated young woman who had first arrived at the races that day.

*

277

That night she surprised him yet again. They found that they were in the same dinner party at a house in De Vere Gardens. After dinner, as the guests left the house to go to the Hyde Park Hotel, Lainey had glanced towards Kensington High Street and announced: 'Let's get the bus.'

The other girls had taken up the cry and started tripping up the road. After walking a few yards Lainey had turned around. 'Come on, you men,' she called. 'Don't be so stuffy. I know you're not, Harry Wrightson. Come and join us. You can get your car later.'

In the end the whole dinner party had boarded a number seventy-three bus much to the astonishment of its conductor and driver.

Lainey was setting the pattern for what were to become known as her wild and high-spirited antics. When she walked through a door everyone knew that it was going to be a good evening.

Once they arrived at the hotel Harry lost sight of her. That was just as well, he thought. He had spent most of the day with her and it would be best to circulate now. He could always find her later and they could have a nice slow dance when the lights had been turned down.

The Hyde Park Hotel's ballroom was on the first floor. He wandered up the stairs chatting to friends he met on the way. Candida Leach was standing at the top talking to a group of girls. Harry walked up behind her and slid an arm around her waist.

'Candy, darling, how about a dance?' he asked.

'I'd love it.' She smiled up at him sweetly as she slipped her arm through his. As she followed him, she threw a triumphant glance over her shoulder at the other girls.

Cynthia Pugh smiled back with just the right degree of reverence in her eyes. Without shifting her glance she spoke softly to the group around her.

'Candida already sees herself as the future Lady Wrightson,' she murmured.

'Lucky her. He's so handsome,' one of the girls sighed.

'She's not there yet.' It was said smugly. 'And rather her than me. By all accounts he behaves like a complete bastard to all his girlfriends.' There was a hint of malice in the voice of Candida Leach's best friend.

As they walked into the ballroom Harry noted that tonight it was Ian Stewart's band who were playing. The band-leader sat at the piano looking very distinguished with his grey hair and moustache. Harry took Candida in his arms. She was not the greatest dancer because of her height, but he had to admit she looked good. She knew it too, though. One of the maddening things about Candida was that whenever he danced with her she was always looking around the room to see who was there that she knew and who was watching her. But for the moment she was looking at him, her eyes nearly level with his due to her high-heeled shoes.

'Everyone's here tonight, aren't they?' she said.

'You should know, Candy dear. From your vantage point at the top of the stairs they must have all filed past you.' He gave her a cynical smile.

Candida felt a tingling in her spine. She looked at him alluringly. 'I'd call it advantageous,' she countered. 'You found me easily enough.'

He threw back his head and laughed. 'That's what I love about you, Candy. You're so modest and unassuming.'

'My dear Harry.' She was gazing at him intently now. 'We're two of a kind. You'd hate a meek little lamb, you'd be bored stiff. You like to indulge in a jolly good gossip and you thoroughly enjoy getting the better of people – look how you treated me over the dress show. I should hate you for that, but I don't. I find you a challenge, Harry, I like sparring with you. You could do worse, you know.'

'That sounds like a proposal.' He raised one eyebrow. 'Just what are you proposing, Candida?'

She stared at him unblinkingly. 'Nothing – yet. I'm having far too much fun and so I'm sure are you. But think about it, Harry.'

'Are you rich?' He loved being outrageous with her.

'Enough.' It was her turn to laugh now. 'I'm sure that's high on your list of priorities.' She drew away from him, indicating it was time to end their dance. 'Come on, I'm sure that you've got other fish to fry. I certainly have.'

It had taken all her strength of character to break away from him, but it was part of the game she was playing and the stakes were high. As they walked towards the bar she turned to him.

'By the way, I didn't see you at the Derby. Don't tell me you were too busy working?'

'I was there. I saw you in the distance,' he lied. 'You looked marvellous as usual.'

'How sweet of you to say so,' she simpered, as she was immediately whisked back on to the dance floor by another young man.

Later on Harry danced with Grace Clover. Tonight he was pleased at the girl's inability to converse as it gave him the chance to think over some of the things Candida had said to him. She had not made him out to be a very nice person, had she? He did not like Candida Leach, but she amused him. Did he really just like playing games with people? Was he really a male version of her? God, he hoped not. One thing he was certain of was that life with Candida would be a drag. He would rather be bored by someone like Grace. He shivered at the thoughts running through his mind, and felt Grace move a little closer. Heavens! The girl had feelings after all. He folded her right hand to his chest and slid his right hand down her back to her bottom, pressing her closer. He closed his eyes and a picture of Lainey on the big wheel came into his head. She was laughing and her hair was flying wild in the wind. A surge of exquisite excitement welled up inside him and he pressed the girl even closer, then felt her tense up and pull away. He blinked owlishly as the room came back into focus. Oh Lord, it was Grace he was dancing with, not Lainey. What had she thought? Had she felt his desire through that thin dress of hers? Obviously she had – she was blushing furiously.

'Come on, Gracie, let's get a drink.'

She broke her golden rule of drinking only fruit juice and asked for a Scotch. As he handed it to her, Harry noticed a familiar figure walking towards the stairs.

'Excuse me,' he said to the embarrassed girl. 'I'll be back in a minute.'

'Of course.' Grace's eyes were fixed on the floor.

Lainey was halfway down the stairs when Harry caught up with her.

'Are you going already?' He had noticed that she was carrying her evening bag. 'We haven't had a dance yet.'

She smiled at him. 'I'm very tired and it is one o'clock in the morning. I have to be up early as I'm doing this modelling course at Lori Lawley's.'

'One dance, and then I'll take you home.'

She shook her head. 'No, Harry. Really. I must go, and you don't have to take me home. I can easily get a taxi.'

'I insist.'

'But you don't even have your car.'

'Then I'll take you in a taxi.' He took her arm firmly and led her outside.

"Oh dear," she thought as she got in. "What have I let myself in for? I'm really much too tired for a struggle."

There was no struggle. From the minute that she settled herself in the taxi Lainey's eyelids fought a losing battle to stay open, and by the time the taxi reached Hyde Park Corner they were closed completely. Harry hardly dared to breathe as he put his arm around her, and her head fell gently on his shoulder. He looked down at her and was overcome by an extraordinary feeling of tenderness. How she affected him – this beautiful uncomplicated girl. She was not calculating like Candida or inhibited like Grace. She didn't play games – and neither did she want anything from him. Was that why he wanted something from her? If so, what

281

was it he wanted? He wanted to put his arms around her and hold her as he was doing now, but with her full approval. He wanted to feel proud of her as he had at the dress show when she had been the centre of attraction. For the first time in his life he had the feeling that he was out of his depth.

The taxi came to a halt outside the Carrington's flat. Lainey raised her head sleepily. 'I must have dozed off,' she said. 'I'm sorry that I wasn't very good company.'

'You're always good company.'

'Dear Harry, you're always so gallant.' It was said sincerely.

"I'm not at all, usually. It's you that makes me so," he thought, but dared not say it. Not wanting her to disappear into the hall he desperately searched for something else to say.

'Are you going to Ascot?' Somehow he would get another day off work and take her on Ladies' Day to the Gold Cup.

Her face lit up as she said, 'Oh yes, Charlie will be down from Cambridge and he's going to take me.'

Damnation, Harry thought. That bloody brother of hers. He had never particularly liked Charles Carrington at school. He had been too studious and moralistic, and Harry's crowd had thought him a bit of a drip.

'That'll be nice,' he responded automatically.

'Yes, I haven't seen him since April. I've missed him.'

She stood on the step, unsure of what to say next. Harry leaned forward and kissed her briefly on the cheek, while behind him the taxi waited with its meter ticking over.

'Night then. See you sooner than soon.'

'You're right.' She laughed and relaxed. 'Good night, Harry and thanks for bringing me home.' She unlocked the door and went inside, closing it behind her.

As Harry gave the driver the address in De Vere Gardens where he had to collect his car he again silently cursed Charlie Carrington. It would have been so enjoyable to have another whole day to spend with Lainey. In the dim dark recess of his mind he did not like to think of her spending too much time with any other man, even her brother. At this moment he felt totally frustrated. Well, there were places he could go to alleviate that. He paid off the taxi and let himself into his car.

In the morning he telephoned Grace Clover and asked her to accompany him to Ascot Races. The young lady had obviously recovered her cool. She replied politely that she would be delighted.

CHAPTER ELEVEN

The Season progressed steadily. Lainey was taken to the Fourth of June at Eton by a seemingly straight-laced up-tight Old-Etonian now enlisted in one of the Guards regiments. However, after a few drinks consumed while watching the cricket in the afternoon, the young man had shed his inhibitions, and later that evening during the firework display had tried to do a striptease. He had been forcibly restrained by several of his friends who had thrown him into the river.

Grace has been horrified when she was told about it.

'My, oh my. What did you do?' she asked.

'Do?' Lainey had giggled. 'It was so hot that I'd have joined him for two pins.' She registered Grace's disapproval and grinned. 'In the river, I mean, not going starkers.'

'You English can be very strange at times.' Grace did not have much sense of humour.

Lainey's eyes were full of devilment as she said, 'Oh we are. Do you know that I went to the dogs last night, Grace?'

'I beg your pardon?' Grace looked baffled.

'Yes, a whole crowd of us went greyhound racing at White City, and afterwards we went to the Hammersmith Palais de Dance. It's one of those old-fashioned dance halls where you have to know all the right steps and they take it frightfully seriously.' She paused dramatically and opened her eyes very wide. 'Do you know that Harry Wrightson and I were chucked out for going under twenty-five miles an hour?'

'I haven't got a clue what you're talking about, but it sounds real crazy.'

'It was. I've never laughed so much in my life. That Harry can be great fun when he lets himself go.'

'Well, I hope that he doesn't let himself go too much when he's with me,' Grace said tartly. 'He's asked me to go to Ascot with him.'

'Has he?' Lainey was surprised. Somehow she would not have thought that the gregarious Harry would be interested in the quiet American girl.

She discussed it with Vivien when she saw her later.

'Are you jealous?' Vivien asked.

'Good Lord no. He did ask me first – though I didn't tell her that.'

'Why on earth did you turn him down?'

'I'm going with Charlie.'

'For heaven's sake, Lainey. He's your brother. He wouldn't mind if you got a better offer.'

'There's no better offer.' Lainey's chin was set determinedly.

'Have you ever thought that Charlie might want to take someone else?'

'No. He wants to go with me.'

Vivien sighed. It was always the same with Lainey. Charlie came before anyone else – including her parents.

'What are you going to do when he gets married, Lainey? You can't hold on to him then.'

'That won't be for ages,' Lainey laughed. 'And I don't hold on to him, Viv. I just love being with him and we see each other so little these days. Surely you can understand that?'

"No, I can't," Vivien thought. "There's something too possessive in your relationship. You've got to make way for other people. You're not children anymore."

Lainey sat in front of her dressing table brushing her long shining hair. She swept it up on top of her head – she liked it that way because it made her look more sophisticated. The fashion at the moment was what was called a beehive, which entailed lots of back-combing and was very full. It reminded her of the paintings of the de Pompadours and was not very flattering. She much preferred a gentle updressed chignon, and fortunately she had the bone structure and figure to carry it off. If she took up modelling professionally that was how she would wear it. For the moment, however, she thought it better to let the white-gold cloud hang loose around her shoulders. It was the way it suited her best – hadn't Harry told her that not so long ago? Always believe a man.

She wandered over to the bathroom where she was running herself a steaming hot bath. It was only half-past six, so she had plenty of time to relax before tonight's dinner party which didn't begin until after eight.

She lay there, letting the bubbles of foam encompass her and inhaling the sweet aroma of Elizabeth Arden's 'Blue Grass'. She closed her eyes and allowed her mind to wander. The middle of July had arrived already, and next weekend was to be the highlight of hers and Vivien's Season. They were to share a dance to be held at Doves Place which was Vivien's home.

Alfie Hurst had insisted that their house should be the venue as it was bigger than Mattingham and could be easily adapted to accommodate a lot of people. Lainey smiled to herself as she thought of all the preparations that had been going on between her parents and the Hursts. Alfie was a wonderful organiser and had employed a great many people. There was to be a magnificent marquee on the lawn where the dancing would take place and there would be a bar at one end. Jennifer and Miriam were to be in charge of the flowers and they had discussed colour schemes for hours on end. All the guests were being organized into houseparties and dinner parties and the dance would begin at half-past ten.

The two families were each having their own dinner parties as they did not live far from each other, but the Carringtons had to be at the Hursts by ten o'clock. As Alison and Charlie were twenty-one, they were also included on the invitation. Charlie had asked some of his friends from

Cambridge and Alison had asked a few of her nursing friends.

Lainey ran some more hot water into her bath. Was she enjoying the Season so far? Yes, of course she was. She was popular and never lacked for partners, and had been invited to all the major social events. That day at the Derby when she had ended up going over to the heath and riding on the funfair with Harry had been particular fun. She sighed. She had wanted to dislike Harry. She had wanted to teach him a lesson for humiliating her at that Pony Club dance, but she couldn't help liking him. He was good-looking, dashing and not at all boring and they got on well together. He was also willing to disregard established conventions. That evening at the dog track and then at the dance hall had been hilarious. Yes, he was good fun. She wondered whether he found her attractive. So far he hadn't even tried to kiss her. Maybe he had meant it when he had told Charlie three years ago that she wasn't that great. Other men kissed her and held her very intimately when they danced with her, but not Harry Wrightson. What was the matter with her? She knew that he had quite a reputation with women, so he obviously didn't fancy her. She was just good old Lainey, the girl you had fun with between love affairs. It had irritated her to see him at Ascot with Grace Clover. Harry and Grace had gone with Julian Fenner and Vivien, and Viv had said that they had had a super time. Grace, apparently, had been quite talkative and Harry had laughed a lot and been most attentive. Lainey had said acidly at the time that he was probably after a rich wife.

Why had she been on the defensive, Lainey wondered. She certainly wasn't harbouring a secret passion for Harry Wrightson. No, it was the thought of Grace as an alternative to herself that had niggled. She would not have minded so much if it had been someone like Candida Leach. That she could have understood.

And what about Charlie? Had she enjoyed herself at Ascot

287

with him? He had arranged for them to join up with two of his undergraduate friends and their girlfriends, when she had thought she would have him to herself. More than once she had found her eyes straying to groups of her friends who were laughing and teasing each other while Charlie and his friends discussed subjects which were completely alien to her. But, yes, of course she had enjoyed herself. Being with Charlie was what mattered. She didn't see him nearly enough, but that would soon be different. In the autumn he would start at Guys Hospital in London, but for the moment he had the summer free. He would come to some of the dances and maybe they could go abroad together in August.

But Charlie had had other ideas about that. He had mentioned something about going to Cornwall with his friends and Alison and some other student nurses. 'Of course, you can come too,' he had said, 'but I'm sure you'd have more fun at all the parties which will be taking place in Scotland.'

'Why don't you come with me?' she had asked. 'We could have fun together. I never see you these days.'

'Lainey, Lainey.' He had put his arm around her shoulders and given her a little squeeze. 'We're so different – you and I. I want so little out of life and you demand so much – you can't be happy if you deny yourself.'

'I won't be happy if I never see you.' She had turned to face him and wound her arms around his neck. 'I adore you, brother mine. You mean more to me than anyone else in the whole world.'

'I adore you too.' She had felt him shiver slightly as he extracted himself from her clasp. 'But we're not children any more, Lainey. We both have separate lives to lead.'

'That's what Viv sort of said.'

'She's right, squirt.'

'You haven't called me that for years.' She had smiled at the memories. 'I used to hate it. I don't any more.'

'We've both grown up.'

'Yes,' she had said quietly, 'and now it's not allowed.'

'Lainey, I don't think . . .'

She cut him off with her next remark. 'I have been seeing quite a lot of Harry Wrightson, you know. I find him very attractive.'

'What? For God's sake, Lainey, you're not serious. The man's a shit!' She had felt a stab of excitement run through her. Charlie never swore, but she had known exactly how to provoke him.

'Oh, I don't know. He's very sexy,' she had goaded him.

'Don't talk like that. It's coarse.' He had looked worried. 'He's not a trustworthy person and I don't like to think of your associating with someone like that.'

'I think I'd make a rather good Lady Wrightson,' she had mused with a grin.

'Don't kid yourself,' he had replied acidly. 'Wrightson needs a very rich girl to help him keep up that estate of his. You don't come anywhere near the mark. He may find you attractive, but if you ever give yourself to him he'll treat you the same as he's treated all the others.'

'We'll see.' She had set her chin determinedly as an idea formed in her mind.

'What's that supposed to mean?'

'That we'll see if Harry treats me the same as all the others.'

'Lainey, you wouldn't?' He had sounded horrified.

She had given him a wide-eyed look and said: 'Go to bed with him? I don't know. Maybe.'

'I didn't know that my sister was a tart,' he had flashed at her.

'What do you want me to be, Charlie?' she had retorted angrily. 'A virgin until I go to my grave?'

'Don't be silly. You know what I mean. Nice girls aren't easy.'

'So now I'm easy, am I?' She had been furious. 'Tell me, Charlie, how many easy girls have you had?'

'It's different for a man.' He had had the grace to blush.

'But you don't respect them afterwards.'

'Why is it different? Girls have the same urges as men – you, as a doctor, should know that.'

'Lainey, you're my sister.' He had sounded bewildered. 'I love you and I don't want you to be hurt.'

After that the fight had gone of out of her. Her shoulders had sagged. 'I know,' she had replied, 'but I already am.' She had looked up at him then as she said, 'Why can we never have what we truly want?'

'Because it would be wrong,' he had whispered.

Lainey came back to earth as she heard her mother's voice calling up the stairs.

'You are going to be late if you lie in that bath any longer.'

'Coming.' She reached for her towel and stood up.

'You can be anything you want,' she told herself, as she began to rub herself dry. 'And you can have any man that you want. And you will. I promise you that you will.'

The day of Saturday July 11th dawned bright and clear. The Carrington house-guests were due to arrive after lunch. Charlie had not said a word when Lainey informed him she had invited Harry Wrightson to stay. She had also – rather perversely – invited Grace Clover. Altogether, there would be twelve people staying in the house including the family, and eight more local people would be coming to dinner.

The two sets of parents had taken a final look at the marquee at Doves Place that morning, and Jennifer and Miriam had given their flowers a final watering. The colour scheme was yellow and white, enlivened here and there by patches of orange and green which peppered the generous flower arrangements. Two large glass chandeliers hung from the central pole and a white trellis frame, draped with ivy, enclosed the dance floor at one end. A red carpet protected by a bright-coloured awning stretched from the French windows in the drawing room all the way to the tent, just in case of rain, but it did not look as if this would be needed.

The three girls had chosen their dresses specifically to

accompany the background decor. Lainey was to be in moss-green chiffon, the brown-haired Vivien had picked a pale-peach satin, while her darker sister, Alison, was to be in a strong shade of gold. All three dresses were very striking and, more importantly, very different from each other, so that each girl looked stunningly beautiful in her own way.

Outwardly the Carrington dinner party was going well. Only four people noticed any emotional undercurrents and none of them would have been able to say exactly what they were.

From the moment that Lainey walked into the room Harry Wrightson was transfixed. The beautiful green Grecian-style dress clung to her figure, suggesting everything yet showing nothing. Her thick hair had been swept back from her face and was held in place by two jewelled combs. Her skin was as smooth as alabaster and her beautiful face was delicately touched up with the minimum of make-up enhanced by a soft pink lipstick. To Harry she resembled a priceless porcelain figurine. She was something that he was afraid to touch yet wanted so badly.

Three people noticed his look and all interpreted it differently. The first – Charlie – thought: "Bastard. I can see you lusting after my sister. Well, you won't get her. I'll make sure of that."

The second – Grace – thought: "No one has ever looked at me like that. I wish he would. I know my mother has always told me you can't have everything in life – some people are beautiful and others are very rich, but it is usually the rich that win."

The third was Lainey herself, who thought: "Yes, there is something different about the way he looks at me. I do have a hold over him – maybe it's because he thinks I'm unobtainable. He's used to having anyone he wants, but not me. Well, I can have some fun with him, and I needn't worry about hurting him – he's good company but he doesn't have a heart."

*

Anthony and Jennifer Carrington sat at one of the tables in the marquee watching the young people on the dance floor. It was after midnight and the lights had been dimmed. Couples were swaying gently together, arms entwined.

'I'm so proud of her.' Tony looked over to where Lainey was dancing with Harry. 'They make a handsome couple, don't they?'

'You old matchmaker.' Jennifer patted his arm affectionately. 'She's only seventeen. She's got all the time in the world. I don't want her marrying too young.'

'Of course not,' he laughed. 'But he's a nice young man, isn't he?'

'He has been charming to me.' She thought for a minute, then added. 'I don't think Charlie is very taken with him, though.'

'Charlie wouldn't think anyone was good enough for his beloved little sister.'

'That's true. He's very protective and I'm sure that she listens to him far more than she does to us.'

'Yes, they get along a lot better than many brothers and sisters.' Tony paused. 'Do you think now we should tell them the truth?'

'No.' Jennifer spoke quickly. 'Don't let's ruin the close relationship that they have. If they found out that there was no blood tie, they might lose something – some feeling between them. Besides,' she added, 'you are her father far more than Alan ever was. You've brought her up and made her what she is today and she loves you. Much better to leave well alone.'

'Yes, I suppose you're right.'

'I know I'm right.' She spoke emphatically.

Tony shifted his glance once more and spotted Charlie who was dancing with Alison. 'What do you make of that?'

Jennifer followed his glance. 'I hope it works out,' she said. 'She's a lovely girl. She would be perfect for Charlie, and can you imagine having the Hursts for in-laws? How lucky could he be?'

'Now who's matchmaking?'

'I wouldn't dream of it.' She rose to the bait. 'They must sort themselves out, but wouldn't it be wonderful?' She put her arm through his. 'I can't imagine anything nicer.'

From the moment that Charlie Carrington had walked into her house that evening, Alison Hurst's expression had changed. From being just a nice-looking girl in a stylish dress, she had become suddenly radiant. Her eyes had lit up and a becoming blush had highlighted her normally sallow complexion, while her dark hair with its auburn lights — usually hidden under her nurse's cap — gleamed from the vigorous brushing it had received a few hours before.

Charlie had held her hands in his and told her that she looked lovely. What was lovely, Alison wondered. Compared with Lainey she was nothing, except that beauty, they said, was in the eye of the beholder. Well, that certainly helped, and so did the fact that the beautiful Lainey was Charlie's half-sister. Otherwise she Alison would have never stood a chance. She had been in love with Charlie ever since she could remember and throughout their childhood he had always been kind to her, even though she was only a girl. He was not handsome in the strict sense of the word but he was distinguished. He was tall and thin, scrupulously clean and tidy, and wore horn-rimmed glasses which suited him, just like his father.

The two families had always been very close and had spent a great deal of time together, yet Alison alone had appreciated the change in the relationship between Charlie and his sister as they grew older. When they had been children he and Lainey had been so very close and now she felt it was as if they had become wary of each other. She didn't quite understand it but, whatever it was, she Alison had been the one to benefit. She had become Charlie's confidante and they had grown much closer.

As she danced with him now in the semi-dark she thought

of the secret that they alone shared. It had happened when they were both eighteen, just after Charlie had passed his driving test and been given a rickety old car by his parents. He had driven over to Doves Place to see her on a hot summer day. To begin with he had merely leaned against the stable door while she fed and watered Vivien's pony in preparation for the commencement of her younger sister's school holidays. It was only when she had finished and was returning the buckets to the feed room that she had turned around to find him behind her, shutting the door. She remembered how she had caught her breath at his sudden proximity and watched helplessly as he took off his glasses and put them in his pocket. Then he had pulled her gently towards him and they had exchanged their very first kiss. His lips had felt warm and dry and his arms had seemed so strong and firm, yet there had been no feeling of claustrophobia like that she had experienced with other boys. She had felt totally at peace. As he let her go he had whispered, 'One day we're going to get married.'

She had just nodded – too overcome to speak.

Neither of them had ever mentioned that day to another living soul, but they knew. There were times, like tonight, when she could sense that something was bothering him, but she never pressed him and knew that he was grateful for that. She had noticed the looks that he had shot in his sister's direction for much of the evening and felt sure it was something to do with Lainey that was agitating him – though what it was, she couldn't imagine. Alison never thought nasty thoughts about anyone, but at that moment she felt she would like to shake Lainey Carrington for whatever she had done to upset Charlie.

The dance ended at three o'clock in the morning. As the final notes were played by the band, Harry, who was dancing with Grace, released her gently. She smiled shyly up at him and he smiled back. She was a nice girl – not the most talkative, but after the super-charged feelings he experienced from being around Lainey he found her company very restful. She was quiet and unassuming – "boring," said a voice deep down inside him.

"Nonsense." He squashed it. "Probably very easy to live with."

He looked across the marquee to where Lainey Carrington was standing laughing and talking to various friends who had come up to say good-bye. Blast her, he thought. What did a man have to do to get through to her? Why could he never say any of the things he wanted to when he was with her? What made him act with so much caution? She couldn't possibly be a long term proposition – she didn't have anything like the wherewithal to support a crumbling country estate – but there was some strange compulsion inside him to try and win her over, for however short an encounter. He did not question why.

He walked over to her, leaving Grace to get her coat.

'Lainey, it has been a lovely party.'

'Yes, hasn't it.' Her eyes were sparkling and her face was flushed.

Her brother Charlie was standing beside her with one of the co-hostesses. Harry registered his frosty glance. No love lost between us, he thought.

'Harry, will you drive me home?' Lainey fluttered her eyelids slightly.

Harry raised one eyebrow speculatively. She was flirting with him and she had never done that before. He saw a glower form on Charles Carrington's face. Stupid sod. Would he try to interfere? Well, he'd show him. He turned to Lainey and put his arm carelessly around her waist. 'Of course I will, *chérie*. Just tell me when you are ready.'

Why did he have this feeling that their remarks, although addressed to each other were really directed at Charlie?

'I'm ready now.' She smiled alluringly.

As they walked away she turned back and called to her brother, 'Don't forget Grace, will you, Charlie darling?'

Alison sighed as she watched the little scene. Most people had to cope with difficult mothers-in-law or predatory females of some kind. If she and Charlie were to have a future together, she was going to have to accept this strong emotional tie between him and his sister. He would never hear a word against her and it was not in Alison's nature to say one. All the same, she wondered, what was it between those two? Was she the only one who saw it, or was she being paranoid? What did they really want from each other?

'I'll get the car.' Harry took his keys out of his pocket.

'I'll come with you.'

'But it's in the middle of a field. You'll ruin that dress.'

'Well, I'll just have to hitch it up, won't I.'

They walked across the drive and down a path to the field gate. She paused for a minute as she surveyed the long grass.

'I'm going to get grass stains all over my satin shoes,' she observed.

'That's easy.' He grinned at her. 'I'll carry you.'

He swept her into his arms and set off across the field. Lainey laughed delightedly, and placed one arm around his neck. 'Am I heavy?'

'No, light as a feather.'

'How gallant you are, Harry.' She was teasing him.

'You always say that.'

'But it's true. I suppose you've had lots of practice.'

For some reason the remark stung him. He put her down and bent to open the door. In the fraction of a second that he was not observing her she looked towards the house. The figure of her brother was framed in the light from the open front door facing in their direction.

As Harry straightened up she flung her arms around him and hugged him impetuously. 'Oh Harry,' she cried. 'This has been the best day of my life.'

A current of desire ran through him as he pressed her to him, feeling his body harden. My God, how he wanted her and for once she seemed almost obtainable. And yet, frustratingly, there was nothing he could do. There were too many people around – he couldn't even kiss her without causing comment.

'Steady,' he said huskily. 'You might drive me to do something you could regret.' He unwound her arms and settled her into the car.

'Not you, Harry.' She smiled up at him trustingly. 'You've changed since I first met you. You're much nicer.'

"It's you who has changed me," he wanted to say, but kept quiet.

It was only when they were halfway home that she spoke again.

'Harry?' she asked. 'We've had great fun this year, haven't we? Will it continue after the Season is over?'

'Why shouldn't it?' His voice was terse.

'I just wondered. We've all done such crazy things. Will we still meet up and do them – the crowd of us?'

"I don't care about the crowd," he wanted to say. "I care about you."

God! That didn't sound like Harry Wrightson. He didn't care about girls, he just had fun with them. "Careful, Harry," he told himself. "Don't let her get to you. She could upset all your well-laid plans."

'I don't see why not,' he answered her question.

'I mean,' she pressed, 'when it's time for the next Season to begin, will you forget about us all and move on to the new crop?'

'You make it sound like a business.'

'Well, isn't it?'

'No. It's supposed to be fun.'

'Oh, it is.' She laid her head back against the seat as an enigmatic little smile hovered around her lips. Was there a hint of triumph in that smile, Harry wondered. He shook his head in confusion. She had so many different moods, she constantly baffled him.

When they reached her home she had changed again. As

she presented her cheek for the customary peck she had that familiar wide-eyed innocent look on her face.

'You won't forget me in years to come, will you?' She was serious. 'You'll always be my friend?'

'Of course.' He cleared his throat and tried to sound matter-of-fact.

'Wonderful.' She flashed him her radiant smile and ran down the corridor to her room.

Harry shook his head feeling more bewildered than ever. Forget her? Jesus, he wished he could! As for always being her friend. Didn't she know the effect that she had upon him? How could you just be friends with someone when you were attracted to them as much as he was to her?

It was five o'clock in the morning and Lainey could not sleep. Her throat was dry and she felt desperate for a drink. Eventually she got out of bed, wrapped her cotton dressing gown around her and tiptoed down to the bathroom at the end of the corridor where she swallowed two glasses of water. That was better. She wondered why her throat had felt so rough. She didn't drink alcohol so it couldn't be that. It must have been all the excitement.

She started to walk back towards her bedroom, and then stopped and listened as she thought she heard a noise. Footsteps were coming up the stairs. She heard a cough – Charlie. She would know that cough anywhere. Instinctively she looked around and noticed that she was standing outside Harry Wrightson's bedroom. Without quite knowing why, she put her hand on the doorknob, and then, as Charlie appeared at the top of the stairs, withdrew it in a quick little movement bound to attract attention.

'Lainey, what are you doing up at this time?'

'I wanted a glass of water.'

'In Wrightson's room?' His voice was very cold.

'No, silly, in the bathroom.' She fixed her eyes at a spot on the floor.

'Don't lie to me, Lainey. I saw your hand on that door handle.'

'I'm not lying.' She looked up at him defiantly.

'For God's sake, Lainey.' He grabbed her roughly by the arm and propelled her along the corridor to his room. He pushed her inside and shut the door behind him. 'Now, tell me, just what the hell is going on.'

'It's none of your business.'

'Yes it bloody well is. You're at home, Lainey. If you can't behave elsewhere, you can damn well behave here.'

'How dare you make assumptions about my behaviour. You have absolutely no reason to do so.'

'You have just given me one.' His face was white with rage. 'What do you think Mother and Father would think if they knew that their daughter was rushing around trying to creep in or out of young men's bedrooms?'

Lainey looked up in alarm. Surely he would not tell their parents? Oh, why had she started all this?

'You wouldn't do that,' she said shakily. 'It's not true.'

'Ah, you don't want to be found out, do you?'

'There's nothing to find out, so don't you go making trouble.' She wheeled round to face him. 'I don't presume to cast aspersions on your affair with Alison Hurst.'

'I'm not having an affair with Alison. I wouldn't dream of it.'

'My ever-so-noble brother who doesn't sleep with nice girls.' She was now thoroughly worked up. 'What do you do? Just pick on tarts like me?'

'Lainey, you're crazy. Don't do this.'

'Am I?' Her voice had risen an octave. 'I've had enough of your bloody self-righteous attitude. If I love someone, I intend to sleep with them whenever I want to. To my way of thinking, that's not being a tart.'

'If you love them you can marry them, and I'm sure you don't love Wrightson.'

'I don't want to get married, Charlie, but that doesn't stop me having all the feelings that you men get, does it? If it's not wrong for you, then it's not wrong for me.'

'Yes it is. You're a woman.'

'Bullshit, Charlie. You're a hypocrite.'

'Shut up. You'll wake the whole house.' He put a hand over her mouth. She bit him hard. 'Owch! You bitch.' Without thinking he slapped her hard across the face.

They stood there facing each other, trembling with emotion. Lainey's eyes were watering and Charlie could see the imprint of his hand on her reddening cheek.

'Oh God, Lainey,' he whispered. 'What are we doing to each other?'

With a sob she flung herself into his arms. She could feel the erratic beating of his heart as she pressed herself against him. His body responded too as she had subconsciously known that it would. She felt the strength of him through her thin dressing gown, then his arms went around her drawing her even closer. First he kissed her stinging cheek, tasting the salt of her tears as they ran down her face, then she turned her head slightly and his mouth met hers. Their lips parted, and suddenly they were kissing passionately with all the hunger of an emotion for so long denied. Lainey felt that if she died now of a heart attack it wouldn't matter. This was what she had always wanted – what she now knew that he wanted as well.

Eventually they drew apart.

'I love you, Charlie,' she said simply. 'There's never been anyone but you.'

He looked at her vacantly for a moment before stumbling away blindly and sinking on to the bed with his head in his hands.

'Oh my God,' he said brokenly. 'What have I done?'

'You haven't done anything.' She sat down beside him. 'We love each other. We always have, but we've only just acknowledged it.'

'Don't say that. You're my sister.'

'Half-sister,' she said gently.

'It doesn't matter. It's wrong. I feel so ashamed.'

'It can't be wrong to love each other.'

'It's the wrong kind of love, Lainey.' He lowered his voice to a whisper. 'It's a sin.'

'No.' She tried to put her arms around him, but he shook her off.

'Leave me alone, Lainey.' He pushed her away as he rushed over to the window and opened the curtains. He was breathing heavily and his hair was dishevelled. The grey light of dawn filtered through the window, giving the room a ghostly appearance. When he spoke his voice trembled slightly. 'Get out of here, Lainey. Go back to bed. We'll never speak of it again. It never happened.'

'But Charlie . . .'

'Out. Now.'

She walked to the door, then turned back. 'Just answer me one question – honestly – and I promise to do as you say.'

What is it?' He sighed with exasperation.

'Do you love me? . . . I mean – really love me?'

'Oh Lainey.' He could not stop himself from looking at her and she gasped as she saw the naked longing in his eyes. 'Must you extract the last drop of blood? Isn't it obvious?'

'Say it.' Suddenly it was terribly important that he must tell her.

He clenched his hands and lowered his head. 'I love you,' he whispered. 'God forgive me, but I do.'

'Thank you, darling Charlie,' she said humbly as she slipped out of the door and closed it quietly behind her.

By the time Lainey got up, Charlie had left the house. Her mother told her that he had gone over to the Hursts to help with the aftermath of the dance. As the afternoon passed by the house-guests left one by one, but still Charlie had not returned.

Later that evening Lainey and her parents had dinner on their own. It was a very quiet meal.

'I suppose it is a bit of an anti-climax now.' Tony smiled at his daughter and patted her hand in an understanding manner across the table.

'Yes, a bit.' She gave him a thin smile. 'But Charlie will be back soon and we'll have the summer together.'

'Oh, didn't he tell you?' Jennifer looked surprised. 'He's changed his plans. He's going to Spain with Alison and some of her nursing friends.'

'No. He didn't tell me.'

'Well, he knew you wouldn't want to go, darling. Anyway, you're going to Scotland for all the parties up there.'

Lainey picked at her food and as soon as she could she excused herself from the table on the pretext of being very tired.

'I think they've had a bit of a tiff.' Jennifer said, as her daughter disappeared from the room.

'They'll get over it,' Tony reassured her. 'They are very different. I think it's a marvel that they don't row more often.'

'Yes, it is really.' Jennifer laughed.

'It's just that she's growing up, and sometimes Charlie is over-protective and she resents it. And then, of course, there are times like now when he wants to go off without his little sister and she feels left out. Teething troubles, darling. It'll all come right. You'll see,' said Tony confidently.

CHAPTER TWELVE

The rest of the summer hurried by. Lainey went to Scotland and thoroughly enjoyed herself. She was taken to the Edinburgh Tattoo where she watched, fascinated, as the lone piper sounded the Last Post from the battlements of the castle. Then there were the Oban Games where she admired the Highland dancing and saw huge men tossing the caber. The final climax was the Skye Balls, which entailed two consecutive nights of non-stop dancing until dawn at a hotel in the small town of Portree on the Isle of Skye.

The Scottish dances were fun. They still practised the old-fashioned custom of issuing dance cards, and Lainey was gratified to find that hers was filled well before each evening had started. She quickly mastered the complicated reels and twirled her way through the movements with great pleasure and abandon.

Not all the débutantes had gone north for the Scottish Season – some had prefered to holiday in the sun. The Clovers had taken a villa in the South of France at Antibes and Grace had asked a few friends to join them – including Harry Wrightson, Julian Fenner and Vivien. Lainey had not been invited. She had shrugged her shoulders when she had learned about it and commented that it did not take a genius to know why she had not been included. In any event, looking back on it, she thought that Scotland had most probably been much more fun. Even staggering across a grouse moor on a rainy afternoon had its own kind of charm and these Scots certainly didn't stint themselves when it came to providing mouth-watering meals.

Yes, it had been a fabulous month. As she sat in the train heading back to London she wondered whether Charlie had

had as good a time. Funny, she hadn't thought about him at all while she was away. She felt slightly guilty. Well, he had told her not to, hadn't he? She sighed as she thought back to the Monday morning after her dance. As she had drawn back the curtains in her bedroom she had seen him outside packing things into his car. She had dressed hurriedly and run downstairs and out into the yard.

'Charlie,' she had called. 'You didn't come back for supper last night.'

'No.' He had straightened up as he had replied. 'I stayed at the Hursts.'

'Was Alison still there?' She had sounded accusing.

'Yes, she was.'

'You like her very much, don't you, Charlie?'

'Yes, I do.' He seemed nervous.

'Charlie, I'm so sorry about Saturday night. It was all my fault. I wanted to make you jealous.' She had had to tell him.

'Don't, Lainey.' He had turned away from her. 'It's not all your fault. It's mine too.'

'I don't want to lose you. I couldn't bear it.'

'You won't lose me. Lainey.' He had taken off his glasses and rubbed his right eye in a gesture just like their father. 'You're my sister – I'm your brother – remember?'

'I can't help but remember, can I?' She had sounded bitter.

'Lainey, we agreed . . .'

'I know. I know. I promised to forget the whole incident, but don't shut me out.' She had put out her hand to touch his arm but he had flinched before she could do so. 'We will still be friends like we used to be, won't we?'

'It'll take time, Lainey.' He had sighed deeply. 'At the moment we need to be away from each other. I must lead my life and I see now that you must lead yours.'

'Will I see you when you are working in London?'

'Of course you will. I'll come to the flat to see you and Mum and Dad.'

'Is that all? No more heart to hearts? No days out together?'

'Not for the moment – maybe later.'

'I see.'

'No, you don't.' His voice had been low and firm. 'You should, but you don't. Think about it, Lainey. Give us both a chance to find our own happiness.'

She had set her chin determinedly. 'Happiness is being with someone you love, or so I always thought.'

'Lainey, oh Lainey.' He shook his head sadly. 'You have to learn to let go.'

'I don't want to,' she had whispered.

'I know, but you must.' He had jumped into his car and started the engine. 'You must, for both our sakes.'

The train slowed down as it approached King's Cross station. Lainey stood up and lifted her suitcase from the overhead rack. Back to the real world. Back to starting her professional modelling career. Back to more parties in the mini-Season which stretched until Christmas. And back to Charlie.

"It'll be all right," she told herself. "We'll go back to being just like we were before, and one day he'll see that I was right and that it's not wrong to care."

As she stood in the long queue for taxis she wondered how things would have been if he hadn't been her brother. Well, there wouldn't have been a problem, would there? That was the trouble, wasn't it? She never really thought of him as a brother – more of a step-brother. Wouldn't that make everything easy? She sighed. But he wasn't a step-brother, she knew that. He was a half-brother and the Bible said that was a sin. Incest. She shivered. It hadn't felt in any way incestuous – if it had, she wouldn't have wanted it, would she? Why did she want something that was so wildly unobtainable? Was it that to love Charlie was safe – he was a blood relation and would never abandon her, whatever she did or said? He had always come to her defence and she was sure that he always would. Why did she want more?

"You can't have him," she told herself. "You'd better resign yourself to that."

A little voice inside her whispered so softly that she could hardly hear it: "There's no such word as can't."

It was in October that the invitation was issued. It came from the committee who ran the International Débutantes Ball in New York City and said that they would very much like the Lady Candida Leach and Miss Alaina Carrington to be their guests for two weeks at the end of December and beginning of January 1960 and to represent Great Britain at the ball.

Lainey was thrilled. Even the thought of going with Candida did not deter her. In fact Candida had been quite friendly lately. It had been established that she and Lainey shared the honour of being named 'Deb of the Year' and a shared honour was better than no honour. Now Candida acted as if they had a bond which no-one else had been worthy of. They were the best and the best should stick together.

The two girls were to fly via Frankfurt where they would board a Lufthansa plane to New York, as Lufthansa was one of the many sponsors of the event. They left on Boxing Day so that they would have time to recover from the time difference. It promised to be quite an adventure.

A chauffeur-driven car met the girls in New York and whisked them straight to the apartment of the chairman of the International Committee. The driver told them that he would wait and then take them on to where they would be staying.

Mrs Margadol breezed into her spacious living room and viewed her two latest arrivals critically. The committee always insisted that the girls who represented their countries and states should be beautiful and it was a policy which she heartily endorsed. She smiled as she held out her hand to the two English girls. They were both gorgeous – just what the

Americans would be expecting. And, in addition, one of them had a title.

'I'm so glad that you are here, dears.' She smiled fondly at them. 'I know that you're going to have a fabulous time. I thought that you'd like to be together, so I've arranged for you both to stay with Mrs Prebble. She's Senator Prebble's wife, you know,' Janie Margadol gushed. 'He's from Maine. Mrs Prebble joined our Committee this year as she is organising her granddaughter's début. It will be nice for you to meet Mary-Beth and then she can help introduce you around. Of course, she doesn't live with them – her mother died a year or so ago and she lives with her father on Park Avenue – but she spends a lot of time at her grandmother's apartment in Seventy-Third Street.'

They were then introduced to the two girls that Janie Margadol had staying with her. The first was a German baroness and the second an Italian contessa. Neither of them spoke very fluent English, but they smiled and nodded and were able to converse at great length with each other.

When they were eventually allowed to leave Candida and Alaina collapsed into the car, bursting with laughter.

'I don't think that we were smart enough to be allowed to stay in her apartment,' Candida giggled.

'I think you're right.' Lainey agreed. 'It was "Contessa this" and "Baroness that" all the time, wasn't it?'

'Do you think the Senator's wife will be the same?'

'Probably. And if she's a grandmother she must be old. I just hope that she doesn't impose a curfew on us every night.'

'She'd better not try,' Candida grinned. 'I, for one, intend to have a whale of a time while I'm here.'

'So do I.'

Fortunately for the two girls, there was very little similarity between Janie Margadol and Karen Prebble. Karen thought Janie a typical Committee lady, and found her gushing manner slightly irritating. But then one had to put up with these people, for they were the organisers and did all the hard work. There were the people on committees who 'did' and there were the people who 'sat', and Janie Margadol was one of the doers while Karen Prebble sat. Karen was quick to acknowledge that Janie was essential, however irritating she could be.

She had been flattered to be asked to have two of the international girls to stay. She would have preferred to have had the Italian girl instead of the second English girl, but Janie was such a snob that she had taken her before anyone else had had a chance. Still, the two English girls had been voted joint 'Debs of the Year' so they were obviously well-to-do, and they would be nice friends for Mary-Beth. In fact, she could hear them chatting with her granddaughter now, as they had arrived just a moment earlier.

She decided to give them a few more minutes to get acquainted before she walked into her living room. Both strangers stood up. How well-mannered the English were.

'How do you do.' Karen held out her hand. 'I'm Karen Prebble. I'm so glad that you could come. Which of you is Candida?'

'I am.' Candida took the hand and gave her a sunny smile.

"How big she is," Karen thought. "She must easily be six feet tall. She makes the other girl look so delicate. How lovely the other one is. She looks vaguely familiar, but I can't think why.'

She turned to her granddaughter. 'Mary-Beth, dear, I have to go out, so why don't you show the girls their room and make sure they have everything they need. I'm sure they'll want to have a rest after their long tiring journey. Why don't you come back and have dinner with us later. Your grandfather will be here and he'd love to see you.'

'Oh, I can't Gran. I'm sorry. Daddy and I are having dinner with Linda.'

Karen clicked her teeth in exasperation. Linda was a

young widow who was a buyer in one of the larger department stores. Alan had recently started to go out and he was seeing Linda quite often.

'I'm sure that they wouldn't mind at all if you came here instead.'

'Gran, I'd love to, but I can't.' The young girl touched her grandmother's arm gently. 'You see, Linda asked me especially. It's her birthday and we're celebrating.' She turned to Lainey and Candida. 'But I'll come by in the morning with my friend Jeannie, and perhaps you'd like us to show you some of the sights?'

The next two days passed very quickly. On the Sunday the two American girls kept their promise and trailed Lainey and Candida around the city, pausing briefly for a delicious hamburger lunch at P. J. Clark's. That afternoon a tea-dance was held at one of the big hotels – the social round had begun.

On the Monday morning they were woken up early by the Prebbles' maid and taken to the airport. There they were joined by the German baroness and the Italian contessa, and were asked to pose on the steps of a Lufthansa aircraft while the press snapped away. The pictures appeared in the papers later that day.

That evening there was a large cocktail party at the Plaza Hotel. It was very crowded and Lainey found that her head was beginning to ache from the heat and the smoky atmosphere. She tried to concentrate on making polite conversation to the admiring young men who surrounded her, but after an hour she began to wish desperately that she could get out and breathe some fresh air. She made a feeble excuse and walked towards the door, leaving three baffled young men looking after her. As she slipped outside they all agreed that English girls were strange – beautiful, but very strange.

The enormous foyer was busy. As she walked towards the

main entrance Lainey wondered what she should do with herself. She couldn't very well go back to the Prebbles' apartment even though they had given her a key. It would be tantamount to admitting she had failed to be invited out to dinner. Suddenly she heard her name being called. She turned around to see Mary-Beth standing a few feet away talking to a tall thin young man wearing glasses. For an instant her heart lurched as she thought it was Charlie, but as she walked over to them she realized the similarity was not really that strong. His build was the same and the fact that he wore the glasses, but he wasn't nearly so handsome as her beloved brother.

Mary-Beth introduced them, 'This is Jimmy Foxton. Jimmy, this is Lainey Carrington, whom I told you about.'

'Hi there.' He smiled down at her. 'You're even prettier than Mary-Beth said you were.'

'Thank you.' She smiled back at him. No, he wasn't handsome, she thought, but he looked interesting, and as she shook his hand she noticed he had long sensitive fingers.

'Jimmy's a musician,' Mary-Beth volunteered. 'He's studying music at Harvard.'

So that explained it. Only musicians and doctors had hands like that.

At that moment Candida appeared escorted by two swains. When she saw Lainey she whispered something to her escorts and then ran over to her friend.

'They wanted to take me out to dinner,' she giggled. 'I said that I would hate to upset one of them, so they both decided to take me.' She glanced at Lainey. 'What are you doing? Why don't you join us and even up the numbers? They want to go to the Colony for dinner and then on to El Morocco's to dance. It should be a riot.'

Lainey hesitated. The combination of the headache and then seeing this man who had reminded her so much of Charlie had dampened her party mood.

Mary-Beth saw her indecision. 'Lainey's coming with us,'

she said. 'Jimmy promised his cousin Phil that we would join up with him for dinner and so she is going to even up our numbers for us, aren't you, Lainey?'

'OK. See you later – much later.' Candida winked and rejoined her faithful admirers.

'You will come, won't you?'

'Well, if you're sure.'

'Of course we're sure.' Jimmy patted her shoulder. 'I'll go and call the terrible Phil and get him to join us.' He walked off in the direction of a telephone.

'I thought you said . . .' Lainey looked at Mary-Beth accusingly.

'Sure I did. You wouldn't have come otherwise,' Mary-Beth grinned at her.

'But you might have wanted a cosy evening together.'

'Not at all. We've known each other for ages – we can have plenty of those in the future.'

'Oh!'

'Jimmy and I have known each other since we were at school. He helped me through the time when Mom died. We're going to get married one day, but at the moment he has to finish Harvard, and Grandmother is insistent that I make my début.'

'Is he going with you to the International Ball tomorrow?'

'Yes. He's my civil escort. We're allowed to pick those for ourselves – unless we come from miles away like you foreigners. The military one gets provided though. You'll see how it all happens at the rehearsal tomorrow morning.'

'It sounds hilarious,' Lainey laughed.

'I'm sure it will be.'

'Mary-Beth, do you mind being parted from Jimmy so often?'

'Yes and no.' The other girl smiled softly. 'I talk to him all the time and we trust each other completely.'

'It must be wonderful to be like that.'

'It'll happen for you too.'

'What'll happen?' Jimmy had sneaked up behind them.

'Lainey will find someone great like you.'

'Mary-Beth's biased.' He ruffled her dark curly hair affectionately. 'Well, people, let's get going. Phil's meeting us in the village in twenty minutes.'

'This is really going to help your education,' Mary-Beth laughed. 'It's very informal and Bohemian. I believe you have an area similar in London called Chelsea. We're a bit overdressed tonight, but it doesn't matter.'

Afterwards Lainey thought that evening had been one of the most pleasurable she had spent in America. She found herself very drawn towards Mary-Beth Jefferson. The girl was natural and friendly and they felt an immediate empathy together, though in many ways they were very different. Mary-Beth was not quite as tall as Lainey, and even though both girls had thick healthy hair one had bouncing brunette curls while the other had long straight white-blonde tresses. Both had brilliant blue eyes.

In character too there were similarities and differences. Lainey was ambitious to achieve and would never be happy in second place, while Mary-Beth was a home-maker. The height of her ambition was for Jimmy to be successful in the musical career he wanted so badly. Lainey was also the extrovert and Mary-Beth was inclined to be quieter. But after spending two evenings together – the second of which was spent at Small's Paradise in Harlem where they all danced rock 'n' roll and jive – Jimmy announced that it was like being with two sides of one person.

'You even look a bit alike,' he asserted. 'If it wasn't for the dramatic difference in your colouring, I could believe that you were sisters.'

'Idiot.' The girls laughed light-heartedly, but they were secretly pleased.

The day of the International Débutantes Ball was something that Lainey would never forget. It was to be held at the

Astor Hotel and the rehearsal took place in the morning. Each girl was allocated two escorts – a civilian escort, either of her choice or else selected by the Committee, and a military escort provided from the naval college at Annapolis. When she had been announced she would take the arm of her civilian escort while her military escort carried the flag of her country or state, and walk between the two young men to the centre of the grand ballroom to make her curtsey to Society. Meanwhile, the orchestra led by Tony Cabot would play appropriate music. As at Queen Charlotte's Ball in London, all the girls had to wear white and all the civilian men white-tie and tails. Decorations were also to be worn. The naval cadets would of course come in their dress uniforms.

The rehearsal was fun. They all met their naval escorts for the first time and the girls from abroad met their civilian escorts – if they had not met them already at one of the parties given in their honour during the previous two days. After having a quick lunch in various small groups, they all went their own ways to hairdressers and then to spend a quiet hour or so relaxing before the big night.

It was a beautiful evening. The Astor Hotel which was situated on Broadway and Forty-Fourth Street provided a perfect setting. Tables of eight or more had been placed around the dance floor, and the receiving line had been called for eight o'clock while dinner was at nine. After this there would be the presentations, and once these were over it would be on with the dance.

The foreign girls and their escorts had all been put on the same table to make them feel more at home. Mary-Beth was at the Prebbles' table with Jimmy and her father and Linda and several other young people. Alan Jefferson was feeling very proud of his daughter. She looked lovely in her simple but beautiful white dress. Her face was flushed with excitement and her brilliant blue eyes sparkled with happiness. Alan didn't really like big social gatherings, but he wouldn't have missed this for the world.

313

The presentations were inclined to drag on a bit and he did not concentrate very hard on all the girls who came forward. Pretty teenagers dressed in white were inclined to look very similar. Linda noticed that his attention was wandering and put her hand on his arm before it was Mary-Beth's turn. Alan smiled at her gratefully. He lifted his head and watched proudly as his daughter walked gracefully in on Jimmy's arm. She was representing the state of Massachussetts where Alan's family originally came from. She made a perfect curtsey and his heart swelled with pride. He swallowed a lump which had formed in his throat and blinked rapidly as he felt a smarting in his eyes. How different from her mother she was. Rosemary should have been like this, but instead she had been poisoned by her unreasonable jealousy and suspicions. Thank goodness Mary-Beth was emotionally stable, and not only was she a beauty – most important of all – she had found a kind and decent man who loved her. There was no doubt in Alan's mind that Jimmy Foxton was the right man for her. Of couse, they were both very young yet, but they were being sensible. Their love would last – of that he was sure.

For a second he felt a gnawing sense of loss. Why had it been ordained that he should never have this? Why had the beautiful girl he had married been forced to suffer the way she had? Why had he had to meet the love of his life – for that was how he thought of Jenny – when it was too late? Jenny, oh Jenny, what has happened to you? Who did you marry? Are you happy now? Is it just me who can't get rid of this empty feeling? For a second he felt the sensation of being very close to her, yet he knew it was ridiculous. She was thousands of miles away in the peaceful English countryside. In his mind she would never grow old. She would always remain a young girl in her early twenties.

'She was great, wasn't she?' He was brought back to earth by Linda's voice.

'Yes, I was very proud.'

The presentations were over. Alan stood up as Mary-Beth came rushing back to their table.

'Sweetheart, you were wonderful. I'm very proud of you.' He gave her a quick hug.

'Thanks, Daddy.' She smiled up at him. 'I was real nervous.'

'You certainly didn't look it, did she, Linda?'

'Certainly not.' Linda kissed her on the cheek.

Alan looked on approvingly. "They get on so well," he thought. "She's such a nice woman, I'm lucky to have her for a friend. If I ever marry again it should be Linda."

It was later in the evening that he saw her. He felt his eyes drawn to her as if by a magnet. She was the loveliest young girl he had ever seen, sitting at a table across the room surrounded by young people, yet seeming oblivious to them all. There was a far-away expression in her eyes and she was gazing at someone or something behind him. Alan couldn't turn around because he was dancing with Linda and the dance floor was very crowded. As he stared at her he saw a look of raw yearning transform the beautiful face and he drew in his breath sharply. What or who could have caused an expression of such abject misery in one so young?

'Are you all right, Alan?' Linda had noticed him falter.

'Sorry, I'm not the best dancer in the world.'

'I think you're just fine.'

He sighed and glanced back to the girl. She was chatting quite animatedly now with the people at her table. Had he imagined it? No, it had definitely been there, that look of despair. She covered it well, that's all. He had a sudden strange feeling that he knew her, but that must be nonsense for he would never forget a face like that. Maybe, it was just that he recognised what she had been feeling.

As he left the hotel, Alan knew that he could never ask Linda to marry him. It wouldn't be fair. He was still in love with Jenny and he could not settle for second-best.

*

Lainey hugged herself as she lay in bed after the ball. It had been a very glamorous evening and she had enjoyed every minute of it – except for a brief moment when she had seen Mary-Beth and Jimmy dancing. They had looked so happy and very much in love, and for an instant she had felt an unbearable pain. This girl, whom she liked so much after knowing her for such a short time, was so lucky to have a man like Charlie to love her, and for her it was acceptable when for Lainey it would never be all right. They were alike in so many ways – she and Mary-Beth – and yet Mary-Beth could have her Jimmy and she, Lainey, could never have Charlie. Would she ever come to terms with that fact? Oh Lord, it didn't bear thinking about. She'd better go to sleep. Sleep cleared most things, and tomorrow would be a new day.

The rest of the time in America was spent in a whirl of ever increasing social activities culminating in a weekend at Annapolis where the girls had been asked to a naval ball. Lainey and Candida enjoyed it all thoroughly. They were very popular with the cadets and never lacked for partners.

They were due back in New York on the following Monday as there was to be another charity ball on the Tuesday, then they would fly back to England on the Wednesday.

'You know, I really wouldn't mind living over here,' Candida confided in Lainey on the Sunday morning. 'The Americans are so friendly and generous. They put Englishmen to shame.'

'I thought you told me that you could never give up your English lifestyle?' Lainey reminded her.

'I know, I did, but I've changed my mind.' Candida's eyes lit up. 'American men are much more courteous. They put someone like Harry Wrightson to shame. People like him think that having a title and a crumbling estate means that you should feel honoured to be asked out by them. Well, I've got news for him now.'

'He's always been OK with me.' Lainey had decided to forget about the incident three and half years ago.

'That's because you were never romantically involved with him,' Candida said smugly.

'Did you have a big thing with him?' Lainey knew that there had been something between them.

'Yes, for at least two months at the beginning of the Season.' Candida gave her a superior smile. 'But I got bored, so I told him to take a flying jump.'

This was not true but it sounded good just saying it, and Lainey was not to know.

'Well he seems to be consoling himself with Grace Clover,' Lainey grinned.

'Yes. I wonder if she'll land him.'

'I wouldn't have thought he was ready to settle down.'

'Who said anything about settling down? My father's been married for twenty-three years and he still makes a fool of himself with his women.'

Lainey looked up at the bitterness in Candida's voice. She felt awkward. What should she say? 'I'm sorry,' she said softly.

'Yes, well . . .' Candida gave a brittle laugh. 'My mother's resigned to it. She ignores it – pretends it doesn't happen.'

'Perhaps she loves him.'

'Then she's a fool.' Candida tossed her head defiantly and walked over to the dressing table. She started to brush her hair forcefully. 'I'm never going to put myself in that position. When I get married, it's going to be to someone well-off who will lead the sort of life I want and give me the things that I want. Love won't play a large part. As long as we like each other and get along, that'll be more than enough.'

'I don't think I could settle for that.'

'Beauty won't necessarily bring you happiness, Lainey.' It was not said spitefully. 'In fact, it usually attracts the wrong kind of people with the wrong ideas. I think that we've already found that out. We start by wanting everything, but if we're clever we should decide early on to settle for the most that we can get.'

Lainey didn't answer. She started dressing while she digested what Candida had just said. It was funny how sharing a room with someone for two weeks could change your view of them. Poor Candida. Outwardly she appeared to have everything. She seemed confident and self-assured, but she wasn't really, was she? Lainey felt that somewhere along the line Candida had been hurt deeply – by her parents perhaps? She had acquired a tough veneer to combat whatever it was she had learnt. Was she right to think the way she did? No. And yet . . .? You couldn't have everything could you? She, Lainey, knew that. She was going to have to learn to settle for second-best – whatever that might prove to be. Suddenly, she felt an overwhelming longing for Charlie – just to talk to him, to know that she hadn't lost him completely. In the distance she heard the telephone ringing.

'Lainey, it's for you.' Candida held out the receiver.

'Goodness! I wonder who on earth . . .' Lainey ran across the room.

'Hello . . . hello?' The telephone crackled in her ear.

A voice said: 'Long distance calling Miss Alaina Carrington.'

'This is she.' She put her hand over the receiver as she looked at Candida. 'I think it's home. I wonder what they want.'

'Please hold,' the voice continued. 'I'm connecting you now.'

And then she heard his voice: 'Lainey, is that you?'

Her heart started to beat violently as her face lit up. 'Charlie! This must be mental telepathy. I was just thinking about you. How did you find me?'

'That number you telegraphed us from New York. They told me where you were. Lainey, darling, you'd better sit down – if you aren't already.'

She heard the catch in his voice. 'What's wrong?' She sat on the bed.

'It's Dad. He's had a heart attack . . .'

'Oh God, is he . . .?'

'No, but it's touch and go. Can you come home immediately?'

'Yes, of course.' Lainey felt numb with shock.

'Cable me your flight number and I'll meet you.'

'Yes, I will.' She replaced the receiver.

'What's happened?' Candida sat down beside her.

'It's my father. He's had a heart attack.' Lainey stared in front of her. 'A bad one. I have to leave at once.'

'Oh Lainey, how awful. Is there anything I can do?'

'Yes, please. I'm going to try and get a flight from Washington, so would you tell the Prebbles as I don't think that I could talk to anyone at the moment. I'll write to them as soon as I can.' Lainey's voice broke and the tears began to fall.

'Of course I will.' Candida put her arm around Lainey's shaking shoulders. 'And I'll bring the rest of your luggage back with me.'

'Thanks, Candida.' Lainey tried to smile at her. She picked up the telephone. 'And now I'd better call the airport.'

Charlie was waiting for her as she walked through customs at London Airport the next morning. One look at his face was enough to tell her what had happened. She collapsed sobbing into his arms as he held her tightly. His cheek was next to hers and his tears mingled with hers. 'He died late last night,' he whispered.

'Oh no.' She couldn't stop the crying as the tears rained down her face, blinding her.

Charlie stroked her back and held her tighter. 'You cry all you want,' he said. 'Let it come out. It's the best thing to do.'

The busy airport bustled around them and passengers did not give them a second glance. They were used to such scenes as drama played a large part in airport life. Partings and reconciliations – they could both be emotional.

As they sat in Charlie's car and drove to Mattingham, she said, 'I never said good-bye.'

Charlie took one hand off the wheel and entwined his fingers with hers.

'It's all right, Lainey.' He squeezed her hand. 'I'm sure that he knows.'

'Charlie, I don't know how I'm going to get through the next few days.'

'We'll manage, Lainey darling. We have to. We have to be strong for Mother.'

'What would I do without you?' She attempted a weak smile.

'You won't ever have to.' Still his hand was clasping hers. 'You're my sister. I realize now that whatever happens I can't cut you out of my life.'

For a moment her heart soared, then it sank again. Did he realize that he had called her darling twice in the last twenty-four hours? Did he realize the implications of what he had just said?

"Oh Charlie," she thought and sighed. "Did it really have to take this to bring us close again?"

CHAPTER THIRTEEN

Tony's death had shocked Jennifer profoundly. Even though he was eighteen years her senior, he had only been fifty-eight when he died. He had worked too hard – she had often told him that, but he had been so dedicated and had been healthy all his life. It seemed impossible that out of the blue he had been struck down by a massive heart attack and died the same day. She was going to miss him dreadfully.

Why was it that it always rained at funerals, she wondered after it was all over. It had been depressing enough without the addition of grey skies, a bitterly cold wind and that driving rain, but thank goodness for the children. Lainey and Charlie had sat on either side of her in the little country church and the Hurst family had been behind them. She was lucky to have them all. They had been a tower of strength to her.

The church had been packed – not only with friends, but with many of Tony's professional colleagues. He had been very well respected and his obituary in *The Times* had been a fitting tribute to a wonderful man.

He had been a wonderful man, Jennifer thought as she sat at her desk trying to sort through all his papers. He had loved her and the children so much and had worked so hard for them. They had done him credit – Charlie and Lainey. Charlie was clever and conscientious and had always enjoyed a wonderful rapport with his father who had been delighted when Charlie decided to become a doctor. Lainey had also always been her father's girl. Yes, Tony had always thought of her as his, and she had almost been more of a daughter to him than to Jennifer. She had always been able to wrap him around her little finger. Jennifer smiled to herself. It was said, wasn't it, that mothers and sons were especially close as were fathers and daughters? It was true, but strange in their case, as she was not Charlie's mother and Tony was not Lainey's real father – but only she knew that now.

What would she do now? She was forty years of age and already twice widowed. Tony's solicitor had informed her that she had been left financially secure. She had smiled sadly when he had told her. Dear Tony, he had always thought ahead and it was typical of him to have made provision for his family in case of an untimely death.

She was not a town person, and now that she would not have to accompany her husband to business functions she knew that she would sell the London flat. She would be far happier living at Mattingham where the Hursts were not far away and she could see more of Miriam.

Alfie had offered the ultimate solution to the only problem that had worried her. He had informed her that he was in the process of buying a little mews house just off Eaton Square for Vivien and Alison to share until they got married. However, Alison would hardly ever be there as most of the time she lived in the nurses' home, and so Vivien needed someone to share with her. The timing was perfect, and as Vivien and Lainey got on so well together it was obvious they must become flatmates.

Within a month of the funeral, Lainey moved into the pretty little house in Ebury Mews. Upstairs it had two bedrooms and a bathroom and downstairs there was a light and pretty living room, a kitchen and a cloakroom. French windows from the living room led to a small paved patio where they planted an assortment of spring flowers in two black-and-white wooden tubs.

Miriam had been responsible for the decor and Alfie had paid. Vivien took the larger bedroom which had room for two beds, so that she could share it with Alison on the odd occasion that might be necessary.

'From now on, you're on your own,' Alfie informed his younger daughter. 'It is important that you learn to understand the value of money. You must budget for all your expenses and, as long as you are both working, you should be able to live very well.'

Both girls were very excited and determined that this should be a great success. Vivien had just begun to work in her father's company. She was starting at the bottom and would work for a time in every department until she was thoroughly acquainted with all aspects of the business. She was very like her father in many ways. She shared his belief in his dream and was equally determined that Hurst and Lever should have a reputation for producing the best quality and the best value in their field. She knew that her father would not treat her preferentially and that if she was ever to have a place on the board she would have to earn it, but she had no compunction about doing just that.

Lainey also was beginning to build a reputation for herself as a model. She had started her professional career back in the autumn of the previous year and had been surprised at the number of jobs she was given. Because of her tall willowy figure she was in great demand for fashion shows. It was tiring work and not half as glamorous as she had thought it would be, but she loved most of the clothes she was given to wear and her extrovert personality delighted in the lights and music of the actual performances.

Fittings were the real killers though, as she had to stand for hours while outfits were pinned on her. Self-important designers would scream at her if she dared to rest a foot and she found that she was so tired at the end of the day it was an effort to go out in the evening. She started rationing herself to two nights a week.

She hardly ever saw Harry, but he too had changed his job and was busy running an expensive leather accessories shop which had recently opened in Bond Street. It was a new venture sponsored by Grace Clover's father. Lainey had smiled when she heard about it – Grace obviously had her tabs well fixed on Harry.

She saw Charlie on his free weekends when he was off-duty and could come home to keep their mother company. During those times it was almost like it used to be. They would go for long walks and talk about their work – he was doing his internship at one of the big London teaching hospitals and seemed to be exhausted whenever she saw him. He did not like the city – he never had. She knew that he would not be really happy until he qualified and was able to join a country practice.

Lainey was happy. She was becoming very successful and she was back in favour with her beloved brother. He had no spare time to form an attachment to anyone else, so for the next couple of years she could feel safe in the knowledge that she was his number one confidante, as she had been once before.

But there was a slight difference to how it used to be. This time there was a nagging feeling of impermanence – as if something would soon erupt.

It did, sooner than she had bargained for.

Lainey was over the moon. Marcel Lefauvre had asked her to fly to Paris to be one of the models in a charity fashion show which would be held at the Ritz Hotel at the end of April. She would arrive on a Monday and have two days of fittings before the show on the Wednesday evening, and would be back in England for the weekend.

She rang Charlie to tell him.

'That's wonderful. My international sister. You never stop. Are you coming home this weekend? If so, I'll drive you down. I want to discuss something with you.'

'Tell me now.' She wondered what it was.

'No, you'll have to wait.' He was being deliberately mysterious. 'I'll pick you up on Saturday morning at the usual time.'

'Pig, I hate you.'

'See you Saturday.'

Charlie seemed on edge when he picked up Lainey from Ebury Mews that weekend. He was not very talkative on the way down to Surrey, but as Lainey had had a busy week she was quite content to sit back and daydream.

She wondered idly what was bothering him, but she didn't ask as she knew he would tell her when he was ready. There was one doctor at the hospital with whom he found it very difficult to get along, so maybe they had had words? That would not be very like Charlie, and yet he did have a stubborn streak in him. He always stuck up for what he thought was right and fair. Could a personality clash result in Charlie having to leave that hospital? "Don't be silly," she told herself. "It needn't be anything like that. It's probably just some silly misunderstanding which can be sorted out in no time."

As they approached Mattingham village, Charlie turned the car in the opposite direction from their house. He drove to the edge of the woods and parked in a gateway.

'It's such a beautiful morning.' He smiled apprehensively at his sister. 'Let's go for a walk before going home.'

'Sure.' She smiled back at him. So now he wanted to tell her.

They climbed over the gate and set off down a path between the trees. At first he was silent, as if he wasn't sure how to begin, then as they reached a clearing he spoke: 'I'm engaged . . .'

'Engaged in what?'

'No, you've got it wrong. I'm engaged to be married. I proposed to Alison and she said yes.'

'What!'

He gave a nervous laugh. 'Well, aren't you going to congratulate me?'

Suddenly she felt as if the sun had gone in. She stumbled away from him and leaned against a gnarled oak tree. 'Why are you doing this?' she asked as she stared at the ground.

'I love her, Lainey, and she loves me. We're very well suited.'

'How can you say that?' She almost spat the words out as she turned her gaze on him. Her eyes were bright with unshed tears. 'How can you say that to me after what we both admitted to each other . . .'

'Lainey, you promised . . .' He looked anguished.

'I promised to forget it because you made me, but I can't – I don't want to. I love you and I know that you love me. You said that we needed time. You said that time healed, but it doesn't always. We can work it out, Charlie. I know we can.' She put a hand on his arm and felt him shiver at her touch. 'Meanwhile don't do something that you could regret for the rest of your life.'

'Lainey, there's nothing to work out.' He forced himself to take her hands in his. 'There can never be a you and me in that way – we know that. Alison's a wonderful girl. She's what I need – and you're wrong, I do love her. It's the right kind of love. It's gentle and it feels good.'

'She'll be second-best. You'll always feel for me – you know you will.'

'She won't be second-best, Lainey. She knows about you and me.'

'You've told her?' She was aghast. 'Everything?'

'No, not everything.' He blushed and his voice shook. 'Only that we are very close and that I love you a lot and that nothing will ever change that.'

'You've just changed it.'

'No, no, I haven't. You're my sister and I'll always love you.'

'It's not enough,' she whispered.

'It has to be.'

'Wait just a little while. You don't have to rush into this.'

'We've already told the parents.'

'I see.' Her voice was tight. 'I'm the last to know. Vivien didn't say a word.'

'She didn't know, Lainey. Alison's telling her now. This evening we're all going over to the Hursts to celebrate.'

'That's great!'

'Can't you try and be happy for me?'

She didn't answer.

Harry Wrightson glanced at his watch. He was cutting it rather fine, but if he ran he could still just catch the plane. He flung a tip at the porter, grabbed his suitcase and his briefcase and rushed into Heathrow's Terminal Two. Bloody traffic. He had a meeting in the bar at the Crillon scheduled for this morning, followed by a lunch and then a visit to a Paris trade show in the afternoon. George Clover would not be very pleased if he fucked up on his first important meetings with overseas clients.

There was a queue at the Air France desk but the flight number for the Paris plane was still showing. Thank God for that. He joined it, dropping his heavy suitcase with all the leather samples inside it on the floor. He took his copy of *The Times* from his jacket pocket and started to read the front page. Suddenly he felt himself being shoved from behind. He put out his hands to stop from falling and collided with a woman in front of him.

'What the hell?' He turned around to see a harassed porter who was sweating profusely as he unloaded an overburdened trolley.

'Sorry mate.' The man gave him an apologetic grin. 'It's like a mad house down here on a Monday morning.'

Harry nodded curtly and turned back to the woman. 'I'm so sorry. I couldn't help it . . . Good Lord, it's you! What are you doing here?'

'I might say the same to you.' The reply was cool.

"Oh no!" thought Lainey. "I would have to run into someone I know." She had not had much sleep over the past few weeks and was feeling decidedly off-colour. The news of Charlie's engagement had hit her hard and she had counteracted it in the only way she knew how. She had accepted every invitation that she received and had stayed out late and worked flat out as well. Her name had appeared in the gossip columns as having been at one or two particularly wild parties. She had known that Charlie would see it and that it would upset him. She'd show him. If he had felt guilty about his love for her, he could now feel guilty about the way she was behaving. Let him suffer as she was.

As always Harry felt the familiar feelings of excitement well up inside him. How long was it since he had seen her? It was before she went to America with Candida. Heavens! It was now late April. That was five months ago. He hadn't realized how much he had missed her.

She looked thin – too thin. Her lovely eyes were covered by a pair of very dark glasses and she wore practically no make-up. Her face was pale and there was a droop to her shoulders. Why was she so obviously depressed? Oh, of course, her father had died recently, hadn't he?

'Are you going to Paris?' he asked her.

'It looks like it, doesn't it?'

Why did she always manage to make him feel gauche? They had reached the desk. He took her ticket and handed it in with his. 'We might as well sit together, don't you think?'

'Fine.' She didn't appear too interested.

He would not be put off. He saw their luggage safely on to the conveyor belt, then took her arm and steered her across the departures hall.

'You didn't say why you were going to Paris?'

'Marcel Lefauvre has asked me to model for him at a gala at the Ritz Hotel on Wednesday.'

'That's wonderful. What an international girl you are.'

"Jesus! Was he going to talk just like Charlie as well?"

'Don't patronize me, Harry.'

'I wasn't.' He raised an eyebrow. He did not remember her being touchy like this. 'I meant it. I take my hat off to you. You've become a very successful lady.'

'I'm sorry, Harry.' She gave a deep sigh. 'It's not you. I'm very tired and I'm inclined to take it out on whoever's around at the time.'

'That's OK. Now, are we going to sit together or not?'

'Yes, of course, though I warn you I'm not very good company at the moment.'

When they had settled themselves into their seats he leaned across and put his hand over hers. 'I'm sorry about your father,' he said. 'You must miss him a hell of a lot.'

'Yes, I do.' He heard the catch in her voice.

'How's your brother?' He was making conversation.

'He's just got engaged to Vivien Hurst's sister.'

'Well, that must be marvellous news. You're all such friends, aren't you?'

'Yes, we are.' She didn't sound enthusiastic at all.

'She's a nurse, isn't she? It sounds like a perfect match.'

'They should have waited.' She said it bitterly. 'Daddy is barely cold in his grave.'

God, she was prickly. Harry spoke carefully. 'Sometimes a loved one can help to ease the pain. It was three or four months ago, wasn't it, Lainey? You can't mourn indefinitely.'

'I could have helped him if he'd let me.'

'Family can be too close on occasions.'

'How the hell would you know?'

'I have a step-father and two half-brothers and a half-sister. I know what it can be like sometimes.'

"No you don't," she thought. "You haven't got a clue. If you did, you'd be shocked – even a playboy like you would be shocked at what's between Charlie and me."

She changed the subject. 'Why are you on this plane?'

'I'm going to Paris on business for George Clover.'

'Oh yes, I heard that you were working for him now.'

She took off her dark glasses and he was shocked to see how drawn her face was. It looked all the more so because she had her hair tied back with a chiffon scarf. She must have noticed his expression for she chose that moment to pick up her handbag and excuse herself.

While she had gone, he looked at the luggage label on her make-up case. It said: Hôtel de la Tremoille, Rue de la Tremoille, Paris.

When she returned he saw that she had rouged her cheeks and applied some lipstick.

'Where are you staying?' he asked casually.

'They've put me at a place called the Hôtel de la Tremoille. It's very close to the Rue du Faubourg St. Honoré where Marcel has his salon.'

'What an extraordinary coincidence.' Harry threw back his head and laughed. 'That's where George has booked me.

'Maybe it's the best value in town.' It was the first time she had smiled the whole morning.

'Well, at least we can share a taxi.'

As they stood waiting for their luggage, Harry left her for a few minutes to find himself a telephone. First he telephoned the Hôtel de la Tremoille and made sure he could get a room, then he cancelled his reservation at the Crillon in Place de la Concorde, and lastly he left a message for his business associates that he would be a few minutes late.

CHAPTER FOURTEEN

Marcel Lefauvre was delighted that he had managed to get Alaina Carrington to come over to Paris for his show. It was to be a really big affair to which most of Paris Society had subscribed. It was indeed an honour that the charity's committee had voted to show his clothes. He would now be classified among the very top designers.

By bringing over Lainey he was – how did the English say it? – producing a rabbit out of the hat? She would be a great surprise to the audience. The Paris models were well-known for their sophistication, but this girl would bring with her a breath of fresh air with her cool roselike English beauty. They would love her.

It had been a late decison on his part. He had tried other girls in his lovely wedding creation and had not been satisfied. Then he remembered the haunting looks of the girl in the show he had staged the previous year in London. She would be just right. He had to have her. He had put through a call to Lori Lawley at once.

He had been told that Lainey was very booked up since she had started her professional modelling career, but of course for the chance to do a Paris show they were sure that something could be arranged. Marcel had smiled to himself. Another sign of his undoubted success.

He was going to put her in only three outfits – the most romantic dresses of his summer collection and of course, she would end the show in the bridal dress. Every man in the room would fall in love with her and every woman would see her daughter in the dress. Perfect. Mitzi, Suzy, Alys and the others would not be best pleased that the limelight would fall on a stranger – imported at that – but *c'est la vie*.

Marcel looked at the gold carriage-clock on the mantel-piece. It was almost midday. She should be here soon. He would have liked to fetch her from the airport, but there was still so much to do. Then again it was probably better that he hadn't. He didn't want to be seen making too much fuss of her, for it might promote bad feelings between her and the other girls.

And then she was there, walking through the door, and he knew how right he had been to choose her. She was a little thinner, maybe, and her face was paler, but that was most probably nerves concerning her first major assignment.

'Lainey, *chérie*.' He rushed forward and embraced her warmly on each cheek. 'You had a good journey? The hotel is all right?'

'Marcel, I'm so thrilled to be here.' She removed her dark glasses and gave him her brilliant smile. Goodness, he'd forgotten the colour of those incredible eyes. 'Everything's fine. I'm still gasping for breath at the beauty of Paris.'

'We must make sure that you have the time to see something of our city.' He smiled proudly. 'Now, you must meet Arlette.'

A tall thin woman stepped forward and nodded her head. Her sleek black hair was pinned in a severe bun on top of her head and she wore a very tailored black dress.

'Arlette is my head vendeuse.' Marcel continued. 'She has been with me for . . .'

'Long time,' the woman interrupted with a heavy accent. '*Elle est ravissante*,' she said quietly.

'We have much to do.' Marcel rubbed his hands together. 'But first we will go for a quick lunch so that you do not faint from exhaustion before your first fittings this afternoon.'

Lainey enjoyed her first day in Paris. The little restaurant that Marcel took her to for lunch was crowded and busy. It was a city in a hurry, she thought. Everything was bustling from the waiters inside to the people milling about on the pavements. Traffic drove at crazy speeds and drivers had little patience as horns blared and voices yelled veiled insults at fellow travellers when they were held up for longer than a few seconds.

Even though it was only the end of April, it was warm and sunny – so different from home where it had been raining when she left. It was easier to relax here away from all the people she knew. "I needed to get away," she told herself. "I couldn't face all those smiling faces telling me how happy they were for Charlie and Alison. Here, I won't be reminded. Here, everything is new and exciting and I intend to have fun. I want to see it all."

But how was she going to do that? She didn't know anyone in Paris, and Marcel had told her that he would be very tied up before the show. She sighed. Maybe it had been a lucky coincidence that Harry Wrightson had been on the plane, and an even greater one that he should be staying in the same hotel. Would he ask her out? Perhaps. Maybe he had business meetings every night? Not Harry. He wasn't that dedicated. He would want to live it up a bit while he was here. But maybe he had lots of friends here? He knew so many people he was bound to have people here that he would look up. Was she going to have to spend the next two nights alone in her hotel room?

"I don't want to be alone," she thought. "I don't want the time to think. I want to go out and do crazy things – with an attractive man at my side. Someone who's fun and who doesn't care. I don't want to care ever again."

But what did she want? Was it excitement? Paris was exciting, wasn't it? Was it happiness? She didn't think that she'd ever truly feel that again. Was it achievement? She was already learning that the more you achieved, the more you wanted. Was it sex? The idea made her cheeks redden slightly as she stood engrossed in her daydream while being pinned into one of the dresses. She felt a thrill of apprehension run up her spine. Maybe what she needed was a really good affair. She was eighteen years old and she didn't know anything, so maybe it was time she learned. But who with – Harry Wrightson? Why not? They wouldn't hurt each other. She gave a secret smile which made her look mysterious and alluring. How would she go about it? She would have to encourage him, wouldn't she? She had never done that. Was it too late?

And then again, he had never made a pass at her – not since that first meeting when she had been only fourteen. Did he find her unattractive? Nonsense. Her chin went up in a determined fashion. All women who presented themselves as ready for action with a man like him would be considered fair game. "I must be a bit more subtle than that," she thought. "I'm not going to be just anybody. I'm going to be the one he will remember. I'm going to be the best."

By the time the fittings were over, Lainey's spirits were restored. She had set herself another target and now, she must achieve it.

To compensate for not being able to entertain her for the next two evenings, Marcel had insisted on dropping her off at her hotel at the end of the afternoon. Lainey had assured him that she would be fine. She was very tired, she had insisted, and she needed an early night.

As he watched her walk gracefully past the doorman and into the hotel, Marcel had shaken his head. Such poise in one so young was unusual, but still he worried about her. He wanted her to have a good time during her first trip to Paris. Tomorrow he would make sure that someone was available to escort her for the evening.

The taxi drew away from the kerb then braked sharply as two other cars almost collided. The driver started yelling and gesticulating. Marcel sat back and prepared to wait. He glanced out of the window. A tall man was walking towards the hotel clutching a briefcase. There was something familiar

about him which made Marcel lean forward. As he drew
level the young man turned his head in the direction of the
shouting. "I know him," Marcel thought. The man grinned
at the disturbance, then hurried into the hotel.

It wasn't until he was paying off the taxi driver that it
came to Marcel. It had been Lord Wrightson he had just
seen – the same young man who had come to visit him while
he had been in London. He had been so in love with the
Carrington girl then. It had been written across his eyes – a
Frenchman could tell – but hadn't there been someone else?
Oh God, yes! It had been the half-brother, hadn't it? He,
Marcel, had seen the same look in her eyes when she had
looked at him – or had thought he did? He had had that
terrible premonition of disaster.

Well, thank goodness he had been wrong. So they were in
Paris together – the handsome Lord Wrightson and Alaina.
No wonder she didn't mind being left to her own devices.
She hadn't said a word, so she obviously didn't want it to be
known. Marcel smiled fondly. Who understood better than
the French? He would say nothing.

Lainey lay in the bath and let the water envelop her. There
was nothing like hot water to ease aches and pains, she
thought. Standing for hours on end having clothes pinned on
you was very tiring, especially after an early start and a long
journey. Should she telephone Harry and suggest that they
meet downstairs for a drink? Or should she go down to the
elegant reception room and sit there, hoping that he would
come in?

She was saved from making a decision when the telephone
rang. She hopped out of the bath and padded into the bedroom.

'It's Harry. How was your day?'

'Fine. How was yours?'

'Busy. Look, would you like to meet downstairs for a drink
in half an hour? I have to dine with a manufacturer at nine,
but I expect you're busy too.'

'Half an hour would be fine.' Damn! He would have to be doing something. She'd been silly to think otherwise.

She made herself up with extra care and wore a deceptively simple wool dress. She fluffed her hair out so that it framed her face – he liked that, didn't he?

He was waiting for her when she walked into the room. He smiled and stood up. 'You look lovely, Lainey, but then you always do.' He gave her cheek a peck. 'What will you have to drink?'

She gave him her famous shy smile. 'You flatter me.' She sat down. 'I'm exhausted, but after lounging in the bath I feel gloriously relaxed. I'll have a glass of wine, please.'

He raised his eyebrows. 'I didn't know that you drank alcohol?'

She sat back in her chair. 'It's the new me,' she stated. 'I'm in France now. I can't insult them, can I?'

'No, I suppose not.' He sounded amused. He summoned a waiter and gave him the order. 'What else is included in the new you?'

'Not too much.' She leaned forward and picked some nuts out of the bowl on the table. He could not help but be aware of the swell of her breasts through the soft fabric of her dress. He drew in his breath sharply. Did she have any idea how provocative she was being? She nibbled the nuts one at a time, savouring their taste, then pushed the bowl away. 'Don't let me eat anymore or I'll ruin my dinner.'

'Where are you going?' He couldn't stop himself from asking.

'Nowhere. I wanted an early night.'

'I wish I didn't have this business dinner. We could have painted the town together.'

'But you do, and I'm tired.' She rested her hand briefly on his arm.

Was she flirting with him, he wondered. She never had before. That's what had made her so different. He glanced at her sharply, but, no, her expression was serious and those eyes were wide and innocent.

336

'Maybe tomorrow, if you're free?'

'All right, but don't worry if it doesn't work out.'

"It bloody well better," Harry thought as he hailed a taxi. "To have her all to myself in a city like Paris is too good an opportunity to miss."

The concierge handed Lainey a note when she came back the following afternoon. It said: Meet you in the foyer at eight-thirty. Don't dress up. We're going to the Left Bank. Luv, Harry.

For a second she felt disappointed. So he wasn't going to wine and dine her at one of the chic Paris restaurants as he would someone like Grace Clover. She was good old Lainey with whom you had fun. Fairgrounds and dog tracks and now the Left Bank. He did not need to spend money on her as he didn't want to impress her. She was a chum, 'Oh well, Lainey,' she told herself. 'Forget your ideas about being a vamp. It just isn't your scene.'

How wrong could she have been? No other place could have beaten this for atmosphere. It was a warm evening and the many little pavement cafés were filled with students eating al fresco. At first they walked for what seemed like miles as they explored the area, then, at around ten o'clock, they chose a restaurant right on the river to eat at. Fairy lights decorated the outside and pairs of lovers wandered by, stopping occasionally to kiss as they leaned over the stone balustrade.

Lainey thought it was the most romantic setting that she had ever seen. Here she was on this warm evening with a highly attractive man, and yet it wasn't quite perfect. He should have been treating her like a lover too – not like one of the boys! What was wrong with her? Oh, she couldn't fault him. He treated her with the greatest respect. Wasn't that what she'd always wanted? It wasn't his fault that now she wanted something different. He didn't even know. "Well, what happens now?" she wondered. "How do I change

337

things?" She smiled at him tentatively. For the first time that evening she felt tongue-tied.

He noticed her sudden shyness. 'You look just like you did when I first met you four years ago,' he said.

'Do I?' That was very astute of him, she thought. She felt like it too.

'It's funny, isn't it. I thought you were eighteen then, and now you could be fourteen.'

'I was very naive then.'

"You still are, thank goodness," he thought.

'You were so lovely – even then. I'm afraid I made an awful idiot of myself.'

'I think I did as well.'

'Your brother Charles was livid. I thought he was going to slosh me.'

'Yes.' Her voice had become terse. Why did he have to mention Charlie on tonight of all nights?

'He doesn't like me. He never did at school.'

'You're very different.'

'Thank God.' He gave a dry laugh.

'Yes, thank God.'

He raised an eyebrow. 'I thought you were very close?'

'We are.'

'Are you pleased about . . .'

She interrupted him: 'Are you going to marry Grace Clover?'

'What?'

'Well, you work for her father and I gather that you take her out a lot.'

'That doesn't mean . . .'

'Do you love her?' She leaned towards him.

'No.' He felt decidedly warm. 'Lainey, what the devil . . .'

'But you might marry her?'

'I don't know.' He ran a hand through his dark hair. 'Lainey, what is this? The Spanish Inquisition?'

'Do you find her attractive?'

'She's OK. What's it to you?'

'Just curious. She's moderately attractive, you're not in love with her and yet you might marry her. Is it because you need a rich wife to keep up your estate?'

"Oh God," he thought. "I've really blown it. If she could ever have been interested in me, it'll never happen now."

'You make it sound so tacky,' he said quietly. 'You know it takes two to strike a bargain.'

'A bargain? Is that what it's called?'

'It could be that Grace would like to be an English Lady.'

'So you'd both sell yourselves?'

'I don't think of it like that. We get along. It would probably work.'

'You're probably right.' She sighed. 'It's better than being hurt.'

He was beginning to understand. 'Have you ever been in love, Lainey?'

'No, and I don't want to be – ever.'

'You may change your mind one day – women are notorious for that.'

'Never.' She was emphatic. She raised her eyes from the table. 'I'm sorry that I cross-questioned you. Thank you for being so honest.'

He gave her a cynical smile. 'That's a laugh. You thank me for making myself sound like a complete shit.'

'But you're not – not completely.' She grinned as her mood changed. 'You acknowledge what you are, Harry, and what you want. That's fair, isn't it?'

'You're a strange girl.' He shook his head.

'Do you find me attractive, Harry?'

'You know damn well that I do.'

'No, I don't. You could just be being gallant again. You've never even tried to kiss me in all the times that we've been out.'

'There are some girls that a man respects.'

'You didn't when I was fourteen.'

'For heaven's sake, Lainey, I thought you were much older. Are you never going to forget that night?'

'You told Charlie that I wasn't that great.' She looked down. 'Did you mean it?'

'Did he tell you that?' He felt anger welling up inside him.

'No, I overheard you.'

'I didn't mean it. I was feeling rather stupid and extremely cross with that sanctimonious brother of yours. Before I realised who you were, I thought that he was just plain jealous.'

She got up and walked quickly over to the balustrade. She leaned over and tried to regain her breath. Oh God, it had been there even then when she was fourteen – that feeling between Charlie and herself. He had felt it then, and she was feeling it now. Would they never stop hurting each other? Would she be able to console herself with someone like Harry? It wouldn't be a long-term affair as she didn't have Grace's assets, but here in Paris no one would know. It was time that she learned to be a woman.

'Lainey, what's the matter?' Harry was standing behind her.

'Hold me,' she whispered. 'I want you to hold me.'

She turned around to face him and he saw that her eyes were very bright. He stepped forward and took her in his arms. She was surprised at how comforting it felt as for a while they stood completely still and the world walked past them. No one thought lovers out of place in this city. She pressed herself closer and felt his body respond. A delicious thrill of desire ran through her. She moved her head ever so slightly and his lips found hers instantly. They were cool and dry and his breath smelled fresh. It started as a gentle kiss, but almost immediately became more passionate, and at one point they were hardly aware that they were two separate people. When eventually they drew apart, they were both amazed at the intensity of the feelings which had passed between them. Harry leaned against the stone balustrade and let out a long sigh. His arm was still around her and she rested her head on his shoulder.

'Do you have any idea how difficult it is going to be for me to stay in that hotel just down the corridor from you?' he said shakily.

'You don't have to,' she said softly. 'I want you to be with me.'

'Are you sure that's not just the wine talking?' He squeezed her shoulder gently.

'No, it's not.' She pulled away and stood facing him. 'I've never made love before, Harry, but I want to now. I need to. I need to find out what it's all about and I want you to teach me. We like each other and I think we understand each other. We find each other very attractive, don't we?'

'You must know that, after what's just happened.' His voice was hoarse.

'Well, what do you say?'

'It's not the most romantic offer I've ever had.' He gave her a rueful smile.

'But we don't want romance, do we? We don't either of us want to feel guilty. We can't hurt each other or anyone else. You need never worry that I would make things difficult for you when you have had enough, because we know that we're not in love.'

'I don't know what to say,' he stuttered. 'I don't want you to wake up tomorrow morning and regret this – neither do I want to disappoint you.' He felt his face redden.

'Dear Harry.' She threw her arms around his neck impulsively. 'The only way that you could possibly disappoint me is by refusing me. Don't turn out not to be the man I think you are.'

He gave a hollow laugh. 'I'm not a complete bastard, you know, despite what you may think.'

'I think that I'm going to enjoy making love with you.' She grabbed his hand and pulled him after her as she scanned the street for a passing taxi.

*

As they sat silently in a taxi on their way back to the Hôtel de la Tremoille, Harry wondered at this change of events. He should be over the moon that this girl who had bewitched him for so long and whom he had always felt was out of his reach, was now his for the taking. Had she been any other woman, he would not have hesitated for a second, but with Lainey it should be different. He did not feel that love between them should be casual in any way – even thinking that made him feel guilty. Having an affair with Lainey – he knew – would change his life. He was crazy about her. He'd never felt like this about anyone before, but he couldn't pick her up and then drop her. She'd got to him already and goodness knows how vulnerable he would be after they became lovers. And she'd just said that she wouldn't make things difficult for him when he'd had enough! How could he ever have enough of her?

He knew that he shouldn't start this. For some unknown reason he knew that he was going to get hurt, but how could he refuse her? To turn her down would be unthinkable – especially as he wanted her so much. "We men are very weak," he thought. "We like to think that we are the conquerors, but really we are the conquered."

He wanted Lainey Carrington – correction, he loved her. Oh God, what an admission! Therefore, he was willing to take her on any terms – and he would. The one thing he knew that he must not do was to reveal his true feelings for her. If he did, she would run a mile.

"I'll play it her way," he told himself. "Who knows, one day things might change."

From the moment that he entered her room Harry took charge. He undressed her quickly, feasting his eyes on her body as he did so, and then let her do the same to him. He pushed her gently back on to the bed and lay down beside her, kissing her eyes, her mouth, and then the pulse that beat in her throat, before fastening his lips on to each of her nipples in turn. He felt the shivers of desire run over her as all the while he stroked her soft skin. He knew that he couldn't keep this up for long. If he did, then everything would be over before it had started. He rolled over quickly and positioned himself over her. As he tried to push into her he met the expected resistance. He had never knowingly made love to a virgin before.

'Relax,' he whispered as he kissed her again. He pushed again, and her eyes flew open as she uttered a soft cry and he felt himself slide inside her. Oh the relief – the joy – of being part of her. He started to move. He hoped that he wasn't hurting her, but it was impossible to stop. Her arms were holding him tightly. Suddenly he felt her body responding to his rhythm as they moved together, faster and faster until he could contain himself no longer.

As he lay spent beside her he reached for her hand and entwined his fingers with hers. 'Forgive me if I hurt you. I couldn't help myself. You're so lovely.'

'You didn't hurt me.' She squeezed his hand.

'Next time, I promise you, will be much better. It won't all be over in a few seconds.'

'It was wonderful.' She turned her head and smiled at him. 'Can it get better?'

He smiled at her naivety. 'Much better. And better and better and better.' He put his arms around her and drew her close.

Harry awoke before Lainey and watched with pleasure as she slept. Her hair was tousled and the sheets which barely covered her nakedness were crumpled. To him she looked gloriously abandoned. What a remarkable girl she was and what an incredible night it had been. They had made love three times and he felt marvellous. As he had predicted it had been better each time. She was a quick learner and wanted to please him as much as he wished to please her. He leaned over now and kissed her gently on the mouth. Her eyes flickered open.

'Hello. How are you this morning?'

'Terrific.' She stretched her arms above her head making her breasts almost disappear.

'Don't do that or I'll have to ravish you all over again.'

She looked at her watch. 'You can't,' she said. 'I have to get up. I have a rehearsal this morning at the Ritz. Don't forget that the show's tonight.'

'And what if I won't let you get up?'

He made a grab for her, but she side-stepped him neatly and ran into the bathroom. She turned on the water and stepped into the shower. The next thing she knew he was there beside her.

'It's much more fun to shower together,' he said as he ran the soap over her body. 'Come here.' He caught her to him, their bodies slippery from the soap.

'Harry, I shall be late,' she protested weakly as the warm water gushed over them.

'This will only take a minute,' he whispered as his mouth closed on hers.

She felt his hardness between her legs. With one swift movement he lifted her off the ground and pushed himself into her. She felt the familiar thrill of excitement run through her as she gave herself up to his love-making.

'You beast,' she said afterwards as she walked back into the bedroom, a towel wound around her head. 'Now look what you've done. My hair's soaking wet. What am I going to do?'

'Surely they'll send you to the hairdresser before this shindig?' he grinned remorselessly at her.

'Yes, I've got an appointment at Alexandre this afternoon, but what am I going to look like for the rehearsal?'

'Wonderful as always. Tie it back with that silly scarf.'

'Oh, you . . .' She punched him in exasperation.

'I'm getting out of here.' He feigned alarm. 'It's not safe. I'll see you tonight.'

'No you won't. I'm working.'

344

'Not when I'll be seeing you.' He winked at her.

'I might be too tired.'

'Not you. You're insatiable.'

'Go.' She threw a pillow at him as he disappeared out of the door.

He was a wonderful lover, Lainey mused to herself during the day. He was much more considerate than she had imagined he would be – more so than most men, from what she had been told. Not that she could judge as she hadn't known any other men, but girls gossiped and from that she had learned that a lot of men tended to be more concerned with their own needs. She felt a glow inside her. It had been so satisfying – so warm. In spite of herself she liked Harry Wrightson. It must be because they had been honest with each other from the beginning. If she didn't feel the way she did about Charlie, she supposed she could have mistakenly imagined herself a little in love with him. Thank goodness she knew better. "I hope that he doesn't tire of me too quickly," she thought. "This affair could be my best armour against Charlie."

"And your most effective weapon," said that little voice buried deep inside her.

The fashion show was a great success. Marcel was delighted with his models and with the audience's reaction to his collection. He kissed all the girls on both cheeks and told Lainey that he had never seen her look more ravishing. He knew that the orders would pour in.

It was near the end of the evening that he saw them in the foyer. Marcel had just come out of the men's room and now he walked over to them.

'Lainey, are you leaving already?'

She turned around. 'Yes, Marcel. I'm very tired. I was going to look for you to say good-bye before I left.'

'You won't forget the photographs tomorrow?'

'No, of course not. I'll be there.' She was going to be photographed for a fashion magazine in the three dresses that she had worn in the show. 'I'm sorry.' For a minute she looked embarrassed. 'Where are my manners. This is Harry Wrightson. He's an old friend of mine from London. Wasn't it a coincidence, we were on the same plane on Monday.'

'How do you do.' Harry held out his hand.

'*Enchantez*.' Marcel grasped it. He raised an eyebrow. So the young man had not told her about the incident last year.

'If you will excuse us.' Harry put an arm around Lainey's waist.

'But of course.' Marcel nodded his head. '*Bonne nuit*.'

Did she blush slightly, Marcel wondered as he watched them leave. There was no mistaking the look in the young man's eyes. He adored her. And what about the lovely Lainey? Did she love him? He would have said that she did – and then again, perhaps not?

CHAPTER FIFTEEN

Neither Lainey nor Harry went home as originally planned that Friday. He hired a car and they drove to Fontainebleau for the weekend. They stayed at a small hotel opposite the palace gates and spent the time making love and walking in the woods. It was so peaceful. Lainey had laughed to herself when she thought this. Peace. It was what Charlie wanted, not she. Why did he always have to come into her thoughts when she least wanted him to? Why did it make her wonder that if making love with Harry was so great it might be even more so with Charlie? It was a silly question really. With Charlie it was love, whereas with Harry it was just a blending of the senses. Sex. Wonderful mind-blowing sex. That didn't last forever, did it? It eventually played itself out. Then you were left with nothing – unless you loved one another. She should pity the woman who would eventually fall in love with Harry. It would be a one-way relationship. He had said so, hadn't he?

"Harry and I should marry each other," she thought. "It's a pity that I'm not rich enough for him. That way we wouldn't hurt each other and we wouldn't be hurting anyone else." Except Charlie. Poor Charlie – to see the woman he loved and couldn't have married to a man he despised. How . . . satisfying?

They returned to London on the Sunday evening and since Harry had parked his car at the airport he drove her back into town.

The little mews house was in darkness when they arrived.

'I expect that Viv's in bed – or maybe she stayed down in

the country tonight.' Lainey helped him take her luggage to the door. 'Do you want to come in?'

'No, I'd better not. I think that we both need a good night's sleep.'

'Yes,' she giggled as she unlocked the door.

He lugged her cases into the hall and then pushed the door closed.

'One for the road – to keep us going until next time.' He swept her into his arms and kissed her hard.

'Will you miss me when you're tucked up alone tonight?' she said against his mouth.

'Minx.' He pressed her even closer to him and felt the instant electricty between them. 'I thought you'd worn me out, but it seems that you haven't. I'd better go while I still can.'

At that moment the sitting room door opened and a man appeared in the light.

'What the . . . Oh, . . .! Where the hell have you been?'

Lainey and Harry sprung apart.

'Charlie,' she said. 'What are you doing here? You know perfectly well where I've been. I've been in Paris.'

'With him?' Charlie nodded his head in Harry's direction.

'Yes.' Her head went up defiantly. 'Harry was on the same plane and he brought me home.'

'I see.' It was said with meaning.

'No you don't.' Lainey's eyes blazed. She turned to Harry. 'Harry, please go before my brother makes a fool of himself. Thank you for bringing me home.'

'Yes, well, if you're OK. I'll call you tomorrow.' He got into his car and drove off. Jesus! That Carrington was an idiot. No wonder there was friction there. He had suspected it from something she had said that night on the Left Bank. He still treated his sister like a kid and she obviously didn't like it. One thing was clear, if he had thought that Charles Carrington had an influence over her once, that wasn't the case now. Thank God. In fact, it might just work to his advantage.

'What the hell is this all about?' Lainey was seething. 'How dare you cause a scene in front of a friend of mine.'

'I've rescued you once from him. I'm not going to do it again.'

Alison appeared from the sitting room.

'Lainey, you're back.' She smiled and then noticed the glowering faces of the brother and sister. 'What's the matter?'

'Alison, keep out of this.' Charlie turned back to his sister. 'Were you in Paris with him?'

'Yes, he was there too – on business.'

'Ha! He hasn't done a hard day's work in his life.'

'That's where you're wrong. He's working very hard for Grace Clover's father.'

'How convenient,' he sneered. 'You're a fool, Lainey. Wrightson's just playing with you.'

'Charlie,' she said quietly, 'I've had enough of your jealousy. Don't pretend that you were worried about me. You knew that I was all right. I sent Mother a cable saying that I wouldn't be back until tonight. You can't make me feel bad about Harry, because I don't.'

'You mean that you *are* having an affair with him?' He sounded aghast.

Suddenly something inside her snapped. 'Yes I am,' she shouted. 'And it's bloody marvellous. He's the most wonderful lover and we can't get enough of each other.' She started to walk up the stairs.

'You're a fool. He'll never marry you. He needs a rich girl like Grace.'

A gleam came into her eyes. 'Oh yes he will,' she said, 'if I decide that I want him to.'

'Don't kid yourself.' His shoulders slumped. 'Do you love him?'

For what seemed like an age they stood looking at one another in silence, then she turned and walked on up the stairs.

"Oh Charlie," she thought as she collapsed on her bed. "What on earth has love got to do with it?"

Alison touched Charlie's arm as he stood there still gazing up the stairs.

'She's only trying to shock you,' she said quietly. 'It's because she knows that you don't like him. She's not really behaving badly.'

'Yes, she is,' he replied without turning his head. 'She wants to hurt me and she's succeeding.'

'But why on earth should she want to do that?'

'Because . . . oh, it's a long story. We've always been so close – too close.'

'You have to stop feeling responsible for her, darling. You're not her father, and even if you were she's an adult now. She must be allowed to make her own mistakes and learn from them.'

'I suppose so.' He gave her a weak smile. 'You're so good for me, Alison. The best thing I ever did was to ask you to marry me.'

'There you are then.' She gave him a quick hug. 'So give her some air, Charlie. If you don't voice your disapproval, Lainey will soon get tired of playing her little games.'

She felt him tense up. 'It's not like that – at least, I understand why she does it. We've always understood each other so well.'

'Then why . . .?'

'I couldn't possibly begin to explain.'

'But . . .'

'The subject's closed.' There was an obstinate expression on his face. 'Come on, I'll drive you back to the nurses' home.'

'But I was going to stay here the night. I'm not on duty until tomorrow afternoon and I wanted to spend some time with Vivien tomorrow.'

'I'd rather you didn't, not tonight – please?'

She looked at him with concern. Oh dear, she really didn't

want to get into any fight between him and his headstrong sister. Maybe it would be better if she wasn't there in the morning to listen to Lainey berating her brother.

'All right, Charlie,' she said meekly as he shut the door firmly behind them.

That summer of 1960 passed in a blaze of excitement and success. Lainey's career went from strength to strength as did her affair with Harry Wrightson. Although she had to travel a great deal throughout the British Isles, she found these absences only served to ferment their relationship.

At first she had thought it fun to be the 'other woman', as she styled herself, in Harry's life. She knew that he took out Grace Clover at least twice a week, and, judging from the way that he couldn't wait to get his hands on her, Lainey knew that he wasn't making love with Grace. If anything, his passion for her, Lainey, had increased – and if she was truthful, so had hers for him.

When Lainey was in London they would nip off to secluded restaurants where they would not be recognised. They would deliberately prolong their meals together, savouring their mounting excitement until neither could stand it any longer, then they would rush to his car and drive at a crazy pace through the streets of London until they reached his flat in Chelsea where they could fall into his bed and satisfy their need. Afterwards he would drive her back to the little house in Ebury Mews – she would never stay the night at Harry's unless Vivien was away.

It was when the social events of the summer Season began again that Lainey felt the first pangs of dissatisfaction. It was Grace whom Harry took to the Derby and to Ascot. The Clovers had tickets for Glyndebourne and of course Harry went with them.

She shouldn't care, Lainey told herself. After all, this was just fun. He didn't owe her anything – and she didn't want him to. They went to the circus on Clapham Common and to the funfair afterwards. They went on boat trips down the Thames and riding in Richmond Park. These were all the things that you did with a friend and they were fun, but somehow she was irritated that he didn't ask her to any of the smart events.

Charlie never mentioned her relationship with Harry again, but she couldn't help noticing a certain look in his eyes once or twice when there was a picture of him in the *Tatler* or *Queen* at some function with Grace. It was an 'I told you so' expression, but it didn't have a self-satisfied quality. There was more of a feeling of sad resignation, and that irritated her too.

Harry, as well, was suffering from increasing feelings of doubt. This affair with Lainey Carrington was getting out of hand. He really enjoyed being with her and found that when she was away on modelling assignments he was bored and edgy. Who was she with and what was she doing? He had never been jealous before. It was a completely new experience and he didn't like it.

He should be delighted at his progress with Grace Clover. The girl was obviously nuts about him and her father was making it quite clear that he approved. She was a nice enough girl – intelligent too – but, oh dear, these American girls were so intense. Julian Fenner had been quite right when he had said they had no sense of humour. Could he really spend the rest of his life with someone like that? Very soon he would have to make up his mind. The Clovers would not stand for him messing their daughter about. They had been very generous to him, and it was all due to them that he had a well paid job that had given him a chance to prove himself – and he had. The London shop was starting to do well, and Harry himself had been as surprised as most people at his ability to run it smoothly. He realised, though, that Grace was part of the deal, although it had never actually been put into words. No Grace would mean no job, and no job and no Grace would almost certainly mean the end of one stately home.

"This summer," Harry had promised himself, "I'll have this summer. Who knows, this affair may have played itself out by the end of the summer."

But it didn't. It was getting better and better. Not just the sex – that was and always had been magical – but the liking and the laughter and the feeling that for the first time in his life he was giving something to a relationship and not just taking.

Was it the same for her? Sometimes he thought that they were so close and at others she would get that far-away look in those beautiful eyes and he couldn't be sure. One thing he was certain about was that the minute he announced his engagement to Grace, Lainey would be out of his life.

He sighed as he remembered an evening spent recently with Candida Leach. Lainey had been away and he hadn't been able to face the thought of spending that evening with Grace. On the spur of the moment he had rung Candida and taken her to the Stock Pot and then on to the Blue Angel to dance. She wasn't a bad girl, he had conceded afterwards. She was quite amusing really – if you appreciated the bitchy, slightly cynical way her mind worked. Had he been like that? For the first time he questioned it. True, he had never known his father, but he had a step-father and two half-brothers and a sister. Did he resent them? In his opinion they were spoilt and unruly and he knew that Aunt Lavinia felt that as well. He was also well aware that his stepfather resented the fact that he, Harry, would inherit Tenterden Park. As far as his mother was concerned, he had settled early on in his life to the fact that her love was not directed at him – it was always the three screaming half-broods, as he called them – and so he had acted accordingly. It was self-preservation. If you didn't allow yourself to love someone, then they couldn't disappoint you. Gradually Tenterden had become the love of his life as he knew they could never take that away from him. He, as Lord Wrightson, would inherit the house, and he had vowed he would do everything in his power to keep it. It would be his children who would one day live there and eventually inherit it. And so on and so on.

And now something utterly unforeseen was taking place. He was beginning to question his logic. Was it right to sacrifice so much for the sake of a house? After all, it was only bricks and mortar, wasn't it? If he did make this so-called sacrifice, who could tell if the next generation would manage to stay there? What if he didn't have a son? To do all this for a son as yet unborn – not even conceived? An incredible thought struck him. What if Lainey was pregnant? He felt a thrill of unexpected warmth and pleasure at the idea. That would solve everything. He would have to marry her and things would be taken out of his hands. She would not be able to run away from him. It was a wonderful thought, but it left him as quickly as it arrived. There was no way that she could be pregnant. He had been far too careful.

He enjoyed his evening with Candida. For the first time in a long while he was able to relax. Even during those fun-filled days with Lainey there was always that underlying passion, and with Grace one had to be so careful not to offend her and to appear chivalrous in the extreme.

Candida had long since given up her designs on him and was now walking out with an Italian count. She made no bones about the fact that she wanted to live in style.

'If it's not to be a stately English mansion, then a *palazzo* in Tuscany will have to do,' she told Harry.

'The wonderful thing about you, Candy, is that you never change.'

She had smiled at him. 'Oh, but I have, Harry. Style is still essential, but it's no longer so exciting.'

'You were right when you said last year that we were very alike, but I can't help feeling that we're too young to see life this way.'

'It's not our fault,' she replied seriously. 'It's the way we were brought up.'

'Do you like your parents?' he asked suddenly.

'Sometimes, and sometimes I blame them for the way they've made me feel.'

'I understand.' He nodded.

'I knew you would.' She put a hand over his in friendship. 'Are you going to marry Grace?'

'I suppose so.' He sighed. 'What else can I do?'

'Nothing. We've all been brain-washed.'

'We don't have to accept it.'

'But we *do*, Harry. That's why we're so alike.'

'But not for each other.'

She gave a cynical little laugh. 'No, definitely not for each other.'

That evening with Candida had helped put things into perspective, Harry thought. He had obligations to fulfil and a lineage to uphold. Tenterden had been handed down for generations. It had survived the Civil War and it must survive Harry Wrightson and stay in the family. The summer was drawing to a close and it was getting near to the time when he must shoulder his responsibilities.

But how did you say good-bye to a girl with brilliant blue eyes who melted in your arms every time you held her? How did you kiss her for the last time and enjoy the rapture of making love to her, knowing that it would never happen again? Would she care? She had spoken with such conviction in Paris, being adamant that neither of them was in love. But he was in love and he'd had no idea that it would be as painful as this.

"Don't think about it yet," he told himself. "There are still a few more weeks left. Don't spoil them – enjoy them."

But in the autumn Harry was granted a six-month reprieve. Annabel Clover was taken ill and Grace had to fly back to Texas. It turned out that she would be away for the whole winter as George then paid for his daughter to accompany his wife on a three-month luxury cruise to help her convalescence. Grace telephoned him constantly and Harry

355

made all the right remarks to reassure her. April 1961 seemed a long way off.

After Christmas while his mother and step-father were skiing in Switzerland with the half-broods, he organised a houseparty for a hunting weekend. Julian Fenner had asked him if he could bring a friend with whom he worked in the City as this friend and his wife were longing for a chance to spend a day with the Quorn Hunt. Harry had asked Lainey and Vivien as well. He knew that Vivien Hurst was an accomplished horsewoman, but had been surprised when Lainey said that she wanted to go too.

'Are you sure you'll be all right?' he had asked her. 'I mean, it's quite hairy if you've not had much experience. It's very different from riding in the park.'

Lainey had thrown back her head and laughed. 'I've ridden all my life, Harry Wrightson. Just because I don't have a horse any more doesn't mean I've forgotten. Two weekends with Viv beforehand will get me right back in the swing of it.'

He had been amazed at her prowess on the day. He had put her on the quietest horse in the stable, and not only had she looked exquisite, but she had proved that she could cope admirably as well. He had felt so proud of her. At the end of the day when she handed the horse back to the girl groom, she told him that she hadn't enjoyed herself so much for ages.

That night he watched her at the local hunt ball as she danced with everyone in their party. How beautiful she was and how self-assured. How right she looked in these surroundings. At dinner he seated her opposite him at the other end of the table. She should always be there – not someone like that cold fish, Grace Clover. The old house needed warmth and laughter and . . . children – her children. They would be lovely children. Harry knew that he was very handsome – it was something he felt no need to be modest about. Suddenly the thought of marriage to anyone other than this woman seemed intolerable, but there were so many obstacles. Firstly, how did he broach the subject to her? She said that she didn't love him, but he didn't know if he believed that. How could they be so good together if that was the case? And they were good together in so many ways. Something was stopping her from acknowledging it – even to herself. What was it? There was no other man in her life – he was sure of that, wasn't he?

That wasn't the only problem. How did he survive at Tenterden without money? "I'll just *have* to get money for myself," he vowed. He looked across the dance floor to where Julian's friends Paul and Suzie Drew were dancing. During the weekend Paul had intimated that there could be a good opening in his company for a man like Harry. At the time Harry had laughed. Why should he go and work his balls off in the City when he was doing very nicely thank you with George Clover's company? If he married Grace he would become a director and would never want for anything. George's little girl was the apple of his eye. Whatever Gracie wanted, Gracie got, and that included him!

There was big money to be made in the City, in finance, but it meant plenty of hard slogging. He wasn't stupid – Harry knew that. He was just idle. Well, the days of being a playboy were over. "I have a lot to think about and work out," he told himself.

As they danced together later that night, Lainey snuggled up to him as she said: 'I've had a wonderful day, Harry. All that excitement out hunting and now this lovely evening. I feel so . . . I don't know, but I just can't wait to make love.'

He held her close as he felt his body respond to hers.

'I know, I want to too,' he said into her hair. 'But not tonight.'

'What?' She pulled away slightly so that she could look at him.

'There are other people in the house. It wouldn't be right.'

'Isn't it a bit late to start safe-guarding my honour?'

'No,' he said crossly. 'I don't want anyone sniggering behind our backs. It wouldn't be right – not for you.'

'I'm sorry.' Did she look wistful for a second? 'I forgot the situation.' She gave him a mocking little smile. 'Dear Harry, you're always so gallant.'

'I'm not really and I do wish you wouldn't keep saying that.'

'I'm sorry.'

'And stop apologising.'

'What's the matter?'

'Nothing.' He grabbed her hand and pulled her roughly towards the bar. Why had she managed without knowing it to make him feel a complete shit? The situation as she saw it was that he was supposed to be getting engaged to another woman in the spring, yet here he was amusing himself with her. He was a shit, wasn't he? Well, he was going to change all that – because of her. "What if she won't have me? What if she really only wanted this affair to be brief?" He knew that he had to catch her at the right moment – when she was vulnerable – then she'd say yes.

"It'll happen," he told himself. "Be patient and it will happen."

'Are you in love with him? You're positively glowing.' Vivien sat on the end of Lainey's bed. It was Sunday night and they had returned to London.

'No, you know I'm not.' Lainey was irritated.

'I think you're kidding yourself.'

'I'm not. We're just having fun. We both understand that.'

'I'm sure.' It was said dryly. 'I still think that you're going to miss him like hell when he gets engaged to that tedious Texan.'

'I might miss the sex.' Lainey blushed. 'He's incredible.'

'Yes, well, I don't want a graphic description.'

'Viv, do you think I'm awful because I'm having an affair with Harry?'

358

'It's none of my business. I just don't want to see you get hurt.'

'I won't, I promise.'

'Don't you feel guilty about Grace?'

'No.' Lainey sounded off-hand. 'I don't think it's a great love-match, so why should I feel guilty?'

'Ah! So that makes it all right, does it?'

'What are you driving at?'

'Nothing.'

At that moment the telephone rang. Vivien picked it up.

'Mum, hi . . . lovely to hear from you . . . Yes we had a super time. What? . . . Oh, that's great. When? . . . Fantastic. I'll tell Lainey at once . . . OK. I'll speak to Ali tomorrow . . . Yes, I'll be down next weekend and we'll celebrate. Bye.' She replaced the receiver.

'What's that all about?' Lainey felt a prickle of unease.

'That was Mummy to say that Ali and Charlie have finally set their wedding date. They're going to get married on the last Saturday in April. That gives us three and a half months to prepare. Isn't it terrific?'

Lainey felt ill. She clenched her hands together so tightly that the knuckles went white. Oh God, she wasn't going to be sick, was she? She drew in a deep breath and the feeling passed as she forced herself to answer lightly: 'Yes, simply terrific.'

The weekend of Charlie Carrington's wedding was cold but clear. Lainey went down to Mattingham on the Friday evening. She would spend a quiet night there with her mother and Charlie before the wedding on the following day.

She had asked Harry Wrightson to the wedding. He would come down from London the following day and join them at the Hursts' house where the wedding was being held, then he would spend the rest of the weekend at Mattingham.

At ten o'clock Jennifer announced that she was going to bed. Lainey and Charlie were left in the study by the fire. It

359

was the first time that they had been alone together in many months and they both felt awkward. After a long pause she said: 'I do hope that you will be happy.'

'Thank you, Lainey. I hope you mean that,' he said quietly.

'Oh I do. I do,' she said earnestly. 'I really am trying.'

'That was what I was afraid of,' he sighed.

'I can't help it if I still feel . . .'

'Lainey, don't.' His voice was curt. 'I can't deal with it.'

'I know.' It came out almost like a sob.

'Lainey, why did you ask Wrightson tomorrow?'

'Can't you guess?'

'Yes.' He said it so softly that she could hardly hear him. 'I was just hoping that you would tell me something different.'

'I have watched you and Alison over the past year and I have felt such pain when I see the two of you together. She has got someone who should belong to me – who loves me as much as I love him. In any other circumstances it would be us getting married tomorrow. I'm sorry, Charlie, but I can't help wanting you to feel what I'm feeling. I want you to see me with Harry and know that there is nothing you can do about it.'

'You are very cruel.'

'Sometimes you have to be cruel to survive.'

'I'm glad that we're going away.'

'What do you mean, going away?' She was alarmed.

'I'm joining a practice near Ripon in Yorkshire.'

'But I'll never see you.' She was aghast.

'Believe me, Lainey. It's better for both of us.'

'I hate you, Charlie.' She advanced towards him menacingly.

'Don't.' He put his hands in front of his face to ward her off. 'Don't touch me. I just want to be free of you.' He stumbled past her and out of the door.

She ran after him and watched as he rushed blindly up the

stairs. Her chest heaved and her eyes glistened with unshed tears. "You never will, Charlie," she thought. "You never will. Whoever we marry, we are never going to forget the way we feel about each other – not for as long as we're both alive."

It was a pleasant wedding, Harry thought. The bride looked radiant. She was not the classic English rose like Lainey, but in her own way she was a very attractive girl with her olive complexion and her long thick blue-black hair. She didn't resemble her younger sister at all, but took after her mother. There was a slightly Biblical quality about her. You could imagine her starring in one of those Cecil B. de Mille epics. A really good person – not of today's world.

Carrington seemed a bit on edge, but he supposed that most bridegrooms felt like that. At one point during the reception he had caught him looking at his sister with something almost akin to hatred. What had gone wrong there? They used to be so close – why, that ass, Carrington, had been livid when he had brought Lainey back from Paris, hadn't he? He'd behaved more like a jealous lover. Something deep inside him stirred uneasily, but he didn't dwell on the thought.

He wondered why he had accepted Lainey's invitation to this wedding. He knew that Carrington couldn't stand him, yet Lainey had been adamant about wanting him there. Why should she want to annoy her brother on his wedding day? He shouldn't have come. He didn't want to be caught up in their private war, whatever it was about, but Grace was returning to England the following Monday and this could be the last time he spent with Lainey. Nothing had happened to change that situation. No opportunity had presented itself. How could he make things change? He looked around the room to find her, but she was nowhere to be seen. People were starting to drift outside as it was nearly time for the bride and bridegroom to leave.

He found her in the drive standing on her own. She was engrossed in her own thoughts and there was a look of intense misery on her face. He walked over to her.

'Hello little one.' He put an arm around her waist.

'Hello, Harry.' She gave him a watery smile.

'What's all this?' He brushed a tear tenderly from her cheek.

'I always cry at weddings.'

'I gather it's a well-known fact.' He grinned down at her encouragingly.

A shout went up and the new Mrs Carrington appeared on the doorstep with her husband behind her. She paused for a moment, her face wreathed in smiles, then she closed her eyes and threw her bouquet. Lainey gasped as it landed in her arms. She still looked dazed as she kissed the couple good-bye, then they were away in their car with tin cans clanking behind them.

Harry glanced down at the flowers. Were they an omen? Would she be the next bride – his bride?

As they drove back to London the following night she said: 'Harry, can I stay with you tonight? I don't want to be alone.'

'You know you can.' He wanted her so much and the thought of Grace arriving on Monday was very depressing.

They made love feverishly as if they both knew that this could be the last time. Afterwards she turned away from him and curled herself up in a tight little ball. He thought he saw her shoulders shaking.

'What is it?' He touched her tentatively.

'I'm so miserable,' she mumbled.

'Why, darling?' It was a slip of the tongue but she appeared not to notice.

'Everyone I love or like seems to leave me.'

'Meaning who exactly?'

'Daddy died and Charlie's going to be living miles away. I'll never see him.'

'You've still got me.' He rolled over and took her in his arms.

'No, I haven't. Grace gets back tomorrow and then I'll never see you again either.'

'That's not true.' He rubbed her back soothingly.

'Harry, I'm not continuing this once you get engaged to her. I may have behaved badly where she's concerned already, but at least you weren't engaged. I do have some scruples.' She pushed him away and sat up. 'I think that I'd better go.'

'But I thought you were going to stay the night.'

'I've changed my mind. I don't think it's such a good idea after all.' She started to pull on her clothes.

He jumped out of bed and caught her to him, ignoring her protests.

'Don't go,' he said as he kissed her face and her hair. 'I couldn't bear it if you went. I don't love her. You know that I never did. It's you that I want – I always have. The thought of spending the rest of my life with that humourless inhibited woman leaves me cold. Marry me, Lainey. We need each other.'

'What did you say?' She stopped struggling and faced him.

Suddenly he felt gloriously free. He'd said it – he'd actually said it. He took her hands in his and spoke slowly and distinctly. 'I said, marry me, Lainey. We're so good together – you know we are. You loved Tenterden, I know you did, and you looked so right there.'

'But I'm not rich. I can't help you keep Tenterden.'

He laughed nervously. 'It doesn't matter. I've been offered a job in the City, and I'm going to take it. If I work hard, the prospects are very good.'

'But I don't love you and you don't love me. This attraction that we feel now could wear off.' She looked apprehensive.

Why couldn't he tell her that he adored her – that all he wanted to do was to make her happy? He knew that was not what she wanted to hear – she probably wouldn't even believe him.

'Has it worn off in the year that we've been together? If anything, it's even stronger.'

'But . . .'

'No more buts. Yes or no?'

She looked at him silently for a long time, then she sat down on the bed.

'Yes,' she whispered.

'What?' he stammered.

'Would you let me continue working?'

'Yes, of course, as much as you like.'

'Then yes, I'll marry you.'

'Oh Lainey.' He tore off her shirt and pushed her back on the bed as he pressed his naked body tightly against her.

She wound her arms around his neck. "I don't love him," she told herself firmly, "but I want him and I need him. I'll be a good wife to him and I'll make him proud of me." She felt the familiar thrill of excitement that she experienced every time he made love to her. She cried out as he entered her, but he couldn't make out what she said. He felt her nails rake his back as their love-making became more frenzied.

Afterwards, as he still lay on top of her, a little smile hovered on her lips. "Who said he'd never marry me?" she thought. "I knew that if I wanted him to, he would. I vowed way back in Paris that I would be the one he'd remember, that I'd be different from the rest, and I am. Everything and everyone is obtainable – you just have to want them enough. Even Charlie could be mine one day."

CHAPTER SIXTEEN

Once she had agreed to marry him, Harry wasted no time.

'Let's get married as soon as possible,' he said. 'What are you doing this week?'

'I'm working today – if I ever get there.' She looked at her watch. It was seven o'clock in the morning.

'And for the rest of the week?'

'Not much. It's a slack time of year just before the collections. I'm supposed to go and see Alfie and Viv later in the week about something to do with Hurst and Lever.'

'Put it off. We'll drive to Scotland tonight and get married at Gretna Green.'

'But we can't just take off. What about your job? Are you crazy?'

'Yes, and anyway I'm going to be changing my job.'

'But what about our parents ... and Grace is arriving today. Shouldn't you tell her?'

'Grace is the past. She was a girl I took out. I never made love to her and she's been away for six months. For all I know, she could have found someone else.'

'But she's coming back to see you – you know that.'

'Well, I won't be here.'

'Ah!' Now she understood his hurry. 'You want to present her with a *fait accompli*?'

'Lainey, I can't stand scenes – few men can. Now, what do you say? We can telephone our parents from Scotland as soon as we're married.'

His excitement was infectious. What an adventure it would be. Who wanted a big Society wedding? Not her, and apparently he didn't either. When she turned towards him her eyes were sparkling. 'Yes,' she said breathlessly. 'And anyway, I've worn enough brides' dresses to last me a life-time.'

Later that morning Harry told his astonished staff at the shop in Bond Street that he would be away for the next four days on business.

'Please get in touch with Miss Clover and tell her that I will speak to her later in the week,' he told his secretary.

The girl raised an eyebrow, but said nothing as she scribbled on her notepad.

At lunchtime he walked down the street to Cartier's and purchased a simple gold wedding ring.

'The lady should really try it on if it's to fit exactly.' The salesman looked down his nose at the piece of string with which Harry had measured Lainey's finger.

'Yes, well, there's no time for that.' Harry signed a cheque and pocketed the little box.

As he reached the door the salesman thawed slightly. 'May I be so presumptuous as to offer you my sincere congratulations, m'lord?'

'You may . . . and thank you.'

The next thing he wanted to do was to drive to Tenterden. If he got a move on he could be there and back in four hours – just in time to collect Lainey from Ebury Mews at five-thirty. With luck his mother and Oliver would be out. There was something he wanted to collect.

The telephone was ringing as Harry walked into his flat at half-past four.

'What the hell do you think you are doing?' It was his step-father's voice on the other end.

'Oh, hello Oliver. Nice to hear you.'

'Cook has told us that you were down here this afternoon and went to the safe. Your mother has just found that the Lady Sophia ruby has gone. Did you take it?'

'As a matter of fact I did, Oliver. It is mine after all. It was left to me.'

'Don't you think that you owe us an explanation? You come into this house and help yourself, and then leave without a word.'

Harry fought to control his anger as he said, 'I think you are forgetting, Oliver, that it is my house, and when I am twenty-five next year you won't even be living there. As for an explanation; I'll be giving that to my mother tomorrow.'

'And what exactly do you mean by that?'

'You'll find out tomorrow, Oliver, so you'll just have to contain yourself until then.' Harry replaced the receiver.

He flung some clothes into a suitcase and ran downstairs to his car.

Lainey was waiting anxiously by the door when he arrived.

'Quick,' she said. 'Let's go before Viv gets back from work.'

He smiled. 'So you don't want to give any explanations either.'

'I left a note saying that something had come up, and not to worry.'

He settled her into the car and jumped in beside her. Lainey threw back her head and exhaled deeply. 'I can't believe that this is really happening,' she said as they drove off.

'Neither can I.' He took one hand off the wheel and ruffled her hair.

'Are you sure this is what you want?' She looked apprehensive.

'Yes, absolutely.'

He didn't ask her the same question.

Neither of them noticed Vivien Hurst as she turned the corner, but she saw them. "Isn't Grace getting back today?" she thought as she walked on down the mews. She unlocked her front door and picked up the note which was on the floor. "Dear Viv," she read. "Something has come up. I'll be away for a few days, so don't worry. Luv, Lainey." On the bottom was scrawled, "Wish me luck."

For a moment she gazed at it with a puzzled expression on her face, and then a sudden idea struck her. "Oh my God!" she thought and put a hand to her mouth.

'Mother, it's me, Lainey.' Lainey held the telephone to her ear.

'Lainey, darling, where are you? I tried to call you yesterday, but Vivien said that you'd had to go away and she didn't know where you were.'

'I'm in Scotland. Mother, sit down. I've got something to tell you. Harry and I have just got married.'

'What?'

'I said that Harry and I have just got married. Oh, don't be cross, please. It's what we wanted. No fuss or anything.'

'Oh, Lainey.' Jennifer sat down. She felt shattered.

'Please be happy for us, Mother. It ... well, it just sort of happened this way.'

'But darling, you're so young and it's so sudden.'

'Mother, we'll be back this weekend and we'll come straight to see you.'

'But darling, I don't understand your rush. I like Harry. Why did you feel that you had to run off?'

'It's a long story – and no, before you think it, I'm not pregnant. It's something between Harry and me. Please say that you forgive us for not doing it the conventional way?'

'Darling, you're my daughter. I only want you to be happy.'

'I am, oh I am. You're wonderful.'

'I love you too, darling.'

Jennifer shook her head numbly as she put down the telephone. Oh to be young and in love. You could do such crazy things. She knew that Lainey had been seeing a lot of Harry Wrightson and he had certainly looked smitten with her last weekend at Charlie's wedding, but would they regret this sudden rush of blood to the head?

368

'She's like I was at that age,' she thought. 'It's almost like history repeating itself. I rushed off and married Richard because I was so sure that I was doing the right thing, but if I was to be completely honest with myself I have to admit that it wasn't. I confused love with pity which isn't the same thing at all.' She couldn't help giving a little cynical smile. Now here was her daughter rushing into marriage at the same age with a distant cousin of her first husband. Would the result be the same? There was no need for pity where Harry was concerned – as far as she knew – and these days the young were not usually virgins, like she had been, when they married. She wondered what Alan would have thought of his daughter marrying so young. Alan, she hadn't allowed herself to think of him for so long. What did he look like now? Was he middle-aged and bald? She was forty-one, so he must be forty-five. Was he still with his neurotic wife? Did they have a family of their own?

"Oh Alan, I miss you," she thought. "I loved Tony very much and we had a wonderful life together, but he never quite filled that part of my heart that will always belong to you."

She took a piece of paper and wrote a note to Charlie and Alison at their hotel in Majorca. It wasn't until she was posting it that she realised her daughter hadn't mentioned the word 'love' at all.

'How was your mother?' Harry leaned down and put his arms around Lainey's neck as she sat at the dressing table brushing her hair.

'Fine. She likes you.' She smiled at his reflection.

'I'm glad that someone in the family does.'

For a second her face assumed a closed-up expression. 'What my brother thinks is really of little consequence.'

'I know that you don't mean that.' He kissed her cheek.

'I do.' The inference was that the subject was closed.

'I have something for you.' He pulled a small red-and-gold leather box out of his pocket.

'For me?' Her face lit up with excitement. 'Oh!' she gasped as she opened it. A large ruby and diamond ring sparkled up at her. 'Oh, Harry, it's magnificent, but . . .'

'It belonged to my grandmother,' he said quietly. 'She left it to me on the condition that it became my wife's engagement ring.' He slipped it on to her finger. 'I'm afraid there was no time for that, so here it is now.'

'It's beautiful.' She looked up at him. Her eyes seemed even bigger than usual. 'I shall treasure it.'

"And I shall treasure you," he thought.

When Charlie Carrington opened the letter he read it briefly before walking far away down the beach. He sat himself down on a rock, and when he had made sure that he was entirely alone he put his head in his hands and cried.

The marriage of Lord Wrightson and Alaina Carrington was news within a very short space of time. By the time the couple arrived back in London, their pictures had been in most of the national daily papers and in some foreign ones as well. Lainey was amazed at the interest which they had aroused. They were inundated with letters and telephone calls.

The news had apparently reached America and Lainey was thrilled to receive a letter from her friend Mary-Beth Jefferson. Mary-Beth went on to say that she and Jimmy Foxton were getting married the following summer and she hoped that Lainey and her husband would come over for the wedding.

There was little chance of that, Lainey thought. Now that Harry had changed his job he was having to work very hard and he was determined to make a lot of money in the financial world. She herself was being offered even more modelling jobs, partly due, she was sure, to all the publicity over her marriage. They needed all the money they could make so there would be no expensive trips for the moment.

It was during the autumn of that year that Alfie and Vivien came to Lainey with a proposition.

'We meant to talk to you about this earlier in the summer,' Vivien said. 'But what with your marriage and then we found ourselves with other business commitments. We've got a very exciting new idea.' She turned to her father. 'Dad, you tell her.'

'Well, Lainey.' Alfie folded his hands and surveyed his daughter's best friend who was also very dear to him and his wife. 'Hurst and Lever have decided to break into the cosmetic world. We have approached a company to supply us and the brand name will be exclusive to us. What we need is a good sales pitch.'

'And that's where you come in,' Vivien broke in. 'We want to sign you on as the Hurst and Lever girl to advertise our new range of make-up and nail products. You would have to work exclusively for us for two years. What do you say?'

'You should do it,' Harry said when she told him. 'While I approve of your working, I don't like the idea of you traipsing all over London, going to various auditions and working all hours of the day and night. Before we were married I never realized how exhausting it must be. You look positively shattered some evenings. If you become the Hurst and Lever girl, you'll know exactly what you are doing and you'll be working for people you like.'

'I want to, but I don't want anyone to say that it's favouritism.'

'Lainey, sweetheart, looking the way you do, who could possibly accuse them of that?'

'You're being gallant again.' There was a gleam in her eyes.

He took a good-natured swipe at her. 'Go and phone them and tell them you'll do it.'

'OK, OK. Anything for a quiet life.' She picked up the telephone.

Harry settled down to read some business reports. He was enjoying his new job. To his surprise he had discovered that he had quite a flair for putting deals together. He also had a nose for the right investments. Who was it who had said that you had to speculate to accumulate? Well, he wasn't going to go mad, but there were one or two nice little profits showing on his portfolio. If he continued this way they might well be able to move into a house or a decent-sized flat in the near future.

He reached in his pocket for his cigarettes. As he pulled them out a piece of paper fell on the floor. He picked it up and smiled as he glanced at it. It was a short note from Candida. It said simply: 'Well done. You broke the mould. I hope that you will be happy.' He sighed as he tore it up and threw it in the waste paper basket. She wasn't a bad girl, was Candida. He hoped that things would turn out all right for her as well.

CHAPTER SEVENTEEN

"Everything happens in April," Lainey thought. "I was born on April Fool's Day – that's a joke for a start – and I met Harry in Paris in that month. Charlie got married in April and I married Harry." She stared around her. So much had happened during the past year. Harry's meteoric rise in the City had enabled them to buy a house in Radnor Walk, and as she sat surrounded by packing cases she could hear the decorators whistling in tune to their radio as they painted the hall.

Was she happy, she wondered. She had a wonderful job. She was famous at the age of twenty. Her face was in every fashion magazine and on posters and billboards all over the country. Everywhere she and Harry went they were treated like a golden couple, and they were, weren't they? What more could she want? In June when he would be twenty-five, he would legally inherit Tenterden and it now seemed within the realms of possibility that he might be able to keep it. She should be happy for him and she was. So what was wrong with her?

He wanted to start a family and she didn't want to – not yet. The subject seemed to come up all the time and usually ended with both of them becoming very disgruntled. She noticed that he was drinking a little more than he used to, but she chose to ignore it.

It was now the end of April 1962. The next day she was flying to New York to launch the new cosmetic line in Hurst and Lever's new store there. Harry was not best pleased about this.

'How long do you think that you're going to be away?' he asked her.

'I think it'll be about a month,' she said. 'Uncle Alfie is going to be there to supervise everything, and Viv is coming out for the last week.'

'What the hell am I supposed to do with myself, if you're gone for so long?' He spoke peevishly.

'Harry, you're so busy anyway that I hardly see you now. I'll be back before you know it.'

'I don't like to think of you living it up with all those racy New Yorkers.'

'For heaven's sake, I'm not going to have the time – and I don't know anyone there except Mary-Beth Jefferson who's just about to get married. Anyway, I'll be with the Hursts and they won't exactly be living it up.'

'It's time that you settled down and produced my son and heir.'

'That wasn't part of the deal.'

'What deal?' He looked aghast.

'We agreed that this marriage would work because we're good together. It has to be fun and therefore I need to work. I enjoy working and it gives me my own identity – and we also need the money. There's plenty of time for a family.'

'You're my wife and I want you with me,' he said sulkily.

'You don't own me.' She put her hand on his arm, but he shook it off.

'Don't I know it.' He poured himself half a glass of neat whisky and proceeded to drink it. He swayed a little unsteadily on his feet. 'I never really had you, did I? There was always some part of you that I couldn't reach. What the hell do you really want, Lainey? Do you actually know?'

'You're being ridiculous – and of course I know what I want.' Her voice was cold.

'Well, what is it, as it doesn't seem to be me?'

'It's not my fault if you indulge in too much of that to perform.' She eyed the empty whisky glass disparagingly.

'You bitch.' He raised his hand as if to strike her, then lowered it.

'I'm sorry,' she said. 'I shouldn't have said that. We're both under pressure. I have to go to New York, Harry. It's part of my contract and I want to go. Maybe it's a good thing. Maybe we need some time away from each other.'

'Aren't you worried as to how I could amuse myself while you're away?'

She looked at him honestly. 'No, Harry, I'm not. You must do whatever you want. I can't stop you, whether I'm here or not.'

'Don't you care?' He couldn't stop himself from asking the question.

She was saved from answering as the telephone rang. She picked it up.

'Charlie, how lovely to hear you.' Her voice had become soft and warm.

Harry clenched his fist. That bloody brother of hers. Trust him to ring up in the middle of one of their fights. He poured yet another glass of whisky and swallowed it in one gulp.

When Lainey put the telephone down she looked pale.

'What did that bloody brother of yours want?' Harry had not been listening to the conversation.

'Um . . .?' She appeared to be lost in thought.

'Was he trying to stir things up? He never liked me, did he? I bet he's just waiting for the chance to get you away from me.'

'What?' She looked vague, then she assembled her thoughts. 'Actually, he didn't mention you.'

'Well, what the hell was that all about? You were on the phone for long enough.'

'He rang me to tell me that Alison is pregnant.' Lainey's face had gone white.

'That's the first sensible thing that I've heard tonight.'

'I'm going upstairs to finish packing.' She dashed out of the room as a wave of nausea overcame her.

*

The first week in New York was very busy. There were magazine interviews and publicity pictures. The Hurst and Lever store had been opened six months before and was on Madison Avenue in a prominent position quite close to Bloomingdales.

Alfie had booked them into the Plaza Hotel which was very central. Lainey had written to Mary-Beth Jefferson and there had been a letter waiting for her when she arrived. Mary-Beth said that she would be in the city for a couple of nights during the first week of May as she had to have her final fitting for her wedding dress, and perhaps Lainey could have dinner with her then.

The two girls went to dinner at Twenty-One and spent hours gossiping and catching up on their news.

'I can't tell you what a shock it was when I heard that you had had to dash home from Annapolis when your father died,' Mary-Beth said. 'It really seems incredible that we haven't seen each other since.'

'It seems like only yesterday,' Lainey said. 'I'm so glad that I'm going to be here for your wedding.'

'Yes, that's really terrific. Why don't you come down and stay with us – if you've finished with your job. We have a lovely house at Southampton where we go every summer, and we're having the wedding there. If you came down on the Thursday before, we could have a couple of days together. I'm sure that someone would drive you back afterwards.'

'That would be wonderful. I'll check with Uncle Alfie, but I think everything will be over by then. Viv – that's his daughter and my closest friend – is coming over just in time for the promotion party that week. I know that they're planning to stay until after that weekend as she has never been to America before. If I come back after your wedding on the Saturday, we can spend the rest of our free time together.'

'Great. That's all arranged then.' Mary-Beth placed her

elbows on the table and fixed Lainey with a stare. 'Now, tell me all about this dishy husband of yours. Fancy you being married before Jimmy and me – and to an English Lord. Lady Wrightson – it sounds terribly grand, doesn't it?'

'Idiot,' Lainey giggled. 'I don't even notice it.'

'You wouldn't. Well, what's he like? Do you have a photo?'

'No, I don't – not with me anyway. Well, he's very good-looking, I suppose, in a very English way. He's five years older than me and we get along very well.' She blushed slightly.

'I should hope so too.' Mary-Beth punched her affectionately on the arm. 'You said that he has this great mansion?'

'Yes, it's the ancestral home, but we don't live there yet. It's going to cost a mint to look after it. Harry's got to work like a Trojan for us to be able to afford to stay there.'

'It looks as if he's doing just that. You said that he couldn't take the time off to come over here with you?'

'Yes, he is.' Lainey sighed.

'What's the matter?'

'Nothing.' She looked startled.

'Come off it. You know that even when we had only just met we were able to sense when something was wrong – remember how Jimmy called us the terrible twins?'

'I'd forgotten.'

'No you haven't. Now tell Auntie Mary-Beth.'

Lainey gave a nervous laugh. 'It really isn't anything. I just think that he's getting too possessive. He didn't want me to come – even though he knows that I'm under contract to Hurst and Lever for two years. He wants me to stay at home and produce endless babies, and I don't want to – not for a long time. He knew that when I agreed to marry him.'

'Lainey, for God's sake, don't you look in the mirror? What man wouldn't be worried about letting you out of his sight for weeks on end?'

'It's not like that. You wouldn't understand and I can't explain.'

'Lainey, what is this?' Mary-Beth looked worried. 'You talk about agreeing to marry him and saying it's not like this. Don't you love him?'

'I like him and he likes me and we're very attracted to each other. Neither of us wanted to fall in love. We give each other what we both need – at least I thought we did, now I'm not so sure. Harry has started drinking heavily. Marriage is beginning to have its problems.'

'Maybe he's discovered that he loves you.'

'Oh no, it's nothing like that. Harry's incapable of love.'

'Oh Lainey.' Mary-Beth shook her head. 'Do you always believe everything you are told?'

'No, of course not. But *that* I know.' She spoke crossly. 'Anyway, it's different for you and Jimmy. You've always loved each other – and only each other. Nothing's ever stood in your way.'

Mary-Beth looked up sharply. 'And what has ever stood in your way?' she asked.

'No, I didn't mean it like that.'

'Then how did you mean it?'

'Mary-Beth, this is getting heavy. It's not really important. I shouldn't have said anything. There's really nothing wrong that Harry and I can't work out with each other. We're both under pressure from our jobs and all the adjustments that one has to make in the first years of marriage. We'll be fine.'

"I wonder," thought Mary-Beth as she dropped her friend off at the Plaza after dinner. "I reckon that you married on the rebound, Lainey, and that hardly ever works."

The final promotion of Hurst and Lever's cosmetic range was in two days' time. This party would also launch their new perfume which was to be called 'Intuition'. The publicity pictures of Lainey looking mysterious and yet knowing were to surround the room where the party was to

378

be held, and even Lainey had to admit that the New York photographer was a genius. They were the best pictures that had ever been taken of her. The following month they would be in every fashion magazine in the country. She would be famous this side of the Atlantic as well as in her own country. Already one of the biggest modelling agencies in the city wanted to sign her up. She was quite glad that she was under contract to Hurst and Lever for another eighteen months, as she could imagine Harry's face if she informed him that she wanted to do more work in America.

As she walked into the Plaza Hotel after a particularly hard day's work she saw a familiar figure surrounded by luggage standing at the check-in desk.

'Viv, you're here at last.' She ran over and hugged her friend. 'How was your trip? Are you frazzled?'

'Hi, I'm feeling terrific. I'm so excited that I'm actually here.'

'How's everything at home?'

'Fine. I called your mother and she's OK, and I tried to get Harry but he was always tied up so I never did manage to speak to him.' Vivien's cheeks went slightly pink, but Lainey did not appear to notice.

'Let's go up to your room. I can't wait to tell you everything that's been going on over here.' They walked towards the elevator. 'Did you say that you'd tried Harry? Well, I'm not surprised that you didn't get him. He's so wrapped up in the financial world these days that even I hardly see him at all.'

'Yes.' Vivien spoke quietly.

After the bellboy had deposited her luggage and closed the door behind him, Vivien turned to Lainey as she unzipped her overnight case. 'I must just have a wash. I feel really scruffy after that long flight. I won't be a second, and then we'll talk about everything you've been up to.' She took out her spongebag and disappeared into the bathroom.

Lainey sat down on the bed and prepared to wait. A

newspaper was sticking out of the open case. "Oh good," she thought, "an English paper." She took it out and started to read. It was nice to read news from home. The weather was still dreadful – that made her feel good as New York was pleasantly warm. She turned the pages until she came to the gossip column. Suddenly she caught her breath. Was she seeing things? There, staring her in the face, was a picture of a rather tipsy Harry draped around Candida Leach. The write-up insinuated that, while his wife of barely one year was away modelling in New York, the dashing young Lord Wrightson was consoling himself in the arms of his ex-girlfriend the Lady Candida Leach. It went on to say that before his dramatic elopement with the beautiful Alaina Carrington, handsome Harry had been seen constantly in the company of Texas heiress Grace Clover whose father he had worked for.

Lainey closed the paper quickly and put it back in Vivien's case. So that was why her friend had looked uncomfortable when she had mentioned about not being able to get hold of Harry. She felt a deep sense of resentment welling up inside her. "Here I am working my tail off while he acts like a playboy at home. I've always known that he's not in love with me, but I'll be damned if he makes me a laughing stock." She felt the threat of tears in her eyes. Now why on earth should she want to cry? It must be because he had made her feel so angry. That's right, they were tears of anger. "He's not worth it," she told herself. "I thought that he had grown up – that he was beginning to shoulder his responsibilities – but I was wrong. Leopards never change their spots. Charlie was right when he said that this marriage would be a disaster – but he'll never know that. I'll deal with Harry in my own way. And I was right about Harry. He doesn't have a heart – but I always knew that, so he can't break mine."

Why, then, did she cry herself to sleep?

Harry Wrightson gazed at the morning paper as he tried to

swallow his coffee. The bastards. So they had put that wretched photograph in after all. He sighed with frustration. It had not been at all like they made it sound. OK, he had taken Candy out to dinner – but purely as an old friend. Her boyfriend had been somewhere in Italy and they were both feeling depressed. How unfortunate it had been that he had chosen a restaurant where some filmstar was having a party. The press had known about it and in the middle of dinner a photographer had arrived. He had recognised Harry and Candida and had made it sound as if they were included in the show-business party. Some write-up, wasn't it? Candy had been twitchy about it too. Her count wouldn't like it either, he supposed.

He stifled a yawn. It hadn't been a late night, but he was working so hard that even eleven-thirty seemed too late. He ran a hand through his hair. What would Lainey think if she saw this? Their relationship was fragile enough at the moment. "Oh Lainey," he thought. "Why do I have to love you so much? Why can't you love me? Is this going to louse things up completely, or won't you even care?"

She would care, but for the wrong reasons – he knew that. She had her own ideas about him which he had helped to instill. She would never believe in his innocence or in his love for her.

On the other hand maybe she would be jealous, and maybe this article would give her a jolt. Maybe, just maybe, it would make her realise that she did love him after all. He sighed. Pipe dreams – that's all they were – but at least they were something to hold on to.

Lainey's work in New York was finished. The promotion had gone extremely well and both Alfie and Vivien were delighted at the amount of interest and praise that their new products had received. Now that it was all over, Alfie had promised his daughter and her friend a week in the city, so that they could sightsee and have fun.

Mary-Beth collected Lainey from the hotel a few days later on the Thursday afternoon before her wedding. It had worked in very well as she had had to come into the city to pick up her wedding dress. It now lay on the back seat of her car in a fine cloth bag.

'I'm so glad that you're going to meet Daddy at last,' she said sunnily as they set off for Long Island. 'My grandparents will be staying too, so you'll see them again. I can't wait to show you everything. The marquee is going to look so beautiful and the flowers are going to be gorgeous. Jimmy is coming to dinner tonight and he's longing to see you again . . . oh, and . . .'

'Mary-Beth, stop it.' Lainey was laughing. 'If you don't concentrate on driving this car, we'll never make it.'

'Sure we will.' The excited American girl flashed her friend a happy smile.

When they finally reached their destination Lainey was impressed by the large attractive old house. Like most of the other summer homes in that area it was built of clapboard and shingle and had a large porch attached. It was surrounded by three acres of garden, which at this moment seemed to be a hive of activity. The marquee was in the process of being hoisted and Mrs Prebble was gesticulating in various directions as she instructed the hundreds of workmen.

'Grandmother is in her element,' Mary-Beth grinned. 'It's just like giving me a Season all over again.'

Karen Prebble turned and saw them. 'Ah, there you are, darling.' She detached herself from the workmen and walked across the lawn. 'Alaina, how nice to see you again. Mary-Beth is so delighted that you can be here.' She patted the back of her immaculate hairstyle. 'I'll show you to your room. Cook has planned dinner for seven-thirty, but I expect you'd like to relax until then.' She turned to Mary-Beth. 'Your father said that he hoped to be here by dinner.'

'Great.' Mary-Beth kissed the older woman's cheek.

'Don't you bother to come in, Gran. I'll show Lainey her room.'

'Well, I am rather busy.'

'See what I mean?' Mary-Beth whispered as the two girls set off in the direction of the house. 'She's loving every moment.'

Alan Jefferson pulled up outside his house a little after seven o'clock that night. It had been hot driving down from town. The temperature was uncommonly warm for the time of year and the humidity was high. He noticed that his daughter's car was already there and he heaved a sigh of relief. He realized that he was over-protective of Mary-Beth. But she was all that he had and he loved her very much. He worried every time she drove that nippy little car of hers.

He supposed that her English girlfriend was here as well. Funny how she'd struck up such a friendship with someone she hardly knew. The girl was reputed to be very lovely – even the hypercritical Karen had acknowledged that. Well, she'd have to be, wouldn't she, if she was a top model and about to be on all the Hurst and Lever advertising? Mary-Beth had told him that she was married to an English Lord and that they were trying to salvage a crumbling estate. Quite a task for such a young couple, he thought. It served to remind him of his days at Edgeglow during the war. Strange how many similarities there were. Jennifer hadn't been much older than Mary-Beth and she had been saddled with a house she could not afford to keep up. That was why she'd taken in the children who had been evacuated. A familiar pang of loss hit him. He had tried so hard to put her from his mind, but to no avail. His relationship with Linda had suffered simply because she wasn't – and never could be – the right woman.

He had been honest with Linda and she had said that it did not matter. But it mattered to him and he had ended the relationship. It wasn't fair to either of them to continue. Since Linda, there had been no women in his life – at least none that mattered. Oh, he was not a monk, but casual dalliances had never been his style and they weren't now.

Maybe he should try and find out what had happened to Jennifer – if only to put his mind at rest and tell himself once and for all that she was out of his reach and happily married. Now that Mary-Beth would no longer be at home, he would be even more lonely than before. Maybe it was the right time to do some discreet investigation. "I'm forty-six years old," Alan thought. "I'm still in good shape and my hair hasn't turned grey. My friends think that I am very fortunate. I have money, position and a successful career. To them that is everything. They think I'm better off without a wife, but most of them are divorced or having affairs. They would never understand my way of thinking in a hundred years."

He got out of his car and reached inside for his jacket and his brief-case. As he straightened up he told himself that he must put on a happy face for this wonderful occasion. His only child was marrying a great young man. They had been crazy about each other for ages and there was no doubt in Alan's mind that it would be a successful marriage. But, oh dear, how lonely it would be after she had gone.

'Daddy, this is my friend Lainey Wrightson whom you've heard so much about.' Mary-Beth gave her father a quick kiss and held out her hand in Lainey's direction.

'Lainey, I've been looking forward to meeting you.' Alan released his daughter and looked across the room. As he met the eyes of the young woman sitting on the sofa he drew in his breath sharply. "I know this girl," he thought as a strange feeling of déjà-vu came over him. "I could never forget a face like that."

'I know that this sounds like the cliché of all time, but haven't we met before?' he asked her as he shook her hand.

'I don't think so.' She smiled at him a little uncertainly.

Her handshake was warm and firm. How beautiful she was – not a bit as he had imagined her. He had thought that because she was a well-known model she would be very sophisticated and over made-up, but she was quite the opposite. There was a frank openness in those lovely eyes which even in such a short space of time made it easy to see why she had captivated his daughter and her future husband.

'You probably saw her in the distance at the International Débutantes Ball two years ago,' Mary-Beth bubbled. 'Lainey represented England. That's how we met, remember?'

'Yes, that must be it,' Alan replied a shade too heartily. He still wasn't convinced. He felt that he already knew this girl, even though he had never met her. It was a strange unsettling feeling. He wondered if she felt it as well.

After dinner Alan stood at the window and watched the two girls as they walked across the lawn. They were laughing and joking together. "I wish that I'd had more children," he thought suddenly. "It would have been nice for Mary-Beth to have had a sister."

'They're very alike, aren't they?' Jimmy Foxton had walked up behind him.

'What?' Alan was surprised.

'Very alike and very different. When we were all in New York two years ago I kept telling them that it was like knowing two sides of one person. Terrible twins, that's what I called them.'

'How strange.'

'Sir?'

'I felt as if I knew her. I said so before dinner.'

'Yes, you did, didn't you? I expect that it's because in so many ways she resembles Mary-Beth.'

'But they don't look . . .'

'Oh, I'll admit that their colouring is very different, but there are certain similarities, don't you think? Take those extraordinary deep blue eyes of theirs and their bone structure. They are both tall. But they have remarkably small bones. Look at their hands and their feet – and then they have several gestures that they both do quite automatically which are the same. It's quite fascinating.'

385

'I'm surprised at a young man of your age noticing things like that,' Alan smiled.

'You have to be able to recognise and feel things in my profession.'

'Yes, of course, how silly of me.'

'One day, perhaps, I'll write an opera about something along those lines.' Jimmy looked dreamily out of the window. 'Something along the line of two sisters maybe who never met until they were grown-up. It would be strange and haunting, so that when they meet for the first time they feel that they know one another, even though they've never met before. Maybe they both love the same man – yes, that's it, then it can be a wonderful tragedy.'

'What you have, my lad, is a wonderful imagination.' Alan clapped him on the shoulder. 'But stick with it. I've no doubt that one day you'll be a great composer.'

The following day it rained. Mary-Beth was distraught. 'It just can't do this tomorrow,' she cried as she paced the room like a caged animal. 'The garden looks so pretty. I couldn't bear for it to be a wash-out. It would be most unfair.'

'The trouble with you, my girl, is that you've not got enough to do, so you are driving us mad with your constant worrying about something over which only God has control.' Karen Prebble spoke brusquely. 'Why don't you go up to the attic and sort through those boxes of clutter that have been there since your father bought the house. You never know what you might find – some long lost treasure, though I doubt it. Anyway, it would be a worthwhile job and would keep you occupied so that you stop making us all paranoid. I'm sure that Alaina will help you, won't you, dear?'

'Yes, of course.' Lainey got to her feet. 'Come on MB, it'll be good therapy as you Americans say.'

The two girls spent the rest of the day totally engrossed in sorting through things which had been accumulated and discarded over the years of Mary-Beth's childhood. They laughed when they found old photographs of her as a baby and as a little girl.

'Oh, there's that teddy-bear that I had when I was six.' Mary-Beth grabbed a very dishevelled toy that only had one eye and had obviously been well-loved. 'I lost him and cried for ages, then Mother told me that she'd thrown him out as I was too old for that sort of thing.'

'That was rather unkind,' Lainey said.

'Mother was like that.' Mary-Beth didn't seem to harbour any malice. 'She couldn't bear the thought that either Daddy or I could love anything else.'

'Yes, but a teddy bear?'

'I know. It was very sad. Daddy really had a tough time with her. She had several breakdowns before she died.'

'He never married again, did he? It seems strange, as he's so good-looking, and he's not that old, is he?'

'No.' Mary-Beth sat on her heels. 'There was Linda two years ago. I really thought that he might marry her. She was real nice too, but somehow he chickened out. If I didn't known him so well, I'd be inclined to think that there was someone else – maybe someone who's married or something, with whom he's madly in love. Sometimes, when he doesn't know that I'm watching him, I see this far-away look in his eyes.' She shrugged her shoulders. 'But it's not that. It's not his style. He's too honest and too upright. He wouldn't steal someone else's wife.'

Was it her imagination, or did her friend's face go pink, Mary-Beth wondered. A thought struck her. Had Lainey been on the rebound from some married man when she married her husband? She opened her mouth to ask a question. But Lainey anticipated it.

'Come on,' she said in a matter-of-fact tone of voice. 'We've got one more crate to go through. We may just finish before dinner.'

'Oh, I've had enough. Let's call it a day.' Mary-Beth looked into the crate. 'It looks like there's only a few more old photo albums.' She leafed through the one on the top. 'Oh yes, they're pre-war and some of Daddy in the war. They don't need sorting. He won't want those thrown out.'

'Can't we look at them?'

'Not now, I'm parched. I need a drink before we change for dinner. You can come up here and take a look tomorrow morning if you like while I'm at the hairdresser.'

'Yes, I think I will.' Lainey smiled at her. 'I love looking at old photos, it's fun.'

'Yes, well, I've seen them all a hundred times before. Are you sure that you don't want a hair appointment?'

'No really. I always do it myself, except when modelling jobs demand some ridiculously exotic style.'

'OK then. Now, are we going to get that drink?'

Mary-Beth's fears had been groundless. Saturday morning dawned bright and clear. By ten o'clock the sun had come through the clouds and was rapidly burning away the few that remained.

Everyone was busy, running in all directions and doing last minute adjustments. Lainey had offered to help but had been told there was nothing she could do. It would be better, she thought, if she kept out of the way. Mary-Beth had gone off to the hairdresser.

"I'll go and look at those albums," she thought. It was funny, but Mary-Beth's father intrigued her. She liked him, but she found him slightly unsettling. "He seems so familiar," she thought. "There's something so trusting about him. I feel as if I could tell him anything and he would help me. It's like when I was a little girl and I fell over and cut myself. I would go rushing to Daddy and he would make it better. I miss him. There's no longer anyone whom I can run to with my problems. But I couldn't have told him about Charlie and me, could I? Mother's wonderful, but she'd never understand either. Daddy always understood me better than Mother. Why do I feel that I could tell Alan Jefferson? Why do I feel he would understand?

"I'll start with the photographs," she told herself. "If I want to find out more about the man, I can at least look at pictures of him when he was young. They may tell me something."

The first album she unearthed was dated 1938/9. There were pictures of a very handsome young man standing by a small single-seater aeroplane with his arm around a beautiful young girl. That must be Rosemary. She looked very healthy and full of life then. So, he was a flier. Lainey wondered if he had been in the airforce during the war. He had aged well, she thought. He had filled out a bit, but he had remained in good shape. He no longer had that lean earnest look that often characterised young people. She flicked through the book and then rummaged in the crate for the next one.

The first photograph showed him in his wartime uniform. He really did look extremely handsome. Good Lord! She looked closer. It was an RAF uniform. He must have been in the British airforce. She turned the page. There were pictures of a place called Millington. Wasn't that in Wiltshire? So, he had been stationed in the West Country. Hadn't Uncle Alfie been there? She felt a thrill of excitement. Maybe they had known each other? On the other hand, Uncle Alfie had become a prisoner of war very early on. She turned the page, now totally fascinated by the old browning prints of fighter planes and the men who flew them.

'Lainey, I'm back,' Mary-Beth called from downstairs.

Hurriedly she put down the album she was looking at, and it was then that it happened. A photograph, which had not been pasted in, fell out on to the floor. Lainey bent down to pick it up. As she turned it over she felt herself go icy cold from the shock. The picture was of a very beautiful young girl, and written across the right-hand corner was: 'To darling Alan with all my love, Jenny.'

For a moment she stood transfixed, just staring at the photograph, then she started to shiver as the reaction hit her.

That photograph – that very same photograph – was the one that her father had kept on his desk in Harley Street right up until the day he died. Her mother looked so beautiful in it. Up until this very second, she had thought that the look in her eyes had been put there by her father, but now . . .?

'Lainey, come on. It's lunchtime.'

'Coming.' She forced herself to come back to reality as she hurriedly stuffed the offending picture in her pocket.

"I'll deal with this later," she told herself. "I can't begin to think about it now."

CHAPTER EIGHTEEN

It had been a beautiful wedding, Alan thought as he stood watching the workmen on the following morning as they started their clearing up. Mary-Beth had looked so happy and so had her young husband. They were good kids – both of them. He was certain that they would get along just fine. How very fortunate it was that Mary-Beth had not inherited her mother's temperament. It really was amazing that she was such a well-adjusted girl.

She had only had one maid of honour and that had been her great friend Jeannie Mason – in fact it had been Jeannie and her parents who had given the lovely Lainey a lift back to New York. His thoughts lingered on Lainey – he would have liked to know more about her, though he didn't know why.

At one point in the wedding service, when the rector had told Jimmy he could kiss his bride, Alan had happened to look across at Lainey and been shattered to see a look of abject misery on her face. Had she been in love with Jimmy? No, not possible. She hardly knew him. Maybe she was not a happily married woman. Maybe this wedding reminded her of something that she had not been so lucky as to experience. Suddenly he realised where it was that he had seen her before. It *had* been at the International Debutantes Ball. She had been the young girl whom he had noticed sitting at a table while he had been dancing with Linda. She had had the same look on her face then as she did today.

When he looked back at her, she had composed herself and was smiling in the direction of the happy couple. Last time he had thought that he had dreamed it, but this time he knew that he hadn't – on either occasion.

He had talked to her briefly during the reception and had been surprised that she had asked him so many questions about his time in the airforce. He had been reticent with his answers. He didn't like remembering that time of his life, as it brought back too many other memories with it.

'I wasn't there for that long,' he had told her. 'I was shot down in July 1941 and, because of my injuries, they shipped me home.'

'I see.' Her little face had had a strange look on it. Surely she didn't think that he had chickened out?

When she had come up to say good-bye she had opened her mouth to ask something, and then apparently thought better of it. Instead she had simply shaken his hand and thanked him for his hospitality.

Alan had wanted to tell her to stay in touch, but somehow the words didn't come out. He had just nodded and smiled and said that it had been a pleasure.

The telephone was ringing. He walked back into the house to answer it.

'Hello?' He picked up the receiver.

'Mr Jefferson?'

'Yes.'

'It's Alaina Wrightson. I'm sorry to bother you right after the wedding.'

Alan felt an overwhelming sense of joy. How was that for mental telepathy?

'Lainey, I'm so glad you called. I was just thinking about you.'

'Were you?' Her voice sounded wistful.

'What can I do for you?'

'I wondered whether you would possibly have the time to meet me when you get back to New York. There's something I want to ask you?'

'Yes, of course. Why don't I take you to dinner tomorrow night?'

'Well, if that wouldn't be too much of an imposition.' She sounded hesitant.

'Of course it wouldn't. I shall look forward to it.' Alan tried to lighten his tone of voice. 'It isn't every day that I get the chance to take out a lovely young girl who's young enough to be my daughter.' He laughed nervously.

He heard her draw in a sharp breath. 'Yes. Well ... if you're sure, that would be very nice.'

"Good Lord!" Alan thought. "Does she think that I'm coming on to her?"

'I'll book a table at the Four Seasons. Mary-Beth always likes it when I take her there.' He wanted to sound reassuring. 'I'll make it for eight o'clock. Shall I pick you up at the Plaza?'

'No,' she said quickly. 'I'll meet you there.'

After he put the telephone down Alan felt a prickle of unease at the base of his spine. What was he getting himself into?

"I hope that I'm not going to make a fool of myself," he thought. "I'm too old for all that, and she's the same age as my daughter – I must keep reminding myself of that."

That night he didn't sleep well. He dreamed of a young girl with bright blue eyes who was beckoning at him. Behind her there was someone in the shadows, and as hard as he tried he couldn't make out who it was. And all the time the young girl was smiling and beckoning and saying that it was all right.

But what was all right?

Alan woke up in a sweat. He got out of bed and opened the curtains. The sun was shining. He looked down on the traffic which was already heavy on the street.

'Stop fantasizing,' he told himself sternly. 'There is nothing odd about this girl phoning you up. She probably wants to discuss something to do with her career.'

Yes, that was the reason. The world this morning looked far too normal to be holding any dire secrets for him.

As Lainey walked towards him in the restaurant, Alan was

aware of how heads turned. The head waiter who led her across the room was obviously impressed as well. The young Lady Wrightson was beauty at its best – pure and understated. Alan was convinced that most people in the crowded room felt better for having witnessed her entrance.

'I'm sorry I'm late,' she smiled as she sat down, facing him.

'You're not. I wanted to be here when you arrived.' He smiled back at her.

'What will you have to drink?'

'I'd love a gin and tonic.'

'The English seem to like that.'

'Do we?' She gave a light laugh. 'What makes you think that?'

'I suppose because I knew an English girl once – a long time ago – who used to love drinking gin and tonic. I have always associated it with England.'

'My mother likes it.'

'There you are then.'

'Yes.' She looked thoughtful.

'Shall we order?' He handed her the menu. 'Everything's delicious.'

They spent the next hour talking about the wedding and about life in America. It was only when they got to the coffee stage that Alan realised that Lainey had completely avoided talking about herself or her life in England. Instead, she had managed to keep the conversation focused exclusively on him and Mary-Beth. Clever, but why?

'Well now, young lady, just exactly what did you want to ask me?'

Lainey placed her elbows on the table and clasped her hands together. 'It's about when you were in the British airforce during the war.' She looked at him intently.

'That was a long time ago – before you were even born.' Alan knew that he sounded a trifle too hearty. 'I wasn't there for that long unfortunately. I was shot down and suffered severe damage to my eyesight. I also had a spinal injury so they sent me back home.'

Was he making excuses for his failure to complete his active service in the war, he wondered.

'When you were there you were stationed at a place called Millington in Wiltshire. I know that from the photographs in your old album. I wondered if you knew Uncle Alfie.'

'And who is Uncle Alfie?' He felt a little easier. 'I didn't mix much with the top brass, I'm afraid,' he laughed.

'Oh, he wasn't top brass.' She gave a nervous little smile. 'He was just an ordinary pilot. Alfred Hurst. You may not have known him. He got shot down over enemy territory quite early on and spent most of the war in a prisoner of war camp.'

'Alfie Hurst? Of course I knew him.' Alan looked amazed. 'He's your uncle?'

'Not my real uncle.' She took a sip of wine. 'He's always been a great family friend. I work for him, you know. He's the Hurst of Hurst and Lever.' Her eyes never left his face.

'Good heavens!' Alan ran a hand through his hair. 'I had no idea. How incredible. I always knew that he would do well for himself, but this is truly amazing.'

'He's here in New York at the moment and so is his younger daughter, Vivien. She's my best friend. They're staying at the Plaza as well. Maybe you would like to call on him?'

'Yes, yes I would. How simply incredible.' Everything about this evening seemed unreal – and it was happening just at the time he had wanted to find out about Jenny. Maybe Alfie Hurst had kept in touch. Maybe all it would take would be a meeting with him. He began to feel very excited. 'Imagine,' he said half to himself, 'the last time I saw little Vivien she was barely a year old.'

'Yes, I thought you would know her.' Lainey opened her handbag and took out the photograph. She handed it to him.

Alan felt the blood rush to his head. 'Where did you find this?'

Was it Lainey's imagination or did his voice tremble slightly?

'It fell out of your album. It wasn't fixed in.'

'Why did you take it?'

'Who is she, Alan?'

'Jenny,' he whispered. 'Jenny Woodward.' His face looked grey. 'What is this all about, Lainey?'

She handed him the picture.

'A similar print to that one sat on my father's desk all his life,' she said softly. 'I always thought that that light in her eyes was for him.' She choked and her eyes glistened with unshed tears. 'But it wasn't, was it? It was for you.' She paused and then delivered her bombshell. 'I'm Jennifer Woodward's daughter. You must have known my father as well. He was Anthony Carrington.'

'Oh my God!' Alan felt as if someone had hit him on the head hard. 'I can hardly believe what I'm hearing.'

'It's true – and there's more.'

'Not here. We should talk in private. Will you come back to my apartment?' He looked at her hesitantly.

She nodded.

They didn't speak a word on the taxi ride up town. It wasn't until they were were inside his Park Avenue apartment that he said, 'I loved your mother very much.'

'You still do, don't you?'

'How could you possibly know that?' He was taken aback.

She gave him a sad little smile. 'When you've longed for something all your life that is forbidden to you, it's easy to recognise the signs in someone else.'

He remembered the look he had seen on her face at the wedding.

'What has been forbidden to you, Lainey? Surely you're too young for that?'

'No younger than my mother was, but we'll come to that later.' Her voice had an edge to it.

'Lainey, I never wanted to hurt your mother. I loved her very much.'

'I'm not standing judgement on you, Alan.' She put a hand on his arm. 'Believe me when I say that I think her life has been far happier than yours. My father was a wonderful man and they were very content together.'

'Was?' He looked up sharply.

'He died two years ago.' She stood up and walked over to the window. 'And no, before you ask me, she hasn't remarried.'

There was a silence while he digested this piece of information. Jenny was free. He could see her again – if she would want to see him again, that is. One thing he knew was that he wanted desperately to see her. He felt exhilarated – over the moon. Lainey's next words brought him down to earth.

'There is something I have to know,' she said, still gazing unseeingly out of the window.

'Yes, anything. What can I tell you?'

'Assuming that you obviously did have an affair with my mother, when did you last sleep with her?'

Alan froze. 'Lainey, it was such a long time ago. Surely it can't matter now?'

'It does matter. Please, answer me.'

'I don't know.' He ran a hand through his hair distractedly. 'I was shot down in July 1941. I suppose it was just before then. Why?'

'Would you say that she was sleeping with my father when she knew you – or even before she knew you?'

An icy hand gripped his heart.

'No.' His voice was hardly audible. 'Tony loved her – I could see that. But he knew about your mother and me. He knew that I could never marry her because of Rosemary and he knew that we couldn't help the way we felt about each other. I'm glad she married him. He was indeed a wonderful man.'

'Alan, I'm as confused as I think you are.' She turned from the window and he saw that tears were flowing down her cheeks.

'Lainey, honey, what is it?' He took a step towards her, but she avoided contact with him.

'My birthday is April 1st 1942. April Fool's Day – that's a joke, isn't it?' She tried to smile through her tears. 'That means that I was conceived in July 1941. Mother married Father in the autumn. I always thought that wartime promoted situations like that. No one ever mentioned you. I was always led to believe that I was Tony Carrington's daughter – so was Charlie, my so-called half-brother. But I'm not, am I? Tony Carrington was not my father – you are.'

'Jesus!' Alan sat down on the nearest chair.

Lainey came and sat opposite him on the sofa.

'It explains so much,' she said. Her voice had risen an octave and sounded very excited. 'It explains why Charlie and I felt the way we do about each other.'

'Little three-year-old Charlie Carrington?' He looked up at her bleary-eyed as he tried to take in what she was saying.

'He's twenty-four and a qualified doctor.'

'Lainey, I can't quite believe all this. I feel as if I'm in the middle of a very strange dream.'

'Think of my name.' She spoke earnestly. 'Alaina. If I'd been a boy I'd have been called Alan, wouldn't I? Think of how alike MB and I are. We have the same eyes – everyone agrees on that. What they didn't realise was that we both have your eyes. We're the same height with the same bone-structure. I'm blonde like you and my mother while she's dark like her mother. Jimmy was right when he laughingly said that it was like being with two sides of the same person. That's what we are, aren't we?' She looked at him seriously. 'When I first met you I felt that in some strange way I already knew you. Did you feel that too?'

He nodded dumbly.

'Oh, you can't imagine what a weight this has taken off my mind.' Her wet eyes sparkled.

'What do you mean?' Alan was suddenly alarmed at her

nervous exhilaration. 'And what did you mean about the way you and your brother felt about each other?'

'But don't you see? He's not my brother, is he? We thought it was wrong to have those feelings about each other. We had to suppress them. He married Alison – Viv's elder sister – to get away from me and I married Harry to teach him a lesson, because I knew that Charlie couldn't stand him. None of that need have happened if only we'd been told.'

'Did your parents know about your feelings for one another?' Alan was trying to make sense of the situation.

'No, of course not. There's a dirty word for what we thought we felt about each other.'

'Oh Lainey, I don't know what to say.' Alan registered for the first time the possibility that this beautiful young girl could be his daughter. 'This has all come as such a tremendous shock. I don't know what to do.'

'I want everyone to be happy.' She sat down next to him and flung her arms around his neck. 'I never knew that I could be so happy.'

'But, honey, don't jump the gun.' He hugged her to him. 'Although it sounds more than probable, only your mother can verify this.'

'She will. I know she will. Anyway, I know that it's true. I don't need her to verify it. Oh, I can't wait to tell Charlie.' She stood up and put on her coat.

'Lainey, don't go. Not yet. We need to talk more – especially about you and Charlie. You're married, my dear, and so is he. Don't act in a hot-headed way over this. It would be so wrong and I think you could regret it deeply.'

'I won't.' She smiled at him fondly, but he could tell that she wasn't really listening.

'Please don't do anything rash.' He gripped her hands. 'Meet me tomorrow and we'll discuss all this some more.'

'Yes.' She smiled and gave his cheek a quick kiss, then she

hugged him briefly. 'I shall sleep so well tonight,' she said as she left.

One person who did not sleep well that night was Alan Jefferson. His thoughts were in utter confusion. It had been one thing to tell himself that now he would try and find out about Jennifer Woodward, but quite another to suddenly have all these facts thrown at him out of the blue by this lovely girl who professed to be his daughter.

There was no doubt in his mind that this girl was special to him. He had felt that from the moment he had first set eyes on her. "Oh Jenny," he thought. "What did I do to you? What did I put you through? I wish that you could have told me. I wish that I could have known this beautiful hot-headed daughter of ours while she was growing up." Yes, he was as certain of that as Lainey was. She was his daughter. He had been reckless and incautious as a young man, and though Mary-Beth had not inherited that side of his character, Lainey apparently had. What was this obsession with Charlie Carrington? From the look that he had seen in her eyes on several occasions it must be quite something. That look was all-consuming – dangerous? "Oh Lainey, sweetheart," he thought. "Don't act rashly. It could ruin your life."

What was her husband like, he wondered. She had said that Charlie didn't like him. Was that genuine dislike or simply a dislike of anyone that she would have married? Was she happy with him? Or was it just as she said, that she had married him to spite her would-be lover?

What would she do now? Charlie was married to the Hurst girl. What an unbelievable mess. Parents tried to do right by their children, but so often they were proved wrong. Clearly, Tony and Jenny had decided to keep up the pretence that Lainey was their daughter and therefore avoid any possible scandal. They would never have dreamt that a brother and sister could be attracted to one another. And who could ever have foreseen that Lainey would meet Mary-Beth and become friends with her – and find that photograph?

It was obviously meant to be. It was meant to be for a number of reasons. The predominant one was that it was up to him, Alan, to do something about Lainey and Charlie before they did something that they would both regret.

As soon as he got to work the following morning, Alan telephoned Lainey at the Plaza hotel. He felt himself grow cold as the impersonal voice on the other end of the line said that Lady Wrightson had checked out earlier that morning. Oh God! Where had she gone? What was she going to do in the heat of the moment? Had she already booked herself on to a flight back to England? How could he find her and stop her from doing something that would turn so many people's lives upside down? Jennifer no longer lived at Edgeglow – that much he knew – but Lainey had not said where they lived now. He put his head in his hands as he tried to think clearly.

Of course! He slammed his hand down on his desk. Alfie Hurst was here with his daughter. He would know. He was the person he must talk to before he embarked on a trip to England. Alfie would be able to tell him so many things and it would be wonderful to see him again.

Alan pressed the intercom in front of him. 'Nancy, get me Mr Alfred Hurst at the Plaza Hotel, will you please – oh, and then book me on a flight to London, England.'

'Yes, Mr Jefferson.' His secretary's voice showed no surprise.

As Alan waited for the telephone to ring, he suddenly remembered that Alfie would have no idea of his relationship with Jenny. It had all happened after he had been taken prisoner. Oh Lord, he was going to have a lot of explaining to do.

CHAPTER NINETEEN

'Well, well, so you came home three days ahead of schedule.'
Harry walked into the bedroom as Lainey was unpacking.
'What brought this about? I'm sure that it wasn't a rampant
desire to see me.'

'I came because I wanted to. Don't make me wish that I
hadn't.' Lainey's face was set and her movements were
nervous and jerky.

'I always seem to say the wrong thing,' he mumbled with a
sigh. 'I have missed you, you know.'

He put his arms around her awkwardly and bent his head
to kiss her. She accepted the kiss coolly.

'Have you?' she asked dispassionately.

'You know damn well that I have.' His hands were moving
over her body rousing her senses in spite of herself. With a
concerted effort she pushed him away.

'I read the *Daily Express*. I know what you were doing
while I was away.'

'It wasn't like that. I swear to you that it wasn't like that.
You must let me explain.'

'Spare me your weak excuses.' She turned away.

'Well, what about you?' Suddenly he was incensed. 'What
am I to think when this man keeps ringing you from
America?'

'What are you talking about?' She rounded on him.

'Alan Jefferson. He called yesterday and again today. He
said that you must speak to him as soon as you arrived, so
don't act "holier than thou" with me. I suppose that this
girlfriend of yours has a randy brother.'

Lainey had gone white. 'It's her father and . . .'

'Oh, so now you're into older men . . . and I always

thought that you were so pure. What a joke that was. I thought that there was something between us – something that neither of us would ever find with anyone else. Well, tell me, my lovely devious bride, what does he do to you that turns you on even more than when you're with me? What little sexual tricks has he got up his sleeve?'

'Oh, you bastard!' She slapped him as hard as she could across the face. 'Oh.' Her hand flew to her mouth. What had she said? It wasn't Harry who was the bastard, it was her, Lainey. She felt the tears welling up inside her as she stared at him silently. She could see the imprint that her hand had made on his cheek.

'Never do that again,' he said very softly. 'And never call me that.'

'I . . .' She gulped as she looked mesmerized into his eyes. There was a cold hard glint in them. She remained transfixed as he started to take off his clothes.

'And now I'm going to show you exactly what there is between us,' he informed her.

'No.' Suddenly she found that she could move.

'Yes.' He pushed her down on the bed and ripped her blouse as he hastened to pull it off her.

'Harry, no. I don't want to.' She struggled, but he was too strong for her. 'Not now – not like this.'

'Yes, now. You're my wife and I want you now – and so will you, you'll see.' He held her arms with his hands and imprisoned her legs with his knees as he nuzzled her neck and bit her shoulder, then he fastened his mouth on her left nipple and teased it gently with his tongue.

"Oh God, don't do that," she thought. How treacherously her body was behaving. He knew all the ways to make her respond. One of his hands was now pulling away her remaining clothing and she was helping him to do it. As he entered her she gave a cry like a small wounded animal. His mouth was instantly on hers, searching and probing deep into her. Her arms went around him – one raking through his hair and the other pressing his buttocks deeper and deeper into her. At that moment she could not have enough of him, nor he of her.

It was not a gentle love-making, it was harsh and full of a wild need. It was exciting and in the end deeply satisfying.

When at last it was over, Lainey curled on her side in the foetal position and cried as if her heart would break.

'You see, you can't deny it,' Harry said as he put an arm around her. 'We're so good together.'

'No,' she whispered.

'Lainey, darling, we need each other.' He drew her to him and kissed her forehead gently. 'I love you, and, if you would only acknowledge it, you do love me.'

'No.' She broke away from him and sat up shaking violently. Her eyes were glassy as she said, 'You're not capable of love – I know that and you've already proved it.'

'I can explain that. It's not what you think. Just give me the chance to explain. It's you that I love and only you. It always has been, ever since I met you.'

'Don't say that. I don't want to hear it.' She looked distraught as she ran a hand through her dishevelled hair. 'I hate you for the way you make me feel. It's not love, it's . . . oh, I don't know what it is.' She stood up and ran to the door. 'I have to ring Charlie,' she said as she disappeared.

'That bloody brother of yours,' he shouted after her. 'Sometimes I think that it's him you've wanted all along.'

He followed her out into the corridor. She had stopped dead in her tracks and her hands cupped her flaming face. It was as if she had turned to stone.

'Lainey.' Harry was alarmed. 'What is it?'

Slowly she came back to life. 'Nothing,' she said calmly. 'Nothing that you would ever understand.'

She walked on down the stairs.

'I could try,' he whispered, but he knew that she couldn't hear him.

He heard her pick up the telephone and dial a number. After a few seconds he heard her say: 'Charlie? Thank God you're there. I've got to see you. There's something that I've got to tell you.'

There was a pause while she listened to whatever he said, then: 'Yes, I'll do that . . . and Charlie, I've missed you so much.'

"Oh God," thought Harry dully. "I'm right – I was only trying to make her angry but I'm right – she's in love with her brother."

As Jennifer drove up the drive she noticed a strange car parked outside the front of the house. Funny, she wasn't expecting anyone. She reached across to the passenger seat and picked up her box of groceries. As she straightened up she had a quick look at herself in the mirror. What a mess, she thought. She had no make-up on and her hair was longer than she usually wore it and tangled from driving with the windows open in the hot weather. She hoped that it was no one important who had come to call.

'Oh Mrs Carrington.' Bert, the weekend gardener, met her on the doorstep. 'You have a gentleman caller. I've put him in the living room.'

Jennifer smiled to herself at his quaint old-fashioned way of speaking.

'That's all right, Bert. Do you know who he is?'

'Couldn't rightly say, ma'am. I didn't like to ask like, but he's an ever-so-nice gentleman.' Bert had his cap in his hand and was mopping his brow with a slightly grey handkerchief. 'I hope I did the right thing?' He looked worried.

'Of course you did.' Jennifer patted his arm. 'Thank you, Bert.'

She walked into the house and dumped her shopping in the hall. Then she crossed it and opened the drawing room door.

The man had his back to her as she entered the room. He was looking out of the window into the garden.

'I'm so sorry that I was out when you called. I . . .'

The sentence never got finished. As he turned around to face her, she gasped and put out a hand to clutch the back of the sofa and steady herself.

'Hello, Jenny,' Alan said softly.

'I can't believe this. I must be dreaming.'

'No, you're not. It really is me.'

Jennifer was beginning to feel light-headed. She ran a hand through her hair as she tried to think of words to say.

'I look such a mess. I wasn't expecting anyone.' She knew that she was babbling.

'You look wonderful.' His voice was warm – just as she had always remembered it. 'You look exactly the same as you did – when was it . . .?'

'Twenty-one years ago,' she whispered.

'Is it really that long ago?'

'Yes.' It came out almost like a sigh.

With a monumental effort she forced herself to move around the sofa and hold out her hand. 'You look pretty wonderful yourself.' She gave him a weak smile. 'No grey hairs and you haven't put on very much weight.'

He caught hold of both her hands in a spontaneous gesture. 'It's so good to see you, Jenny. So very good.'

She made herself look into his eyes and what she saw there made her heart leap, just the way it used to do all that time ago. She sat down, drawing him down beside her.

'I've thought about you so often,' she said as her eyes still held his. 'I wondered how you were and if you were happy. Did things work out for you, Alan?'

'In a way, but Rosemary died four years ago. I have a lovely daughter who has always been a great comfort to me.'

Alan noticed that she had tensed up at the mention of Mary-Beth, but all she said was, 'Poor Rosemary. So things did not get better between you both?'

'Not really – I thought that they would when Mary-Beth was born, but I was kidding myself as usual. She ended up

by being as jealous of Mary-Beth as she was of anyone else.'
His gaze intensified. 'She was in and out of nursing homes
until she finally died of an overdose – I've never
acknowledged that to anyone before, not even to myself.'

'Poor Rosemary,' she said again.

'And what about you?' he stood up and looked down at
her. 'How have you been, my . . .' He had wanted to say 'my
love', but he didn't dare – not yet.

'I've been fine.' A slight blush crept up her cheeks. 'I
married Tony Carrington – but you must know that. I have a
daughter˜too.' The blush had increased, then faded as she
said, 'Tony died two years ago. It was very sudden. He had a
heart-attack.' She stood up and walked quickly towards the
French windows which were open. 'It's very hot in here,
isn't it? Let's go outside. I think I need to walk around.'

Alan followed her down the stone steps on to the lawn.

'He was a marvellous man,' she said as they strolled
through the garden. 'He loved us all so much. He wanted to
give us everything. I often told him that he worked far too
hard, but he was so dedicated. I was lucky to have him and
yes, to answer your question, I was happy.'

'I'm glad.'

They had reached the wall at the bottom of the garden and
stayed there, looking out over the field in front of them.

After a long pause, Alan said, 'I've missed you so much.'

'Yes, I know,' she replied without looking at him. 'I felt it
– maybe because I've missed you so much as well. How did
you find me?'

'I ran into Alfie in New York.'

'Really?' Now they were beginning to talk like old friends.
'After all these years, how did you find him? He's done so
well, hasn't he? Do you know that his daughter Alison
married Charlie?'

'Yes, he looks marvellous and I was amazed at what he has
achieved, and yes, I know about Charlie.' He laughed at her
enthusiasm.

'Well, did you meet my daughter, Lainey? She was out there doing a big promotion for Alfie.' For a minute she looked apprehensive. 'You'd like her. She's lovely and full of life and fun and . . .' She didn't know how to continue.

'Oh, my Jenny,' he said softly. 'Where have all the years gone? I have so much to tell you and so much explaining to do.'

'So have I.' She trembled and her eyes filled with tears. 'I don't know where to start.'

'Not yet,' he whispered and drew her into his arms. He pressed his cheek against hers and held her silently for a long time as he fought the urge to cry himself.

At last she stirred and he felt the old familiar thrill of excitement run through him.

'I love you,' he said. 'I've never been able to stop loving you.'

'I love you too.' She touched his face with her hand – making sure that he was real. She relished the feel of him – the smell of him. Slowly he lowered his lips to hers.

It started as a gentle kiss, but gradually all the yearning and the longing of a love so long denied took over. It was an exquisite pain that came close to being unbearable, but was impossible to stop. Their bodies seemed to be on fire.

'It's not too late for us, Jenny, is it?' he whispered hoarsely into her hair.

Before she had a chance to reply they heard shouting and a distraught Harry rushed out of the house and across the lawn.

'Jennifer, Jennifer, where are you? Oh!' He paused as he saw her disentangle herself quickly from Alan's arms. 'I'm sorry to barge in on you.' He was covered in confusion.

'Harry. What a surprise. What on earth's the matter?'

'It's Lainey,' he said. 'She's gone. I couldn't stop her. You've got to do something before it's too late.'

'I had no idea.' Jennifer sat at the kitchen table with Alan

408

drinking black coffee. It was late in the evening of what had turned out to be a very disturbing day. 'I mean, well, I never would have imagined that that was how they felt about each other. Tony and I often discussed whether we should tell Lainey who her real father was, but we saw no point in confusing her, and we thought that it might have upset her relationship with Charlie. They used to get on so well. We didn't want them to think that there wasn't a blood tie.'

'You were right.' Alan rubbed her shoulder comfortingly. 'I was well and truly out of the picture and there was no need to make her feel that she was . . .'

'That she was a bastard?' She looked up at him reproachfully. 'She wasn't that – and you know it. She was born out of the love we had and still have for one another. After I got over the shock of losing you so much sooner than I expected, I counted myself as incredibly fortunate at finding that I was pregnant. You left me a part of yourself without knowing it and I've always been eternally grateful.'

'Oh my darling.' He hugged her to him. 'She's beautiful – our daughter – almost as beautiful as her mother. You know that when I first saw her I knew she was something special. I felt something, although at the time I didn't realise quite what it was.'

'What are we going to do, Alan?' She turned to him with a worried expression in her eyes.

'All we can do is talk to her. She's an intelligent girl. She's had one hell of a shock and she's obviously gone to discuss it with her best buddy who is, and always has been, Charlie.'

'But if they really feel that way about each other.' Jennifer still could not quite believe it. 'Think of the damage they could do. They're both married, and Alison is expecting a baby.' She shook her head. 'I feel so sorry for Harry. He really loves Lainey and I'm beginning to think that she has led him a hell of a dance all on account of this apparent obsession with Charlie.'

'Darling, she can't get up to much. If she goes to see Charlie, he has his wife there. They won't be alone.'

'Yes, of course, you're right.' She smiled at him fondly. 'I'm taking things to the extreme. Oh Alan, I'm so glad that you are here. I've been alone for a long time. You've no idea how good it feels to have someone here that I can rely on. The Hursts have been wonderful, but it's not the same.'

'I'm never going to leave you again,' he said seriously.

'How can you say that after just one day?'

'I can and I do. Trust me.'

'I do,' she sighed.

At that moment the telephone rang. Jennifer went into the study to answer it. When she came back into the kitchen her face was white.

'That was Miriam Hurst,' she said. 'She rang just to chat, but in passing she mentioned that Alison had been with them for the last three days. She came down to see Alfie and Vivien now that they have returned from New York.'

She walked silently back into the study with Alan behind her. She picked up the telephone and dialled Charlie's number in Yorkshire. After a long time she put the telephone down.

'There's no answer,' she said dully.

CHAPTER TWENTY

Lainey caught the train from King's Cross on the Friday afternoon. She had already telephoned Charlie about the time she would be arriving and he had said that he would meet her.

What was so important, he wondered, that she had to see him right away. He hoped that she wasn't going to start pressurizing him again about their feelings for one another. It wasn't fair – not to anyone.

Maybe he shouldn't see her, but she was his sister and he cared for her. Maybe her marriage to Wrightson had become unendurable? Well, he wouldn't be surprised. He had never liked the man. It had torn him apart when Lainey had married him, and that's why she had done it, hadn't she? She had told him that she wanted him to know that feeling. "Oh Lainey, how cruel you are. Was I really that cruel to you? What else could I do?

"Alison's a wonderful girl. We're going to have a baby very soon. I'm happy with her – much happier than I would ever be with you, Lainey. With her I can feel some sort of peace. I'm not like you, Lainey, not really, even though we are half-brother and half-sister. I don't want any of life's great excitements. I want to live quietly in the country where I can look after my patients and be anonymous. You would never settle for that, my dear sister. You and I could never work, even if we were not related by blood."

As he drove to the station, he wondered what sort of advice he could possibly give her. How do you advise someone who is so close to you that all you want to do when you are with them is all those things which are forbidden? Would he say or do something stupid? Oh Lord, why wasn't

Alison at home? Everything would be all right if she was there. But she wasn't. She was staying with her parents in Surrey and he should have been there this weekend. It was his weekend off, but when Lainey had telephoned he knew that he had to stay and see her. She had sounded so distraught. Why hadn't he told Alison that that was what he was doing? Why had he made that weak excuse about having had to change weekends with one of the other doctors?

'Hi.' Lainey jumped down from the train carrying a small overnight case. 'I just couldn't wait to see you.' Her face was wreathed in smiles as she kissed him briefly on the cheek.

"Silly me," Charlie thought. "I'm building a mountain out of a molehill. She looks fine. Whatever is troubling her can't be that bad. It's just Lainey being Lainey. All that I'll probably have to do is listen to some rather exaggerated story and then tell her not to be so silly and send her home."

The drove back to his house across the moors, laughing and talking about her time in America. How silly of him to worry so much, but how wonderful that she was here. It was just the two of them – like it used to be when they were children, sweet and innocent. Or had they never really been that? Had there always been – even in those early days – something that qualified as more than brotherly and sisterly love between them?

'I'm glad that you're here.' He covered her hand with his. They were sitting in a local restaurant that he and Alison went to from time to time. 'I've missed you too. Perhaps we can be best friends again now. I think that the time we spent apart was a good thing, Lainey. It made us realize so many things. Don't you agree?'

'Maybe.' She smiled wistfully. 'I wonder how you will feel when I tell you what I've got to tell you.'

'Is it that bad?' The wine was making him feel mellow.

'That depends.'

'Well, don't keep me in suspense. What is it?'

'Not here.' She stood up. 'I'll tell you when we get back home.'

'Why are you being so secretive?'

'That's what it's all about – a secret.'

'Ah.' What was she planning? A secret for whom?

She was quiet on the way home and Charlie didn't feel like making conversation. He felt peaceful. The quiet before the storm, he thought later.

'Now, are you going to tell me what this secret is all about?' He poured himself a glass of whisky and sat down facing her in his sitting room.

'You're not going to believe this.' She sat on the sofa twiddling her fingers nervously.

'Well, are you going to try me?'

'I'm not your sister.'

'What?' It was the last thing he had expected to hear. 'Are you crazy or something?'

'No. It's true.' She fixed him with her brilliant blue eyes. 'I never was your sister. Your father is not my father. My father is an American. He had an affair with my mother during the war, and I was the result. He was wounded and sent back to the States in July 1941. When Mother found out that she was pregnant, your father married her.'

'Are you serious?' He was incredulous.

'Of course I'm serious. Why do you think I'm here?' she snapped.

'How do you know this?' he whispered hoarsely.

'I met my father while I was in New York. Of all the most incredible coincidences, it was his daughter that I became friendly with the last time I was there. This time I went to their house for Mary-Beth's wedding and I found a photograph of Mother in an old album. It was the same one that was on your father's desk in his office. Well, of course, I questioned him about it and it all fits.'

'But Lainey, it was just a photo.'

'No it wasn't. She had written on it – "To darling Alan,

413

with all my love Jenny." Did you ever hear Mother called Jenny? Well, I asked him whether he had had an affair with her and he told me that he had.'

'Lainey, you didn't.' Charlie was astounded.

'I had to, didn't I? It turned out that he last slept with her in July 1941. She married Daddy I mean your father – in the autumn and I was born on April the first the following year. Make of that what you like.'

'Did you ask Mother?' Charlie had always called Jennifer 'Mother'.

Lainey nodded. Well, it was only a little white-lie. She had not been able to bring herself to go and see her mother just yet. Her mind had been in a turmoil. Even though she had liked Alan Jefferson and had known that Anthony Carrington must have always known that she was not his child, her thoughts had been so mixed up; and overriding everything else had been the knowledge that Charlie wasn't – and never had been – her half-brother.

'Lainey, I don't know what to say.'

'Tell me you love me,' she said and held out her arms. 'Tell me that you've always loved me. We don't have to feel guilty or unclean any more. It's all right. We're not freaks. What we felt for each other was right. It was right from the very beginning.'

'Oh Lainey.' He moved over to the sofa and took her in his arms.

She covered his face with hot feverish kisses before fastening her lips on to his. He kissed her softly as she pressed herself closer and closer to him.

'Make love to me, Charlie,' she said against his mouth. 'I've wanted you for so long and I know that you've wanted me. Oh Charlie, I love you so much.' She started to unbutton his shirt and ran her hand along his chest. It was smooth and hairless – so different from Harry's.

'No.' With a super-human effort he pushed her away.

'What's the matter? What's wrong?' Her eyes smouldered with passion.

414

'This is wrong, Lainey.'

'How can it be wrong? You want me as much as I want you. You don't have to feel guilty any more. I'm *not* your sister.'

'There are other kinds of guilt, my love.' He hung his head as he spoke, but all Lainey noticed was that he had called her 'his love'. 'We are both married,' he continued 'I do love Alison and she's having our child.'

'Well, I'm married and I don't have those feelings of guilt.'

'Oh Lainey, what a lot you have to learn about life.' Charlie shook his head sadly. 'Sometimes we can't just take what we want. We have no right to make other people suffer. I would get no pleasure from that and nor would you. There has never been a right time for us and there never will be.'

'How can you say that?' Her eyes blazed. She stood up and ran out of the room.

'Where are you going?' He was alarmed.

'To bed. On my own.' She sobbed, rushed up the stairs and into the spare bedroom. She slammed the door and he heard the key turn in the lock.

In spite of himself Charlie smiled a sad smile. Did she really expect him to follow her?

It was a hot oppressive night. Thunder rumbled in the distance, and Charlie lay in bed unable to sleep. In the end he gave up the idea and switched on the light. He peeled off his cotton pyjama jacket and felt marginally more comfortable.

The thunder was getting nearer. Did she still hate it and feel frightened of it, as she had when she was a little girl, he wondered. In those days she had often burst into his room and curled herself up in a ball under his eiderdown at the foot of his bed. No matter how many times he assured her that there was no chance of their house being struck, she always grimaced and flung herself under the covers when the lightning flashed and was followed by crashing thunder.

The bedside light flickered and then a peal of thunder shook the house. It seemed to be right overhead. Suddenly the bedroom door was flung open and he saw her standing there, shivering in spite of the intense heat in her thin nightgown. Her eyes were enormous and protruding with terror.

'I'm sorry, Charlie. I don't mean anything devious – really I don't. It's just – well, you know how terrified I am of thunder.'

He swallowed nervously. "Oh God," he thought. "Does she really have no idea how provocative she looks standing there in that flimsy piece of material that I can almost see through?"

'I remember.' His voice was barely above a whisper.

'May I stay – just for a little while, until the thunder stops?'

'Just until the thunder stops.' His mouth felt dry. 'Here.' He held out his pyjama jacket. 'You'd better put this on.'

'It's so hot.' She sat down on the bottom of his bed.

'Do as I say.' He raised his voice and spoke abruptly.

She looked at him for a long moment with surprise showing in her eyes, then she lowered her gaze as she said meekly, 'Yes, Charlie.'

The lights flickered again and she cowered. As the thunder cracked, they went out.

'Oh no, I can't bear it. Where are you? What's happening?' She sounded hysterical.

'It's all right. It's only a power cut. I'll go and find a torch.'

'No, don't do that. Stay with me. Please stay with me.'

'Lainey, try to relax. It's all right – really it is. Nothing is going to happen.'

'How can you say that? We're all alone on these God-forsaken moors. It's far worse than it was in Surrey.' She burst into tears.

'Don't, darling, please don't.' Charlie's voice cracked slightly. He reached out a hand to grasp hers.

It was all the encouragement that she needed. She flung her arms around his neck and pressed herself tightly against him.

'I need you so much,' she sobbed as she stretched herself out beside him.

Charlie felt the frantic beating of her heart against his chest as he lay there, immobile for a second, then with a groan he turned and gathered her into his arms.

"I've lost," he thought. "The battle's over. There is a limit to a man's strength. I've always wanted her, that is why I've always been jealous of the other men in her life. I've always felt so guilty – so unclean – about feeling this way, but she has been right all along. Lainey always said that she knew there was nothing dirty about the way we felt about each other."

Oh, the relief of knowing that it would not be a sin. Thoughts of Alison and the coming baby were banished into a distant corner of his mind. It was as if someone had turned a key and locked them away. At this moment there was nothing except for the girl in his arms – the girl he had always wanted and had thought was for ever unobtainable.

He kissed her softly and gently – almost reverently. Her body was tense with expectancy. He was aware that she hardly dared to move lest he would stop as had always been the case – until now. He knew that nothing could stop him now.

'It's all right,' he murmured against her mouth. 'You've won. I can't leave you now. I can no longer deny the way I feel about you. It's as if a terrible load has suddenly been taken off my mind. I love you and now I can say it without feeling that I'm different – odd or peculiar. It's perfectly natural.'

'Don't talk.' She hugged him closer as she felt his hands exploring her body. 'Just feel.'

When he entered her she cried out. For a moment he paused, afraid that he was hurting her.

'Don't stop.' Her fingers caressed his back as she moved her body more insistently.

'I don't want to hurt you.'

'You're not hurting me. You could never hurt me, but I don't care if you do. I want to feel it all – pain and pleasure.'

'Oh, my love.'

She felt a quickening in his rhythm and then he gave a deep sigh and was still. She continued to hold him close. It was over so quickly, but the next time would be better – much better. Of that she was sure. The first time you both expected so much and the waiting and the anticipation always shortened the act – at least that's what Harry had told her. The next time would be the one to remember.

Why was she thinking of Harry right now? How disloyal could she be? As if to atone for it she kissed her lover gently as she snuggled up to him and the thunder receded into the distance.

'The storm is over. Do you want me to leave?'

'No, oh no.'

'I'm glad. I'll never be frightened of thunder again.'

The following morning when Charlie woke up she was no longer there. For a minute he thought that he had dreamed everything. He sat up and rubbed his right eye. When he looked up Lainey was standing in the doorway holding a laden tray.

'I made us breakfast,' she smiled shyly.

Charlie sighed with relief. 'For a moment I thought I'd been dreaming.'

'It was no dream.' She set the tray down on the bed. 'I've made us scrambled eggs and bacon and toast and coffee.'

'How spoiling. I don't usually get treated to breakfast in bed.'

As he realized what he had said, a look of intense guilt flashed across his face, followed by another of total confusion.

'It's all right,' she said softly. 'Eat.' She handed him a full plate. 'This weekend is for us – whatever happens next, at least we will have known this. It had to happen, Charlie. What has always been between us was too strong to be denied. Maybe after this weekend we will be able to find some sort of peace. No one is going to get hurt – I promise you that.'

'Someone always gets hurt, my love. Even if it is just the two of us.'

'Which is better, Charlie, to live constantly yearning for something and always wondering what it would have been like? Or to live the rest of one's life knowing how wonderful it was between us?'

'I don't know.' He put down the plate of untouched food.

'I do.' Lainey removed the tray and slipped into bed beside him.

'Oh Lainey, why is it that I can never think straight when you are near me?'

'Don't try – not now. I can't either. You are all that I've ever wanted. I'm just so thankful that fate gave us this chance.'

The second time that they made love was longer and more intense. Yet, why was it that afterwards, as Lainey lay in Charlie's arms, she felt something was missing? The man that she had wanted for so long was hers. He would never deny his love for her again. He worshipped her, she knew he did, and she loved him – of course she did. She had always loved him. Then what was wrong with her? Why did she feel – what was it? Was it a sense of being let down? No, not possible. How treacherous to even think that way . . .

That afternoon they walked over the moors arm-in-arm, sometimes hand-in-hand. He would often stop and hug her and kiss her, but it was always so gentle – so reverent. Lainey was used to passion – to strong physical contact. She wanted it now.

Charlie's philosophy of love was so different from hers. He believed that love was a delicate feeling that should be nurtured through gentleness. He treated her as though she was a piece of priceless porcelain – as though she might break at the slightest rough treatment. Lainey wanted more – more force, more lust . . . more . . . Oh no! Was that what it was – what it always had been?

That night she tried to force the pace, but he wouldn't let her.

'Relax, darling. There's no need to for you to feel that you have to prove your love for me. I know it and I adore you.'

"I don't want to be adored," she thought silently. "I want to be needed. I want to be used – the way Harry uses me. I want more, and he can't give it to me."

Tears came into her eyes as she thought: "Why am I thinking of Harry again? He doesn't love me – he never has. It's Charlie who loves me – whom I've always loved. I've got what I always wanted, so why am I thinking of Harry?"

She turned on her side to try and sleep.

'Don't turn away.' Charlie put his arms around her. 'I want you to sleep in my arms.'

"Oh God," she thought as she let him hold her. "What have I done?"

By the Sunday afternoon she couldn't wait to leave. The feeling of suffocation was overwhelming. Her thoughts were in utter turmoil. It seemed that everything she had believed in had turned around and nothing was as it should be – everything was confused.

Charlie did not seem to notice her uneasiness. His thoughts were on other things.

'Darling, you were so right to come here,' he told her as they got in the car to drive to the station. 'I can see things so much more clearly now.'

'Charlie, I think we need time. I . . .'

'I'm glad you said that, darling.' He smiled at her lovingly.

420

'I love you and I know that I want to be with you, but I can't let Alison down – not while she's pregnant. It will have to come gently. We will have to wait for quite a while, but it will be easy now that we know how we feel about each other.'

How easily he dismissed Harry, she thought.

'You don't understand.' Her voice was dull. 'That's just it. I don't know how I feel any more.'

'What do you mean?' He sounded alarmed.

'Charlie, you always said that we were incompatible. I think that you could be right.'

'Don't be silly. That was only when I thought that you were my half-sister.'

'No it wasn't. You said that I wanted so much more out of life than you did and I think that you were right.'

'What are you trying to tell me?'

'I think that this could be a mistake.'

'What . . .!' For a second he took his eyes off the road.

'Charlie, look out.'

They were approaching a corner. The car came out of nowhere. It was trying to overtake a lorry which was coming towards them. There was nothing that could be done – nowhere to go. One minute the day was sunny and warm and the next it was plunged into the darkest of nights.

CHAPTER TWENTY-ONE

For two days Lainey lay delirious in the hospital in Leeds to which she had been taken. A frantic Harry had been contacted at once and had arrived even before Jennifer and Alan.

During her ramblings the doctors and nurses had only been able to distinguish the word 'Harry' and it was her husband now who sat by her bedside holding her hand as she tossed and turned in her anguish.

Her injuries could have been worse. She had a few broken ribs and severe cuts and bruising, but she had been lucky, they said. Her brother had been killed immediately on impact. He had obviously swerved to try and save his passenger.

As Harry sat through those long hours waiting for his beautiful young wife to wake up, he wondered what had taken place between her and Charlie. What had Carrington felt when he had been told that they were not related? How honourable had he been in the end? Why had Lainey called out for him, Harry, and not for the man she had run off to?

Was it possible she had realized that Charlie was not what she really wanted? Harry had always wondered why she wouldn't acknowledge her love for him – why she went out of her way to deny it existed. Now that he understood, was it too late for them? What would her reaction be when she was told that Charlie was dead? He thought that he knew Lainey better than she knew herself. She would be overcome with remorse – especially if she had been coming home to him, Harry.

He sighed as he squeezed her limp hand, and closed his eyes. "Dear God," he prayed silently. "Don't let it be too late for us. I'll give her all the time she needs, if only she'll come back to me."

Her eyes fluttered and then opened.

'Where am I?' She looked disorientated, but as her vision cleared she was able to focus on him. He thought that for a moment her eyes lit up. 'Harry?' she said. 'What happened?'

'Don't try to talk, darling.' He smoothed the hair on her forehead. 'You've had an accident, but you're going to be fine.'

'Am I?' She looked confused. 'What did I do?'

'Later, darling. Now you must try and rest'

'No, I want to know now,' she said fretfully.

'You had a car crash, but you're going to be fine,' he repeated.

'Was I driving? Did I hurt anybody?' She clutched his hand as she tried to sit up.

'Lainey, it's all right. Lie back.'

"Oh God," he thought. "What answers do I give her?"

The doctors had said not to tell her about Charlie's death – not yet. Not until she had had a chance to recover.

'You must rest now.' He tried to smile reassuringly at her. 'I'll be back later. Don't worry, Lainey. You'll be out of here in no time.'

'Yes, I'll try. Where's Mummy?'

'She's here. She'll come and see you as soon as you've had a sleep.'

'Where's Charlie? Is he here too?' She frowned as she tried to remember something that was evading her.

'Yes,' Harry whispered. Well, it was only a little lie, wasn't it?

'Poor Charlie.' She was starting to ramble again. 'I love him so much, but it isn't enough.'

Harry's heart leapt. Had he heard her correctly? Had his suppositions been correct?

'Don't talk any more, darling. Just try and get some sleep.'

He got up and kissed her cheek, before walking out of the room and closing the door quietly behind him.

He was halfway down the hospital corridor when he heard the scream. He stopped dead as a cold hand seemed to grip his heart, then he turned and ran back towards Lainey's room, reaching it at the same time as a doctor and two nurses.

Lainey was lying in the bed with a haunted look on her white face.

'I've remembered,' she cried as she saw him standing in the doorway. 'I was with Charlie. Oh, my God, I've killed him, haven't I? He's dead and it's all my fault.'

'No, no, you're wrong,' Harry's mouth was dry.

'Don't tell me I'm wrong. I know. I can feel it. Oh no, I can't bear it.' She started thrashing about wildly.

The two nurses rushed forward as the doctor turned to Harry.

'I think that it would be better if you left, Lord Wrightson. You can come back and see your wife later.'

'But . . .' Harry stared at his wife in anguish.

'Go. Get out of here.' Lainey's eyes looked tortured.

The doctor nodded his head. 'It's better if you let us deal with this,' he whispered, and closed the door firmly in Harry's face.

Jennifer sat in the hospital waiting room for what seemed like an eternity. Her face showed utter devastation as she gripped Alan's hand for support. Across the room a white-faced Harry stood staring out of the window.

Since she had regained consciousness, Lainey had wanted to see no one and the doctors had told them that a visit from any one of them would only upset her more.

Jennifer gave a tremulous sigh and Alan put his arm around her and tried to speak reassuringly. 'She's going to make it, darling. She's our daughter and she's strong. She's a survivor and she has youth on her side.'

'Oh God, I hope you're right. I couldn't bear to lose both of them.' She buried her head in his comforting shoulder as she whispered, 'He wasn't just a step-son, you know. I'd known him since he was three months old and I raised him from when he was sixteen months old. I loved him as if he was my own. He was everything that a son should be. We were the happiest of families, and Tony and I were so proud of our children – we did think of both of them as being *our* children.' She sniffed pathetically.

'I know, my love, and you were right to think that.' Much as it hurt to admit it, Alan realized that Tony Carrington would always be the father that Lainey would acknowledge. The best that he could hope to be when she recovered was a friend – a good reliable friend. He'd be more like a step-father if he married her mother, and he fully intended to do that.

'Were we so wrong to keep it from them that they were not related by blood?' Jennifer looked up at him with tears in her eyes.

'I don't know.' Alan ran a hand through his hair. 'With hindsight, maybe, but who was to know how they felt about each other, and, not knowing it, why disrupt a happy family.'

'Poor Alison.' The tears started to flow down Jennifer's cheeks. 'She loved Charlie so much. There was never anyone else for her. And now her baby will never know its father.'

'At least she has her family with her, darling. They are very devoted, aren't they? And she doesn't know about the way Lainey and Charlie felt about each other. To Alison it is a devastating accident and that's how it must stay. Don't give her any reason ever to doubt her husband's love for her. She's young and in time she will find another man to love her and her baby.'

'She's a wonderful girl – almost a saint, and I mean that sincerely. Why is it that truly good people often have so much to bear while the bad ones seem to get away with so much?'

'I like to think that the good people are being tested for something better in the hereafter.' He held her close to him.

'And the sinners?'

'They have no consciences, therefore they seldom question what they do.'

'Do you think that Lainey is like that?'

'No, of course not.' He spoke adamantly. 'When you truly love someone, it isn't a sin. Was it a sin all those years ago when we were at Edgeglow?'

'I never allowed myself to think so then, but you *were* married to Rosemary, though nobody suffered or died because of us.'

'Jennifer, darling, nobody has died now as a result of this relationship. Charlie's death was an accident – a terrible accident – but he could never have avoided that car.'

'I suppose so, but I can't help thinking that I'm paying for something that I shouldn't have done, and that in a way Lainey is having to pay for my sin as well.'

Alan felt the tingling of alarm start to travel up his spine.

'Don't shut me out, Jenny. Don't go away from me now that I've found you again.'

'I won't, Alan. I never could resist you and I've always loved you, even though I loved Tony too. I'm selfish enough to believe that at our time of life we are entitled to some happiness, and I feel that you were brought back into my life for a reason. You're here just when I need you most, and whatever happens I hope that you're going to stay.'

'I love you,' he said hoarsely into her hair.

'I love you too.'

Harry turned from the window and saw them in each other's arms. He swallowed a lump in his throat. "At least something good has materialized from all this heartbreak," he thought sadly. His eyes glittered brightly as he turned away and looked outside again. "Please God, it will also happen for me."

It was three days later when Lainey finally said, 'I want to see my mother.'

426

Jennifer was shocked when she walked into her daughter's room. Lainey had lost a lot of weight that she could ill afford to do. Her face looked pasty and her eyes which were usually so large and bright had sunk back into her head.

'Hello, darling. How are you feeling?' Jennifer attempted a weak smile.

'Numb.' Lainey had a glazed expression on her face. 'How else could I feel, knowing that I have just been responsible for my . . . I mean Charlie's death?'

'Darling, it wasn't your fault.' Jennifer sat down beside the bed. 'The police said there was no way that Charlie could ever have avoided that car. It was passsing a lorry on a corner. There was simply nothing that he could have done.'

'You don't understand. It was my fault – so many things were my fault. I shouldn't have even been there. If I hadn't been there, it would never have happened.'

'You mustn't think like that. You have every right to go and see your brother.'

'But he wasn't my brother, was he? He never was. Why didn't you tell us?'

'Oh Lainey, what can I say?' Jennifer swallowed hard. 'We thought it was for the best. In every way, except genetically, Tony was your father. He loved you so very much. No one dreamed that you and Charlie would become so close – so attracted to one another. You were brought up as half-brother and half-sister and we didn't want to disturb that special relationship.'

'We thought we were freaks,' she whispered. 'He felt so guilty. I always knew that it wasn't wrong to feel the way I did – I never knew why, but I did – but Charlie was always so honourable. He never deviated from what was right and proper.'

'Lainey, I'm so sorry. We try to do what's right for our children, and it so often turns out to be the wrong thing.'

'I've ruined so many people's lives – Alison's, her unborn baby's and . . .' She gulped and put her hand to her mouth.

'I ended Charlie's. I don't deserve to be here. I should have been the one who died, then everything would have been all right. Everyone could have got on with their lives. Instead of that I'm the one sitting here wishing I was dead.'

'Darling, don't say that. We love you. Alison doesn't blame you. It was just a terrible accident. She's being brave – and you must be too.'

'You don't understand.' It was a chilling cry from the heart. 'Oh, I know that we couldn't have avoided that car – don't think that I don't know that.' Her voice was bitter. 'It's all the other things that I've done that I have to live with. I've been so selfish. All I've ever thought about has been myself. I've never stopped to consider other people's feelings and now I've got to atone for it for the rest of my life.' She closed her eyes and great wracking sobs rent the air.

Jennifer felt so helpless. What could she possibly say to her daughter that could in any way help to ease her pain? Every word that she could utter would sound so trite. If Tony were here he would be able to soothe her. He had always been a master at that.

Could Alan help his daughter? Or would the sight of him only upset her more? She had refused to see Harry since the day she had opened her eyes. Why was that? She had been calling his name while she had been delirious and now she wanted to have nothing to do with him.

Harry was being a tower of strength to them all, but the strain was showing and in the last week he had aged considerably. Lainey was lucky to have a husband like Harry, Jennifer thought. She hoped desperately that her daughter would realize that before it was too late.

Tomorrow was Charlie's funeral, but they had not told Lainey that. Jennifer hated having to leave her. She needed to talk to someone, but who? She obviously didn't want to confide in her mother.

As she got up to go, Jennifer leaned over and stroked her daughter's cheek.

'Lainey darling, you can't take all the blame – whatever you think you've done. It takes two to do anything. If Charlie were here, he would tell you that. I know he would.'

'I'm tired, Mother.' Lainey sounded exhausted. 'I'd like to be by myself. Don't try to make me feel better because you can't succeed. I know what I've done and I've got the rest of my life to pay for it.'

Alison Carrington lay on her bed in her old room at Doves Place and gazed up at the ceiling. She had to rest, they had told her. 'They' were the doctor and her parents and her sister Vivien. They were all being so kind and thoughtful and she knew that it was awful of her to feel so smothered. She caught her breath as she thought suddenly, "I'll never see him again." It hadn't really sunk in before today, but seeing the casket actually lowered into the ground had somehow made it real and not just a terrible nightmare. There was something so final about graveyards. Life ended there. Soon there would be a headstone and crocuses that came up every spring, and in time – a very long time – Charlie would become a happy memory and not this gnawing pain for which there was no antidote.

Of course no one knew what she had had to live with for years. If they had they would have been shocked and sickened by it. Sometimes she thought that Vivien guessed, but they had never discussed it. Alison would never be disloyal to Charlie.

"I've known since we were children about the hold Lainey and Charlie had over each other," she thought. "I knew about it and I saw what it was doing to Charlie. I thought that I could be his salvation, and I was for a while until something happened which even I couldn't foresee. The source of their guilt was taken away from them when they learned that they weren't brother and sister. I'm sure that their feelings were too strong to be denied. That weekend in Yorkshire had to be. They had to know how real their obsession was." She blinked back the threatening tears. She had once thought that, if only they could physically make love, they would find that it was not all that they had imagined it to be. There is something about forbidden love that makes it all-consuming.

Alison had known immediately that Charlie was lying when he had telephoned her to say he could not join her at her parents that weekend. He had said that he had to change weekends with one of his colleagues, but he was a poor liar. She knew that Lainey was back from America and that she was not down at Mattingham. Vivien had telephoned her at her London home and she wasn't there either, although Harry had answered the telephone.

Alison had known right away where Lainey was, and even though she had not known then that they were not related, she had felt that the future of her marriage hinged on this weekend. What had happened? Now she would never know. What had really killed her beloved Charlie? Having lost the guilt about his feelings for Lainey, had he been swamped with new guilt over what he might have done to her, Alison, and their unborn child?

She ought to hate Lainey Carrington – Jefferson – whoever she was, but she didn't. She wasn't an evil girl – maybe a little thoughtless, but her only crime was in loving someone too much. This obsession couldn't have been any easier for Lainey than it had been for Charlie or herself.

There was a tap on the door and Vivien stuck her head around it.

'Are you all right?' She looked concerned.

'Yes, fine.' What a ridiculous answer. What she really meant was that she was as fine as could be expected after burying her husband that afternoon.

'I thought you'd like to know that Lainey's going to be OK.'

'I'm glad.'

'Are you?' Surprise showed in her sister's voice.

'Yes, really.' Alison felt as if a weight had just been lifted off her chest, enabling her to breathe more freely. She looked up and saw compassion in her younger sister's eyes. "She knows, too," she thought. She held out her hand and Vivien walked across the room and took it in both of hers as she sat down on the bed.

'How do you feel, Ali?' she asked. 'I mean, how do you really feel?'

Alison smiled serenely. 'Peaceful – and grateful,' she said softly. 'Poor Lainey. What did Charlie leave her with except heartbreak and torment? She doesn't deserve that. But look what he left me.' She laid her hand on her already swelling stomach. 'I have our child.'

Lainey stayed in the hospital for three weeks, and during that time she refused to see Harry. Her thoughts were still very confused. In some strange way she had convinced herself that by finding out and at last admitting to herself that she loved her husband, that had been the reason for Charlie's death.

Why had she allowed Harry to make her feel that way about him? Why hadn't Charlie been able to measure up? Why had she insisted on having everything?

"I'm a piraya," she told herself. "I devour the people that I try to love. I'm no good to anyone. I've always been a selfish, thoughtless bitch, and now God has taught me a dreadful lesson. Charlie was right when he said that I had a lot to learn about life. I thought I knew it all and I didn't know a thing. He was right all the way down the line. We have no right to make other people suffer. There is no pleasure in it, only anguish, and there never was a right time for us. He was always weaker than I, so I was able to break down his defences and force the issue. I should be so proud of myself – so very proud of being able to manipulate people to do my bidding, no matter what the cost might be to others. Oh God, how I hate myself."

She went home to Mattingham and refused to see a soul. On fine days she sat in the garden. She spoke when she was spoken to, but would not be drawn into any long conversations. She would never let herself get close to anyone in the future. When she was well enough she would go away somewhere – anywhere – and live her life on her own. That way she would not be able to hurt anyone ever again.

Her mother was going to marry her father – at last. That was nice. She was glad that she had managed to do at least one good thing for someone.

She still couldn't bring herself to see Harry. At some time she would have to – to tell him that it was over. Her mother and Alan kept telling her how much Harry loved her, but that wasn't right. He never had. And if he had – how terrible for him. It would be as bad as her obsession for Charlie. Yes, she had finally admitted to herself that that was what it had been. She had been obsessed by him. He had been the only person who had ever voiced any disapproval of her, and so she had always wanted to shine in his eyes. In the end she had. She had made sure that she had, and where had it got her? It had been the same as with everyone else – he had lost his appeal for her. She had achieved nothing and lost everything.

'Lainey, you have a visitor.' Alan came out into the garden.

'I don't want any visitors. You know that. Please tell whoever it is to go away.'

'This young lady is very determined. She insists on seeing you.'

'Oh God, it's not Alison, is it?' She looked horrified.

'No, it's not. It's me.' Vivien appeared beside her.

'Oh Viv, go away, please.'

'Is that any way to greet your best friend.' Vivien sat down on the grass in front of her.

'How can you possibly be my best friend after all that's happened?'

Alan disappeared discreetly back into the house.

'Lainey, it's time that you stopped wearing the hair shirt and playing the martyr. Nobody blames you for Charlie's death. It was just a terrible terrible accident.'

'You don't understand – nobody does.'

'I do – Alison does too.'

'How could she? I've ruined her life.'

'We do, Lainey.' Vivien spoke earnestly. 'We know what you meant to each other. Alison knew that when she married Charlie.'

'But I did some awful things. You'd hate me if you knew.'

'It's not awful to love someone – really love someone.

'But I always thought that he was my brother – that's awful.'

Vivien clasped her friend's hand.

'It's only awful if you let it become so, Lainey. It's the feelings of guilt that are awful, not the feelings of love. Nobody's perfect. God didn't make us that way. We all have to learn from each other.'

'What can anyone possibly learn from me?' It was said bitterly.

'Love.'

'What did I really know about love? I got it all mixed up.'

'Harry loves you, Lainey, and I think you love him. You just never were prepared to give him a chance.'

'Don't be silly, Viv.' Lainey gave a sad little laugh.

'It's true. I had a long talk with him. He's always fought for you, Lainey. Who do you think got you reinstated in the Berkeley Dress Show? Harry did. He told me he took Candida out to lunch and practically blackmailed her into telling Marcel Lefauvre she no longer wanted to wear that bridal dress. He had been furious when he heard how she had got you thrown out.'

'He hardly knew me then,' she mused.

'He's not a bad man. He was a bit wild when he first came to London, but he's settled down and is taking his responsibilities very seriously.'

433

'He always wanted to keep Tenterden. Everything he did was because he wanted to keep that place.'

'I know. He was even prepared to marry that insipid Grace Clover. I suppose it would have been a good bargain – to exchange money for a title – but you changed all that, Lainey. He fell in love with you and he couldn't let you go. You changed his life, Lainey. You made him what he is today. Because of his love for you, he went out and got himself a good job and became a success. He became independent. He had to, if he wanted to keep that house. You didn't have the kind of money that Grace had but, much more important than that, he learned to respect himself.'

'I wish that I could believe you, but I know better. We used to have terrible rows and he started drinking, and then, when I was in America with you, he started messing about with Candida.'

'Lainey, get it through your thick skull that he was not "messing about with Candida" as you call it.' Vivien sighed in exasperation. 'He was lonely and she was an old friend. He just took her out for dinner. It wasn't his fault that they happened to go to a restaurant where some filmstar was giving a party. That's why there were photographers there. They weren't even at the party.'

'And you believe him?'

'Yes, I do. The man loves you, Lainey. He's desperately unhappy. He told me that he always knew you didn't love him, but thought that it didn't matter – or rather, it did matter, but he thought that eventually you would see that you were wrong. He said that there had to be something between the two of you, because it was so good for you both.' Vivien blushed slightly. 'The physical side, that is. And he said that he always thought that you and he were friends.'

'We were. I really liked him, but he started drinking and we kept arguing.'

'He was unhappy, Lainey, and he felt you were cheating him – oh, not in the physical sense, but emotionally. You

434

simply would not acknowledge what there was between you. You know, I think it would have been better for everyone concerned if you and Charlie had consummated that love of yours much earlier. I think that would have been the only way to free yourselves from each other.'

'Viv, how can you say that? He was married to your sister.' Lainey looked shattered.

'Half of him was – the same way that half of you was married to Harry. It's a pity that you didn't find out sooner that you weren't brother and sister. You could have saved yourselves so much heartache.'

'I don't know how you can say that.' Lainey closed her eyes in anguish.

'Someone has to,' Vivien said gently.

Neither of them spoke for what seemed to be an age, then Vivien turned to her friend. 'Will you see him now? He wants so much to see you.'

'No, not yet,' Lainey whispered. Her eyes were still shut and her hands clenched. 'I have so much to think about. I have to go away – to be by myself. You understand that, don't you?'

'Yes.' Vivien nodded. 'Don't take too long, that's all. Life has to go on. There's still a lot to live for.'

The calm tranquil waters of Lake Ullswater acted as a soothing balm to her soul as Lainey took long walks in the August sunshine. Is this what Charlie had meant by longing for the peace of the countryside? Not really, she thought. Charlie's peace was that of organized emotions. He had fought against passion all his life. Its very existence had frightened him. He had wanted his life to be calm and tranquil like the placid water in front of her. Stability – an unexciting placid life with no ups and downs. She, Lainey, had always wanted more. Why? Why had she always had to force the issue?

"I'm only twenty years of age and already I've ruined so

435

many people's lives by my thoughtlessness. What is left for me? I don't deserve to be happy again. Vivien said that life has to go on, but does it? Wouldn't everyone be better off if I was dead?"

It was a frightening thought. A shepherd passed her on the hillside. He smiled and waved.

"You wouldn't do that if you knew what I was really like," she thought. She looked at the dark silent water. It would be so easy.

"Coward," said a voice from deep inside her. "Taking the easy way out?"

'I've never been a coward,' she said out loud.

"You are not all bad," said the voice more insistently. "You made a terrible mistake, that's all, but we all make mistakes. You have to pay for it, but you already know that. To jump in that lake and submerge would be a sin – far worse than any that you have committed so far. No, what you have to do now is try and put things right."

'How do I begin to do that?' she asked the countryside.

"By living your life as best you can."

'How's that?'

"That's something you must work out for yourself."

'I will,' she whispered. 'I promise that I'll try.'

She saw him the moment that she walked out on to the hotel terrace. He had his back to her as he stood leaning on the stone balustrade looking across the lake.

'Harry?' she said tentatively.

He turned around and she gasped as she registered the haggard expression on his face. Had she done this to him? Had she really been so wrong about his emotions where she was concerned?

'I had to come,' he said tightly. 'I had to see you, since you made no move to contact me.'

'It's all right.' She walked over and stood beside him.

'How are you?'

436